"It's g   nigl

Old Maizie, the wag   tress—took a bracii

"What do you mean, long night?" Camp slopped coffee as he filled Emily's mug.

"Hear that thunder gettin' louder?" When Camp nodded, Maizie went on. "Well, I'll need your help keepin' those horses in line. We'll be in a helluva fix if they stampede."

Emily hovered on the balls of her feet. "I'll help ride herd, Maizie."

Camp grasped Emily's waist and swung her around. "You'll do no such thing! The middle of a potential stampede is no place for a woman."

The light of battle sparked in Emily's eyes. "What does that make Maizie?"

He gulped. "Sorry, Maizie. But you're an old hand at this."

Emily smirked. "And you're Clint Eastwood?"

Maizie tipped her face to the rain and laughed. "Entertaining as this is, I gotta cut it short. Time to quit flappin' your gums and saddle up."

Dear Reader,

I recently traveled the Santa Fe Trail. Not by wagon train (like the characters in this book!) but by automobile. It was still quite an experience.

The day we set out was a muggy ninety. Halfway through our trip the wind came up. It howled across the plains, flattening the tall prairie grass…and anything that got in its way—like me. Yet in places where the wagon tracks curve toward the distant horizon, I swear I heard the creak of wheels and the sound of tears cried for the many left buried beside the trail. The land has not softened over the years.

In Dodge City, Kansas, clouds moved in and it started to rain. By the time we reached Oklahoma the rain turned to snow. We inched across icy Glorieta Pass for four hours, trying to reach Santa Fe—safe in a car. My hat certainly goes off to the pioneers! Especially the women.

I was surprised, if not appalled, to learn that only recently have historians begun to acknowledge (in some cases, grudgingly) women's true role in the opening of the American West. In *Anything You Can Do…* I've tried to spell out some of the myths—and perhaps debunk a few.

I hope you enjoy meeting Camp, Emily, Sherry and all the other participants in the wagon train reenactment. Their experience has its share of adventure and comedy—and unlike that of some *real* pioneers—a happy ending.

I love hearing from readers! You can write me at P.O. Box 17480-101, Tucson, Arizona 85731.

Roz Denny Fox

ANYTHING YOU CAN DO...
Roz Denny Fox

Harlequin Books

TORONTO • NEW YORK • LONDON
AMSTERDAM • PARIS • SYDNEY • HAMBURG
STOCKHOLM • ATHENS • TOKYO • MILAN
MADRID • WARSAW • BUDAPEST • AUCKLAND

ISBN 0-373-70776-2

ANYTHING YOU CAN DO...

ANYTHING YOU
CAN DO...

Most Historic accounts of western trailblazing are written by men, about men, to eulogize their feats.

—Catalyst that provoked the wagon train reenactment.

CHAPTER ONE

NOLAN CAMPBELL, professor of history, stared woefully at a skinny white Christmas tree standing in one corner of the staff lounge at his Columbia, Missouri, college. The tree was virtually smothered in pink ornaments and cellophane bows. Several strings of hot-pink bulbs flashed intermittently, and every few seconds his conservative blue tie turned a ghastly shade of green.

Two colleagues brooded beside him. Camp, as he was known by his peers, gestured toward the tree with a glass cup too dainty for his masculine hand. "Fake or not, Lyle, Christmas trees should be green. What's wrong with the world today?"

"Plenty," snorted Lyle Roberts. "Especially with the people in charge of this party. Did you get a load of those dinky sandwiches at the buffet table? No crust and less filling. Takes four to make a decent bite."

"Who planned this do?" asked Jeff Scott, economics prof. "Invaders from another planet?"

"Yeah," Lyle said sarcastically. "Aliens. In other words, our women's studies department. Hey, that reminds me of a joke I heard. How do Columbia housewives call their kids to dinner?"

Camp and Jeff shrugged.

"They say, 'Come on, kids, get in the car.'" Lyle tittered. "Women don't cook anymore."

Unlike his associates, Camp didn't laugh. "I eat out a lot, too," he said, recalling all the evenings he stopped at a café near his home rather than face a solitary meal. "It's a sign of the times, I guess. Home is no longer the focal point of a family." Camp's gaze traveled to a huddle of women instructors. "Eight-plus hours at a job doesn't allow time for domestic chores."

"Are you kidding?" Roberts exclaimed. "Modern women have erased the word *domestic* from their vocabularies. I've said it before and I'll say it again—my great-grandmother's generation spawned the last real women. In her era they cooked tasty meals on wood stoves. No boxed crap of undetermined origin. She planted a garden and sewed for herself and the kids. And she was happy doing it."

"Get a life, Lyle." Camp's sister, Sherry, department chair for women's studies, left her group to confront the men. "Try stepping into this century. Women pioneer in a *lot* of fields. Politics, medicine, corporate America—to name a few. And Lyle," she added sweetly, "we live longer than Great-grandma did."

Lyle wagged a finger in her face. "If settling the West depended on coddled women like my ex-wife, civilization would be permanently stalled east of the Ohio."

She batted his hand away. "Those so-called historic facts about the West are fantasies dreamed up by men. And if you think women today are all pampered, spend an hour in the Women's Hub listening to the battered ones left penniless by well-heeled exes."

"Really? My ex spends the child support I pay her on cosmetics and manicures."

Camp insinuated himself between the two. "Sherilyn,

you missed the crux of our conversation. Lyle's referring to basic evolutionary changes—like, if modern women had to wash without a machine, cook without gas or electricity, they'd have difficulty surviving."

"That's right," Jeff interjected. "Economically speaking, women still expect men to be the hunters, the main breadwinners in the family."

"Oh, pu…leeze! Like you three men could skin a bear and put him in a pot." Sherry thumped her chest. "*I* could live primitively. Thank goodness I don't have to."

Camp lifted a brow. "Toss your electric toothbrush, hot comb and microwave, sis. Then we'll talk."

"Horse feathers. You history types always lament the loss of the *good old days.*" Her sarcastic sneer was suddenly replaced by a wide smile. "The other day I received a brochure at the Women's Hub advertising a wagon-train reenactment along the Santa Fe Trail. Led by a woman, incidentally. Her train leaves Boonville, Missouri, in June, if I recall. Sponsor a few women on that trip, brother dear. See how they compare with your precious pioneers."

Lyle hooted. "Don't waste your hard-earned money, Camp. I daresay they wouldn't make it as far as Independence."

"Oh, yeah?" Sherry met him glare for glare.

"It's a silly notion," Camp said impatiently. "Just accept that today's women are softer."

"Camp's spouting sour grapes," a woman behind them shouted. "Because Greta Erickson refused to spend *her* life shackled to that hundred-year-old house he'll be restoring for the rest of *his* life."

Pain licked ever so fleetingly through Camp's brown eyes.

Sherry dealt the speaker a dark look. She could grumble at Nolan and call him bossy. That didn't mean she'd stand for others picking on him. Greta had hurt him.

Yet it was Lyle who spoke up. "Greta thought Camp's house was fine until she met Mr. Gotbucks, who upped the ante with a fancy new rambler in a gated subdivision. Man isn't important to a relationship anymore. Only the perks he provides."

"Bull, Lyle. One of these days you'll have to eat your words." Sherry thrust out her jaw pugnaciously.

Camp felt the discussion was getting out of hand. "I might consider your experiment, Sherry—if you'd agree to drive one of those wagons." He knew his sister's penchant for luxury and figured that'd end the argument.

"Go for it, girl. Show him." The other women egged Sherry on.

Sherry mulled it over. Spending a summer vacation plodding across the dusty prairie was the last thing she wanted to do. However, she knew a couple of women who were capable of making these men eat their words. Gina Ames, a freelance photographer who last year backpacked across the Sierras. And Emily Benton, Sherry's counterpart at a college nearer St. Louis. Widowed young, Em had returned to the workforce to pay off a philandering husband's debts rather than take one penny from wealthy in-laws determined to drive a wedge between her and her two kids.

Deciding to settle the argument once and for all, Sherry hooked her arm through her older brother's and steered him toward the stairs. At six foot two and leanly muscled, he cut a dashing figure. Too bad these guys from the history department were all several generations too late. "I'll grab that brochure on the wagon train before I leave on Christmas break. We can discuss my proposal some more at Mom and Dad's. I assume you'll be there for Christmas dinner."

"A forty-year-old man should have someplace more

exciting to spend Christmas than with his parents,'' Camp said glumly.

"You're not forty—you're only thirty-eight.'' She punched his arm playfully. "If you add years it makes me older. I prefer to think that at thirty-one, I'm in the prime of life.''

"Prime, huh? Then why are *you* spending the holiday with Mom and Dad instead of serving plum pudding to some lucky guy?''

She smacked him harder. "Very likely for the same reason you're not fixing stuffed goose for a special lady.''

Nolan rubbed his shoulder. "So Lyle was right—you can't cook.''

"You really are a Neanderthal moron sometimes, Nolan. Women are quite capable of surviving without a man. I certainly don't need one around.''

He frowned as she stomped off. Nolan had forgotten how bulldog-stubborn she could be. Wasn't she ever lonely? He was. Thrusting his hands in his pockets, he clattered down the stairs. "I'd just like to find a woman who enjoys the simple things in life,'' he muttered as his steps faltered on the bottom landing. Wrenching the door open, he stepped out and breathed in a lungful of noxious city fumes.

"Ugh!'' For a minute Camp stared at the cars whizzing past and actually recognized merit in his sister's challenge. Give women a chance to prove they could cope as well as their pioneer ancestors. The real question, though: could *anyone* today, man or woman, give up modern conveniences for an entire summer? "Hmm, the answer to that does have the makings of a great academic paper.''

Absently, Camp dug out his car keys. For two years his department chairman had been hounding him to write and publish. A comparison-and-contrast piece on modern versus pioneer women might be the ticket. Although, if such a comparison was to be real and valid, information would have to come directly from the women involved.

Driving home, Camp played with the idea. What if he leased and stocked a few wagons in exchange for the participants' feedback? That'd work. But to remain an impartial observer, he'd have to dissociate himself completely. By following the train on horseback, say, and sleeping in a tent. Except he hadn't ridden a horse in— how long?

Bad idea. Okay, what if he stopped at motels along the route, instead? That way, he could input the women's findings every night on his laptop computer and all but have the paper written by trip's end. Suddenly, what began as an irrational dare sounded pretty darned good.

With a grin, Camp turned off the highway onto the graveled lane leading to his old farmhouse. What better opening for this paper than to point out the author's dependence on a most modern convenience—a computer? Both witty and modest, if he did say so himself.

Sherry would never know what a coup she'd handed him.

BY THE TIME Christmas dinner was over—a dinner during which her brother talked of nothing but what he now referred to as *his summer project*, Sherry regretted having butted into the men's conversation, no matter how irritating. All she'd been trying to do was shake them out of the past. Now here was Nolan reading excerpts from his stupid history books about the he-men who'd tamed the West. The simple fact was, her brother needed some modern woman to boot him into the twenty-first century. Him *and* his pals.

"Suppose the wagon train does still have room?" Sherry asked as they stood together on the porch, preparing to make mad dashes to their separate cars through the falling snow. "How will you choose your guinea pigs?"

Camp chucked her under the chin. "Did you see *Field of Dreams*? The movie where Kevin Costner cleared his cornfield and put in a baseball diamond? I'll lease Conestogas and women will wade out of the corn rows to volunteer."

"Dream on." Sherry jerked away. "You may look a little like Kevin, but even he had to work to entice players to his field."

Camp flipped up his jacket collar. "Let's have it, Ms. Nineties Organizer. How should I attract female adventurers?"

"Advertise in the local newspaper and neighboring college papers. Of course, you'll need an application form that'll weed out kooks. To prove I'm a good sport, I'll help with that. Heck, I'll even mail your applications."

"Hmm. I thought maybe word of mouth around our campus would be easiest."

"Taking all your participants from one pool will skew results, Nolan. Besides, aren't you afraid colleagues will steal your idea? You know how much pressure there is to publish these days. Which reminds me—what about professional liability? Participants should sign a release giving you permission to use their input. And that would be easier if you offered a small stipend. I mean, you *are* asking women to give up vacation plans or work."

"I hadn't thought of liability. What makes you so savvy?"

"I am woman," Sherry said smugly. "So…shall I put together an application?"

"Sure. I guess," he muttered. "Although sending defenseless women on the trip outlined in Maizie Boone's brochure will probably give me nightmares."

"Poor baby." Gritting her teeth, Sherry stepped into

the driving snow and left him standing there. She hurried home to call Gina Ames, the wilderness photographer. After twisting Gina's arm and making her promise not to reveal their friendship, Sherry said that her friend should be on the lookout for an application.

Next morning, Sherry decided to visit Emily Benton.

"Sherry, what a delightful surprise," exclaimed the attractive redhead who answered Sherry's knock. "I thought you were my kids. They're at a neighborhood snowball fight. Come in and warm up. I was just making tea." She released the chain and opened the door to one half of a small duplex. Emily hung Sherry's coat on a wrought-iron coat tree, then skirted a shiny new bicycle, two boxed TVs and the components for two or more computers as she led the way to a tiny kitchen.

"Wow!" Whistling through her teeth, Sherry absently handed over a box of homemade cookies she'd brought. "Fencing stolen goods are you, Em?"

Emily frowned. "My in-laws' presents to the kids. It doesn't matter that our house won't hold all this stuff. It's their latest ploy to convince me to move in with them." Her blue eyes frosted. "As if I'd let them get their hooks in Megan and Mark after the way they overindulged Dave."

Sherry slid into the compact eating nook. "Maybe they feel bad because their son turned out to be such a rat. Guilt does funny things to people."

"A Benton suffer guilt? Hah! It's always someone else's fault. Dave's backers lacked vision. His womanizing was my fault. Don't you know I spent too much time volunteering at church and at the kids' schools?" She poured water over tea bags with a trembling hand. "Sorry for dumping on you, Sherry. The holidays have been a trial. If I didn't owe Toby and Mona so much money, I'd take the kids and move to Alaska or Timbuktu. I told you

Dave's folks literally own this town. I had to look long and hard to find a place to rent that didn't belong to them or one of their companies. I desperately need the job at the college here, but..."

"I wish we had an opening in our department. My dean may retire at the end of the school year. New deans almost always hire additional staff."

"What if he doesn't retire?" She gave a small shrug. "I'm checking the ads in the *Chronicle of Higher Education*. So far, nothing."

"At least let me offer you a short-term reprieve." Sherry dropped a brochure on the table and quickly described her brother's project.

Before Sherry had finished talking, Emily was shaking her head. "There's more to this, right? Something you're not saying. Oh, no—I hope you're not planning to set me up with your brother. You're one of the few people who know what a nightmare my marriage was. I'm sure your brother's a nice man, Sherry, but I'm not interested. I don't care if I'm thirty-four and life is passing me by, I'm just not interested. Okay?"

"Boy, have I bungled this. I'm not setting you up, Em. I love Nolan, but I wouldn't wish anyone that chauvinistic on a friend. I'm doing this because...well, you could call it gender rivalry."

"Do I ever understand that. Megan just turned fourteen. She's constantly lording it over Mark, who's only twelve and still pretty much of a kid. To tell you the truth, Sherry, a wagon train in the middle of nowhere sounds like heaven. A whole summer without grandparents, shopping malls and TV." She fingered the brochure. "Will your brother want children in his study? What makes you feel he'd choose me? Oh, I can't go, Sherry, I really need to teach summer school and earn some money." Jumping up, she began to arrange cookies Sherry had brought on a plate. "I heard through the grapevine that Dave's parents want me to default on my loan. It'll give them leverage to petition for custody of the kids. You wouldn't believe how many times they bailed Dave out of bad land deals. On the last scheme, he lost all the front money for building a casino."

Sherry got up to hug Emily. "Those creeps. Hey, I forgot to mention that Nolan's trip comes with a small stipend. You need a break, Em. Fill out this application exactly the way I've penciled it in. Then mail it. Just don't tell Nolan we're friends." With a final bracing hug, Sherry left her to chew on the idea.

CHRISTMAS WAS a dim memory in Camp's mind and spring break loomed on the horizon before he got around to selecting candidates for his trip. Today, in spite of a drizzling rain, he was set to interview prospects. Not that he had many.

He refilled his coffee cup, sharpened several pencils and returned to his desk to frown at the three applications he'd received. Three! After weeks of advertising, only these few women appeared willing to spend their summers trekking the Santa Fe Trail.

He hadn't expected a flood of would-be adventurers, but considering that he was providing a virtually free summer vacation and paying his participants for their time, Camp had imagined he'd have more than three.

He'd already leased four Conestogas through Mrs. Boone's Frontier Adventures outfit. They weren't cheap, so it was fortunate that he'd shamed Sherry into going or he'd be paying for an unused reservation as well an extra wagon. Yesterday, she said she'd talked her roommate, Yvette Miller, into going, too.

Camp smiled. Yvette had grown up next door. He knew for a fact that she traveled with a hundred pounds of luggage—half of it cosmetics. Maybe she'd have even more now that she repped for an exclusive line of women's apparel. At this rate, his paper would write itself.

He sipped coffee and gazed out the window at the gloomy sky. Assuming the applicants were all suitable, that still didn't allow room for last-minute cancellations or unexpected illnesses. The way it stood, Sherry's wagon would have two drivers. Each of the other women would be forced to drive the entire route alone.

"So?" he said out loud. "Sherry claims they're as strong as pioneer women."

Unfortunately, Camp knew another of the applicants. Brittany Powers. A starry-eyed college sophomore better suited to modeling than anything athletic. She'd been in two of his history classes. Camp suspected she had a crush on him. Such things happened on occasion. He was very careful never to give these young women any encouragement, and most of them soon found boyfriends their own age. Brittany hadn't as yet.

But perhaps he was reading too much into Brittany's reasons for going on this trip. Maybe she really *was* interested in American history. Well, the list of questions Sherry had helped him design for the interviews should reveal how committed each of the women was. He'd conduct Brittany's meeting with his office door open. That ought to give her the right message. Before telling the secretary to send her in, Camp donned horn-rimmed glasses that were like window glass. He figured they gave him a nerdy look.

"Hi, Mr. Campbell." Brittany sashayed past the department secretary, tossing a tangle of blond curls over one shoulder. Camp simply pointed at the chair she was to occupy.

"I'm so excited about this trip," she gushed. "Summers are positively boring." Crack went her gum.

Camp shuddered as he sat behind his big oak desk. Lord, he hated gum-chewers who felt five sticks were a minimum. "You don't have a regular summer job you're turning down then?" he asked politely.

She scooted forward and batted heavily mascared lashes. "Are you kidding? That's why this is so perfect. Otherwise, I'd just veg out at the house."

"Really?" Nolan picked up her application, along with a sharp pencil whose lead he promptly broke. Grabbing another, he eased back in his chair. "What's your main goal after you graduate, Brittany?"

She looked at him coyly. "To marry somebody rich."

"Ah." Camp relaxed. Everyone knew professors weren't rich. Briskly, he worked through the remaining questions. Brittany's answers weren't as clear as Camp would have liked, but given her age and lack of focus, they were what he'd expect.

It was the way she hung on his every word and followed his slightest move with cosmetically enhanced baby blues that made him nervous. And yet they'd be well chaperoned when he collected the data sheets once a day. That fact let him continue. "It's not a vacation, Brittany. I'll expect you to keep an accurate daily log, which I'll incorporate in my academic paper."

"Kind of like a diary, you mean? Oh, cool. My best friend says my diaries could be published as bestsellers."

Camp's doubts concerning Brittany's motivation tripled. But in the next breath, she made an issue of saying her parents wanted her to do this, so he handed her a release form to sign. Not that she needed parental consent—after all, she was nineteen. It just made him feel better knowing she'd discussed it with her folks.

Assuming his best teacher-to-student smile, Camp ushered her back to the door. "I'll be handing out more detailed information later," he said. "Tomorrow, in class,

I'll lend you a book on the history of the Santa Fe Trail. The trip could take ten weeks. It's no picnic. I want you to be prepared."

"Oh, I will be, you'll see." She gazed at him adoringly. "Out there we'll be more like equals—right? I guess everyone will call you 'Nolan'?"

Camp cleared his throat. He was infinitely relieved at the appearance of the department secretary, heralding Gina Ames's arrival.

A suntanned, robust woman with blunt-cut brown hair, Gina steered the conversation to a professional level the moment she sat down. "I'm a freelance photographer. Two national publications have expressed interest in a photo-journey like this."

Had a plum fallen into his lap? "Gina...may I call you that?" Ignoring the thinning of her lips, he said, "Let your work support my scholastic paper, instead. Are you aware that the Santa Fe Trail was the first highway of commerce? A vital link to our past. And it was the last trail saved under the National Historic Trail Preservation Act."

"Spare me the dissertation, Campbell. I was married to a stuffy historian who considered it crass to sell my photographs to tabloids. He and I parted ways."

Removing his glasses, Camp coughed. "Ri...ght. Outside of funding, the extent of my involvement with the trek is to assure simulated nineteenth-century living conditions for modern women traveling a pioneer trail. Our wagon master, or in this case...mistress, is Maizie Boone. Says she's a direct descendant of Daniel. We haven't met, but on the phone she sounds like quite a character. Claims she birthed eight kids at home and is a grandmother of twenty. Most of them work in the business. There may be a book in all this." He drummed his fingers on the desk, envisioning Gina's photos interspersed with pictures from archives.

"Poor woman. İt's a wonder she's not dead. I have to say I'm glad to hear you're not gathering a harem. I found it curious that you only wanted women. Okay, I'll go—provided I have a wagon to myself. I don't like strangers handling my equipment."

Camp was quick to shove a release form across the table for Gina to sign. Odd woman, but he needed her expertise with a camera. Somewhere out there, he thought, a deserving fellow historian was no doubt kicking up his heels. "I'll be in touch," Camp promised, trailing her to the door.

What a diverse group this was shaping up to be. Camp rubbed his hands together. He couldn't wait to meet Emily Benton. The name Benton came from pioneer stock. Last week he'd read an article on a *Jessie* Benton's travels. Daughter of a once-prominent senator, Jessie had married a man known for his explorations along the Oregon Trail. According to Jessie's letters, she loved trail life. She dispatched regular chores easily, and at night, by firelight, she pieced intricate quilts by hand.

Camp had visited the historical society in the hope of finding her journal. As it turned out, they had little trail history from a woman's perspective. He'd never imagined that he might have difficulty finding data to compare or that Sherry was right—history books all seemed to be written by men.

"Hey, Camp," called the department secretary. "There's nobody else waiting."

He glanced at his watch. "Mrs. Benton's scheduled at four."

"Well, she's not here. I'll buzz your intercom when she shows."

Camp returned to his desk. He had papers to grade. But

the minute he hauled them out, she'd probably walk in. Then again—he checked the wall clock—she was already fifteen minutes late. If this was indicative of Emily Benton's punctuality, she might not be a good candidate. Maizie Boone had made it clear that she didn't mollycoddle anyone. Camp knew *he* wouldn't want to cross the gruff wagon mistress.

Ten more minutes of fidgeting and he was ready to write Emily off, pioneer name or not. He pulled out a folder of tests and was busily grading when a disheveled redhead in a rumpled blue suit stumbled through his doorway. She promptly dropped a bulging briefcase of the type mature students preferred over backpacks. Papers and books spewed from the doorway clear to Camp's desk.

Mumbling to herself, she scrambled awkwardly on hands and knees to collect the mess.

Startled as he was by the intrusion, Camp jumped up to lend a hand. From the array of textbooks, he judged her to be a student. And not a very good one if the low grades on the papers he scooped up were any indication.

He frowned. She must be from his overcrowded freshman lecture course, An Introduction to American History. Surely he'd remember her otherwise. But he'd left strict instructions at the desk that he wasn't available to students this afternoon. Maybe she'd be more organized next visit.

"Here," he said gruffly, stuffing papers neatly into her satchel. "I can't meet with you today. See Bess at the outer desk. Tell her to make you an appointment tomorrow during my free period. I hope rescheduling isn't terribly inconvenient."

"Well, it is." The smoky voice climbed. "I raced home from work, took my son to baseball practice and waited to make sure it wasn't canceled due to rain. It wasn't, so I drove my daughter across town to a friend's house. Freeway traffic was impossible." She shifted the bulky case.

"If I'm keeping you from happy hour, we can make this brief." She scraped two stubborn locks of fiery hair from a pale forehead, revealing angry, wisteria-blue eyes.

From his superior height, Nolan Campbell scowled at her, prepared to deliver a rebuke that would let her know in no uncertain terms how unwise it was to talk back to one's professor. The rebuke stuck in his throat, squeezing the breath from his lungs as he was sucked, spellbound, into those amazing blue eyes. Twice Camp opened and closed his mouth, feeling as if he were going down for the third time. Unable to lay claim to a logical reason for clammy hands and suddenly incoherent speech, he floundered back to his desk and flopped into his chair with all the grace of a beached whale.

Something must be terribly wrong. He had to get rid of this student quick. "Look, I'll give you a few seconds. What is it you need?" he croaked, sneaking two fingers to his wrist to take his pulse. It bounced erratically. Oh, God! Maybe it was his heart. He was at that age. And he didn't eat right. If he didn't die, he'd lay off cheeseburgers.

Camp blinked at the woman who'd followed him to his desk. Sweat popped out on his brow. Did she have sense enough to dial 911 if he fell off his chair? Not according to the scores written in red on the papers he'd picked up.

"What do *I* need?" Eyes narrowed, she thumped her bag and purse to the floor and perched gingerly on the edge of the chair that faced his desk. "Did I land in the right room? Are you Nolan Campbell?"

He nodded, keeping his gaze on the tiny frown lines that crinkled above her perfect nose rather than risk a second collision with those killer eyes.

"Then *we* have an appointment, Mr. Campbell. At least, I doubt there's more than one Nolan Campbell at this college who plans to take a wagon train over the

Santa Fe Trail.'' Dimpling prettily, she said, ''I'm Emily Benton, by the way. And I believe that's my application you're turning into confetti.''

Shocked to see his fingers shredding her application, Camp dropped the paper as if it were a hot potato. Things went from bad to worse as his gaze shifted to a spiky heel dangling enticingly from a shapely foot. He snapped his eyes to her face again.

Her smile broadened, and Camp felt as though he'd been kicked in the stomach. This time he had a clearer grasp of his symptoms. It'd been so long since he'd experienced lust that he'd failed to recognize the signs.

Emily Benton was nothing like he'd imagined. In addition to huge, captivating eyes, she had an air of fragility that made her totally unsuitable for his project. Why, the woman didn't have enough meat on her bones to attract a buzzard.

Camp closed his eyes and massaged his temples. ''So,'' he said, dragging one hand over the hollows in his cheeks, ''Judging by the address on your application, I assume you're attending our sister college. Instead of trekking across the prairie this summer, Mrs. Benton, I suggest you sign up for bonehead classes to help bring up those abominable grades.'' His words were cold, Camp knew. But her application stated she was a widow. She probably needed extra schooling to ensure a better job to help raise those kids she'd mentioned. Actually, he was doing her a favor, turning her down.

Not only that, he didn't want to deal with the tension of seeing her every day—something he was loath to admit. Folding his hands, he squared his shoulders and met her eyes. Almost.

''Student? Abominable grades?'' Emily clapped a hand to her head a moment. Then it dawned. ''Oh, the papers.'' She kicked the bag at her feet. ''I teach in the women's

program. Those are my students' papers.'' She grimaced.
''They *are* deplorable, aren't they? But I imagine that the
women in our program are lucky to be in class. Some we
barely coached through GEDs. A few of our older students finished high school, but thanks to crafty divorce
lawyers they're being forced into an alien work environ-
ment. Most have no marketable skills, nor have they
cracked a textbook in years.'' Her speech faltered. Why
was she telling him this? According to Sherry, the man
had some pretty dated ideas about women.

Emily lifted her chin, gathering her dignity. ''I hold a
Master's in psychology and one in sociology. I didn't realize a degree was required to go on your wagon train.''

''I, ah, no, it isn't.'' Taking in a deep breath, Camp
forced himself to study her application. Damn, she looked
as if a stiff wind would blow her away.

Emily couldn't say how she knew he was getting ready
to turn her down. But the feeling was strong. She'd promised herself that after the humiliation of dealing with
Dave—after years of trying to be the perfect wife and
putting her career on hold—she'd never beg another man
for anything. Lowering her gaze to clasped hands turning
white at the knuckles, she murmured, ''Please, Mr. Campbell. My children think money grows on trees. I need this
trip to teach them some solid values this summer.''

Camp's stomach churned. He hated looking down on
her bent head. He needed her, too, dammit—to fill his
contracted portion of the train. But the last thing he
wanted was daily contact with this woman. Wait a minute,
though. Pioneer women traveled with children. Emily
Benton and her kids offered a unique opportunity to contrast a contemporary single mother with her pioneer cousins. For goodness' sake, this was business. Nothing more.
Besides, he'd only see her at night when he collected the
data sheets.

"Sign here." Brusquely he handed her a release form. "I'll mail you the final packet of information in a week or so."

Emily didn't trust herself to meet his eyes. Her hand shook as she scribbled her name. If it wasn't for the fact that her in-laws were stealing her kids' affections by buying them everything under the sun, she'd tell this SOB exactly what he could do with his trip. And it wasn't pretty.

"Naturally, men take credit for winning the West. Hollywood says they did."
                    —*Camp overheard a woman tell Sherry this.*

CHAPTER TWO

AFTER POSTING his spring-semester grades with the registrar's office, Camp loaded his laptop computer in the car, along with his suitcase, and headed for Boonville. He felt curiously lighthearted—sort of like Tom Sawyer or Huck Finn. Probably because it was the first year in ten he'd skipped teaching summer classes. Until he'd begun to pack, he hadn't realized how stagnant his life had become. Or how badly he needed a break.

The thirty-mile drive seemed less. Historically speaking, Franklin, across the Missouri River from Boonville, was the "Cradle of the Santa Fe." But old Franklin was destroyed by a flood in 1826, and Boonville took up the slack. Maizie Boone's wagon train, the one Camp had begun to refer to as *his train,* would leave from the original cobblestone square in Boonville. This was real history, not some Hollywood script.

He reached the town's outskirts, slowed and navigated tree-lined streets, looking for the lot where Maizie had told him to park. He rounded a corner and saw them—a complement of Conestoga wagons framed against the riverbank. He gawked. Seeing the wagons up close, Camp suffered his first stab of apprehension. White canvas billowed above gigantic blue boxes, their running gear painted bright red. They reminded Camp of a fleet of sailboats on wheels. Lordy, he'd booked four of those monsters on a dare. Had knowingly filled them with greenhorns—or whatever they called novice trail drivers. With women yet. Women whose stamina he had reason to doubt. With the exception of Gina Ames.

Camp passed a hand over his sagging jaw. He'd agreed to arrive a week ahead of his researchers in order to stock the wagons and rent the draft horses destined to carry city dwellers many miles from the comforts of home.

The image of one particular city dweller, Emily Benton, loomed starkly before his eyes. Camp pictured her, reins in hand, clad in a flowing, flowery pioneer dress—a matching sunbonnet tossed carelessly back so that her riot of red hair caught flame in the afternoon sun.

He blinked hard to dispel the vision. A sudden cool breeze lifted the hair on the back of his neck, as if ghosts from the original Becknell caravans mocked his imprudence in accepting Emily's application. *Why did you?* they taunted.

"Hey, they all read the brochures." Not a woman had backed out, even though he'd half expected it after his secretary mailed out Maizie's six pages of rules and regs.

Camp stripped off his sport coat and tossed it in the back seat. Rolling his shirt sleeves midway up his arms, he sauntered toward the rustic building that housed Boone's Frontier Adventures.

A young, freckle-faced woman sat at a desk, phone to her ear. Karen Boone, according to her nameplate. One of Maizie's many grandchildren, Camp decided, gazing around the cracker-box office. Two chairs flanked a glass-topped table stacked with brochures like the one Sherry had brandished like a red flag to start this madness. Rather than sit, he studied a laminated, parchment wall map boldly marking the Santa Fe Trail. He'd memorized the route, but the old map reminded him of the risks encountered by the original wagon trains. So did the watercolor paintings depicting the old forts along the trail. Perusing each, Camp felt an odd kinship with the pioneers.

"May I help you?"

He spun at the sound of the girl's voice. He'd been so immersed in his own thoughts, he hadn't heard her hang up the phone. "I'm Nolan Campbell." He ambled up to her desk. "I believe Mrs. Boone is expecting me."

The girl's green eyes twinkled. "I could ask which Mrs. Boone. There are fifty here. More spread all the way to Boone's Lick. I've typed your name a zillion times these last few weeks, so I'd guess you mean Maizie. Want a tip? Don't call her 'Mrs.' If you haven't already figured it out, my grandmother is her own woman."

"I gathered that. But based on your smile, her bark must be worse than her bite."

"True, but I'll deny it if you tell her I said so. The image, you understand? Right now she's two miles out of town at her son Micah's ranch. We board the horses there. Let me draw you a map. She said to send you out to pick the animals that'll pull your wagons."

"Me? You mean it's not just a matter of paying rental fees?"

The girl glanced up from her drawing. "Another tip. Don't let Maizie hear panic in your voice. March right into the pasture and examine each horse. Run a hand over their legs and say 'um' a few times. Then casually ask her expert advice." No spark of humor showed this time when Karen passed Camp the map.

"Uh, thanks. For everything," he said, folding the paper several times as he backed out the door.

On the sidewalk again, Camp took a deep breath. What he knew about draft horses you could inscribe in capital letters on the head of a pin. A very small pin. Oh, during his preteen years he'd ridden his uncle's saddle horses. He'd curried them and seen to their care when his aunt and uncle took vacations, but...

"I suppose...a horse is a horse is a horse," he muttered, hurrying back to his car.

He drove the length of the small picturesque town and beyond, to where lush fields of sorghum replaced rural homes. When the road split around a huge, gnarled oak—the one sketched on his map—he slowed the car and began to search for the Boone mailbox. It wasn't difficult to locate. A green valley off to his left suddenly sprouted gargantuan horses contentedly munching grass. It struck Camp how wrong his earlier assessment had been. A horse *wasn't* just a horse. Each of those bruisers could easily make two saddle horses.

Car virtually at a crawl, he whistled through his teeth. "Some of those suckers have feet the size of dinner plates."

Farther along, he spotted someone inside the fence filling water troughs with a hose. Maizie, he presumed. The wagon mistress was everything he'd imagined and more. Calamity Jane without the cigarillo. Iron-gray hair hung straight to the woman's shoulders from beneath a battered, wide-brimmed hat. A shirt of fringed buck leather topped a split denim skirt. Her scuffed Wellingtons were caked with dirt and run-down at the heels.

As Camp climbed from the car, she glanced up and greeted him with a grin that pleated her sun-weathered cheeks into a profusion of wrinkles. His mind had already begun spinning the human interest portion of his paper.

"You'd be that Campbell fella, I suppose," she rasped. "I'm Maizie." After crushing his fingers in a solid handshake, she spit a stream of tobacco less than an inch to the right of his new black loafers. "Them'er pansy-ass shoes, boy. If you got boots in the car, you better fetch 'em. These Clydes, Percherons and Belgian drafts leave ankle-deep calling cards.'' She placed one foot on the bottom rung of the fence and scraped a layer of dark muck onto the wood rail as if for emphasis.

The pungent aroma told Camp he'd been wrong about that being dirt caked on her boots. It also crossed his mind that Calamity's cigarillo might be preferable to Maizie's chew. He jerked a thumb toward his car. "I brought boots. Give me a minute to change." Thankfully, he'd packed his oldest jeans. He doubted if new denim would pass her muster. As he poked the legs of his best worsted wool slacks into his boot tops, Camp wished he'd changed clothes before leaving campus.

"Ready," he said, rejoining her. "How many horses are we talking?" As Karen had suggested, he knelt and ran a hand down the iron-hard leg of a horse with gentle eyes.

"Four per team, and two per wagon spare. I'm a stickler for rotating stock. We have vets meeting us in Fort Larned and McNees Crossing. My son Terrill will deliver us feed and fresh water. We won't run our animals into the ground the way pioneers did. This is a reenactment, not the real McCoy. That's why I asked drivers to arrive a day early. So you'll all learn to hitch, unhitch and handle these babies."

Babies? Hippo babies, maybe. Camp stood. "Uh, Maizie...all my drivers are women. I never mentioned it— never presumed that *my* role mattered. I'm a college professor conducting a study comparing modern and pioneer women. My volunteers aren't exactly the types who work out with weights or anything." Again, Emily Benton came to mind. Smooth, unblemished skin and a waist Camp could span with his hands. If her head reached his shoulder, he'd be surprised. Camp suffered a second wave of guilt as he eyed the tons of muscle. "Why don't I leave the choosing to you," he said smoothly, remembering the last part of Karen's advice.

"Uh-huh!" Maizie stroked a callused hand down the back of a massive brown-and-white horse. "We'll go with the Clydesdales for your ladies. At seventeen to eighteen hands, they're a little taller than the Percherons, but more even-tempered. Perches are bred with Arabians, so they're more feisty. Belgians are the biggest. Strongest, too. Most are nineteen to twenty hands. You men can drive them."

"Well, I..." He tugged an ear. "I'm not exactly going with the train."

"Uh-huh. Where *do* you fit in, sonny? You're laying out a passel of dough for somebody who's missing the fun."

Camp summarized his plans and ended by saying, "I'd prefer others on the train didn't know about my study. I don't want them purposely helping the women. Ruins the results, you understand."

"It's been my experience that people on these trips either start out friendly and hate one another before the end, or they begin every man for himself and finish up pulling together. Thing I can't see...is women with any guts a'tall lettin' you study 'em like pet rats, 'n you stayin' out of the maze." She spit another stream past his ear, pinning him with faded, all-knowing eyes.

"Of course they will. My paper isn't about how *I'd* fare in the wilds. Men haven't gone soft. We still do manual labor."

"Uh-huh." Maizie gave the horse a final pat. "How well do you know women, boy?" she asked, leading the way out of the pasture. "Claim to be an expert, do you?"

Camp's laughter held a nervous edge. "Show me a man who claims to be an expert on females and I'll show you a bald-faced liar. Even so, I know some in my group will stick until death to prove that anything pioneer women did, modern women can do better.''

"Uh-huh!" Maizie dug a stubby pencil and a wrinkled pad from her skirt pocket and wrote out a rental slip for the horses. "Stop by the office and pay Karen. Meet me at the general store on Market Street tomorrow at ten to buy supplies. I hope you've got the muscle to stock four wagons. It's definitely manual labor—loading bags of flour, coffee, sugar, salt, beans, crackers and sides of home-cured bacon.''

Camp took the bill and climbed into his car. Had he made an error taking her into his confidence? The way she said *uh-huh*, a body would think Maizie Boone had a Ph.D. in psychology. He chuckled as he started the car. Her advice, like little Lucy's in the *Peanuts* cartoons, was probably worth the same—about five cents.

WHEN SATURDAY rolled around, the day Maizie had set aside to teach drivers how to hitch and unhitch the teams, Camp expected his research subjects to trickle in one by one. They surprised him, arriving en masse, accompanied by a television crew from Columbia and a woman reporter from the campus newspaper—which didn't please him.

"Whose bright idea was this?" he muttered, sidling up to his sister.

"Yvette's. What's the matter, Nolan, afraid they'll steal your thunder?"

Camp shrugged. "No, but neither do I want them turning this into some kind of farce. Why do you all look like you stepped off the pages of Mule Creek Mercantile's catalog?" The women, all except Sherry's roommate, sported spanking new boots, blue jeans and Stetsons. Yvette was Hollywood all the way, in white jeans and a purple suede halter top trimmed with fringe, feathers and beads. She wore matching purple moccasins. Camp would have bet the farm she'd come dressed like this.

"Ugh! What stinks?" Yvette ran up to them holding her nose. Her pristine moccasins landed in a fresh pile of manure. She slipped, slid, then went down squarely on her rump. "Ick! Yuck," she squealed as Camp hid a smile and stretched out a hand to help her up.

"You're laughing, Nolan Campbell." She smacked his hand away. "Don't touch me." Instead, she accepted help from a member of the press. The instant she was up, Yvette turned on Sherry. "I assumed they'd pull the wagons with something civilized, like tractors." Sniffing the air, she wrinkled her dainty nose. "This is positively gross. I'm not spending ten weeks smelling horse poop." She clapped a palm over the closest camera lens. "Those shots had better end up on the cutting-room floor, my friend. I know the station manager. Grab your stuff out of my car, Sherry. I'm outta here."

Sherry gaped at her roommate's retreating figure. "Yvette, wait! You promised. Darn it! I paid your half of the rent for the whole summer."

The blonde gingerly picked her way to the car, paying no attention. She peeled off her moccasins and threw them in a nearby trash barrel. Hopping the remaining distance on bare feet, she unlocked the car and tumbled inside.

Sherry took one look at Camp's smirk and ran after her friend. "Oh, for pity's sake, Yvette. I'll pay off your Visa," Sherry wheedled. "Come on, this is exactly what Nolan expects. What happened to striking a blow for modern womanhood?"

"You strike it." Yvette knelt on the front seat, leaned over into the back and started pitching Sherry's bedding and duffel bags out on the ground.

"Fine! Leave. Be a traitor." Sherry grumbled as she snatched her things. "And I want that money back!"

Yvette slammed her door, cranked the engine and peeled out of the lot.

Maizie Boone jabbed an elbow into Camp's side. "Uh-huh! What'd I tell you?"

He scowled. "Shall we proceed with the lesson? My sister's capable of handling a wagon alone. The way I see it, I still have four drivers."

Maizie inclined her head toward his dwindling group. "Maybe you haven't been listening to those kids. They've been bellyaching to leave since they got here. Seein' how frazzled the mom looks, I'll bet you a long neck at Sammy's Bar that she splits next."

Camp had sampled the cheeseburgers and brew at Sammy's last night. Good as they were, he didn't want to meet Maizie there to pay off that type of bet. But now that she'd mentioned it, he heard kids squabbling. He zeroed in on them. Neither resembled Emily. The boy was taller than his mother, and sturdier, his hair auburn, not red. The girl was shorter by a head and as thin as a reed. Rings circled each of her red-tipped fingers. Except for the mop of mahogany hair, she'd pass for a younger version of Yvette. Flounced like her, too. *Brother!*

Emily's jaw was locked in place. She didn't look as if she'd give an inch. "I'll take your bet," Camp told Maizie impulsively. He knew, as Maizie didn't, that Emily's kids were the main reason she'd signed up.

He turned, planning to introduce himself to Emily's offspring. Instead, he nearly mowed down Brittany Powers. Camp's eyes bugged. Brittany's fingernails weren't painted red—they were half silver and half black. At least, on the hand possessively clutching his sleeve.

"Nolan," she whispered breathlessly, a speech pattern he'd noticed her developing over the last weeks of the semester. "I'm positively freaked by horses. You'll take care of mine, won't you?" Her fingers walked up his shirtfront and fiddled with the silver medallion he wore around his neck.

He frowned into eyes outlined in kohl and shaded in luminous silver—colors that matched her nail polish but left her looking oddly like a raccoon. Debating how to handle an effective rebuke in the midst of so many people, he caught Emily's expression of disgust. Surely she hadn't pegged him as a cradle robber.

"I'm not traveling with the train," he snapped at Brittany, firmly setting her away. "Follow Maizie. She'll show you how to harness the teams. According to her, the Clydesdales are big, lovable teddy bears. You'll do fine, Brittany."

"What do you mean, you aren't traveling with the wagon train?" A chorus of angry voices almost blew Camp off his feet. Suddenly, Sherry, Gina and Emily all converged, hands on hips, eyes flashing.

Warily, he sidestepped a cameraman, and aligned himself with the wagon mistress. She spit a bead of tobacco, two drops of which splashed on his boot.

"Uh-huh," she mused in that way Camp had come to find exceedingly irritating. "These the gals who'll stick until death to prove you wrong?" she murmured.

Smile plastered to his lips, Camp held up a palm. "Listen...ladies...I figured I'd make you nervous breathing down your necks. Maizie gave me a list of your scheduled stops. I plan to pop in at regular intervals and pick up these data sheets."

"If you aren't going," Brittany said, pouting, "then I'm not, either."

Gina gathered the others to caucus. After a brief discussion, she broke free. "That's about the size of it, Campbell," she said. "If you don't go, we all quit."

"Hooray," chorused the Benton kids. "Let's go home, Mom."

Emily advanced on Camp. "I'll have you know I gave up a chance to teach summer school. I need that stipend. What do you plan to do about it?"

"Look." Camp raked a hand through his hair. Mentally he added up how much he'd already forked out. The money was nothing compared with the fact that he'd promised his department chair a publishable paper by the start of fall term. "You all agreed to be part of my study. No one said I had to travel with the train."

"I thought it was understood," Sherry said.

Gina crossed her arms. "Well, we could go and write any old thing on his data sheets. Skew his study all to hell! He'd be none the wiser."

"Oh, but that wouldn't be right!" Emily exclaimed, eyes bright with concern even after the others silenced her with glares.

As if things weren't already going down the toilet, Camp's colleagues drove in next. Hearing a reporter explain to the newcomers why everyone was milling about, he shook his head and groaned. "Listen to this great front-page caption," the man bragged, "'Local College Prof Fails Test.'"

Sherry snapped her fingers. "Could you maybe add 'Beaten By Women'?"

Camp's knees all but buckled when Lyle Roberts clapped him hard between the shoulder blades. "Camp's just fooling around. I assure you he's one hundred percent committed to this project. *Of course* he's driving a wagon. He wouldn't dream of backing out before every last woman here falls by the trail."

"Lyle!" Camp weighed available options for digging out of this mess.

"Uh-huh," grunted Maizie. "Gonna be the shortest wagon train in history."

"Okay...hold on," Camp shouted. "It's no big deal.

Brittany, you go in Sherry's wagon. Gina asked to be on her own. Emily and her kids will take the third Conestoga, and I'll drive number four. Now, if everybody's satisfied, can we get this show on the road? I have bedding to buy before the stores close.''

It was hard to tell who was more disgruntled by his capitulation, Emily Benton's children or Camp himself. Megan Benton stamped a dainty foot, declaring her mother couldn't *make* her go. As if to prove it, she flung herself down on a park bench. Mark grabbed his boom box and turned it up to deafening decibels, refusing to turn it down as Emily ordered. He glared when Camp walked over and shut it off. Sullen, the boy flopped next to his sister. "This summer sucks.''

Camp was relieved that Lyle and Jeff had trundled off to Sammy's Bar with the last of the nosy reporters. He felt doubly glad they were gone when Maizie gave his team of teddy-bear Clydesdales to strangers—Doris and Vi, two elementary-school teachers from St. Louis who'd joined the trek. Then she delivered to Camp a quartet of nasty-tempered Belgians. One stepped on his foot, possibly crippling him for life. Another continually tried to eat his hair, blowing foul-smelling breath in his face. "Stop it,'' he hissed.

An hour after all the women had mastered the task of hitching and unhitching, Camp remained in the park, tangled in the harnesses and singletrees that yoked the teams together. The face-saver was that a loudmouthed man from Philadelphia had done no better. Philly, as Camp dubbed the braggart, claimed he'd fished Alaska, shot the rapids of Oregon's Rogue River and single-handedly sailed through the Greek islands. That was where Camp tuned him out and got down to business. He'd be damned if he was going to let a few scrawny women and four fat horses make an ass out of him.

By the time he'd performed to Maizie's liking, Camp was more than ready to slug down the beer the woman owed him. But it was four-thirty. He had less than thirty minutes to make it to the general store to purchase bedding. No way would he sleep on bare planks just to prove he was a manly man.

Let the women jeer. He intended to scare up spare batteries for his laptop, too. It turned out no store in town carried the type he needed. Giving up, Camp raced into a stationery store at five minutes to five to buy every ruled tablet they had in stock. At this point he was beyond caring that the pads came only in pink and lavender. Although he drew the line at pencils with grape-and-strawberry-scented erasers.

By the time he poked his head through Sammy's swinging doors at six-thirty, he found the place jammed with Saturday-night locals. Ah, well, he could do without a drink. Maizie had warned everyone it was "wagons ho" at 5 a.m. She didn't sound as if she'd be inclined to wait for anyone shuffling in late. Besides, the wail from the jukebox only intensified Camp's headache, and the smoke was thick enough to cut with a dull knife. All in all, it'd been a most trying day. He recalled passing a mom-and-pop café somewhere between Sammy's Bar and Maizie's office. A quiet dinner appealed more than a cold beer.

He found the place easily enough. But as he reached for the door, Camp noticed Emily Benton and her kids seated in a front booth. Megan and Mark were clearly still sulking, and Emily looked positively grim. The very last thing he needed to round out his day was to step into the middle of a family feud.

"What the hell," he said with a yawn, "I'll skip dinner in favor of extra z's." Retracing his steps, he again resisted the smell of onions wafting from Sammy's. At the corner, he crossed the street and didn't stop until he'd

claimed his room at the motel. Too tired to shower, Camp shucked his clothes and tumbled into bed—the last real one he'd see for weeks. He sighed as the mattress adjusted to his contours. Seconds before sleep took him, he sat up, snapped on the light and set the alarm on his watch, advancing the time to allow for a leisurely shower and a big breakfast.

What seemed like nano-seconds later, the sound of car doors slamming jarred Camp from a pleasant dream. Where he lived—the outskirts of town, almost in the country—nights were so quiet he almost always slept solidly until the alarm went off. Rolling toward the wall, he pulled the pillow over his head. Then someone banged insistently on his door.

"Wrong room," he yelled. Some fool must have stayed too long at Sammy's Bar and as a result, misread the room numbers.

"Campbell? Is that you? Open up!" At Emily Benton's voice he jackknifed to a sitting position, then leaped out of bed. Heart hammering, Camp yanked the door open the length of the chain. It vibrated out of his hand and slammed in his face. Cautiously he opened it again. "What's wrong? Was Maizie right? Are you quitting?" His sleepy eyes failed to register full daylight.

"Me? The others bet that you'd run off during the night. Maizie sent me to check. It's five-thirty. She's fit to be tied."

"*What?* Come in." The chain jingled, then clanked against the door. "Wait," he said in a muffled voice. "I'm not decent." Snatching his watch from the table, Camp shook it, only to discover that it'd stopped shortly after midnight. "Hell and damnation!" He dug in his bag, dragged out a clean pair of jeans and jumped into them. Socks, boots and a pullover shirt followed. Wadding his dirty clothes into the bag, he raced across the room and

threw open the door. "My watch stopped. The battery must have died. You're saying everyone's already hitched their wagons?"

"Everyone except you. Maizie's...annoyed. The wagons are probably strung the length of Broadway by now."

Camp's curse was muffled by the growl of his stomach. "I'm starved," he said. "I skipped lunch and dinner yesterday." He rubbed his jaw. "I haven't shaved and my teeth feel scuzzy."

"Well, it's too late now. You'll have to get something out of your stores."

"You're kidding?" His steps slowed. "Beans, rice, flour, coffee—those are Maizie's idea of stores."

Emily failed to cloak a look of pity. "Sounds like good pioneer fare to me. Isn't that the object of this trek? To simulate what happened in 1821?"

Because she'd spoken the truth, Camp shut his mouth and accepted his fate. Except that Emily had been wrong on one count. Maizie hadn't gone ahead. She'd waited to chew him out.

Pinching the bridge of his nose between thumb and finger, Camp endured her verbal flogging. This he could definitely do without.

Amid a rousing send-off by townsfolk and a marching band from Santa Fe Trail High School out of Overbrook, Kansas, Camp's four horses decided to act up.

Maizie's son, Robert, and his boy, Jared, occupants of the final wagon, helped subdue Camp's nervous team. If Robert Boone had looked less like his mother, or had been built less like a linebacker, Camp would have tried bribing him into going after coffee and a couple of Egg McMuffins. Or he would have if Mark Benton hadn't kept leaning around the canvas-covered bows of Emily's wagon, leering at him.

By the time they pulled out, a full hour late, Camp was

ready to strangle the kid. And just where was the boy's mother during all of this? The starchy woman who'd jerked Camp out of bed at an unholy hour, acting as if he was a no-good slacker.

Emily Benton had absolutely no control over those brats. Camp recalled her saying in the interview that she wanted to remove them from the harmful influence of overindulgent grandparents. He'd sympathized and silently applauded her. Now he discovered that she herself was turning a blind eye to the antics of her little darlings.

If he had children... But why even get into that? A family was out of the question when you didn't have a wife. The only woman he'd asked to fill that bill had dumped him. After she'd accepted his ring, Greta decided she didn't want to spend vacations renovating a musty old house or being dragged through museums. He *hadn't* dragged her. Those things were a big part of who he was. But Greta's departure still hurt. Oh, he'd pretended to shrug off the loss as inconsequential—had even set about playing the field—which only left him more confused.

As the wagons stretched out, and the sun spread fingers of pink and gold across an endless blue sky, Camp realized it was a mistake to have this much time on his hands to let his mind wander. Colleagues saw him as a man in control of his destiny. Intelligent, happy and smart to remain single. Sherry's pals saw him as a callous guy on the make. Both groups were off base. When he wasn't busy, he was lonely as hell. The older he got, the more he wanted a close relationship of the sort his parents enjoyed. And children of his own. Nice, well-behaved kids.

He shifted on the hard wooden seat, staring blindly at the rumps of the plodding horses. No doubt about it, he was going to be pretty darned sick of his own company long before they reached Kansas, let alone Santa Fe, New Mexico.

Emily Benton grabbed her son, who was once again leaning too far off the seat. "Mark, what's so interesting about watching where we've just been? Why don't you crawl in the wagon bed and play a board game with your sister?"

"Are you kidding? Megan wouldn't lower herself. She's probably got her nose in one of those horror stories she sneaked into her duffel. Besides, I'm bugging the old far— I mean dude. The one who shut off my tunes. He knows I'm slagging him and it drives him nuts."

"What old dude? And what's 'slagging'?" Emily asked absently, overlooking his slip of the tongue as she debated trying to roust Megan from her book. Communication of any sort with Megan had been almost nonexistent since Dave died. Emily had great hopes they'd reconnect on this trip. Her daughter was growing up too fast.

Mark jerked a thumb over his shoulder. "Slagging is like to insult somebody. I meant the old dude you guys forced into driving a wagon. The con man."

"Professor Campbell? Mark, don't call him names."

The boy screwed up his face. "I don't care. He reminds me of Dad. All smiles, making himself out to be the big man, while he's conning you into doing the work."

Emily shot her son a sidelong glance. "If you saw all that, why is it so hard for you to see your grandfather's attempts to manipulate?"

"Toby has the bucks to do nice things for us. We're poor."

"Don't call your grandfather by his given name. It's disrespectful, no matter what he and your grandmother say. And we aren't poor, Mark. We're not rich, but you have food on the table, a roof over your head and clothes on your back."

"Megan says Toby has the Midas touch. He's a king

who had rooms full of money. Like Gramps. Why not let him and Mona spend some on us?''

"Oh, honey, it's hard to explain. Gifts sometimes come with strings attached. Like if you accept gifts, the giver considers that you owe him in return. A payback. But his idea of an acceptable payback may not match yours.''

Faint lines etched the child's brow. "I don't get it. Toby and Mona have everything. What could they want from us?''

"Nothing, birdbrain.'' There was a stirring inside the wagon and Megan thrust her head between her mother and brother. ''Mom's jealous because they can do more for us. Mona said so.''

"Megan, that's not true.'' Emily did her best to hang on to her temper.

"It is so, or else why did you drag us on this smelly old trip? You didn't want us swimming in their pool or having them take us to the mall for school clothes. You'd rather let us die out here on some moldy trail.''

Emily gripped the reins too tightly and the Clydesdales ground to a stop. "Megan, must you be so melodramatic? No one's going to die on this trip.'' Her lecture was interrupted by harsh snorts. Turning, Emily saw Nolan Campbell's team pull abreast of hers.

"What's the matter with you?'' he shouted. "Can't you signal or something? I almost ran you down. Are you totally irresponsible?''

"You might have slowed your horses,'' she said through clenched teeth. Mark was more right than he knew. Nolan Campbell seemed just as dictatorial as Dave.

"Sheesh!'' Mark rolled his eyes in disgust. "You'd better fan it, Mom. I told you, the old dude's a loose cannon.''

Emily gazed at the huge wagon inching toward hers.

Snapping her reins, she sped ahead of Camp. "Just stay away from me," she ordered. "From us."

Mark's lips curled in an impudent grin.

Camp coughed and spit out grit thrown from the Bentons' wheels. In a flash of brilliant insight he wondered why on earth he'd wasted time regretting that he didn't have a wife and kids. Especially a wife!

"Historic reality is a far cry from *men's* version of it."

—*Gina Ames's observation on her first data sheet.*

CHAPTER THREE

THE SETTING SUN CAST long shadows behind the wagons before Maizie gave the signal to stop for the night some five miles outside the community of Arrow Rock.

Camp had bounced up and down on the hardwood seat so long his butt felt numb. Blistered even. He wanted desperately to leave his perch, yet he was half-afraid to get down in case he couldn't walk. Too humiliating. *You have to do something, dolt.*

What he did was watch the others unhitch their horses and hobble them in the carpet of grass beneath a stand of yellowwood and hickory trees. His best view was of Emily's wagon, since he'd parked beside her. Damn, but she looked positively chipper the way she hopped down and bent to loosen the singletrees. Camp was struck by an urge to ruffle the wisps of hair escaping her hat. Curls that shone like new copper pennies in the peachy afterglow of the sun.

His gaze slipped automatically from Emily's hair to her nicely rounded backside. It was plain to see why pioneer men chose to walk or ride horses and let their wives drive the wagons. The simple fact was, women had more natural padding than men.

Would you look at that! Padding be damned. Emily Benton had a thick bench cushion covering that hard plank seat. How would Sherry justify *that* bit of comfort?

Camp scowled, then moaned as he shifted his position, checking to see if the other women had cheated, too. They had! Of all the nerve... Yet on another level—the one that hurt—Camp wished he'd been as smart.

"Are you all right?" Emily's quiet question jarred him from his stupor.

He straightened quickly, ignoring the hot prickles shooting up his thigh as feeling returned to one leg. "I'm fine. Just wondered why we aren't circling the wagons."

Her low laughter sent hot prickles of another sort along Camp's already tender nerve ends.

"And you call yourself a historian, Campbell. For shame. Pioneers only circled the wagons to ward off attacks by marauding Indians. Which didn't occur nearly as often as Hollywood would like us to believe, I might add."

He bristled. "Wagon circles are well documented in the journals I've read. They guarded against more than Indian and outlaw attacks. Circles discouraged scavenging by coyote, cougar and bear."

Mark and Megan Benton tumbled out of Emily's wagon in time to overhear the last exchange. "Mo...th...er!" Megan wailed. "We'll all be eaten in our sleep."

"Bears. Cool!" Mark discarded his sullen look for one of delight—the first Camp had seen from either of the kids.

"I'll bet there're rattlesnakes too," the boy announced in a loud, shivery voice, his face shoved close to his sister's.

She shrieked and scrambled back inside the wagon. Camp felt sorry for Emily. She had her hands full with those two.

"Megan, get back out here," Emily called. "It's time to pick up our list of nightly chores from Maizie. It'll be dark before you know it."

"Chores?" Camp looked blank. His stomach felt caved in to his backbone. The apples Maizie dispensed at the noon water stop had barely whetted his appetite. But starved though he was, Camp wanted to record his impressions of the trip before they faded. Every bone-jarring memory.

"Didn't you read the rules you mailed out?" Emily asked. "It's number four. Maizie doles out a list of chores every night. She'll rotate duties so one person doesn't always get the cushiest jobs and vice versa."

"You have the rules memorized?" Camp paused in the painful act of climbing from the high wagon seat. "I barely glanced at the packet. My secretary ran copies and sent them out. Why would I study the rules? I hadn't intended to travel with the train," he said, as if blaming Emily for his change in plans.

"That was evident. Still, you'd better try to borrow a copy, unless you're expecting special privileges."

"Not at all." Camp reacted to her sarcasm.

"Then I suggest you unhitch your team. Everyone else is already headed for Maizie's wagon."

"Bully for them," he snapped, uncaring that he sounded as fractious as Megan had earlier.

Emily pursed her lips. "Let's go, kids." She checked the Clydesdales' hobbles one last time before hurrying off.

Megan Benton didn't budge. Mark sidled up to Camp. "I've never seen a bear. Are they really out there in the woods?"

Camp considered possible answers, then discarded all but the truth. He'd decided on the policy to which his father subscribed—that all questions asked by kids deserved an honest answer.

"Bears were a problem for the original Santa Fe trailblazers, Mark. We're more apt to run afoul of those rattlers you mentioned. If you gather wood, take care. Roll the piece over with your toe before picking it up. Wood provides homes for a variety of spiders, as well as snakes."

"Hot damn!" Mark exclaimed, then rolled his eyes as his sister let out another shriek and climbed to her knees on the wagon seat.

"Mona said the fact Mom's dragging us on this trip shows how weirded out she is. Toby *begged* me to tell some judge friend of his about this nutty plan. I wish I had. We could've stayed home. And I'm not doing any stupid old chores."

"Who are Mona and Toby?" Camp asked Mark, who—without being asked—helped stake Camp's last horse, a Belgian named Renegade. All day Camp had called him numerous other names under his breath.

Mark waited until they'd finished before answering Camp. "Mona and Toby are my grandparents. Since our dad died, they want us all to live with them. Mom won't. They fight about it all the time. Megan and me hear...'cept I don't think they know."

Camp, who rarely got involved in matters that didn't concern him, was moved to support Emily. "Talk to your mother. I'm sure she has valid reasons."

"She'd lie," Megan said bitterly. "Mona says it's Mom's fault that Dad drank too much. She didn't try to understand him."

Camp thought he was hearing more about the Bentons' private lives than Emily would want discussed. He cast around for a way to extricate himself. Unfortunately, it came in the form of Brittany Powers. She ran toward him waving two slips of paper.

"Nolan. Nolan," she yelled, apparently forgetting the

breathy voice. "I have your chore assignment. We're working together. Isn't that awesome?"

Reluctant to be teamed with Brittany, Camp nevertheless accepted one of the slips. "Well, Mark," he said, frowning after reading it, "don't worry about fending off snakes tonight. We're the wood hunters." He indicated himself and Brittany.

"Snakes?" Brittany shivered, cleaving herself to Camp's side. "I hate creepy crawlies. You're just so...oo brave."

Embarrassed, Camp tried peeling the young woman off his arm. "I need to grab a pair of gloves. You'd better do the same, Brittany."

"I didn't bring any, Nolan." She drew out his name. "But I'll tag along and keep you company." She wound both arms around his biceps this time.

Damnation, but she had a grip like a boa constrictor. "I'm sure there's something you can do around here. Let Mark help me." Camp snatched at the boy's shirtsleeve with his free hand. "Okay with you, kid?" He hoped Mark hadn't heard how desperate he was to avoid going into the woods with Brittany. But Mark was definitely astute.

"What's it worth to you, man? Five bucks?"

Little blackmailer. Luckily, Emily returned then. Before she gave her kids their assignments, Camp hit her with a smile. "Would you give Brittany Mark's job and let him go with me?" At Emily's arched brow, he explained Brittany's lack of gloves.

Emily saw how Camp took a step and Brittany moved with him, as if they were joined at the hip. Her husband had had younger women swarming over him, too. Dave had loved the attention. "I'm sure you'd rather Mark lent Brittany some gloves, right?"

Mark seemed surprised by his mother's caustic tone.

Camp was plain angry. For crying out loud, she seemed downright eager to toss him to the wolves.

"What'll I have to do if I don't help him haul wood?" Mark bargained with Emily.

"Locate rocks and build a fire ring for each wagon."

The boy jerked a thumb toward Camp. "I'll go with the dude. Her witchy fingernails'll poke holes in my gloves." He pointed at Brittany. "Ain't never seen nails like hers 'cept at Halloween."

"Twit. If I were a witch I'd turn you into a toad." Brittany gave him an evil eye. She clung to Camp's sleeve a moment longer, then reluctantly let him go. "I don't want to break my nails on rocks, either. Maybe I'll go see what Sherry's doing. We'll meet later, won't we, Nolan? I mean...you're collecting our data sheets, aren't you?"

Her affected whisper was back, Camp noticed with a wince. Avoiding her question, he said, "I suspect all the chores will be hard on hands, Brittany. I'd hate to see you tear a nail badly and, uh, risk infection."

Brittany's hands fluttered. "You are so thoughtful, Nolan. Nobody else cares if I rip a nail clear off. Or an arm or a leg, for that matter."

"I'm sure your parents expect me to judge these situations in their place."

"My folks don't give a damn what I do as long as I'm out of their hair. I'm a burden they'd like to be shut of for good, not just this summer."

Taken aback, Camp didn't know how to respond.

"You guys run along," Emily said softly, coming to Camp's rescue after all. "I'll carry the rocks. Megan and Brittany can push them into circles with their feet if they don't want to mess up their nails."

"Hey, thanks." Relieved beyond words, Camp wasted no time grabbing his gloves and striking off ahead of Mark into the copse of trees. He'd certainly misjudged

Brittany Powers. Since the day she'd walked into his classroom, he'd figured her for a spoiled kid who had everything. Expensive clothes. Car. Enough spending money to feed a third-world nation. Everything but parental love, it seemed.

"Yo' dude," panted Mark as he caught up to Camp. "That Brittany chick has the hots for you."

Camp peered down his nose at the boy. "Don't be silly. And don't call women 'chicks.' I'm Brittany's college professor. I'm old enough to be her father."

Mark stopped and tipped his head back to gaze at his taller companion. "Uh-huh," he grunted. "Guess she digs old dudes, then."

Camp snatched up a long stick and parted the shrubs. The kid sounded so much like Maizie it was scary. "Look, here are three pieces of dry pine. Take them to one of the wagons while I look for more. And don't call me 'dude.' Understand?"

"It's cool if you don't want to talk about your love life. My mom sends me off to do stuff when I make her uncomfortable, too."

"I don't have a lov—we're not—oh, blast." If he wasn't half-starved he'd leave the kid on his own and go log today's experiences. He had some beauts. But undoubtedly there'd be time while the women cooked dinner. Which would be speedier if he hurried back with wood for the cook fires. As if on cue his stomach rumbled again. Camp muttered a silent prayer that the people Maizie had assigned to the chore of cooking would allow plenty for ravenous men.

By the time they finished gathering wood, the sun had dropped. A stiff night breeze carried the smell of wood smoke and the mouthwatering aromas of onions and garlic. Saliva pooled in Camp's mouth as Mark darted off.

Cheery campfires crackled in front of every wagon. Correction: every wagon but his.

In the flicker cast by Emily's dancing flames, Camp saw that someone had shoved rocks into a circle in front of his wagon. If not for the fact that the air had grown chill and he'd prefer to stay warm while he ate, he wouldn't even bother lighting a fire. The minute he finished eating he intended to collect the data sheets and hibernate.

Plans set, Camp strolled nonchalantly past the Benton wagon.

Emily called out, stopping him. "Maizie said to tell you that your wagon tilts left. She wants you to redistribute your load. Even out the heavier stuff."

"I don't have much that's heavy. But sure, I'll get right on it."

"Oh, another thing. Robert Boone has a big can of oil. We all picked up our ration and oiled our harnesses. You'll need to do yours."

Camp tried to see her face, but she stood in the shadows mixing something in a metal bowl. "Anything else?" He spread his feet, hooking thumbs in his belt.

"No. Just start a fire and cook your meal. Robert and Jared hauled water up from the creek for washing dishes. He said to use water from the wagon barrels for cooking and making coffee."

"Wait! You mean we're not eating potluck?"

She raised a sticky hand and brushed a springy lock of hair back with her forearm. "You mean everyone makes a dish and we eat together? No. The rules clearly state that we're on our own for meals."

"But..." The only food he'd fixed over an open fire had been an occasional hot-dog or toasted marshmallows. And that was about thirty years ago. Now he ate all his weekday meals out. On weekends, he popped prepackaged frozen dinners into the microwave. Now he really wished he'd read those frigging rules. The packet probably included recipes. If he'd only known—the store in Boonville where he'd bought his gear stocked boil-in-a-bag meals for backpackers.

Well, he had to do something fast. The kitchen goddess was looking down her nose again. One thing he knew for sure, he'd die before letting the truth of his culinary ineptitude leak out to his research subjects. "Argh..." Camp cleared his throat. "Believe I'll just mosey up the line and see if Maizie has an extra set of rules."

"Not that I want to keep you..." Emily smiled sweetly. "But if you light a fire now it'll be ready for cooking when you return. See...I've put water on for tea. Once the flames die down, I'll set out my Dutch oven." She pointed to a set of stacked pans. "Your coffee will be drinkable while your meal cooks—if you drink coffee, that is," she stammered.

"I do. Rarely this late, but tonight it sounds good."

"All this fresh air. Sharpens the appetite," she said with a laugh.

When Emily Benton laughed low in her throat like that it sharpened *his* appetite, Camp discovered. But not for food.

He shifted uncomfortably. If there was anything he didn't need, it was to lust after a grieving widow—and definitely not one who couldn't seem to control her kids. Grunting his thanks, he withdrew and built a fire without glancing her way again. Five matches later, it stayed lit.

As long as he was going to visit Maizie, Camp decided to ask if he could change places in the line—so he wouldn't be parked next to *her* tomorrow night. He pawed through his supplies, unearthing a fire grate, a coffeepot and the apparatus Emily called a Dutch oven. The coffeepot didn't have a device to hold filters like the one at home. It was galvanized inside and out. Camp figured you filled it with water and tossed in coffee beans.

Only, how many beans? Maizie's supply list had called for generic canned coffee. He wasn't picky about much, but he was about coffee. The minute he found out he'd be driving a wagon, he'd traded in the can for a sack of gourmet beans.

Settling on a handful, Camp dropped the grate over the fire and sat the pot on it before he took off to see Maizie. Cooking wasn't so hard, he thought smugly.

At each wagon, Camp paused to sniff. The elementary-school teachers had potatoes roasting in foil wrap and were frying a thick slab of ham. Vi, the taller of the two, said the mouthwatering confection cooling on a flat rock was cinnamon apple cobbler.

Refusing to lick his lips, Camp left. Robert's and Jared's plates were piled high with beans and franks. Camp skirted the couple from Philadelphia. That guy was so obnoxious he probably made his wife whip up baklava and lamb wrapped in grape leaves so he'd have another opportunity to brag about his trip to Greece.

Camp skidded to a halt at Sherry and Brittany's fire. "Who fixed that?" He pointed to something that had the look of strawberry shortcake.

"Me." Sherry blew on her fingers and scraped them lightly across her shirt. "Emily discovered a patch of wild strawberries along that fencerow. I also made tomatoes, peppers and onions over brown rice. Tomorrow, it's Brittany's turn to cook. We decided to trade off."

Camp swatted at a curl of smoke. "When did you learn to cook?" he demanded "As I recall, you got a D in home ec."

"In freshman sewing—because we didn't have a machine at home. At the condo, I do most of the cooking.

Yvette's rarely around. Here, take your data sheet. Brittany? Where's yours?"

The girl flashed Camp a wide smile. "I'll bring mine later. I'm redoing my nails." She beckoned to Camp. "I'm painting them ravishing red instead of black. Tell that little creep, Mark."

Ravishing red? Camp edged away, remembering what Mark had said about Brittany having the "hots" for him. "He wouldn't have noticed if you'd worn polish or not."

"No polish? Not wearing any color is like…like going naked. But if that's what you want…" Her rapt gaze traveled slowly up Camp's torso.

Reflexively, he closed the top button on his shirt. No way would he touch that statement. "I'll leave you ladies to eat. I'm off to have a word with Maizie." He couldn't retreat fast enough to their leader's wagon. She had stew bubbling in a black pot, and a coffee mug sat within reach of where she straddled a log, mending a cinch.

"Howdy, there, sonny. Did you get the word about redistributing your load and oiling tack?"

"Emily told me. I came to see if you have a spare set of rules—and to ask if I could move my wagon up in the line…say, between my sister and Doris and Vi."

Maizie took a swig of her coffee, eyes narrowed from the steam. "Spare rules are in my saddlebag. Bad idea for you to move. That little gal ridin' with Sherry ain't here to learn trail history, if you get my drift."

"Dammit!" Camp exploded. "She's my student."

"Uh-huh."

"It takes two to tango, Maizie. And I'm not dancing."

"Glad to hear it, boy. Help yourself to the rules. You might wanna hit the sack early, too. Today I went easy. Tomorrow we'll make fifteen miles or bust."

Camp put a hand to his sore butt. "That far? Are you forgetting this train's made up mostly of women?"

She slapped her thigh and cackled. "Ain't the gals I've seen rubbin' their backsides."

"Joke all you want. The trip is young," Camp reminded her as he walked stiffly to retrieve a set of rules. He thumbed through the pages, disappointed to see there were no recipes attached. "You didn't give the women extra help, did you, Maizie?" he asked suspiciously.

"Extra help, like how?"

"Oh, like while you had me hitching nags, maybe someone held a sideline cooking school?"

"I never play favorites with customers. Rule number seven says each wagon fixes whatever food they eat on the trip. Number nine says the same about laundry. Next town we hit, you might wanna stock up on canned soup, boy. It gets old, but it's easy to open and heat. Had a fella went all the way to Oregon eatin' soup three meals a day. He couldn't cook, either."

"I can cook," Camp lied.

"Uh-huh! See that you memorize those rules. We're keepin' a tight schedule."

There wasn't enough light for Camp to study the list on his way back to the wagon. Most people, he noticed, had eaten and were washing dishes. He hadn't even started his dinner. He might have to forgo writing anything tonight. Especially if tomorrow was going to be an even longer day. Every bone in his body hurt now.

The Bentons were dishing up their food as he passed. Bacon, scrambled eggs and biscuits. Golden, fluffy, steaming biscuits. Camp drooled on the top page of rules.

His dad had always made biscuits on weekends. He should be able to remember the ingredients. Flour. Water. Salt. And baking soda? No, baking powder. Darting another glance toward his neighbor, Camp saw Emily serve bacon from the bottom third of her Dutch oven. Biscuits were in the middle, eggs on top. He could practically hear

Mark Benton taunting him for being a copycat. As if he cared.

Digging out a rasher of bacon, Camp popped it into the pan and set it over the hot coals. Estimating, he tossed approximately two cups of flour in a bowl, to which he added a pinch of salt—uh-oh, he'd forgotten oil. How much? Equal parts? Why not?

According to the baking-powder can, it was double-acting. Camp took another guess and shook some in. Wow, the mixture was stiff. He added more water. He had no clue how Emily Benton made her biscuits so symmetrical, but looks didn't count squat with Camp. He plopped spoonfuls of the stiff dough into the Dutch oven's second level—just like Emily had—and turned the bacon before settling the biscuit pan into the grooves. See, cooking wasn't so hard. Oh, but how long should they bake? Twenty minutes? Half an hour? That sounded good. It'd give him time for a cup of coffee before mixing up the powdered eggs.

Yuck! The coffee was barely brown. Camp tasted it. Weak. Very weak. One handful of coffee beans definitely wasn't enough.

Mark and Megan Benton's arguing diverted his attention. Neither wanted to do the dishes. Well, he'd never had to pull KP as a kid, and look at him now. Maybe Emily Benton had the right idea forcing those two on this trip. A body should be able to survive in the wilderness. Especially a man.

Camp sipped his colored water and watched Emily wrap leftover biscuits in foil. She didn't bustle. He liked that she seemed to do everything with an economy of motion. Well, almost everything. She could scramble, too. Take the incident with the papers she'd strewn across his office floor. She'd fluttered like a bird then. A bluebird in that bright-blue suit. Camp grinned. A redheaded bluebird.

Emily glanced up and caught her neighbor scrutinizing her. "You're burning something," she said, pointing to the smoking pan on his grate.

"Oh, shi..." Leaping up, Camp poked at the bacon. "Sorry," he mumbled. "Guess it's time to start the eggs."

She fought a smile as he picked up a small aluminum bowl and held it over the top pan.

"Wait," she yelled. "Did you put oil in the pan?"

Lord, was he supposed to have done that for the other two, as well? Not wanting to appear ignorant, he opened a bottle of oil and poured till it covered the bottom— followed immediately by the egg mixture, which sizzled, bubbled and blackened in no time flat. He snatched it off, then yelped and nursed a burned finger. "What's wrong now?" he snarled as Emily continued to gape at him.

"Nothing." Hooking a loose strand of hair over one ear, she spun and called to Mark, who stood nearby talking with Jared Boone.

Emily was furious that Sherry Campbell's brother had caught her staring like a ninny. Worse, she was doing it again—feeling sorry for a man. It'd been Dave's charming helplessness that had first ensnared her. Emily the nurturer. Vanguard to the vulnerable. A role that became oppressive when her husband's boyish foibles had ballooned into endless affairs and lies. A shudder coursed through her. The sight of Mark loping back fueled her resolve to ignore Nolan Campbell from here on out. She pasted a smile on her face lest Mark see more than she wanted him to see. Though maybe she'd been wrong trying to keep the unpleasant side of her marriage from the kids...

"Mom...Mom! Jared brought fishing gear. He said I could buy a rod and stuff in Council Grove. His dad says we'll be camping on the Neosho River, and that he'll take Jared and me fishing."

"I don't know, Mark," Emily said carefully. "How...how expensive is fishing gear?" After paying bills out of her last check, plus their rent in advance for the summer, she had exactly three hundred dollars in the bank for school clothes and food until she got paid again in September. Not counting the stipend Camp was paying.

Mark's excitement died. He stuffed his hands in his pockets and kicked a rock into the fire. It clanged against the coffeepot and ricocheted off their neighbor's grate. "I didn't wanna go fishing anyhow." Brushing past his mother, he darted between the wagons.

Sighing, Emily massaged her temples. At least Nolan Campbell had disappeared. Her money woes were no one else's business. She freshened her tea and sank onto a log bathed in silvery moonlight. A perfect setting for a mythical hero to gallop through on his white charger. The fantasy, at least, restored her sense of humor.

Megan Benton reached out of the wagon and grabbed her brother as he ran past. "Psst...Mark. Day after tomorrow in Council Grove, call Toby. He'll let you put the fishing stuff on his credit card. Better yet, maybe he'll come get us."

The boy perked up, then slumped again. "Nah, Mom don't want us callin' them."

"Who cares?" Megan jutted her pointed little chin. "Mona and Toby footed the bills while Dad was alive. You tell me why Mom's suddenly so picky."

"How do you know they paid?" he asked, turning to run smack into Camp, who'd stepped to the back of his wagon to throw out his inedible biscuits. The bacon, charred beyond recognition, he'd scraped into the fire.

The boy sucked in a deep breath. "You spying on us?"

"No, but I heard you mention fishing gear." He tossed one of his rock-solid biscuits into the air and caught it. "These'd double as a sinker," he said around a laugh.

Mark dug one out of the pan. "What are they?"

"They're supposed to be biscuits like your mother's." Camp heaved one into the woods. It cracked against a tree. "I'll give you ten dollars for the ones she has left."

"No way!" Megan spoke up. "We're toasting those for breakfast."

"Oh. Tell you what, Mark. I'll lend you my fishing pole in exchange for her recipe. Only...don't mention that I want it."

"Why not?" Suspicion laced Mark's words. "Why not just ask your sister?"

Camp drew a hand over his jaw. "I figure she's gone to bed," he muttered. "It's no biggie. You kids go ahead and turn in. Soon as I wash dishes, I'm headed for bed myself." He fired the remaining lumps of hard dough into the trees, and walked back to the basin where he'd put the other pans to soak. In a final act of despair, he poured out the weak coffee. If he wasn't so tired, he'd double the beans and try again.

From the corner of his eye Camp noticed that Emily sat gazing at the moon. Occasionally she sipped from a cup. If it'd been coffee, he'd have crawled over on hands and knees to beg a cup. But it was tea. He didn't like tea. And besides, neither of them cared to get chummy.

He knew why he didn't want to get chummy with *her*. Obviously she had her reasons, too. That was evident from the way she'd sneaked her data sheet onto the stack the minute his back was turned. The other women had handed him theirs. The only sheet missing was Brittany's. She'd said she'd bring it by, but maybe she'd been too tired.

Speaking of which—Camp yawned as he emptied his dishwater. Leaving the pans to air-dry, he carefully doused the coals. Plunged into darkness, he stood a moment to let his eyes adjust. Gradually he realized that Emily's was the only fire left burning. He considered telling her he was turning in, then decided against it. She must know it'd be pitch-black once she put hers out. Camp hoped she didn't break her fool neck groping her way into her wagon.

He had his shirt unbuttoned and one leg hiked up over the feed trough that hung on the rear of his wagon—when he suddenly froze and thanked providence for Emily's fire. Now he knew why Brittany hadn't brought him her information sheet. She was in his wagon—her blond hair fluffed out over bare shoulders.

Bare. Holy shi...! Camp scrambled out as fast and as quietly as he could. Fear left a dark taste in his mouth. Where the hell was his sister? Did she know what Brittany was doing?

No. Sherry wanted the women to show him up. But she'd never be party to anything so damaging.

Damn. Unless he wanted to ruin Brittany's reputation, he couldn't roust anyone who was sleeping. That left him one option—to throw himself on the mercy of Emily Benton. He tiptoed between the wagons, almost afraid to breathe. Stopping near the front of her wagon, he whispered as loudly as he dared, "Mrs. Benton...Emily."

She jumped up, slopping tea over the rim of her cup. "I thought you'd gone to bed. Why are you prowling around in the dark?"

"Shh." He held a finger to his lips as he cast furtive glances over his shoulder. "I have a problem. I need your help."

He looked so genuinely flustered, Emily found herself agreeing before she'd heard him out. By the time he'd finished his story, anger gripped her chest. "Of all the spineless...weak willed...why didn't you just tell her to leave?"

Her unexpected fury rocked Camp. Before he could gather his wits, she launched a second verbal attack.

"My husband didn't have a backbone, either. He got himself into jams all the time, only with married women." Her voice shook. "He said if I didn't provide him with alibis, he'd divorce me and his folks would see he got custody of the kids." She hauled in a deep breath. "I feel sorry for Brittany, so I'll help—this once. But hereafter, Campbell, stay the hell away from me." She slammed her cup down and hurried past him.

Camp latched on to her arm. "I don't need an alibi." He spun her around. "Believe it or not, I'm concerned about Brittany's reputation. And her self-esteem. No one at home gives a damn." Releasing Emily's arm, he shrugged. "Okay, I admit finding the kid in my wagon threw me a bit. But mainly I thought if *you* talked to her, she'd be less embarrassed."

"Oh." Emily felt like a fool. She was glad of the darkness. What must he think of her after all the things she'd revealed about her marriage?

"Believe me, Emily, I'm open to any suggestion if you have a better one."

She clasped and unclasped her hands. "I'm...sorry I blew up like that."

"Not to worry," he said lightly. "I've had students with crushes before. But never to this extent. I shouldn't have let her come. Hindsight is always 20-20." He sighed.

"I'll talk with her, of course. If it were Megan, that's what I'd want. I, uh, left a couple of flashlights on the log, if you want to take a long walk."

"Thanks, but no. Once you have her out, assuming she's decent, I have a few things to say. I certainly don't want any repeats of tonight."

Emily handed him a flashlight and took one for herself, sizing him up as she slipped past. Twice she glanced back, expecting him to have vanished. He trod silently at her heels. She fought an unexpected rush of warmth pooling in her abdomen. Darn it...she didn't want to have these feelings for *any* man.

The minute they reached the back of his wagon, Camp cupped his hand for Emily's foot and boosted her inside. He listened to the murmur of voices, steeling himself for fireworks that never developed. In a very few minutes Brittany emerged, followed by Emily. The girl wouldn't look at Camp and refused his help down. Once out, she crossed her arms and hunched her shoulders, face sullen. He was relieved to see her wearing jeans and a respectable cardigan.

Forcing her to look up, he said sternly, "Brittany, we need to talk. Emily and I will walk you to your wagon."

"We don't need *her.*"

"You may not, but I do. It isn't my intention to make mockery of your feelings, Brittany. I'm flattered. Any man my age would be. But that's my main point—age. Had I married at the age my peers did, you'd likely be a classmate of my daughter's."

"I don't care."

"Maybe not now, but you would in a few years when I'm gray or bald and you're still young and beautiful," he said with a touch of humor.

"You think I'm beautiful?" Her gaze flew to his, hope blossoming.

Camp floundered. He flashed his light on Emily as a plea for help.

She thought about letting him deal with his own problem. But over all, he deserved an E for effort. Taking pity on him, she slipped an arm around Brittany's shoulders. "Honey," she said as they walked toward Sherry's wagon. "Mr. Campbell's talking ten years from now. He's trying to say that most women reach their full beauty at thirty, while at fifty men start going to pot. *Everything* starts to decline...." Without spelling out details, she boosted Brittany into the wagon. "Hit the pillow, hon. Maizie plans to make fifteen miles tomorrow."

The minute Brittany disappeared, Emily swung toward her own wagon.

Camp fell into step. "You enjoyed saying that about men going to pot, didn't you?"

Her lips tilted up at the corners, but she said nothing.

"For your information, I don't expect my *everything* to decline until I'm ninety."

Throwing her head back, she stopped and laughed out loud.

A husky, pleasant sound that brought Camp's *everything* to attention and made his palms sweat. And made him want to kiss her luscious lips. Fortunately for him, they'd reached her wagon, which brought a return of Camp's sanity.

"If you're ready to turn in, I'll see to your fire," he said stiffly. "It's the least I can do to repay you." Almost formally, he handed back the flashlight she'd lent him.

"No thanks needed," she said, suddenly as brusque as he. "Keep the torch. I have others." Vaulting gracefully into her wagon, she yanked the drawstring, closing Camp out. Emily didn't move or breathe for a minute, knowing he still stood where she'd left him, probably hurt by her abrupt dismissal of his gratitude. But she could ill-afford to crack the door on friendship, to say nothing of the more dangerous currents that Nolan Campbell stirred within her. Considering her bills, her unhappy kids and the problems with her in-laws, Emily had all the trouble she cared to handle. Hadn't she learned her lesson about men?

Men's version of taming the West leads us to believe it was easy—all in a day's work—and even kind of fun. What a crock of lies.

—*Gina Ames. Entry on data sheet following the first day on the trail.*

CHAPTER FOUR

AN OBNOXIOUS CLANGING penetrated Camp's sleep. His eyes flew open, only to encounter darkness. Then he remembered rule number two. Maizie's version of reveille was an old-fashioned triangle dinner bell.

Stifling a groan, he rolled from his back to his stomach. Lord, every muscle in his body protested. Inch by inch he climbed to his hands and knees. At first he tried rocking back and forth to gain leverage enough to stand. "Those pioneers must have been one big callus by the end of a trip," he gnashed between grunts and moans. He'd thought he was in fair physical condition from all the manual labor he did on his house! Wrong. And if *he* had this kind of trouble, imagine how the women must feel.

Lumbering like a giant sloth, Camp crept to the front of his wagon. There, after two attempts, he managed to heave himself onto the slab seat. Yesterday's aches were minor by comparison.

This was an unholy hour to get up. No respectable rooster even crowed before dawn. "Tell yourself this is fun, Campbell," he chanted, recalling the pointed observation on Gina's data sheet. Uncorking his canteen, he poured cold water over his head. "Jeez," His teeth chattered so hard, he clung to the canvas water bag, wondering how long till he could safely lather up and use a razor blade without danger of draining his life's blood.

"You sure look scummy today. Didn't you bring clean clothes?"

Camp set the canteen aside and scowled down at Mark Benton, who wore saggy pants that ended midcalf and a shirt five sizes too big. "Someone who buys his clothes at the Salvation Army reject store has no room to talk." Seeing his remark hadn't fazed the kid, Camp said, "A lot of pioneers only owned one set of clothes, you know."

"Gross. It probably still stinks in Santa Fe. Me and Mom hauled water from the river about an hour ago so we could wash. So did your sister and the others."

Camp refused to be baited. "What's on the morning agenda? More chores?"

"Nope. Mom says we have half an hour to fix and eat breakfast and fifteen minutes to hitch teams and roll."

Shapes began to materialize around fires that sprang to life along the meadow. A whiff of coffee and something cinnamony drifted in on the cool breeze, sending Camp's stomach into a cramped tailspin. He should have buried his pride last night and begged Emily for the rest of her biscuits. Hunched over the canteen, Camp sincerely doubted the truth of what he'd read about Kit Carson—that he'd survived a week on two slices of beef jerky. "Get lost, kid. I think I hear your mother calling."

Mark shook a mahogany sweep of hair from in front of coolly assessing eyes. "Mom said to ask if you needed help starting your fire."

"Certainly not!" Camp jumped down from the wagon, and nearly collapsed when he landed hard. "But…" he gritted his teeth. "It's nice of her to ask."

"Her asking don't mean nothing, understand," Mark informed Camp. "She's always helping strays."

Camp declined comment. Whether aware of it or not, Emily Benton was partly responsible for his condition this morning. After they parted last night, he couldn't seem to stop dreaming about her. He hadn't slept two hours straight. At first he'd tried to write, but her name cropped up far more often than the others in his study. He'd tossed the tablet aside in disgust and crawled into his sleeping bag. He'd continued to dwell on the things she'd let slip about her marriage. Half the night he'd mulled over why a woman with two academic degrees had stayed married to the bastard she'd described. Surely no judge would give child custody to a sleazebag like that.

Automatically, his eyes sought Emily's dark shape. Sometime before sleep had claimed him, he'd begun to realize she possessed more strength than he'd first given her credit for. So why hadn't she flown the coop with her kids? Money? The way Mark and Megan talked, they didn't have any. "Hmm," he muttered to himself. "With her earning potential?" There had to be more to it. Some piece he'd missed.

"Here." Mark extended several scraps of paper. The raucous tune on his boom box assaulted Camp's ears. Did that kid have an endless supply of batteries?

"Well, take 'em," Mark drawled. "They won't bite. Mom wrote down her biscuit recipe, and one for potato soup. Maybe a couple others. You musta asked her. I sure didn't tell her you wanted 'em."

"Th-thanks. Thank her." Camp all but knocked the boy down grabbing for the papers. The top recipe she'd scribbled on the back of an envelope. How to make campfire coffee. In capital letters, Emily had written: GRIND COFFEE.

Camp struck his forehead with a flat palm. At home he

had a small electric grinder. He'd been so rattled at the time he bought supplies, he'd forgotten that he always ground his gourmet coffee beans before he poured them into his expensive, easy-to-use coffeemaker. So, grind them. But how? Tie the beans in a clean handkerchief and smack it hard with the flat of an ax? Okay. That'd work. Quickly he leafed through the remaining sheets. Soup, biscuits, corned beef hash were a few of the recipes he saw. "Tell your mom she's saved my life...again," he said, belatedly recalling the help Emily had given him with Brittany last night. Man, did he need these—even though he hated being called one of Emily's strays. Was that how she saw him? The pitiful professor? His jaw tightened.

"How'd she save your life before? And when?" In the manner of a young tough, the boy removed the old Saint Louis Cardinals baseball cap he wore and reset it on his head backward.

Either Mark was deadpanning or dead serious. In the dim light, Camp couldn't tell which. It didn't much matter; he wasn't about to explain the saga of Brittany. "That's just a figure of speech, Mark. Your mom, ah, loaned me a flashlight." Camp rubbed a hand gingerly over his stubbled jaw, congratulating himself on fast footwork. "It was after you and Megan had gone to bed. I never thought to buy a flashlight."

"Yeah, well she's good at stuff like that. It's what moms are for. I bet you wish you had one."

"I do. She and my dad live in Columbia. In fact, she's keeping an eye on my house and taking care of my dog."

"I meant...I bet you wished you had one on this trip," Mark snickered. "Megan told me how you took your sister's dare. Not smart, dude. They'll whip your butt." The kid disappeared into the shadowy dawn, leaving Camp's sputter hanging on the smoke-laden breeze.

Why let a half-pint kid get his goat? This trip wasn't a contest between him and the women. It never had been. Well, maybe that was how Sherry saw it. Surely Emily didn't. Or was that why she ran hot and cold? Tonight when he collected the data sheets, he'd set the record straight. Right now he'd better scare up something to eat.

Striking a match to the tented kindling, Camp blanked his mind, pulled out a couple of Emily's recipes and went about gathering utensils.

Again it seemed as if he was two steps behind everyone else. Emily and the teachers in the wagon behind her were cleaning up as he sat down to eat. So what? Everything had gone like clockwork today and he intended to enjoy every last morsel. His biscuits and fried potatoes looked perfect. Coffee had never smelled so good—even if he *had* ruined a brand-new monogrammed handkerchief. Part of a set his mother gave him for Christmas. Well, Mom would understand.

Twice, he tried catching Emily's eye to thank her personally for the recipes. She never once glanced his way. He paused, slathering honey on his first biscuit. Strange code Emily Benton lived by. It was all right to do a man favors, but not be his friend.

Oh, well, to each his own. *Her own,* he amended, all but moaning orgasmically after taking the first bite. Camp sneaked another peek in Emily's direction. Couldn't tell where she was. Uh-oh, why was Maizie Boone bearing down on him? He'd seen that look before—the day he showed up late. Camp couldn't imagine what he'd done to displease her today. He wasn't late...yet. Didn't intend to be. So what had put a bee in her bonnet this time?

The closer she came, the more evident it was that she had something serious on her mind. However, Camp didn't care to be flayed on an empty stomach. He deliberately filled his mouth with fried potatoes and eggs, only rising politely as her smelly boots came to a grinding halt four inches from his own cleaner pair.

"Dammit, boy. Renegade took a powder during the night."

Camp plunked his plate down and vaulted the fire, dashing to the edge of the meadow. Sure enough, Goliath, Little Lizzie and Spike all grazed where he'd left them. But not the tobacco-colored Belgian—the one that'd fought him yesterday.

His breakfast turned to rubber sliding down his throat. "How...how far could he roam, do you suppose?"

"Who knows?" Maizie pulled a new packet of chewing tobacco from her pocket and gnawed off a chunk. "Find him," she ordered after she'd softened up the piece and spit a stream into Camp's fire.

"Me? Do I look like the Lone Ranger?"

"If you end up saddle-sore, you'll double-check your hobbles from here on out. It's rul—"

"Rule fifteen," he broke in. "Yes, I know." Camp thought he had rechecked the hobbles. Obviously not well enough.

"Sooner you start, the better. We ain't waitin', mind you. Follow Renegade's tracks from where you staked him out. Once you nab him, hitch your wagon and head out. Pick up our tire tracks and follow us, fast as you can. We'll be burnin' up the miles today."

"What if I don't find him?" Camp had no worry about being able to follow the tracks left by the balloon tires they'd installed on the wagons before leaving Boonville. That was child's play. Horse tracking was another matter. How did you tell one hoof print from another?

"Reckon you'll find him by and by. He's big as a buffalo. Pretty hard to mistake him for a jackrabbit. The land hereabouts is flat as a flitter 'cept for these few trees." A rumble Camp took for laughter shook Maizie's squat frame.

"It's more a worry over some farmer mistaking me for a cattle rustler that concerns me," he said. "So which of these horses do you recommend I ride for the search?"

"I'll saddle my pinto gelding while you put out this fire. Throw the rocks from your fire ring and any extra wood into your wagon. It'll save repeatin' chores tonight. The pinto's name is Mincemeat, by the way. I bought him from a down-and-out cowboy. Guy wanted everyone to think his horse was a mean one. But I guarantee he'll be fine tied behind the wagon. Just see that you tie him tight."

"Yes, ma'am." Resigned to finding his strayed horse, Camp couldn't help but gaze longingly at his first decent meal in two days—now stone-cold. Again he dumped out his potatoes and eggs. He decided to wrap the biscuits and take them along—in case finding Renegade took him longer than Maizie thought.

Telling himself there was no excuse for delay, he set to work doing exactly what she'd outlined, trying to sort out the various horse tracks.

Gina's wagon pulled out, followed closely by the couple from Philadelphia. One by one the others fell into line. Camp climbed aboard Maizie's saddle horse, then just sat. The string of wagons made quite a sight leaving the meadow. Matched teams stepped in unison as chalky canvas ballooned against a deep-blue sky. Today the sky was the exact shade of Emily Benton's eyes. A subtle blend of lavender and cobalt, like the wisteria trailing over his porch at home.

Rather than moon over eyes that refused to seek him out, Camp knew he should get under way. If he found Renegade soon, he might even catch up with the train before they took their first break.

Even so, he waited until Emily, now the last wagon in line, left the clearing. Her hair sparked in the rising sun, reminding Camp of his vision last Saturday, when he first saw the wagons. But instead of a long, flowing pioneer dress, she wore faded blue overalls over a creamy T-shirt. In place of the imagined sunbonnet, a battered Kansas City Chiefs cap failed to restrain her curls.

Try as he might, Camp couldn't seem to turn away. Not until Emily's wagon became a speck in the distance. "Okay, Mincemeat," he murmured to the restless pinto, "Let's find that truant horse."

Renegade's tracks weren't hard to follow. He left a hoofprint the size of a barn door. But the benighted creature had covered a lot of ground. He'd crossed the river and meandered through a field of wheat. It was nearly noon before Camp ran him to ground, and then only because the lead line had caught on a spindly bush—one of many red-leafed shrubs dotting the knoll.

"Thank you, Lord, for the bushes. Otherwise this miserable piece of dog food would have walked all the way to Colorado."

Camp had to cut away woody branches to free Renegade. The sun beat down unrelentingly, so it was lucky for both of them that Camp had remembered to bring a canteen of water. While the horse drank deeply from the baseball cap, Camp checked to see that the animal hadn't sustained any injury. Renegade was fine. He must have dragged the entire length of rope behind him.

"Why couldn't you have stumbled into this patch sooner?" Camp grumbled as he hacked away the last twig with his dull pocketknife. "Come on, you son of a gun," he muttered as the rope pulled free. "Let's move. At this rate, it'll be dark before we meet up with the others."

The big horse turned and gazed at Camp with unblinking brown eyes. He trudged obediently after his rescuer, even going so far as to nuzzle Camp's neck. "So you missed me, did you, you big lug?" Camp laughed and patted the soft nose.

On the return trek Renegade didn't display any of the spirited nonsense Camp had put up with yesterday. As they retraced the route, only man and his beast, Camp experienced a curious satisfaction at having successfully carried out a task that must have been routine to his pioneer brothers. Maybe the ability to hunt and track was passed down through a man's genes. Hmm, it was certainly something to consider.

He wasted no time hitching his team after arriving back at his lone wagon. Once they stood ready, he unsaddled Mincemeat and double-knotted the reins through a metal ring drilled into his tailgate for that purpose. Camp imagined Sherry would be crowing if he came back emptyhanded. Well, she was in for a surprise. He felt pretty smug about his success.

Tracks left by the caravan were distinct. Beyond the copse of trees, the prairie opened into miles of gently undulating hills. Camp unwrapped and ate the last of his morning biscuits. It had taken longer to find his delinquent horse than Maizie's best guess; if he wanted to rejoin the others today, he'd have to crank up the speed. Which turned out to be easier said than done.

Too often his mind wandered to what it must have been like for the early pioneers. No commercial planes overhead like the ones he saw jetting every so often across the cloudless sky. No automobiles whizzing to unknown destinations along U.S. highway 24, which, if he strained, Camp could just hear. The thought occurred to him that, accurate simulation or not, this trip was cheating. It held few, if any, surprises. A reenactment couldn't compare with the excitement—not to mention the dangers—of facing the unknown that pioneers had experienced every day. He'd have to note that in his report.

Camp continued to amble along, drinking in the trill of the songbirds. Much of the earlier soreness had been worked out of his muscles. He was getting used to the roll and pitch of the wagon. Around two o'clock he crossed a small bridge that he recognized from Maizie's brochure. Some distance off the trail sat Neff's Tavern, the Santa Fe Trail's first stage station. All that was left was a stone smokehouse.

There—he spotted it over to the left. Darn, he wished he could spare the time to stop. If the pattern of tire tracks was any indication, the main column had toured the site. Unfortunately the sun had passed its zenith; he needed to push on. As he plodded past the historic spot, Camp swore he'd triple-check every hobble tonight. With a last regretful glance at the place, he hoped Gina Ames had photographed it from all angles.

Somehow bringing up Gina triggered thoughts of Emily again. Camp was at a loss as to why the woman intrigued him. She was unlike any woman who'd ever caught his fancy. Starting with the horny days of youth, he'd tended to pant after statuesque blondes. All clones of Bunny McPherson, the first girl to initiate him into the wonders of sex. Bunny, two years his senior, had been voluptuous and generous. She'd had a sense of humor and zero inhibitions, the type of mentor every fumbling fifteen-year-old boy needed. Bunny knew about things Camp and his pals talked about out behind the barn—like wet dreams and birth control.

Odd, he hadn't thought about Bunny in years. Yet at fifteen, he'd sworn that when he finished college he'd marry her. It wasn't until the week following his sixteenth birthday, after she'd abruptly moved away, that he learned how many of the boys in his high school had the same idea. Most of them quickly found substitutes. Those guys had no discretion—or loyalty. Camp had a more difficult time transferring his allegiance.

That summer, his history club visited the Smithsonian, and he'd found a new love. Museums. Did that mean there was something wrong with him? Because years later, Greta had bitterly accused him of being married to moldy old museums. Come to think of it, Greta had little in common with Bunny.

Did Emily Benton? Not in looks. Emily was the opposite of tall and voluptuous. Not that there was a thing wrong with her proportions. What she did for a pair of jeans was downright sinful.

She wasn't sleek or blond, either. But the riot of wildfire framing her oval face attracted him. A halo of shades that changed color with each flux of light. He'd dreamed the other night about what it would feel like to bury his fingers deep in those corkscrew curls.

He let his mind meander so long that when next he glanced up, he saw the sun dipping low. Surprisingly, he faced the Blue River ford. Someone—Maizie, he supposed—had tacked a message on a withered tree: His name in block letters, followed by "Water your team." Then it read, "Cross here and turn directly into the sun. Stay between the Blue and the Little Blue till you reach Rice Farm. Go straight five miles to our campsite. Hopefully!" Yep, that was Maizie—she of little faith.

At the base of the tree, in a plastic bowl, someone with more trust in him had left three honey-drenched biscuits and a bag of trail mix. Camp grinned. He'd bet his bottom dollar that was Emily's doing. Maybe she really was a reincarnation of Jessie Benton Fremont, the pioneer lady said to have nursed the sick and settled feuds within her husband's caravans on a regular basis.

Camp owed Emily again. Big-time.

He worried about the river crossing, but he needn't have. His team plunged into the water with little urging.

Problem was, they didn't want to climb out. He lost a good half hour coaxing, cajoling and finally leading them. Fortunately, the Blue wasn't deep at this point, only a few inches above Camp's hips. And he didn't mind, as his skin had begun to feel hot and itchy. So much so that he soaked his shirt and put it back on wet.

At first it felt good. But as the afternoon lengthened, the sun beat down without mercy, drying his clothes stiff. The itch came back—worse. His legs, his arms, his neck grew hot and tingly. The more he scratched, the more he itched. Camp tried concentrating on the serenity of the river that flowed in the direction he was headed. And on the beauty of the evening ambers streaking the sky. Nothing worked. Each passing mile became more unbearable than the last. He watched the sun sink into a flat puddle of molten gold, and even the coolness of evening didn't help.

At one point he stripped off his shirt to check for fleas. There were none, and no welts, but rather a bright red, slightly bumpy rash covering his chest, arms and legs. An allergy? To what? His shirt was old and his jeans had been washed a hundred times.

Stars blanketed the sky and a crescent moon had risen by the time Camp spied a row of campfires in the distance. He was quite positive he'd never been so happy to see anything in his life.

Maizie and Robert ran to meet him. Sherry, too. Camp identified Brittany lurking in the shadows with Megan Benton. Gina lounged against her wagon. Only Emily was missing. Funny, but she was the one he wanted to see.

"Yo, there, weary traveler. You're a sight for sore eyes." Maizie grabbed the lead horses and guided his team in a circle until Camp's wagon lined up with the last one in the row. Vaguely he registered that it was Emily's.

Maizie instructed Robert to unhitch Camp's team. She ambled back just as he climbed down. "I was beginnin' to worry, boy. What took you so long?"

Camp snorted. What a stupid question. *She'd* sent him on that chase. Instead of answering, he pushed up his shirtsleeves, continuing to scratch his arms as he passed her. He intended to handle his own unharnessing.

Maizie grabbed his arm and whistled through her teeth. "Looks like Renegade wasn't all you found today. Got yourself a right smart dose of poison sumac, I'd say. I warned the kids and out-of-staters. Didn't think to caution anybody who'd grown up here." Tobacco juice sailed past Camp's shoulder.

"Stop that," he bellowed. "Tobacco chewing is a dirty, filthy habit. Not to mention bad for your health."

Her eyes popped wide. Emily materialized from the blackness, gliding between them. "Camp, don't take it out on Maizie because you're tired and out of sorts."

"I have plenty of sorts," he said curtly. "I also have this damned rash itching me to death. It's a little late to be telling me I should've had sense enough to keep out of the stuff. There's no poison sumac where I live."

"How like a man to yell at women for his own stupidity. I should've known." Throwing up her hands, Emily stalked away.

Camp felt bad. She wasn't to blame for any of this.

Sherry inspected his blotches with a flashlight. "Leaflets three, let it be. I learned that as a kid in Girl Scouts, Nolan."

"That's poison ivy. And I was slightly more concerned with finding my horse than counting leaves. What in my first-aid kit will cure it?" he asked Maizie.

She tucked her thumbs in her belt. "Nothing I know

cures it, boy. Cortisone cream takes away the sting and some of the itch. Water spreads the rash the first couple days, so don't wash.''

"Great. I got plenty wet fording the Blue. That's about the time I really noticed something was wrong.''

"Why did you get wet?" Gina asked. "We never left our wagons.''

"Yeah, well, somebody forgot to tell my team that. Damned animals loved the water.'' Camp thanked Robert nicely for helping him unhitch, but he rechecked every hobble himself. From now on, he'd *know* their tethers were secure.

"Don't touch me,'' Sherry said, jumping aside as he accidentally brushed her on the way past. "I read you can give that rash to people during the weepy stage.''

Camp ignored her. Robert gazed on him with sympathy. However, he and Maizie carefully avoided any contact as they left.

"Well, are you finally ready to concede that we women are better suited to pioneer life than modern man?'' Sherry demanded.

"The trip is far from over. The deal, as I recall, was to determine whether or not modern women have what it takes to get from Boonville to Santa Fe.'' Camp didn't know why he was being surly. He wished everyone would leave him alone.

"Oh, you're so stubborn. You should see yourself. Three days' growth of beard, filthy clothes, and that rash is probably going to close one of your eyes.''

Somewhere, he dredged up the will to grin. "Today, me. Tomorrow, maybe you.''

"Are you ready to bag it?''

"I'm sticking it out,'' he said. "How about you? Had enough?''

"Certainly not. It's just...you're the only brother I

have. A lot's happened to you the last few days. Megan told Brittany how you ruined last night's meal. Speaking of which—what did you do to her? She said it'd serve you right to starve. I thought she had a mega-crush on you.''

"Brittany's a troubled girl, Sherry. Can you take her under your wing? Head her in the right direction?''

"At least she isn't living hand-to-mouth trying to support one or two babies like some of the young women we counsel in the Hub.''

"If she keeps on her present course, it may happen. She's obsessed with finding a husband. She could hook up with some total jerk.''

"Tell me about it. Most of my students wouldn't be in the predicament they're in if they hadn't fallen for the wrong man. Marriage doesn't mean happily ever after.''

"You sound bitter,'' Camp said as they ambled toward his wagon.

"Informed and wary, not bitter. Then again, maybe you're right. It's not only young women who get mixed up with rotten men.''

Camp suddenly realized they were both gazing at Emily's wagon. "Do you know anything about Emily's marriage? Her application said she was widowed,'' Camp said, careful to keep his tone light and his voice low.

Sherry shot him a narrowed glance. "Why would I know? She's your applicant.'' Sherry bit her lip. Had he found out about her bringing in Gina and Emily?

"No special reason. She's your counterpart at her college. I know history profs at other institutions. I thought maybe you two had met at a conference or something.''

"Look,'' she said. "I've gotta run. You're beat. Why don't I collect the data sheets tonight?''

"Would you? Hey, thanks. I'll see what I can do about

making myself presentable." He scrubbed a hand over his ragged, itchy jaw.

"You'd better not shave, Nolan. The rash may be under your beard."

"That's a switch. What happened to my looking as scruffy as hell?"

"Can't a sister have a change of heart?"

"While you're feeling charitable, would you see if you have anything in your first-aid kit that I can put on this rash? I know mine only has the bare essentials."

"I'll look. If I have something, I'll bring it when I drop off your info sheets."

They parted. Camp's first priority was to get out of his dirty clothes and to wash, even if he spread the rash. He didn't want Mark Benton pointing out how rank he smelled. Or Emily. Not that she'd venture that close to him.

He'd just stripped off his shirt and was headed for the enticing *lap, lap* of the half-moon curve in the Little Blue River when Sherry rushed up carrying everyone's data sheets. Camp retraced his steps and tossed the papers in his wagon.

She tagged after him when he started off again. "I didn't have cortisone cream. Ooh, that rash looks awful. I'll bet you don't sleep much tonight. How long will it last?"

"Darned if I know. I've never had anything burn, sting and itch at the same time. I don't suppose there's a closet herbalist around," he joked.

She wrinkled her nose. "Ask Philly—Harv Shaw. He has an opinion on everything."

"Good thing I'm bringing up the rear. If I had to listen to him pontificate, they'd haul me off for assault and battery."

"Murder's crossed my mind. Maizie has the patience of a saint."

Camp laughed. "A tobacco-chewing saint? That's a picture."

"Come on, she's perfect for this job. And she'll add spice to your paper." Sherry stopped short of the river. "Have you asked permission to include her?"

"No. I will before the trip's over." He dug at his rash. "This is driving me nuts. I don't care what Maizie said, I've gotta wash off some of this trail dust. I doubt I'll sleep anyway. Are you up for a game of poker? I'll ask Robert and Maizie to join us."

"Sorry, I'm going to bed. Three more days of eating dust before we reach the park in Council Grove—and then we get two blessed days of rest. I can't wait to find a beauty shop and treat myself to the works. You'd better try to sleep. Maizie says it'll hit a hundred degrees tomorrow."

"I doubt pioneer women had beauty shops along their route," Camp said dryly.

"Or doctors, either. You may have to ride into Independence to see one."

"No, I won't," he called as she left, taking the only light with her. Most of the campfires were already banked for the night. He intended to build one and cook dinner after bathing. Too bad if he disturbed his neighbors. He still half expected Mark Benton to show up and get in his licks. "Trip must have worn the kid out today," Camp muttered. "Thank you, Lord."

The moon, almost a quarter tonight, cast ripples across the water. Camp pulled his boots off, then his socks, and quickly shed everything else. He wadded the dirty clothes into a ball, taking care to drape his clean cutoffs and a towel over a jutting granite rock. Looking neither right nor left, he dived into the icy stream. God, it felt good.

Seated on a mossy outcrop about ten yards upstream, Emily Benton stifled a gasp that threatened to give away her position. She realized now that she should have called out before Sherry left. But she hadn't wanted to appear to be eavesdropping. Emily had never dreamed he'd strip naked and plunge to his neck in water after what Maizie said about water spreading the rash. *Now what?* Should she reveal herself, or try to skulk away unnoticed? If it wasn't happening to her she'd laugh. She'd read this scene a thousand times in books.

As she wrestled with her conscience, Camp charged out of the water and shook like a shaggy dog. Moonlight spilled over his dark hair and broad shoulders, gilding water droplets that slid down his chest. Emily held her breath. Dressed, the man was one to notice. Unclothed, Professor Campbell was a work of art. His chest was wide, muscular and not too hairy. His hips were narrow, his thighs... Emily's mind stalled there as she felt his eyes discover her. "I, ah, I..." She struggled to speak—to lower her gaze. All she did was stare, thinking it'd been so long since she'd been able to appreciate a naked male body. Too long. Her knees jelled.

Cold though he was from his swim, the minute Camp saw her wide eyes, so dark they looked purple in her moonlit face, heat pooled in his groin. For a moment the itch numbed, as did his thoughts. In truth he was far more embarrassed than she appeared to be. "Sorry for the strip-tease. But you might have cleared your throat," he said, snatching up the towel.

Suddenly overcome by jitters, she whirled around.

Realizing that she was shaken, too, Camp gave a lick and a promise with the towel and struggled into his cut-offs. "There, I'm decent," he said, slinging the towel around his neck. "I suppose it's too much to hope that you brought me something to relieve this itch."

Although his voice sounded light and relaxed, Emily was slow to turn back. She was afraid a vision of how he looked emerging from the water would be forever emblazoned in her mind. As she gathered her nerve and finally faced him, her tender heart reacted to his angry rash. "Ouch! Camp...a...a homemade concoction of soda and vinegar works on poison oak and ivy. I'll go mix some." Sweeping by him, she snapped off her flashlight.

"Hey, leave the light on. I'm barefoot."

She hesitated, a dark wraith in the moonlight. "Where are your boots? This dry buffalo grass will cut your feet."

"Yes, Mother."

She tensed again. "Apparently *someone* needs to watch out for you. Have you eaten today?"

"Only what the Good Fairy left at the Blue River ford."

"Oh." Emily hadn't meant for him to know she'd left the food.

"I'm not complaining. And I'll sure accept the soda treatment. How is it you know how to mix some old-fashioned remedy?"

Happy to have her mind off the river incident, Emily explained as they walked. "Trail rides in the wilderness with my dad and his horsey pals. I didn't realize how much I missed those outings until this trip."

"Why didn't you continue the tradition in your own family?"

"My husband—" She broke off, pointing to her wagon, and touched a finger to her lips. "I'll see if I can find what I need without waking the kids. Meet you at my fire. I'll mix the paste and bring it. Oh," she called softly after his retreating form. "In the top section of my Dutch oven there's some leftover stew. It may still be warm."

Camp tried to thank her again, but she'd climbed nimbly over the wagon's tailgate. He dumped his bundle of dirty clothes into his wagon. As he ladled himself a bowl of stew, his thoughts remained on Emily. However, the heat from the smoldering coals soon increased his itching. By the time she returned, he'd sought refuge on his own wagon tongue.

Peering around, she finally spotted him. "There you are." She waved a container. "Come into the light and I'll pat this stuff on."

He set the bowl of stew aside. "Aren't you afraid of catching the rash? Everyone else is."

She shook her head. "On one of our outings, my little brother dismounted in a patch of poison oak. I slathered this stuff on him five times a day or more, and I never broke out. This stuff doesn't hurt. My brother said it felt good."

"I wasn't worried about me. I wouldn't wish this miserable stuff on a dog. But if you're not afraid, have at it."

No sooner had she dabbed the first patch than Camp wished he could retract his words. He hadn't counted on the soft glide of her fingers over his bare skin causing an erection.

Emily had started on his back. Too quickly she moved to his legs. Camp thought he'd burst. "I'll do the rest," he said gruffly as she rose from her kneeling position and stretched toward his stomach. Her touch was bad enough, but when she stood, she left a trail of some sweetly provocative perfume. He'd have bet it wasn't possible to grow harder, but he did.

"Don't tell me you're ticklish?" she teased, coming at him with hands covered in white paste.

He opted for the easy out she offered. "Yeah, I am. Here, do my arms. Stay away from my ribs."

"Chicken." Clucking, she drizzled white goo down his

arms. "How about your face? Is your face ticklish underneath that beard?"

"As a matter of fact, it is. And you're enjoying torturing me far too much, Mrs. Benton. Give me that." Camp nearly upset his cooling stew as he grabbed at the plastic container.

Emily didn't let go. She landed in his lap—and promptly discovered the very reason he'd been trying to keep her away. Their eyes met, his darkening with need. Hers, surprised at first, then pleased, then wary as she released the bowl and scrambled up.

"Look, I wasn't trying..." She clasped her hands tight to stop their trembling, and started again. "I should know better than to tease a man. I'm not looking for involvement. And I don't do one-night stands. I'll write down the ingredients for the paste. When we reach Council Grove, I suggest you buy a book on outdoor survival."

Denial that he wanted either a relationship *or* a fling hovered on Camp's lips. However, she was gone before he acknowledged that it would have been a lie. Apparently his body knew something his mind refused to admit—since the day Emily Benton blundered into his life, he'd been barreling full-speed toward involvement. Question was—what, if anything, should he do about it?

"Dammit," he hissed into the velvety darkness. "I'm not looking for one-night stands, either."

If Emily heard, she didn't reply.

"Our national folklore romanticizes the adventure—the *male* adventure—of conquering the West.
—*Sherry Campbell's data sheet. With elaborate doodles drawn around this statement.*

CHAPTER FIVE

CAMP SAT OUTSIDE the circle of heat from Emily's fire and picked out various constellations in the star-littered sky. He'd long since finished a second bowl of stew. Now he marked time while his dishwater heated.

After the dishes were washed and the fire out, he applied another coat of the soda paste to the areas he could reach. He'd just climbed into his wagon when a movement near the tailgate of Emily's Conestoga caught his eye. At first he thought maybe she'd had second thoughts, but in the bluish beam of the moon, he saw that it was Megan. Curious. A bathroom run? If so, where was her flashlight?

He watched her glance furtively around, then haul something from beneath the coach. A day pack. What the...? A chill snaked the length of Camp's spine.

The girl shrugged into the pack and set off with purpose. Before she slipped out of sight, Camp made the decision to follow her.

He expected her to head for the highway, even though it was a five-mile hike. But she didn't. She'd disappeared. Camp panicked. His heart jackhammered until Maizie's string of saddle horses began to wicker, and he glimpsed Megan tiptoeing among them.

"Where's the ruckus, boy?" Camp nearly jumped out of his skin as Maizie's raspy whisper struck him. Wheeling, he blankly took in her frazzled gray hair and a ratty old sheepskin coat she had buttoned over a long flannel nightgown.

"Megan Benton," he murmured. "She may be running away. Damn...look there. She's nabbed herself a getaway horse."

Maizie chuckled. "The kid won't go far on Dumpster. Robert's hoping to unload that nag in Santa Fe. What're you waitin' for? I reckon you'll catch her at the river."

The rapidly fading hoofbeats spurred Camp to action. "Wake Emily. Tell her I'll bring Megan back."

The wagon mistress nodded.

Camp dashed off, thankful for the moonlight and the stillness of the night that let him follow the sound. Breathing hard, he added a burst of speed as he heard the horse snort and whinny, then falter. Obligingly, the river bank sloped gently. Not so much danger of the horse breaking a leg.

At last Camp saw Megan urging her mount into the water. He cupped his hands to yell and saw the horse slow. The animal pranced a bit, then abruptly sat down in the middle of the stream. A bright moon provided Camp with a ringside view. Megan lost her grip on the mane. Inch by inch she slid down the broad back, over the rump, and hit the water with a loud splat. She bobbed immediately to the surface, gasping and flailing her arms. The horse arched his neck and trotted blithely back to shore, uncaring that he'd left his rider behind, bobbing like a cork.

Camp had one boot off and was tackling the second

when Emily stumbled through the tall grass, followed by Maizie, who puffed like a steam engine.

"What happened?" Emily's face was pasty white.

Shaking his head, Camp splashed into the river after Megan, now drifting downstream.

Maizie finally caught her breath. "Told you," she hollered at Camp around a chortle. "Trait of that horse is to sit every time he lands up to his knees in water. It's why he's named Dumpster. Hope the gal swims." She sobered, peering at Emily.

Still not comprehending, Emily nodded dumbly.

Cold water lapped at Camp's chest as he carried the coughing, sputtering girl to the bank.

Dumpster shook his head and danced out of reach. Maybe it was a trick of the moon, but Camp swore the roan's lips peeled back in a grin. Camp wasn't smiling, though, his eyes glued to Emily's stricken expression.

"Why?" she asked in a shaky voice, stripping Megan of her soggy pack.

The teen glared defiantly. "I was going to town...to call Mona. This trip sucks. It's hot and sticky, and the mosquitoes are as big as helicopters." Huddled in her wet clothes, she burst into tears.

Camp figured Emily would crumble in the face of Megan's crocodile tears. He pictured all three Bentons leaving the train in Council Grove.

"I'm sorry you're unhappy, Megan." Emily's voice held an edge of steel. "I chose this outing, and I make the decisions for you and Mark until you're of age. Your grandparents have no say in the matter. Now dry off and go to bed. Apologies can wait until morning." Emily's stiff gaze skimmed Maizie and Camp briefly before she grasped Megan by the arm and marched her off.

"Un-huh." Maizie sounded satisfied. "Well, don't just stand there, sonny. Rub that horse down and give him an added measure of oats.'' She waddled off, avoiding the swish of Dumpster's cold, wet tail.

Rub *him* down? As if Camp himself wasn't soaked. Obviously, the whole incident had amused Maizie. All along she'd known the outcome. But as his unplanned dip had washed off all his soda paste, Camp was not amused.

Once he sat in his wagon again, dry and slathered with paste, he felt more benevolent. He supposed it was funny that of all the horses Megan might have swiped, she'd picked that one.

Poor Emily. She fought an uphill battle with those kids.

Wide-awake now, Camp decided to compile the data sheets Sherry had collected. He pulled out Gina's. She'd devoted a half page to the invasion of giant mosquitoes at Neff's Tavern. With uncharacteristic wit, Gina stated that at one point she had to fight them for possession of her camera. Camp shuddered. It was just as well he hadn't stopped. It hurt to imagine mosquito bites on top of sumac poisoning.

Sherry grumbled about Brittany's petulance. In between doodles and snide comments, she wrote that she was sick of the same scenery. Camp expected similar criticisms from Emily. Instead, she described the prairie in terms of rich colors and unending vistas. And she wrote eloquently of the sorrow she'd felt visiting the Neff family cemetery, because they'd had lost so many children in infancy. Camp imagined tears in Emily's lovely blue eyes as she poured out her heart.

He tapped his pencil to his lips. Clearly he was going soft on Emily. And he shouldn't. For the sake of his paper, it was imperative that he remain objective.

An admirable plan, but Camp's dreams that night and the next were far from objective. Still, Emily's sympathetic smile and the memory of her soothing touch kept him plodding through the days; her homemade concoction offered him relief from the terrible itch during long, sleepless nights.

The day before they were due to reach Council Grove, Camp noted how everyone's spirits seemed to lift. He felt it, too. His rash had subsided enough for him to shave at last. This morning, he felt almost human. All in all, Camp thought things were finally looking up.

Mark Benton had quit bugging him and had started hanging out with Jared Boone. Brittany and Megan cloistered themselves each evening, trading books and teen magazines. A much subdued Megan, Camp noted.

His mind still on the youngsters, Camp circled to the rear of his wagon to dispose of the water he'd used for shaving. He startled Mark, who guiltily thrust a stack of shiny metal objects behind his back—so suddenly, that he dropped one.

"What do you have there, Mark?" Camp inquired offhandedly. "Are you and Jared collecting coffee can lids to use as slingshot targets?"

Mark grabbed for the fallen items, and in the process dropped two more. Camp saw they were cut in shapes—like road markers. Rusted stakes protruded from each.

He set his shaving kit and basin aside and went for a closer inspection. Being less encumbered than the boy, Camp bent easily and retrieved two that still lay on the ground. His gaze lit on green Conestogas etched on a white tin background and stenciled letters that said: Santa Fe Trail. They were markers. Shooting the boy a glance, Camp saw that he was poised for flight.

Camp stopped him with a look he reserved for students cheating on a test. "Mark, the historical society spent a lot of time and money placing these markers along the trail route. Removing them is a serious matter."

"I found them," Mark said, but he also licked his lips nervously.

"Found them where? The dirt on some of these stakes is fresh."

Mark dumped the markers he still held at Camp's feet. "Take 'em. I don't even want the stupid old things."

"You need to put them back where they belong, Mark. When did you start this collection?"

The boy's color drained. He backed away. "Yesterday. But what difference does it make? Nobody but us'll see 'em."

"A lot of tourists visit the trail. Besides, it's stealing. This trail is under federal protection. There's a fine attached to taking markers—if not a stiffer penalty."

"Then I'll call Toby from town. He'll pay the dumb old fine. So it won't do you any good to run and squeal to my mom."

"I'm not going to tell her, Mark. You are." Camp's voice remained calm as he stared coolly into Mark's mutinous eyes.

The boy hunched his shoulders and kicked at a rock. "It's Megan's fault. She wanted one for her bedroom."

"Did Megan take some of these?"

"No," Mark admitted with a sniffle. "I can't put 'em back. It's a long way, and I'm just a kid."

"You're old enough to be responsible for your actions. I want you to go tell your mother and Maizie what you've done. If you do, I'll help you return the markers. But I won't cover for you."

"Sheesh!" Mark scraped at a lank fall of hair. "Okay, but I don't know why you'd help me."

Camp arched a brow. "I recall getting into a few scrapes at your age."

"You? But you're a teacher."

"I wasn't born a teacher." Camp's lips quirked in a smile. Sobering quickly, he said, "We all make mistakes. The trick is to learn by them and try not to repeat any."

"Toby says you shouldn't ever admit to making a mistake."

Camp shied from touching that statement. On the other hand, someone needed to. "It takes a big man to admit to being wrong. And it makes sleeping easier."

"I guess I know what you mean. I didn't sleep so good last night. I was scared my mom would see 'em." He nudged the markers. "I wish I hadn't done it."

"That's the spirit. I'm proud of you, Mark. Your mother will be, too. Say, can you ride a horse?"

"You bet," the boy bragged. "I've ridden lots of times."

Camp smiled in relief and the two went off in search of Emily.

"What?" she exclaimed after Mark had stumbled through his confession. Closing her eyes, she rubbed her temples. "Honey, whatever possessed you? How will we put them back where they belong?"

Mark jerked a thumb toward Camp. "He said he'd help."

Emily acknowledged Camp for the first time. "How?" she asked, frowning. "We've traveled at least five miles."

"If Maizie agrees, I thought Mark and I could saddle two horses and ride back. We can make it in half the time it took the wagons. Less if we push. I'll ask Robert if he'll allow Jared to drive my wagon until we catch up."

"Yes. I suppose it's the only way."

Because she nibbled worriedly on her bottom lip, Camp cleared his throat. "I could go faster alone. It wouldn't teach him as much. But it's your call, Emily."

Considering what Camp had said, Emily glanced up and caught Mark's hopeful smile. "No," she said decisively. "That's the Benton way out. He did the fiddling—now he needs to pay the piper. I'll go with you to talk to Maizie, son, after you thank Camp for doing this."

After a few false starts, Mark managed a passable thank-you.

"If you leave now," Emily asked Camp, "will you be back before dark?"

"Run that question by Maizie. She may know a shortcut. Otherwise, I guess we'll have to take bedrolls and more in the way of food."

An unexpected smile lit her face. "We know you won't run into the Good Fairy who left you food at the Blue River ford."

Camp grinned as she curled a hand over Mark's shoulder and walked him toward Maizie's wagon. His smile faded as soon as Megan parted the canvas and climbed onto the wagon seat, blowing on newly painted fingernails.

"My brother is such a dipstick."

"Why do you say that?" Camp braced a hand on a wagon bow.

The girl smirked. "Because Toby would hire someone to put the markers back. Why should Mark get saddle sores?"

Camp tucked three fingers of each hand into his back pockets. "Guess you didn't listen to your mom. Comes a time guys and girls need to stand on their own two feet to look at themselves in the mirror." Leaving it at that, Camp walked away. He met Emily and Mark cutting between their two wagons. Emily's eyes were grim, Mark's downcast. Something in his demeanor made the boy appear younger to Camp. Younger and more vulnerable. His heart gave a little crunch. Maizie could deliver a blistering rebuke; he knew that for a fact. Had he done right, making Mark fess up? After all, he didn't have children and he worked mostly with young adults. He'd handled it the way he thought his father might. Maybe there was a better way.

Emily stopped in front of him, her hand resting lightly on Mark's neck. "Maizie read us the riot act." Absently, her fingers smoothed her son's shirt collar. "What he did was wrong. I'm not trying to make light of his transgression. I just wish the couple from Philadelphia hadn't been there at the time. Harv Shaw made it sound like a capital crime. Said kids who'd steal government property would burn flags and...and become traitors." She pulled Mark close as he began to sniff against his sleeve.

Camp felt a surge of anger, soon replaced by an odd feeling of protectiveness toward this mother and child. "Shaw's mouth is bigger than his belt size, which is saying a lot." Kneeling, he forced Mark to meet him eye to eye. "You knew all along it was wrong. Now you're making restitution like a man." Camp gave him a friendly nudge on the arm. "Hey, I see Maizie's bringing our horses. Stuff those markers in a saddlebag and let's be on our way."

Mark edged closer to Camp, his wide eyes on the approaching horses. "Wha...what if a guy hadn't ridden a horse lots of times like he said?"

Camp heard the quaver in his whisper. "You mean," he said, "you've ridden only a few times?"

Shuffling his feet, Mark hitched up his belt but said nothing.

"Uh, Mark," Camp muttered. "How many times—exactly?"

"I sat on a plow horse once," the boy said eagerly. "A farmer Toby knows owned it. But I can ride. I know I can."

Camp straightened fully, his gaze flying to Emily. He did indeed see worry shadowing her deep-blue eyes, and he reached out automatically, wanting to soothe it away. But her eyes went darker. She flinched and ducked to avoid his hand.

"What? Emily...I..." Camp slid his palms against his thighs.

"Sorry." She reddened a bit and looked sheepish. "You startled me." Tugging her son with her, she ran to where Maizie had stopped to shorten the stirrups on the smaller of the two horses. "How gentle is he?" she inquired.

Camp stared after her. She didn't look back. He noticed that Emily rubbed her upper arms as if to ward off goose bumps, even though the sun had bloomed fully and the day was warming. He swallowed a growl. Had there been more to the fear he'd seen in her eyes—more than just the fact that she was "startled"? In addition to sleeping around, had her no-good husband abused her?

Again the pieces didn't fit. She wouldn't have stayed in an abusive relationship. The more he saw of Emily Benton, the more puzzling she became—as if she were two different women.

Maizie whistled, jolting Camp from his thoughts. He jogged over to the trio.

"I gave Mark Silverbelle. She's a honey. Has a gait like a rocking chair. The boy'll do fine, and you've already got a feel for this bronc."

"Mincemeat and I are old friends." Camp stroked a hand down the pinto's nose. "Aren't we, boy?" Rechecking the cinch for himself, he turned to Maizie. "Is it possible to make the round-trip in one day?"

She nodded. "Pour on the coals going. Easy on the return. Follow the river coming back. You'll cut off a lot of miles. Water the horses often. Mark will beg for stops. Expect he'll be hurting. You're probably broke in by now. But I'll ask Robert to go, if you'd rather."

Camp studied Mark. He saw that both the boy and his mother expected him to jump on Maizie's offer. "Thanks, but no. Mark and I will see this through. Will you have Jared drive my wagon?''

Maizie dug in her pocket and pulled out a chunk of chewing tobacco. Suddenly aware of Camp's grimace, she tucked it away again. ''We Boones are Kentucky hill people,'' she said by way of explanation. ''My daddy smoked and my mama chewed. Out here chewin's safer. The least little spark can set off a prairie fire that'll burn a thousand acres of grass almost before an eye can blink. Lost my brother and two cousins to one of them fires.'' She patted her pocket. ''Seein' how you're paying most of the freight, I'll have to say the customer is right. But dang, old habits die hard.''

''I appreciate your trying.'' Camp relieved her of the pinto's reins and nodded as she drew his attention to a packet of beef jerky and a few apples she'd stowed in his saddlebags. As he boosted Mark into the saddle, Camp said, ''At college there're a lot of farm kids who've already started to chew. Last year alone we lost two young men to throat cancer. Death by fire or cancer, it's all a waste. I'd hate to see the kids on this outing go home with the wrong message.'' He pulled himself into the saddle.

Maizie slapped Mincemeat on the rump and stepped aside. ''Be off with you. Anybody ever tell you that you missed your callin', boy? You shoulda been a preacher.''

Camp had his hands full keeping a rein on the crow-hopping pinto.

Sherry joined Emily at her campfire as Nolan and Mark melted into the distance. Maizie had already gone about her business.

''Did that doofus brother of mine lose another horse?'' Sherry shaded her eyes.

Emily sighed. Reluctantly, she told Sherry the whole story.

"He's being noble? Did someone slip a mickey in Nolan's morning coffee?"

Emily bristled. "You know, Sherry, I don't see him as the man you described. Are you aware that Brittany sneaked into his wagon the other night? He asked me to flush her out, but he could've run or treated her like dirt. Instead, he stuck around and talked with her, careful not to hurt her feelings. And he didn't let Mark wiggle off the hook the way Dave would have, and Toby does."

Sherry cocked a brow. "So, are you saying I misjudged Nolan's attitude about women? That it's all my fault we're out here busting our buns, frying to a crisp?"

"You said yourself it had to do with sibling rivalry. Remember that I've lived with a genuine old-fashioned man who really disrespected women. So far, I haven't seen anything about Cam—Nolan that compares."

"I said gender rivalry. Nolan's a historian, and the stuff they teach distorts women's true role. Brittany is his student. Of course he's going to handle her with kid gloves, even if she is a twit. By the way, she and Megan are palling around. I feel sorry for the kid, but I don't think I'd want a daughter of mine sharing beauty secrets with her."

Emily bent over her campfire and poured them each a cup of Earl Grey. Throwing a glance toward her wagon, she lowered her voice. "I wish you did have a daughter, Sherry. Maybe then we could compare notes. Lord knows, I could use some reassurance. Or advice. I'm not happy about the girls' blossoming friendship. But something I've learned about Megan—she goes out of her way to do the things I object to." Emily gripped the cup with both hands and breathed in the pungent bergamot. "I'm the counselor, yet your brother seems to know how to handle my kids better than I do. So, if you have any tips, Sherry, I'm all ears."

A flush stained Sherry's cheeks. "I'm sorry, Em. The last thing you need is a friend haranguing you and adding to your problems. The fact is, teenage girls are a mass of belligerence and hormones. I was. I imagine you were." She sipped her tea. "Nolan's a few years older than me. There was enough of an age difference that he had zippo patience dealing with me storming through puberty. Hey, why are we always discussing him? It's not as if you're interested in him romantically or anything. I know you've sworn off men."

Sherry's words created a rumble of tension in Emily's stomach. Or was it hunger? "Look, Doris and Vi are packing to leave. Megan and I haven't eaten yet. Our oatmeal's probably dried in the pan. Mark disrupted our breakfast coming in with that tale of his. I'm not used to him volunteering information. Generally, I have to pry it out, or have it come back to me through some member of the community who isn't under Toby's and Mona's thumb. And that's darned few."

Sherry tossed out the last of her tea and gave her friend an impetuous hug. "If I had the money from my trust, I'd lend you enough to pay your in-laws so you guys could blow that popstand. What about your family, Em? Is there no one you can borrow from?"

"Over a hundred grand? That's a big chunk of change. My family are all blue collar. They have mortgages and credit card debts like everyone else. Just pray I find a good job on the West Coast. If I got offered a higher salary, I don't believe Toby's toady judge could block my leaving. Do you?"

"I wouldn't have thought he could, anyway. I'm afraid I don't have any legal experience, Em. Not outside of referring needy students who come into the Hub to the Legal Aid Society. Do you think you could make an appointment with them at their Columbia office? How far does Toby's influence stretch?''

''Throughout our county. Plus, he's into politics at the local and state levels. Money talks everywhere. Lord knows he always managed to get Dave off without consequence. I'm almost ready to throw caution to the wind and chance it.'' She managed a humorless smile ''I'll be old and gray before I pay Dave's debts. If I don't do something soon, Toby and Mona will choose a man for Megan to marry and pick Mark's college.''

''What? They don't believe in college for girls?''

''You know they don't. According to Mona, if I hadn't had two degrees Dave wouldn't have felt inadequate and he wouldn't have strayed.''

''Bah, humbug. How can you put up with them, Emily? I'd be in Leavenworth doing ninety-nine years of hard time, I'm afraid.''

''Don't think it hasn't crossed my mind. Luckily, I'm also a coward.''

''Well, pacifist, maybe. I wouldn't call you cowardly. That's one reason I thought of you for this trip. I can't say what or how, but I predict—I feel it in my bones— one of us will do something heroic that Nolan will have to report in his article. Picture this, Em, we'll have redeemed twentieth-century womankind.''

Emily inspected her chapped hands. ''Wouldn't it have been easier to write the article yourself, Sherry?''

''There's still the old glass ceiling. I could write it. Or you. It wouldn't carry the same weight as Nolan's article. Have you been to conferences where papers are presented?''

''No. But heavens, Sherry, we outnumber men in academics these days. There must be lots of women professors who go and present papers.''

''Sure there are. They're accorded about as much respect as you could stuff in a billy goat's navel. When a woman gets up to read, the men in the audience go for coffee or take bathroom breaks. Or they steal her work. Well, I might be exaggerating a *little*, but..."

"In that case, I understand why this excursion is so important to you. I'll try my best not to screw up, pal. And I'll take more care filling out my daily data sheets. Rest easy, Sherry—I'll do my part."

"Good. We women have to stick together. Which reminds me...we'd better get our fannies in gear. Maizie's ready to hit the trail."

"It's so dusty I'm going to put a little distance between my wagon and the teachers'. It's not as if a straggler can get lost. This country's so flat you can see all the way to Oklahoma."

"Kansas City, at least." Sherry screwed up her face. "You're one hundred percent right about the dust. Did you see that road sign advertising Itchy's Flea Market? I'm itchy from all the cottonwood blowing around. I guess we're spoiled in Columbia, with our rolling hills and pine and maple trees. What do you suppose kept pioneers trekking through this desolate land?"

"The promise of Spanish money. I tell you, money rules the world."

Sherry chuckled. "Not my world. Work rules my world. If my boss retires...a big *if*. No sense counting on a promotion. Anyhow, in four years when I come into my trust, I'll be able to afford a house."

"Or you could marry someone who owns a house."

"Emily, I'm shocked! That's no reason to walk down the aisle."

"I didn't mean you'd marry to gain a house. It goes without saying that you'd love the man who owned the bricks and mortar."

"I've decided to remain a happy bachelorette."

"Sure. The tougher they talk, the harder they fall."

"Yeah, yeah!" Sherry waved at Emily over her shoulder.

Emily smiled long after Sherry had boarded her wagon and pulled into line with the main caravan. Sherry was tall, willowy and possessed the most luscious peaches-and-cream complexion of any woman in Emily's acquaintance. She also had a sharp mind and a wonderful sense of humor. It was easy enough to imagine men falling crazy in love with her. Emily knew Sherry hadn't met anyone who made *her* feel that way. But if ever the right man came along, she'd be a goner.

As for herself, well—she was the more likely of the two to remain single. Except that widowed and single were different. Still, the prospect of living alone once the kids flew the nest sent a trickle of dread down Emily's spine. All those years, all by herself... It wasn't the sex she missed. Long before Dave's death, his philandering had driven her into sleeping in the spare bedroom. Listening to colleagues, Emily knew sex could be pleasant. Even fun. No, she couldn't say she'd missed the sweaty coupling Dave called lovemaking. But she did miss the aftermath. The quiet time after he'd fallen asleep when his body warmth reached out, cocooning her in the darkness.

Winter nights were the hardest to get through alone. It was dark by the time she got home from work, and cold. To save money, she lowered the thermostat during the day.

She felt foolish wrapping herself in flannel sheets and dragging out her tattered, childhood teddy bear. He sat like a lump on the empty pillow, neither breathing nor exuding warmth; all the same his presence comforted.

After Dave's plane had crashed, so much crap came her way from Toby and Mona that Emily took her comfort whenever she could find it. A cup of tea with a friend. Rereading a favorite book. Watching a TV game show with the kids. Her teddy bear...

Emily might have daydreamed the morning away had Jared Boone not called out that she was being too slow.

"If you're in a hurry, go around me, Jared. I don't mind bringing up the rear."

"Gram wouldn't like that. She wants a man covering the rear of the train."

"Gram? Oh, you mean, Maizie. Why on earth...? Never mind. I get the message." Emily stewed, until it dawned on her that Jared's directions had probably come through Robert rather than Maizie. It didn't sound like Maizie's philosophy. "Hold your horses, junior," she told him. "I'll get under way when I'm ready."

The boy, who wasn't much older than Mark, gave a long-suffering sigh. "Yes, ma'am. Only, I'm not 'junior.' The Boones have enough juniors without me."

Ah, she thought, *even the management's a little touchy this many days out.* Emily made mental note to add that to her data sheet. She also vowed to remain pleasant throughout the entire trip, even if it killed her.

As the day wore on, that promise grew harder to keep. Mile after endless mile, they slogged past fields of waving grain and red-crested tassels of milo. Twice their path ran parallel to highway 56. Truckers hauling baled hay to market honked their horns. The noise made the horses skittish and difficult to handle. The few cars that passed all slowed down; people opened their windows and cheered the trekkers on. A man on a tractor pulled up next to Emily and chatted. He thought the reenactment was great. He'd lived near the trail his whole life, he said, yet had never found time to drive the route. He warned of thunderstorms brewing in the Texas gulf, and in the next breath wished her Godspeed.

It seemed as if God had traveled at a snail's pace for the last five miles. Emily frequently found herself looking back over her shoulder, expecting to see Mark and Camp overtake them at any minute. Funny, how she thought of him as "Camp," although Sherry always called him "Nolan."

The nickname fitted him, in spite of the fact that camping was foreign to the man. However, he was no slouch on a horse. Emily's heart had beaten faster this morning, watching him ride off, so straight and easy in the saddle. His handling of the pinto was at odds with his ability in other areas of trail life. Emily didn't see him as the type to own horses and muck out stalls. But she'd been wrong about a man before. Horribly wrong.

As the sun began its western descent, the lead wagon turned and set a course into the sun, toward tree-covered undulations. Blessed hills. This turning of the whole column brought Megan out of hiding.

"Where's the town? You said we were stopping in Council Grove."

"We'll be there tomorrow. In time for the morning walking tour."

"I'm not taking any old walking tour. Brittany and I plan to shop."

"You girls had better take notes. Never know when you can use them in a school history paper."

"Brittany said they'll have neat antique stores. We're going to look for old hats, funky jewelry and stuff."

"Hats? Megan, we don't have money for someone else's junk." Emily practically yanked her team to a stop. She did slow enough for Megan to hop off.

"I'm going to ride with Sherry and Brittany. All you ever do is rag on me. I don't need your money. Mona gave me her credit card numbers."

"Megan—you come back here! You're not to charge

anything to Mona, do you hear?'' Her words echoed back from a curve they were rounding. Maizie had already pulled in beside a bubbling stream. Emily decided to un-hitch her team first and argue later. Megan was *not* going to use Mona's credit cards this time.

With dusk settling in, she had more to worry about than her mother-in-law's far-reaching tentacles. There was still no sign of Mark and Camp.

Emily fretted as she and Sherry gathered wood. ''I wonder what's keeping them. They didn't take bedrolls or much food.''

''Speaking of food,'' Sherry murmured. ''Megan wants to eat with us, Em. I said okay without thinking. If you'd prefer, I'll send her back to your wagon.''

''No. Let her stay. That'll be one less thing for us to fight about.'' Emily brought Sherry up to date on her lat-est confrontation with Megan.''

''I'll look for an opening to talk with her,'' Sherry promised. ''I can see your mind's on other things. Do you want me to ask Robert to ride out and have a look around?''

Emily shook her head. ''That's not what our pioneer sisters would do. They'd suffer in silence. I'll be fine, Sherry. I'm sure I'm worrying needlessly. I've been more of a worrier since Dave died in that crash.''

''I understand. Why don't you come eat with us, too?''

''No. I'll be fine. Really.'' Emily patted Sherry's arm as they dropped their last load of wood and prepared to part.

Sherry gave Emily's hand a squeeze. ''I may gripe about Nolan, but he's dependable. Did I mention he's ren-ovating an old farmhouse? Down to the bare wood. Noth-ing is too tedious. You'd be impressed. I'm telling you this so you'll know he's not a quitter. He's totally reliable and he follows through on things. Trust me, Mark is safe with him.''

Emily smiled. ''Thanks. I won't tell a soul you paid him a compliment.''

Sherry screwed up her face. ''On most things, Nolan and I actually see eye to eye. He's not half as bad as his colleagues. Lyle Roberts thinks women are useless.''

''Careful, or you'll talk yourself into siding with Nolan. Go on and fix your dinner. I'm sure he and Mark will roll in shortly.''

But they didn't. Darkness occluded the skyline. Nothing but the wind moved out of the east—the direction they'd travel. The temperature dropped appreciably. Emily fixed a whole pot of navy bean soup in anticipation of their riding in hungry.

Megan slunk back at nine. She climbed in the wagon without saying a word. Emily was too weary to argue about Mona's credit cards. She paced and stared into the black night, drinking cup after cup of tea. No doubt the caffeine was adding to her unrest, making her feel even more jittery. One by one the other fires were extinguished, until only hers and Maizie's were left.

It was after ten, going on eleven. Emily sensed more than heard approaching hoofbeats. She jumped up and ran to the edge of Camp's wagon, clutching a hand over her heart. ''Yes!'' A steady clip-clop shook the ground.

Then, so as not to appear unduly anxious, she walked sedately back to her campfire, poured another cup of tea with shaking hands and sat. The instant the plodding horses appeared, she sprang up. Camp led the horse Mark had been riding. Her son was draped limply across the front of Camp's saddle. ''What happened?'' Emily barely choked back a turbulent cry.

Camp reined in the pinto, awkwardly placing a finger to his lips. ''It's okay, Emily,'' he whispered. ''Poor kid fell asleep. My arm's about to fall off. I doubt he'll wake up. Let me figure out how to slide off, and I'll help you put him to bed.''

Emily steadied the horse, grateful for Camp's offer. It was years since she'd been able to manage Mark's dead weight.

A lack of feeling in the arm and leg that'd borne the bulk of the sleeping boy caused Camp to dismount awkwardly.

"Shouldn't we wake him?" Emily murmured. "Won't he be hungry?"

"At five o'clock we met a family picnicking along the river. They shared sandwiches, fruit and cookies and picked our brains about the Santa Fe Trail. Mark enjoyed the food—almost as much as he enjoyed playing Santa Fe Trail guru.''

"All the Bentons make wonderful instant experts. I'm sure it's in the genes.''

Camp chuckled as he bundled Mark into Emily's wagon. "I see Maizie's still up. I'll go report in and see to the horses. Then I wouldn't object to a plateful of whatever it is that smells so good.''

"Soup. I hope it's still edible. What took you so long?''

"You'll want to discuss that with Mark. I'm afraid his life of crime started a few miles earlier than he let on.''

"Oh.'' She fumbled for words. "I'm really sorry.''

Camp gazed down on earnest features hauntingly etched in moonlight. Moved, he gently held her shoulders. "Mark's a good kid, Emily. But he's easily led. I may not have a right to say this...but after things he let slip today, I'd say you'd be smart to remove both kids from their grandparents.''

Struggling against a lump lodged in her throat, Emily pulled from his loose grasp. "You'd better take care of the horses. I'll go check on the soup.''

Impulsively, Camp caught her arms again. He hated the pinched look that killed the lively sparkle of her eyes. Instinct urged him to kiss away the sadness. Carefully cupping her soft face, he bent and tilted Emily's chin until their lips met. What started out as a desire to comfort flamed on contact. She arched away, frustrating Camp. He wanted more from her than a simple kiss. But the instant she wrenched away, he released her. Confusion clouded his eyes.

Panting, she licked her tingling bottom lip. It'd been years since any man had kissed her with such compassion, let alone with passion. The coil of need clutching her abdomen tempted her to lose herself in body-numbing foreplay. But with Dave, foreplay always led to unsatisfying sex, which caused more problems, solving none. "I'm going to bed," she said brusquely. "Get this straight—I am not a sex-starved widow. My appreciation for what you did for Mark doesn't extend to payback of that sort. The Bentons taught me there's always a price to pay for favors. Help yourself to soup and coffee. And consider my debt to you paid in full."

Camp barely had time to suck in his breath before she vaulted into her wagon bed and jerked the canvas closed. He glared at the flimsy material that he could so easily rip aside. Bone-weary though he was, he was sorely tempted to do just that and set her straight about his intentions. The fire that shot through his veins died as he heard one of the kids stirring and Emily answer in a low, soothing tone.

To top it all, he was as baffled as she by his caveman tactics. One thing Camp did know, he wasn't anything like her husband. Or her father-in-law. Tomorrow he'd have something to say to Mrs. Spitfire Benton. And when he'd finished, dammit, she wouldn't lump him in with the Benton men again.

A restrictive ideology prevailed in the written history of the American West. That men were courageous, women passive and dependent.

—*From Nolan Campbell's notes.*

CHAPTER SIX

EMILY FOUND IT impossible to relax. Blood rushed to her ears—and everywhere else her body had touched Camp's. She burrowed under the covers, then kicked them off, trying to concentrate on the even breathing of her children. As she'd told him, she wasn't a sex-starved widow...but she was sure acting like one. Every time she closed her eyes, she pictured straight, sable eyebrows and softly curled dark hair. Her fingers itched to feel the texture, the traces of silver that feathered his temples. Exactly right for a professor. Nolan Campbell's hands were well manicured but not smooth against her skin. Were they, and the solid muscles she'd felt in his chest and thighs, a result of the carpentry work Sherry said he did on his home?

It wasn't easy for Emily to admit that she liked the feel of Camp's hard, masculine body. Because she remembered being drawn to Dave's athletic build at first. The abuse of his body with too-rich food and an overabundance of alcohol began gradually. He'd developed a paunch well before they stopped sharing a bed. Her numerous attempts to alter his eating habits gave him all the more reason to complain about her to his parents. Looking back, Emily realized that was just an insignificant part of the erosion of respect between them.

Nolan Campbell didn't seem like a man of excess or overindulgence. *Or maybe he was.* Emily ran her tongue lightly over her tender lips. He'd certainly delivered a three-alarm kiss. Unless it'd been too long for her to gauge, she'd venture to say he'd been well on his way to turning that kiss into a four-alarm blaze.

Flopping over on her stomach, Emily punched her pillow into a pulp.

"Mom?" Mark's restless voice floated out of the darkness. "Is something wrong?"

"I'm fine, honey," Emily lied. "Are you hungry? You were asleep when Camp brought you home."

"Not hungry," he mumbled, kicking at his covers.

"Do you want your pajamas on?"

"Nah, don't need 'em. Camp said real pioneers slept in their clothes. He knows all about that stuff." Another, longer yawn. "He's rule, Mom."

Into the silence, Megan piped up. " 'Rule' means he's boss or cool," she grumbled sleepily. "*Good* in mom talk."

"I see," Emily muttered. "Anyhow, I think I do."

"Sheesh, Mom. It's heavy-metal lingo. You know, *metal rules.* I'd have thought you'd be up on stuff like that at college," Megan said scornfully, rising briefly on her elbow.

"In college when you mean good, you say good," Emily retorted dryly. Which wasn't necessarily true, of course. With all the cultures and countercultures a teacher encountered, communication was often confusing. What she did find interesting in this midnight exchange with her children was that Mark had gone from calling Camp a "loose cannon" to deciding he was "rule." Kids—Mark in particular—didn't switch allegiance easily.

Megan huffed a little and turned over. Her breathing soon evened out again. Mark had gone back to snoring softly. As her own blood finally cooled, Emily decided she might have acted rashly, tarring Camp with the same brush she reserved for Dave and his father.

She sat up and reached for her jeans. Pulling them on, she muffled a yawn. Oddly, the conversation with her kids had brought things into focus. If nothing else, she owed Camp an apology for acting like an outraged virgin.

CAMP WAS IN NO MOOD for idle chitchat. Maizie had other ideas. He tried to cut their conversation short, insisting he didn't need or want help with the horses.

"Bah, two sets of hands are quicker than one. You look bushed. I hafta say you did a good deed today, sonny. I found out Jared knew Mark had swiped those signs. He stayed mum because of some warped code these young 'uns go by."

"How can you fault loyalty? Truth is, I doubt Mark will pull that stunt again. I'm just glad I discovered it then, rather than farther afield."

Maizie gave the horse Mark had ridden a last, brisk rub and a scoop of oats. "Mark's the lucky duck. I'd probably have skinned the kid alive if I'd caught him. His mother needs to tune in before it's too late."

"Give Emily a break. She's doing the best she can."

"Uh-huh." Maizie dug in her pocket for a chew, stopped and gave a wry shake of her head. "So are you reforming her, too?"

"Nothing of the kind," Camp replied too quickly. "In the beginning, I felt like you. I know now that her in-laws spoil the kids rotten. I gather they're some piece of work." He paused. "Look, if you want to know any more about the Bentons, you'll have to talk to Emily."

"Fair enough. You hungry, boy? I could probably rustle up some grub."

"Thanks, but Emily left soup warming. I may as well take her up on the offer. Also, I promised to bank her campfire. She and the kids already went to bed. Mark was exhausted—slept the last few miles." Camp massaged the arm that'd held the boy as he eyed the long row of dark wagons. "Appears everybody made an early night of it. What's our agenda for tomorrow? You said about three hours to Council Grove?"

"Yep. On the road by six sharp. We need to arrive in time for the town's summer celebration. There'll be a parade, tours, all that folderol. Guess folks are anxious to hit town for a spell. All except that Ms Ames of yours." Maizie scowled.

"Gina? I'm sure she'll want to photograph the folderol, as you put it."

"Yeah, well, she's got her tail in a tizzy. Had her mind set on filming a patch of sunflowers. We got here too late. She's in a snit. Asked if we could start later. I tried to explain if I adjusted the schedule for one, everybody would expect favors."

"Gina strikes me as being a professional. The snit will be over by morning."

"'Spect so. Well, sonny, I'm scrammin' these old bones off to bed. You better eat quick and grab some shut-eye yourself."

"I will. After I jot a few notes. I noticed someone collected my data sheets. Remind me to say thank-you tomorrow."

"Your sister. I like that gal. She's surprisingly cheerful for having to put up with that ditzy miss you stuck her with."

"Ah, yes, Brittany." Camp massaged the back of his neck. "I should feel guilty, but I'm banking on Sherry's levelheadedness rubbing off."

"Humph, if she doesn't tear her hair out first. Only time will tell. Well, good night, boy. Don't want your food gettin' cold for my jawing."

Camp gave the two saddle horses a last pat, then made a beeline for the only beacon left burning—Emily's still-glowing fire.

Entering the empty campsite, he crouched on his heels to stir the soup. The only sounds were the wind rustling through clumps of tallgrass and the occasional whicker of horses. Loneliness struck Camp without warning. He wavered between partaking of this solitary meal or chucking it in and going to bed.

In the midst of his indecision, the hairs at his nape stiffened. Sensing something or someone behind him, Camp straightened and whipped around, slopping hot soup on his jeans. "Who's there?" His heart beat unsteadily. What would he do if it was Brittany? *Send her back to her wagon, that's what!*

Emily, not Brittany, separated herself from the coal-dark outline of the wagon.

She hadn't meant to sneak up on him. However, once she'd glimpsed his broad back crouched over the grate, her heart began to pound again, and her feet took on a life of their own. Thoughts muddled, Emily had entertained the idea of going back to bed, of saving what she had to say till daylight. Now she'd shown herself, leaving her no choice but to follow through.

"It's just me." Her voice cracked.

"Emily?" Camp rose. The spoon continued to drip on his boots. "Did Mark wake up hungry?" Realizing he still held the spoon, he quickly stuck it back in the soup.

"He's in luck. I stopped to feed the horses and haven't had time to finish this up."

She gave a shrug, eyes on the bubbling pot as though it contained witches' brew instead of harmless bean soup. "Mark's sleeping like a log. So is Megan. I, uh, I came to apologize."

He followed her gaze. "Apologize for the soup?" He sent her a puzzled smile. "If it's scorched you can hardly blame yourself. We were late. Anyway, I'm not fussy."

Sighing, she clasped her hands solidly in front of her. All the while her restless gaze traveled skyward, then swooped to lock on the ground near Camp's feet. "I'm apologizing for my earlier outburst." The last word sank into a whisper. She tried again. "I don't know you well, but I've seen firsthand that you possess more integrity than Toby. More than Dave ever did. Forgive me, I shouldn't speak badly of the dead."

Her tone pricked his conscience. It was too polite. "Don't give it another thought. I was out of line." He glanced at the dark canopy overhead. "I can't even blame my bad behavior on a full moon," he joked.

But Emily found she couldn't laugh. She'd said her piece; now it was time to leave. "I should—"

Camp judged she was about one second from bolting. "You're cold," he broke in. "Come, sit by the fire. You're an answer to my prayer, you know," he said too quickly. "I hate eating alone." He hooked his foot around one of the canvas stools she'd left grouped around the fire ring and offered it with a smile.

Emily relaxed a little. She didn't rush to take the seat.

"Scout's honor. It's not good for a person to eat alone."

"I don't believe you were ever a Scout," she snorted. "And I've never heard that company aids digestion."

"Sure it does. Mine, anyway," he said, grabbing another stool and dragging it close to the heat. He sat down and he calmly filled a bowl with soup. As he spooned up a mouthful, he presented Emily with a long face.

This time her sigh spelled resignation. "Stop that. You know I'm a sucker for cow eyes. Would you like crackers with your soup?" Stepping into the light, she bent easily and plucked a packet of unopened crackers from a metal canister. Gingerly she perched on the stool he'd prepared.

Camp hid a grin. He'd take victory any way he could achieve it. "I'll never turn down food. Emily, this soup hits the spot. It's thick, the way I like it." He accepted a handful of crackers, but stopped speaking as their fingers brushed. He felt a sensation that reminded him—oddly enough—of the shock he'd once suffered when his electric sander shorted out. It traveled to his elbow and weakened his grip.

He and Emily both lunged for the fumbled crackers. Camp experienced hunger of a different nature. Emily exuded a tantalizing scent of coconut and almond that put his hormones on alert. He jerked away, knowing he smelled of leather, horse and sweat.

Her stomach churning, Emily made a big production of closing the cracker packet and returning it to the covered tin.

Something was definitely happening here. Camp fought an urge to taste the creamy pulse that had begun to throb in Emily's neck. He bit into a cracker, instead. Once he'd devoured it, he went back to methodically eating his soup. In the sudden descent of silence, Camp was terribly afraid he'd begun to sound like a dry camel taking on water. But if he stopped...

Emily's scent filled him. He found it almost impossible to concentrate on satisfying his hunger for food. Making a concerted effort to act at ease, Camp stretched his long legs toward the fire. "Tomorrow we roll into Council

Grove," he said inanely. Darn it, he'd never been inane. Normally he was quite articulate.

"Tomorrow. Yes." Emily bent and set the canister down before straightening and crossing her feet primly at the ankles. She didn't know what to do with her hands and finally left them loose in her lap. *What was wrong with her?* Friends generally considered her a witty conversationalist. However, she wasn't quite sure what had happened with that simple touch they'd shared. No. The real problem—she *was* sure.

Frowning, Camp ladled himself a second bowl of soup, although he barely remembered having tasted the first one. He wished she'd quit rubbing one ankle on the other that way. He imagined her naked flesh slowly massaging his calves. Shifting uncomfortably, he muttered in a gravelly voice, "Are the kids looking forward to the tours or to visiting the Last Chance Store?"

"No."

After waiting several heartbeats with nothing more forthcoming, Camp set his bowl aside. In an all-out attempt to sweep the provocative visions from his mind, he viciously rubbed the bridge of his nose. "Hey, help me out here, Emily. If our students gave one-syllable answers, we'd be all over them in a minute."

The absurdity of two adults—professors—floundering for dialogue, worse than shy preteens, propelled a bubble of laughter past the lump in Emily's throat. Leaning toward him, she clasped her hands between her knees. "I deserve to flunk. My only excuse is that I've been out of the singles scene a long time. I'm afraid I saw an accidental touch and a simple kiss as a prelude to hopping into bed. It's my problem, not yours. That's how Dave operated. It's probably not how you act."

Camp's stomach fish-flopped. The glow from the fire picked up a dusting of freckles on Emily's cheeks—a result of these last few days in the sun. What could he say? He felt guilty knowing she'd hit squarely on what lurked in his mind. What it did was make him face facts. In Emily's case, he did operate differently. Everything she'd blurted out was true; this wasn't his normal style. But his reaction to Emily wasn't the way he normally reacted to a woman, either. He sure as heck didn't want to scare her off until they figured out what it was that spiced the air between them every time they got within shouting distance. At the moment she looked about half a step from taking flight. Again. Camp definitely didn't want to screw things up.

He cleared his throat. "At our age, Emily, everyone carries a lot of baggage. Maybe we should just let the past be. Not worry about it?" He already knew she'd had a bastard for a husband—an experience that'd left her wary of men. So what? According to Greta, a man who hung out in museums was a zero in the relationship department, too. So why not keep things superficial? "Do you see any reason we can't be friends?" He carefully steepled his fingers.

"Friends." She turned the word over on her tongue and in her mind, recalling how his lips had made her feel. Heart knocking, she eyed him skeptically. "Define 'friend.'"

"I'm lousy at crossword puzzles—but I'll give it a stab. Friends lend a helping hand, laugh together, maybe eat together. Hopefully, share a common interest or two."

Emily nodded. That didn't sound too threatening. He didn't flippantly say friends were playmates. "In a way..." She hesitated. "We, uh, do have a common interest. Sherry said you're remodeling an old farmhouse. My hobby is refinishing furniture."

"See, I knew we were kindred spirits. Do you work with any special time period?"

"I'm partial to the country-styled hard maples, but I tend to mix and match so long as it's real wood and not veneer. I guess you could say my taste is eclectic."

Camp felt the tension slide from his limbs. "Have you ever refinished kitchen cabinets? That's where I am. Sherry says I should gut the room. I want to modernize, but there's a brick-walled fireplace I'd like to save. And an old icebox I thought would make good storage until Gret—someone called it an eyesore."

"Not after it's refinished. Does your friend know people would practically kill for a real icebox? I'd love to see your place," she ventured softly. "Maybe I could give you a few tips."

"More than likely you'd turn tail and run. Even my parents refer to the house as Nolan's white elephant. They're convinced I'll have one foot in the grave before it's ready for guests. I've been working on it in my spare time for eight years. Four bedrooms and two bathrooms are complete. I've stripped the living-room and dining-room walls and floors. My bedroom and one I use as an office are the only rooms I've furnished. In the kitchen I have a refrigerator, a microwave, and a table and two chairs my folks were throwing away."

"Think how satisfying it'll be once it's finally done. I loved my house. It didn't need as much work as yours, obviously, but I redecorated every room."

"You say *loved* as if it's in the past."

Her face fell. "I had to sell for financial reasons after Dave died. The kids and I moved into a small duplex. Luckily the people who bought the house wanted a lot of the furniture, too, or else I'd be paying storage every month."

Camp read the look. He wouldn't call it luck at all. He thought giving up her house had been tantamount to driving a stake through Emily's heart. "When we get back to civilization, I'll draw you a map to my place. I've already invited Mark, but if you're moved to do a little consulting on the side, I'd be happy to hire you."

"Oh, I couldn't take money. I wouldn't."

"Well, then by all means drop by and toss out opinions."

"I'd like that. I'd like Mark to do more riding. Do you, by chance, have horses?"

"No, but there's a stream behind my house that's great for fishing. I understand Jared's going to teach Mark how. And I do have a lop-eared mutt who loves kids. A ten-year-old golden lab. He and I walk together every morning. He doesn't understand why I don't have time to take him fishing anymore."

"Mark used to beg for a puppy." Her lips tightened. "I was afraid—well, his father didn't like animals. And now," she lamented, "our place is too small."

Camp had to temper the rush of anger he felt. Only— as she'd said earlier—there was no sense arguing with a dead man. Nor did Camp want to sound as if he chastised Emily for staying with the jerk. She said he'd threatened to take away her kids. Not that he fully understood how that could happen. It seemed, on the surface anyhow, that someone possessing the tools to work with disadvantaged women could have used those same tools to break free of her own situation. But there he went, judging her unfairly again.

"Why are you looking at me like that? I'm not kidding, Camp. My place is too small for a turtle, let alone a dog. It wouldn't be fair to the animal."

"Hey, your word is good." He stood, wishing he didn't have these doubts. But the question kept cropping up, and their friendship was too new for him to ask. He faked a yawn. "I'll wash these dishes before the fire dies and leaves me with cold water. Go on to bed, Emily. Maizie plans to be on the road by six.''

''I'm awake now. You go to bed and let me do the dishes.''

''My mother wouldn't believe I'd argue if someone offered to wash dishes. See, you've warped my psyche. Going by the rules in my house, you fed me, so scram, I'll handle cleanup.''

''Could I convince you to repeat this conversation to Mark sometime? His father and grandfather voiced definite ideas on what constitutes men's work compared with women's. Oh, forget it, the kids'll just point out that Toby and Mona have a cook and a maid.'' She jumped up and poured the basin full of water, then set it on the grate. ''I tend to view housework as a team effort. Since that's my philosophy, we'll share cleanup and both get to bed faster.''

Camp was struck by a picture of the two of them winding down for the day and walking off to bed hand in hand. A picture so clear that he stopped folding the stools and stood, gazing hungrily at the delicate feminine curves of her back.

As if sensing his scrutiny, she turned from scrubbing the bean pot. ''Camp?''

''Fine.'' He passed a hand over his eyes. ''I'm all for teamwork. Let's cut the small talk and dig in.''

Because there was no other conversation between them, Emily wondered what in their brief exchange had made Camp act so moody. Just as she'd begun to let down her guard with him, too. Well, she'd had a bellyful of moody men. He needn't worry that she'd press her unwanted company on him again.

''I don't need an escort service to find my way to my wagon,'' she said. A gentleman through and through, Camp padded at her heels, shining a light on the path between their wagons. She didn't respond to his grumpy "good night."

Emily had no sooner climbed into her wagon and closed the flap than she decided it'd been churlish to pretend not to hear him. He had put in a full day helping Mark. And Camp had said to begin with that he was tired. It was another example of her past intruding. Emily hated that she'd reverted to the passive-aggressive tendencies she'd developed to cope with staying married. Darn, why did she always end up owing Nolan Campbell apologies? She'd set out to clear the air and now she was back at square one. Fumbling with the ties, Emily threw open the canvas she'd just cinched shut. She expected him still to be there. But he wasn't.

Just as she considered going to his wagon, his lantern sprang to life. Backlit against a canopy of white was a clear silhouette of Camp removing his shirt. Emily's mouth went dry. He shed his jeans and then... What in the world was she doing? She wasn't a voyeur, for pity's sake. Sucking in a huge gulp of night air, Emily drew her canvas closed with shaking fingers. She stumbled on hands and knees to her bed and dived under the covers without removing her clothes. For a long time she lay absolutely still, her mind locked in battle with an unforgivably acute imagination.

CAMP ROUSED at the faint sound of Maizie's dinner bell. He groaned. That woman loved to punish late sleepers with the clang of iron against all three sides of that blasted triangle.

He sat up slowly and heard the thump of books hitting the floor. Snapping on a flashlight, he realized he'd fallen asleep in the middle of comparing the women's data sheets with what was listed in his texts. According to the books, men like Crockett and Boone shunned towns, preferring to live off the land. *His* group, however, looked forward to the promised layover in town.

And not one woman mentioned that the firewood they stocked here would have to last or else, like their pioneer sisters, they'd be out collecting cow chips to burn. Sherry wrote that she was dying to find a bookstore and a beauty shop. Gina wanted to develop her film. Brittany filled two pages with the plans she and Megan had made: a visit to the rodeo, junk food and shopping. Only Emily mentioned visiting historical points of interest. She named some that Camp had never heard of.

In a moment of weakness, he imagined viewing history through Emily's eyes. Such beautiful eyes. Forced to deal with a quickening in his blood, Camp thrust thoughts of Emily aside. He gathered the papers and bundled them with the others, then dressed and took a walk in the woods. A dip in the icy stream effectively cooled his ardor. By the time he returned, preparations for the day had begun.

Mark and Megan were stuffing their faces with pancakes. Emily didn't seem to be around. Mark glanced up and greeted Camp with a sticky smile. "Hi. Jared's dad says if me and him collect piles of wood this morning, he'll loan me a fishing pole to use for the rest of the trip."

"Him and I, stupid," Megan growled before Camp could say a word. "Instead of dragging us on this crappy trip, Mom should have stayed home and sent you to summer school."

"No more'n you. I didn't get any Ds on my report card."

Megan's brows drew down. "Mona said my teachers shouldn't have given me so much homework. She said they were insensitive to Daddy's death."

"A year later?" Mark jeered. "'Sides, what was different? Dad was never home anyway."

"There's a lot different. Mona and Toby made sure we lived in a nice house. Wait till you're my age and have to explain to friends why you moved to a dinky duplex."

Camp listened to them argue as he built a fire and waited for his coffee to brew. Life must have been hell for Emily. Still was, he acknowledged as he sliced the last of his potatoes to fry with a can of mushrooms. Her in-laws sounded like people who'd stepped straight out of a Stephen King novel. Camp felt like waltzing into that town and telling them to lay off Emily. The idea took shape before he remembered the way they'd parted last night. He stirred the mixture, lamenting how things had turned out.

Sherry ran up, saving Camp from dwelling on the subject.

"Nolan, I'm worried about Gina. She left at dawn to photograph sunflowers. Said she'd be back in half an hour. We're due to leave soon and she's not back."

Camp washed his first bite down with a swallow of coffee. "Gina's a big girl. She probably decided to skip breakfast in favor of a big lunch in Council Grove."

Sherry's troubled gaze drifted along the foothills, where gusts of wind turned the bluestem tallgrass into ocean waves.

"I can tell you believe something's happened to her. Isn't it possible she just lost track of the time?"

"Not Gina. She runs her life on a schedule. A lot of us just buy daily planners. Gina actually uses hers."

"How can you know her so well? You only met two weeks ago."

Emily passed by carrying an armload of wood and abruptly dropped several sticks. She hadn't meant to eavesdrop, but did hear Sherry's gaffe.

Sherry shifted from foot to foot. Her eyes made contact with Emily's in a silent warning.

"Really, Camp," Emily chided, crossing to stand beside Sherry. "You don't have to be very observant to see that Gina runs her life by the clock."

His gaze skipped to Emily's open smile. Darn, how did she manage to throw him into a tailspin with one smile? "You think Gina should be back by now, too?"

"Yes, I do."

"Okay. Let me stow my gear and I'll ask Robert to help me take a look." Camp assumed his offer would appease both women. Instead, Sherry bounced a suspicious glance between him and Emily.

"You wouldn't take my word, but the minute Emily asks, you turn into the Lone Ranger. What gives with you two?"

Emily's cheeks flushed. Camp sensed where Sherry was headed and tried to ward her off. "It was the buildup of concern, sis. I still doubt there's a problem, but I'm willing to take your collective word."

"Oh. Guess I let Brittany influence me. She swears there's a romance developing between you two." Snatching the plate from Camp's hand, Sherry pushed him toward Robert's wagon, missing the look that passed between him and Emily.

"Why don't we go ourselves?" Emily asked. "Aren't we as capable of finding Gina as the men are?"

"Robert's been over this route," Camp countered. "He knows the area. Worst-case scenario is Gina had a run-in with a rattler, and Robert's the best person to deal with that."

Emily's eyes glittered angrily for a moment until she registered Sherry's interest in their spat, and she said through clenched teeth, "No doubt Robert is the best choice."

Camp came within a hair of responding in kind to her sarcasm. Reconsidering, he tugged the bill of his Kansas

City Royals cap over his eyes and went in search of Robert—who was inclined to agree with Camp that Gina had either strayed farther than planned or that she'd lost herself in her work.

Robert dug out a dime. "I'll flip you for who breaks the bad news to Maizie. She's raring to get under way. This isn't going to make her happy."

"Better you take her tongue-lashing than me, old son," Camp said, delivering a friendly slap to the man's back. "Sherry said Gina followed that trail." He pointed to a faint track leading up the hill. "See where it splits? I'll search the east branch. After you tell Maizie, hike along the other side. If neither of us finds Gina by six, let's touch base back at the fork and switch to plan B."

"Which is?" Robert frowned.

"Beats me," Camp said. "I just made up plan A. She supposedly hiked the Sierras alone. I'm counting on her to beat us back."

Robert nodded, and the two went their separate ways. Camp soon discovered that his portion of the trail petered out. He loped to the fork, expecting that he'd engaged in this morning exercise for nothing. He broke into a jog the minute the crossroads—where Robert paced irritably—came into sight.

"Don't tell me," Camp panted, removing his sunglasses to blot away the sweat trickling into his eyes. "No Gina."

"That's right, and this trail dead-ends on the other side of the hill in a cornfield. As far as I can see is farmland. Some fallow, most planted. I'm going back for my binoculars. Hell, the way the wind whistles through the corn stalks, it's impossible to tell if she's out there wandering around."

"You think she might be?"

"It'd be my guess. Philly opened his big mouth last

night and blabbed about this being the place where they've reported odd circles in the middle of cornfields. Circles some fool claims were made by spaceships. If she went in to take pictures and got turned around, it could take her two days to find her way out.''

"You're kidding?''

"'Fraid not. I can tell you've never farmed corn. Some places it grows so tall you can't see daylight.''

"Yes, but can't you just follow a row to the end?''

"Yep, providing you're headed in the right direction. The rows crisscross.''

"I see. Well, let's not waste any more time.''

MAIZIE ANXIOUSLY awaited their return. "Damn,'' she said. "If this ain't a pickle.''

Harv from Philadelphia shoved his way between Robert and Maizie. "Don't waste our time because of some broad's stupidity. I say we go on to town and send a search party back. Your brochure promised a frontier day's celebration. Why should the rest of us miss the parade?''

Maizie glared at him. "Nobody's stopping you, Mr. Big Mouth. But it's a far piece to Santa Fe. If you have trouble with your wagon, don't count on help from trail mates.''

He made an ugly gesture, but he did shut up.

Robert rummaged in his wagon and pulled out binoculars and a rifle. "Gina might have run afoul of a rattlesnake or a rabid coyote.''

Emily handed Camp several clean white dishtowels. "If Gina's injured, you may need to cover a wound or make a sling.''

Camp accepted them grimly. He pressed Emily's hand in appreciation.

"Can Jared and me go?" asked Mark eagerly. "We wanna help."

Searching his mind for some polite way to say no, Camp was relieved to hear Robert say it first. "You guys stay and help the ladies lay in a good supply of wood. Best thing you can do is have these wagons ready to roll the minute we return."

Near seven-thirty the searchers stumbled across Gina's footprints leading into a cornfield, just as Robert had predicted. Forty-five minutes later, Camp grabbed Robert's arm. "Is it my imagination or are we covering the same ground twice?"

"It's not your imagination. She wandered in circles for a while."

Cupping his hands around his mouth, Camp shouted Gina's name. Both men strained to hear over the moaning wind that sounded almost human at times.

Robert shook his head and turned to plunge deeper into the field.

"Wait!" Camp's sharp command stopped him. "This way. I heard a shout." Camp pointed in the opposite direction from the set of tracks.

"You may be right," Robert said excitedly. "Listen." Faintly, they heard what sounded like "Help," above the constant rustle of the leaves.

The men angled diagonally through some forty rows before picking up Gina's tracks again. This time they shouted in unison. The answer sounded weak but clear. Keeping up a running discourse, Camp stumbled through a wall of corn and fell over the woman they sought.

"Thank God you found me. I feel like a fool," Gina gasped through parched lips. "I'd set up my tripod for a close-up of the sunflowers mixed in with the corn. I stepped back and landed in a blasted prairie-dog hole. It threw me into the tripod, which toppled over on me. I'm afraid I broke my left leg and my right arm.''

"The arm is really swollen," Camp concurred. He carefully immobilized her arm with a sling fashioned from the towels Emily had given him. A cursory glance at the odd angle of her leg had Camp fighting a queasy stomach. "Moving you will hurt like hell. If we take you and your equipment, we'll have to immobilize this leg and trade off carrying you."

"Don't think I'm going to louse up your paper, Campbell. I'll need somebody to drive my wagon into Council Grove to a doctor. He'll patch me up.''

Camp didn't want to disillusion her, but he didn't think Gina Ames would be continuing with this trip. There went the professional photographs he'd coveted. Oh, well, accidents happened now as they had to the pioneers—the difference being that Gina's pioneer sisters would have tossed her into a wagon and forged on. She might or might not have healed properly. Today, medical equipment and techniques virtually assured her of a full recovery.

Forcing his disappointment aside, Camp made his decision. No part of this reenactment—or his project—was worth taking risks with Gina's health. She'd stay behind in Council Grove.

"Pioneer women were little more than passive partici-
pants in their husbands' ventures."
—*A statement in one of the standard history texts used by
Nolan Campbell.*

CHAPTER SEVEN

THE MEN TOOK TURNS carrying Gina and her heavy equipment. Camp developed a new respect for the scrappy
woman who worried not about her injuries but for the
safety of her camera and lenses. Her arm and leg had to
hurt badly, yet she never once complained of her own
discomfort.

Maizie, Emily, Sherry, Doris and Vi ran to meet the
returning expedition. Sherry gripped Gina's good hand.

Emily fussed and adjusted her sling. "What can we do
to help, Gina?"

Mark and Jared sidled closer. Brittany and Megan hung
back. The couple from Philadelphia showed no interest
whatsoever in the plight of a fellow traveler.

"That ankle and knee look nasty," Maizie said after
giving Gina's injuries a cursory once-over. "You step in
front of an eighteen-wheeler, gal?"

Through clenched teeth, Gina retold her story.

"Boys." Maizie waved Jared and Mark over. "We
need splints, or the ride to town will be murder. See if
you kids can round up some magazines for braces. We
women will rip up an old sheet for ties."

Mark screwed up his face. "Brittany's got a slug of movie magazines. I ain't gonna be the one to ask her to give 'em up."

Sherry rallied. "I'll talk to Brittany," she said. "You boys hitch Gina's team."

"Sure," replied Jared. "That's easy. C'mon, Mark."

Mark dawdled. "She can't drive a team with that arm," he noted. "Ms Ames, I'll drive for you," he volunteered.

It had been on the tip of Camp's tongue to suggest that Sherry have Brittany drive their wagon, and his sister take over Gina's. Mark's request both surprised and pleased him. Ultimately, however, the decision to let the boy drive or not rested with Emily. Along with the others, Camp anxiously awaited her verdict.

Maizie clapped the youth on the back. "I'm proud of you, Mark. That's a right gentlemanly offer."

Megan hooted. "My brother a gentleman? He's a baby. Who'd trust him to drive a wagon?"

Though it was one of the first smiles Camp had seen Megan crack, he still would have backed Mark on general principles. Except that Maizie beat him to it.

"For your information, missy, at the time of the real wagon trains, a twelve-year-old lad was considered a man."

"Yeah, Megan, so shut your trap." Mark glared at his sister.

"Enough, you two." Emily shook a finger at both. "This is no time for bickering. We need to settle Gina in her wagon before she goes into shock." As Emily spoke, Robert carried Gina toward her wagon. Jared ran to help his dad.

"Gina's white as a ghost," Emily announced at large. "Sherry, do you have any extrastrength analgesic on hand? Does anyone?"

"I do, dear," Doris volunteered. Pointing to her white-haired wagon mate, she said with a twinkle in her eye, "Between us we have a pharmacy of across-the-counter pain medicine. Taking this trip at our age was defying nature. We didn't want to be caught in the middle of nowhere and be a burden with our achy joints."

Emily smiled. "I should be so spry after I retire from teaching. Ask Gina which of your medications she'd prefer, while I help Maizie tear sheets."

"Mom." Mark tugged at her arm. "Is it okay for me to drive Ms Ames's wagon?"

Emily hooked her thumbs through her belt loops. "Ask Camp."

At once Mark plied Camp with reasons he should be allowed to drive.

Camp listened intently, his eyes still on Emily. When Mark wound down, she was the one Camp addressed. "I'm glad you value my opinion."

"You leased the wagons, after all."

"Oh." Camp's smile fractured. "It's fine by me. But the ball's in your court."

Emily tensed, then shrugged. "I have a tendency to try to protect my kids from possible failure. Mark," she said, spinning toward him, her energy building. "I know you've watched me drive the team, but it's a matter of threading the reins properly through your fingers in order to apply even pressure on the driving bit. Please have Maizie or Robert show you the basics."

"You mean I can do it? All right!" Those near enough to hear him grinned.

GINA'S ACCIDENT resulted in a several-hour delay. They all accepted that they'd miss the parade. Robert saddled a horse to ride ahead to set up a doctor's appointment for Gina, and to try to reschedule tours. Jared drove their wagon, a switch that left two young drivers one behind the other. Maizie took it upon herself to exchange Gina's wagon with the Shaw wagon. Of course Harv complained bitterly.

Regardless, Emily was grateful to Maizie. Experience had taught her that mothers weren't always the best overseers of their children in new situations. This way, if Mark needed direction, he'd accept it much more readily from Maizie. Which didn't mean Emily wasn't worrying. Eventually she stopped leaning out to try to see how he was doing. It hurt her neck, and there was absolutely nothing she could do to help him.

Camp watched Emily's head bob out time and again. He knew the agony she felt. It was like that first day on the trail, when they were all new to driving. He'd worried constantly—when he wasn't in pain from the hard plank seat and the jolting ride—knowing he'd gotten everyone into what might be a risky undertaking. It'd given him a devil of a headache, until it occurred to him there wasn't a damn thing he could do except look out for himself.

He laughed now. Then he'd been about as ill-equipped for this job as an ape from the wilds. Both he and Mark Benton had come a long way. Surprisingly, Camp felt a curious paternal pride in what the boy was doing.

Paternal! Camp hauled back on the reins, slowing his team. That revelation was a shock. Or maybe not, considering his protective feelings for Emily. And her family.

In "family," he'd included Megan. Teenage girls were scary. They resided in a mystery world of clothes, makeup and volatile moods. Megan and Brittany provided plenty of fodder for contrast to the young pioneer women Camp had become acquainted with through old diaries.

For instance, Megan and Brittany avoided work like the plague. Given chores, they either dinked around until someone else, usually Emily or Sherry, got fed up and completed the task. Or they grumped and finished their work only after constant nagging. Pioneer girls had toiled from sunup to sundown.

In all fairness he had to say Brittany and Megan were fastidious about their persons. Come hell or high water, their hair got washed daily. Would they, Camp wondered, if faced with the peril of a rattler, neatly dispatch the snake with one of their battery-powered curling irons? Or would they fall apart?

A few weeks ago, his money would have been on the latter. Now, after Mark's surprising turnaround, Camp wasn't so sure. The last few days he'd begun to revise a number of the notions he had held at the start of this trip. *Some* modern women might be wimpier than their pioneer cousins. Not all, by a long shot.

What would Lyle Roberts say about his discovery of the flaws in their teaching texts? He'd probably harp on Gina's dropping out. Camp didn't plan to make an issue of her accident. She had options that weren't available to pioneer travelers, as he'd make very clear in his paper.

AN HOUR AFTER they pulled into Council Grove and set up in a park on the town's outskirts, everyone grouped around Gina with long faces, staring at the splint on her arm and the long white cast on her leg.

"I've hired Mark to drive my wagon and me to Santa Fe," she announced, and named a figure that was more than a generous wage.

Both Emily and Camp sucked in a sharp breath.

Mark, grinning like a fool, dug a wad of bills out of his pocket. "This is the first payment. Enough to buy me a fishing pole of my own. I'll help settle Gina in the hotel room she's rented for tonight, then me and Jared are going fishing with his dad."

Sherry knelt by Gina's side. "If you're doing this to show Nolan that modern women are as tough as his precious pioneers, forget it. Thanks to modern medicine we don't have to suffer the way our predecessors did. Em and I agreed that we'd put our heads together and find someone to drive you home.''

Camp nodded to show he approved. "Gina, I don't think you should stay—''

"I've made up my mind.'' Gina stubbornly waved them away with her good hand. "The doctor said my cast stays on for six weeks. Said I can remove the splint myself in four. We've already arranged transportation home from Santa Fe. There's no reason to disrupt the schedule for me.''

The way Emily and Sherry were glaring at him, Camp was half-afraid to say anything lest it be misconstrued. Except that he agreed with them wholeheartedly. "Gina, how do you plan to manage simple things like climbing in and out of the wagon? Not to mention tending to...to, ah, personal matters.''

More blunt than Camp, Maizie came right to the point. "How are you gonna get to a bush, gal, let alone squat behind it?''

"Mark and I already had this discussion.'' She looked affronted. "Not that my ablutions are anyone's business, but the doctor's providing me with a portable potty. Everything's resolved. Mark will build my cook fires and set up my tripod as needed. For a fee, of course.'' She met Emily's eyes and winked. "Your son is a sharp financier. I predict he'll make a killing in the stock market someday.''

"I don't object to Mark's pitching in,'' Emily said. "But he shouldn't take Gina's money.''

"Sure he should,'' Maizie asserted. "Gina wants to pay, and Mark wants the job. Teaches the kid solid work ethics. 'Nough said if you ask me.'' She turned to Mark and her grandson. "You two run along before them fish stop bitin'. Tell Robert I've got a hankering for catfish for breakfast.'' One by one, she made eye contact with the others in the circle. "Why are y'all standin' around? Go soak up some history. I'll take Gina to her room. Believe I'll sit with her a spell and rest these old bones.''

"Only thing I'm going to soak is my body in a bubble bath,'' Sherry said.

Megan and Brittany didn't have to be told twice to go. They were itching to explore. But before they could cut and run, Emily pulled her daughter aside. "Megan, I'll expect you back at the wagon for supper. Six-thirty, and don't be late.''

"Mo...th...er!'' the girl huffed indignantly. "Brittany and I planned to grab something at the rodeo. I wish you'd stop treating me like a kid.''

"You've been fourteen for all of a month, Megan. I'll concede that you're not a *kid*-kid, but neither are you an adult. I'm willing to negotiate curfew. What time is the rodeo over?''

"Ten,'' the girl said sullenly. "But there's a dance later. Cripes, I'm going to be with Brittany, and she's nineteen.''

"Yes...I know.'' Emily definitely wasn't reassured. After all, she'd witnessed Brittany's assault on Camp. His back was toward Emily, and he was chatting with the older girl. Emily couldn't gauge his reaction. For all she knew, things might have changed between those two. But no—she was replaying old tapes. Camp had handled Brittany with the utmost discretion. Anyway, Emily had no call to be jealous. Nolan Campbell had made it plain that all he wanted from her was friendship.

As if she wanted more from him. So why was she having such a hard time staying focused on this skirmish with Megan?

"Mom!" Megan's lower lip stuck out an inch. "Is it all right to eat at the rodeo with Brittany or not?"

Sensing Emily's eyes on him, Camp turned. He broke into a smile and started toward her, making her blush.

"L-let me check with Camp," she murmured. "Brittany and I are part of his project, remember. He may have specific tours he wants us to take for his study."

"Oh, brother. I knew this trip was going to be a drag." Megan kicked a loose stone. Brittany stood to one side cracking her gum.

"What's going to be a drag?" Camp strolled up, hands casually tucked into his pockets. "According to Brittany, you two ladies have a full day planned."

Megan slanted her mother an angry glance. "Tell that to my mom. She's treating me like I'm no older than Mark."

"No such thing. I'm not sure it's safe for the girls to walk alone at night that's all."

Head swiveling, Camp studied the tree-lined streets, alive in the aftermath of a parade. Families collected in groups, talking. Girl Scouts sold lemonade. Craft booths littered the wedge-shaped park. "Town seems pretty tame to me."

"Yes, but a rodeo and dance..." Emily wasn't ready to give in.

"Sounds like fun." Camp flashed a smile at the girls. "I heard two couples discussing the bands. The first half of tonight's dance is bluegrass music, followed by a local country band. Wouldn't you like to hear them, Emily? That way we can all walk back to the wagons together. Unless you plan to take a room at the hotel."

"No, I'm not..." Emily wasn't sure if he was asking her to go with him to the dance or just to meet afterward. Either way it solved her immediate problem. "Okay." She caved in because of the girls. "I don't know where the dance is being held, so I have no idea how to choose a place to meet. Do you?'' she asked Camp.

"It's somewhere on the rodeo grounds. In a town this size, we're not talking Madison Square Garden. There's bound to be a main gate where we can meet."

The girls didn't look overjoyed, but they nodded. So they could be off and about their business, Camp thought with a grin. "Hey," he called, watching them exchange worried glances as if to say *Now what?* "There's probably a fee for the dance as well as the rodeo. You two have enough money?"

The girls shrugged, but when Emily began digging in her purse, Camp placed a restraining palm on her arm. He pulled out two twenties and passed one to each girl. "Have fun on me. Just know that I may pick your brains later for my paper."

Giggling, they stuffed the bills into their pockets and dashed off.

Emily rifled through her purse until she found a twenty, and slapped it into Camp's hand. "I can pay my children's way."

Camp tested the spark of annoyance he saw in Emily's eyes. "Out-of-pocket expenses should all have been listed on the sheet I mailed out. Maizie forgot to include the rodeo and the dance. I didn't intend there to be hidden costs, Emily."

"All right...if that's the only reason." She accepted the money back, zipped her purse and slung it over her shoulder. "I have to scoot if I'm going to make the one o'clock tour of historic sites. See you later." She took off like a deer in flight.

Camp scratched the back of his neck, then jogged to catch up. "Do you mind if I tag along? I don't mean to crowd you, but I planned on going."

"It's a free country." Her steps quickening, she continued toward the old building that housed the visitors' bureau, where Maizie said the tour started.

Thrown off by her cavalier response, Camp broke stride. Even with his longer legs, he didn't catch up easily. When he did, she ignored him. Darn it, he wanted to spend time with her. If he'd upset her over the money, he was genuinely sorry.

"You must be leading the monument tour," Emily said to a man holding a fistful of maps and brochures. "Am I early?"

He peeled off one of each for her, then did the same for Camp. "This explains the sites. It's a self-guided tour," he said, checking his watch. "Guess you're it for this hour." Snapping his cuff down again, he went back into the building.

Emily scanned the street in both directions. "Where are Doris and Vi?"

"We can give them a few minutes if you like. But considering the loose way this tour is run, they may have already gone."

"You're right." She took a deep breath. "I'm glad you decided to go, Camp. It's not as much fun seeing the sights alone."

"For a minute there, I wasn't sure I'd be welcome."

"I know, and I'm sorry. I was annoyed about your giving Megan that money. My in-laws throw cash at my kids as a way of making me look bad. It doesn't help matters that I have to watch every dime. I know you meant well, but..." A sigh shook her frame.

"I'm the one who's sorry, Emily. I should have asked your permission."

He looked so contrite that Emily felt bad for foisting her troubles on him. She definitely didn't want him thinking she'd make a habit of it. "Maybe this tour isn't even worthwhile. If you have things to do, I really can go on my own."

"I don't have any plans—other than picking up a coffee grinder. In fact, I was going to suggest we have lunch first. Then we'll be able to walk off the calories. Across the street is Hays House Restaurant. Maizie told me it was opened in 1847 by Seth Hays, a great-grandson of Daniel Boone. She said it's the oldest eating establishment west of the Mississippi."

Emily gazed at the old stone building. "I wonder if it's expensive?"

Camp opened his mouth to say it'd be his treat, then thought better of it and feigned interest in the brochure. "Might be worth the price to see the antiques. This says the building's been remodeled, but some original pieces still exist. Oh, maybe you don't like museums and such...." He remembered Greta's snide remarks and curbed his own enthusiasm.

"Are you kidding? I love them. And I love historic houses. Look, this says the fireplace has a hand-hewn mantel." She frowned slightly. "Surely they serve appetizers for people who don't want a full meal."

Camp let her work it out in her own mind. Eventually she smiled and stepped off the curb, preparing to cross the street. He took her arm, pleased that she'd decided to join him. But it went against the grain to have a woman he'd invited to lunch pay for her meal. On the other hand, Emily wore her pride very close to the skin and he didn't want to risk offending her again.

While they waited for seating, they wandered around, checking out the antiques. Even after the hostess showed them to a table, Emily spent more time examining the needlepoint fabric on the chairs than she did looking at the menu.

In Camp's opinion, the dinner salad she ended up ordering wasn't enough to keep a bird alive. As it turned out, his meal would feed three people. As they ate, they discussed a range of subjects. Everything from the tintypes on the walls to their job goals and aspirations. A little at a time, Camp cajoled Emily into tasting most of what was on his plate.

"It's none of my business," he said as the waiter cleared away the remains of his baked apple dessert, "but why haven't you moved if your in-laws make life so miserable? With your education and experience, I'd think you could get a job in almost any college or university."

She rearranged the salt and pepper shakers. "You mean, why don't I quit whining about Mona and Toby and take the advice I give students?"

"In a word, yes." Camp stirred a dollop of cream into his coffee.

Emily practically squeezed the life out of her tea bag. She took a sip, wondering how much to say. "To an outsider, I guess it seems an easy decision. I wish it was."

Camp watched her over the rim of his cup, troubled by her bleak expression. "I've gathered from what you and the kids have said that your life-style changed, went downhill, after your husband's death. The more I see of you, Emily, the clearer it is how you feel about their money."

She set her cup in the saucer, but still held it tight with both hands. "No matter how hard I try, the skeletons in my closet have a way of popping up."

"We all have them," he said dryly.

"Compared with you, I have enough to fill several walk-in closets."

Camp tried to imagine Emily-of-the-sunny-smile with some terrible blight on her record. Nothing came.

Surreptitiously, she studied his blank features. "Ha! I thought as much. Your life has been a bowl of cherries."

Emily grimaced as she polished off her tea. "Don't ever get married, Campbell. When I took vows for better or worse, my life landed in the pits."

He signaled for the check. "The marriage wasn't a total failure. You have Mark and Megan."

"Which brings us to your original question. Why don't I take them and relocate?"

Camp slipped money into the folder. Emily passed him her portion. He let it lie there for a time, but in the end heaved a sigh and added it to the tip.

"My in-laws are the biggest wheels where we live," she said as they rose. "In retrospect it seems foolish, but I never had reason to question where Dave's money came from. He called himself a developer and boasted about finding backers for casinos and posh resorts. I hadn't a clue how many times his parents bailed him out of get-rich-quick schemes. Often, it turns out, and after he died they tallied up the bill. The sum is staggering. It's like a sword hanging over my head. If I moved but missed a payment for any reason, they'd use it to force me back. I'm in a catch-22 situation unless I locate a job with a sizable salary increase."

"Did you cosign notes any of the times your husband borrowed money from his parents?"

"No. But they showed me a pile of canceled checks. They even paid the mortgage on our house."

"If you didn't sign anything, how can they collect from you?"

"I told you the Bentons virtually own the town. They have subsidiaries owning subsidiaries. Three-fourths of the businesses are in debt to them in some way. Believe me," she said bitterly, "I lie awake nights trying to figure out how to take the kids and disappear. But what lesson is that for the children? Even if I ran, there's still a matter of references. And I owe the college credit union on my car. There'd be no hiding."

"What if you consolidated your loans at your new site and paid everyone in your old town off?"

She rose, slinging her purse over her shoulder. "Banks don't exactly rush to lend money to a single mother, to say nothing of someone new in town. They're all good ideas, Camp, but I've examined this mess from every angle. Frankly, I don't see any way out."

He trailed her to the front door, then reached around her to hold it open. "I'd be surprised if Mona and Toby are on the up-and-up. People who'd treat family the way they treat you are bound to be all-round jerks. You want to make them sweat? Sic the IRS on them. Those boys don't owe allegiance to anyone."

Emily laughed. "Remind me never to get on your bad side. You play hardball."

"I really don't. Their hold over you and the town smells fishy. People with that kind of money and power usually cut corners someplace, or they pull a few shady deals."

"Toby was an only child of wealthy parents. He inherited big, plus he has a knack for making money. Mona's major problem is that she spoiled her only son to distraction and refuses to believe he could do anything wrong. Therefore it stands to reason she'd blame me for his excesses."

"I guess you loved him, huh?"

"Everyone loved Dave. He radiated charm. He could have had any woman he wanted. And did, if even half of what I heard later in our marriage was true. The thing I ask myself regularly is why he chose to marry. And why me? The girl he dated before me is a fashion model, and many of the ones who came after could have stepped off the covers of *Cosmo*."

"Don't put yourself down, Emily." Camp took her hand as they strolled down the street. "I suspect old Dave knew exactly what he had in a wife. Pretty, talented, loyal. A great mother to his kids. From the way you've described him, he fits the mold of a man who needed order in his chaotic life. Men like that have to present a picture of normalcy to the world. And they want a son to carry on their name."

"Are you sure your degree isn't in psychology?" Emily raised her eyebrows.

"History, and you know it. But all disciplines intertwine. History teaches that there are Daves in every culture and in every generation. And an equal number of Emilys who become ensnared. History definitely repeats itself. Don't ask me why."

"How did you know that was going to be my next question?"

"You're pretty easy to read, Em. Your face is an open book."

"Great! Gullible as a sheep, that's me." She tried to untangle their fingers, but he wouldn't let go.

Without making it an issue, Camp kept hold of her hand as they wandered from site to site. He dropped it once to peer in the smoked windows of the Last Chance Store, which according to a sign on the door had recently closed for good.

"I'd say chances ran out for the Last Chance," he quipped.

"It's a shame," Emily said. "According to the brochure it was the last trading post where pioneers could buy supplies until they reached Santa Fe. Look, they've built a supermarket on the corner. That's progress, I guess."

"At least the sign says the historical society has taken over the building."

She nodded. "Well, I guess there's only one more point on the tour."

"Lead on." Camp took her hand again, content to let her guide.

"It's a statue of the pioneer mother in Madonna Park." Crossing the street, they headed for a slab of carved gray marble set in a small triangle of grass. A young boy clung to the calico skirt of the woman in the statue. She cradled a babe in her arms.

Camp and Emily gazed without speaking at the care-worn features on the lined face framed by a sunbonnet. Beneath her long dress the woman wore an unflattering pair of lace-up drover's boots that looked too large for her feet, and too masculine. Sadly, there was little softness about the so-called Madonna of the Trail.

"She looks old before her time," Emily whispered. "You can practically see the miles etched in her eyes."

"But determination in the set of her jaw, too." Camp said, backing away to take a picture with a small, disposable camera he pulled from his shirt pocket. He quickly snapped a second shot that included Emily. Her slender, jeans-clad figure beside the statue contrasted *then* and *now* more effectively than any words he might write in his paper.

Emily stuck out her tongue, stuck her thumbs in her ears and wiggled her fingers at him. "I hate having my picture taken. I hope it breaks your camera."

"I hope not. It would be a shame to miss recording something so poignant, don't you think? Even at that, my shots won't compare with Gina's."

"I'm going to stop and see her now. I'll tell her not to worry—that you're taking up the artistic slack—shall I?"

"Somehow I'm not sure hearing there's a camera in my hands will improve her morale."

Emily laughed. "You may be right. Gina is a do-it-myself person. Odd that she trusts Mark to help out."

"I get the distinct impression that, in her estimation, the world would do well without men. Perhaps she sees Mark as young enough to be trainable."

"What's the magic age beyond which a male becomes untrainable?" Emily asked in all seriousness.

Camp contemplated her through his eyelashes. "Does anyone in education believe a person is ever too old to learn? Isn't learning and change exclusive of gender bias, Emily?" He gathered her hand in his again.

"That's idealistic, Camp. Not everyone *wants* to change."

"I'll agree that desire and ability depend on the individual. I assume you have a specific person in mind."

She glanced up sharply. "No. Well, yes...maybe. I know Dave was smart enough to make informed choices. He never did. I'd like to think Mark will. I wondered how long I'll have any influence."

She sounded so discouraged, Camp dropped her hand and slid an arm around her shoulders. "It doesn't sound as if Dave received any positive direction as a kid. I'd say your odds with Mark are significantly higher."

Emily reached up and threaded her fingers through Camp's. "Thanks for the vote of confidence. You're a nice man. I can't imagine why some woman didn't snap you up years ago."

"I, ah, came close to marrying once." It was on the tip of Camp's tongue to tell her about Greta, except he found the whole experience hard to talk about. He was spared by Mark and Jared, who ran up, each dangling a string of fish.

Mark had changed from his sag clothes. Both boys wore overalls without shirts, and straw hats that left them looking like Huck Finn.

Emily broke from Camp to walk a slow circle around her son. "Wow. Do I know you? What a difference. I'm impressed. Also with the fish. Now I don't have to worry about what to fix for dinner."

"Maizie said they're for breakfast," Jared explained. "My dad's gonna take Mark and me out for hamburgers tonight, Ms Benton. Is that okay?"

Emily seemed taken aback. "I, well, that's fine. I'll fix something for myself."

Camp frowned. "I thought we'd eat in town, Emily, and then go on to the dance."

"'We'?" She stopped and raised a brow. "Oh. I assumed we were only going to meet afterward, to walk the girls home."

Camp tried unsuccessfully to hide the disappointment sweeping through him. The last thing he wanted to do was press her into a date if she was reluctant. But she seemed as unsure as he was, so he decided to try again. "I thought I'd asked you to go with me, Emily. If you don't like to dance we can just listen to the music."

"I like to dance. It's been a long time," she said, ducking her head to keep him from seeing her flushed cheeks.

"That's good." He battled a sudden urge to touch her face. To lift her chin so he could read those huge compelling eyes. "I want to dance with you, Em." He winced. "Unless you don't want to dance with me?"

"Of course I do," she retorted, then lowered her voice. "I shouldn't even have to tell you that. But if you want your ego stroked, you're barking up the wrong tree." She nervously clasped and unclasped her hands.

Camp caught both in one of his and let his gaze run slowly from the tip of her toes to the crown of her head. "Looks like the right tree to me," he murmured huskily.

Her breath escaped like a puff of steam. "I'm going by

to check on Gina to tell her what we saw. Perhaps we should just meet at the dance.''

He felt her withdrawing. "This is a date, Emily. Get used to the idea. I'll meet you in front of Gina's hotel two hours from now. That'll give us time for a leisurely dinner. I hope you aren't the type to stand a guy up.'' He winked at Jared and ruffled Mark's hair. "Don't wait up for your mom, sport. I intend to have the last dance.''

As Camp strolled off, Mark grinned slyly at his mother.

Clearly flustered, Emily swallowed three retorts. Finally she gave up and shooed the boys on their way.

"I think cowboys tamed the West. I don't believe what Sherry said, that a cowboy's horse and six-gun were more important than girls."
—From Brittany's data sheet, filled with praise for cowboys.

CHAPTER EIGHT

THE DANCE WAS in full swing by the time Camp and Emily joined the line waiting to enter. At her insistence, dinner had been casual—Coney Island-style hot dogs at a Lions Club booth. They laughed with strangers over the antics everyone went through to keep mustard, catsup and sauerkraut from dripping onto their clothes. Emily called a halt at one. She dabbed mustard off Camp's chin after he ate his second right down to the paper.

He loved seeing the funny faces she made at his pathetic attempts to clean the sticky condiments off his mouth while they waited to get into the dance. The playful banter contributed in part to the subtle difference Camp detected in their relationship tonight. Was it because he insisted they call their evening a date, or because Emily had changed into a dress made of some soft, pale-yellow material? Not frilly, yet it underlined her womanliness, or so it seemed to Camp.

As soon as he paid the nominal entry fee and they stepped inside the converted barn that'd been lit with lanterns and dressed up with hay bales and checkered table-cloths, he noticed a return of Emily's cool reserve.

A large area of the plank floor was packed with people doing circle dances to lively bluegrass tunes. Camp felt the beat of the music through the soles of his boots as he and Emily jostled around the perimeter of the dance floor.

"I don't see the girls." Emily paused frequently to rise on tiptoes and peer through a maze of cowboy hats.

Camp guided her with a warm hand flattened at the small of her back. "We've barely made it a fourth of the way around the building, Emily. At the hot-dog stand I heard someone say the younger crowd often gravitates to the loft, where they have pool tables and free soft drinks."

"Pool? Megan doesn't know the first thing about pool!"

"While we're this close to the stairs, we may as well have a look."

"I suppose," she said grudgingly. "But I'm sure it's a waste of time."

They'd no sooner cleared the top step than Camp heard Emily's sharp exhalation. Following the direction of her gaze, he saw Megan, pool cue in hand, give a saucy toss of her head and bend over the table. Judging by the roar of approval that went up from bystanders, Camp guessed that little Megan, who supposedly didn't know the first thing about pool, was creaming her partner. Craning his neck, Camp saw the girl's difficult, kitty-corner shot spin into an end pocket. Megan, too, looked different tonight. An old-fashioned crocheted hat crushed her auburn curls. A ribbed cotton crop top showed off her narrow waist.

Brittany spotted Camp and Emily. She leaned in front of a tall cowboy, saying something to the cocky winner. As Megan turned slowly, remoteness replaced the animated smile that'd brightened her face a moment ago.

Breaking away from her pals, she stalked up to her

mother. "I thought we agreed to meet at the end of the dance. You can't resist spying on me, can you?"

"Nothing of the sort," Emily denied. "I wanted to let you know we were here. Who are these people you're with? Why aren't you dancing?"

Megan cast a quick glance over her shoulder at a slim-hipped young man in cowboy garb, who'd finished racking the balls. "Come on, Meg," he called. "I hope you don't plan to run off with my ten bucks without giving me a chance to win it back."

"Megan, you're betting?" Emily gasped. "I forbid it. We don't have money for you to throw around foolishly. Whatever possessed you? What do you even know about this…this game?"

Megan blew a large turquoise bubble, let it pop and hauled the gum threads back into her mouth with her tongue. "Dad taught me years ago on Mona and Toby's table. I'm good," she boasted. "How do you think I get spending money? I'd be laughed out of my old crowd on the skimpy allowance you dole out."

Camp saw the color leave Emily's face. He felt her slender body begin to shake. Pulling her into the curve of his side, he panned the group huddled around the table. None looked like high rollers. If she just stepped back a minute, Emily would see they were all clear-eyed, clean-cut youngsters.

Megan's rudeness was another issue, and not one to be dealt with now. Not one that was really his problem….

"Take it easy on these guys, ace," Camp teased Megan as he smoothed a hand up Emily's rigid back. "Your mom and I would hate to see you sucker some poor cowboy out of his rodeo entry fee. Isn't that right, Emily?"

Megan sniffed disdainfully. "I could."

Willing Emily to loosen up, Camp continued to massage her stiff neck. Lazily scoping out the players a second time, Camp let his eyes meet Brittany's. He couldn't tell if her smoldering anger was aimed at Emily or at him. At both of them for being together, he surmised. Too bad; she needed to get past that crush.

"Your mom and I are going down to see if we can convince the band to play some old-fogy music," Camp informed Megan casually. "We'll meet you and Brittany at the close of the dance. Oh, and Megan...if you want the guy in the black shirt to ask you to dance, don't take all his money."

The girl frowned for a moment, then tossed her head and laughed. "My dad had a big ego, too. He hated losing. 'Course, I usually let him win." The laughter died suddenly. Eyes overbright, she blinked them clear and swung gaily back to the table.

Camp sensed Emily gearing up to explode. He didn't know who she was maddest at, Megan or him, but he figured the fallout would enlarge the chasm between mother and daughter. He all but bullied Emily down the stairs.

"How dare you," she said in a furious whisper after he hauled her into a relatively vacant corner below the stairs. "That's my child up there betting. *Gambling.*" Cupping her elbows, Emily began to pace. "Now I find out her...her father taught her. Oh, God! And you...*you condoned it.* You and Dave. I suppose if she'd lost, you would've given her money the way Mona and Toby do." Hugging her waist, she seemed almost ill.

"No." Camp tried to take her in his arms, but she shook him off. "This isn't Atlantic City, Emily. It's Council Grove, Kansas. These are penny-ante games to while away an evening. The stakes aren't high enough to send anyone to the poorhouse."

"You find it funny? I've seen Dave drop a thousand

dollars in a few games of pool. He always thought th
next game he'd win it back.''

"It sounded to me like Megan saw through her dad.
Couldn't you give her the benefit of the doubt? If they
don't come down to dance in half an hour or so, I'll go
put a stop to it and we'll leave. Megan's underage and
Brittany's in my care for the duration of the trip.''

Emily looked moderately relieved, but Camp still
wasn't able to persuade her to dance. Her gaze strayed
time and again to the stairway. Only after she saw the
group of laughing young people trip lightly down the
stairs did color return to her face.

Later, though, Megan and Brittany slipped outside with
two boyish-looking cowboys. Emily fretted that they'd
gone out to sneak drinks.

"It's possible,'' Camp said calmly. "Do you know for
certain that Megan drinks?''

Near tears, Emily shook her head. "But then, I didn't
know Dave taught her to play pool, either. He always had
a glass of gin in his hand,'' Emily said as if that was a
telling factor.

"They may just have gone out for air. Or maybe the
guys smoke. Dance with me, Emily. If this was anyone's
kid but yours, you'd advise her parents to loosen the reins,
wouldn't you?''

She rubbed her temples. "I guess. Yes, I would. But
until this past, awful year, I never believed I'd be sitting
on the other side of the table.''

Camp gathered her in his arms and waltzed her out on
the floor. The bluegrass band had been replaced by a
country group. For their first number, they played a love
ballad. Though his back was to the door, Camp knew the
minute Megan returned. Emily went pliant against his
chest. Not that he minded. Her breasts were soft, and his
chin nestled comfortably atop her silky hair. Her warm

breath tickled his throat. They danced the next four numbers straight, occasionally passing one or other of the
girls. Megan avoided eye contact. Brittany dealt them
frost.

It took three rounds of slow dances before Emily felt
the tension leave her body and began to enjoy herself. She
tried to look at Megan as others must see her. As a pretty,
popular girl. Megan danced with an easy grace that reminded Emily of herself before she'd married Dave. A
jolting thought. And sad. They'd been happy once. The
disintegration of their marriage came on gradually, starting with her first pregnancy. When morning sickness, ex-
panding middle and swollen feet left her drained, Dave
simply went places and partied without her. That Megan
was born in winter only served to keep Emily and the
baby more housebound. At the time she couldn't know
that Dave was on a roller-coaster ride downhill.

"A dollar for your thoughts," Camp ventured, tilting
her chin so he could smile into her suddenly distant eyes.

She gave a start. "A dollar? Talk about inflation."

"Well, you'd drifted so far away, a penny hardly
seemed enough to entice you back. They've announced
the last dance. Shall we brave it or do you want to sit it
out?"

"The last dance? Already?"

Chuckling, Camp molded her close. "We've been
dancing for an hour. I'm running out of steam, while
you're like a kid gathering speed."

His remark coaxed a smile. "Tomorrow I'll pay for all
my youthful ambitions. You'll be fresh as a daisy and I'll
probably look like a hag. I'd just realized when you asked
about my thoughts that I haven't danced like this since
before Megan was born. More like before she was con-
ceived," Emily laughed.

The thought of her making love with that bastard, even

if he had been her husband, spoiled what remained of Camp's good mood. "Emily, are you telling me that a man who loved to party, drink and shoot high-stakes pool never took you out?"

Emily drew away the length of their arms. "I'm not lying. And I'm not angling for your sympathy. There—" she pointed stiffly "—I see the girls heading out the door. Let's go."

Camp twirled her back and folded her into an embrace. "You deserved better treatment, Em. The last thing I want to do is hurt you," he murmured in her ear. "I'm sorry. It galls me to imagine the way that selfish jerk must have hurt you."

The smell of Camp's aftershave and the feel of her cheek pressed to his taut muscles awakened a shiver of need in Emily that she hadn't experienced in a long time. "I think what bothered me most were the cruel remarks Toby and Mona made within my hearing—about things like our not sharing a bedroom after Mark was born. I couldn't bring myself to tell her that Dave had brought his best friend's wife into our bed while I was in the hospital. I found her makeup and a nightgown. I would've divorced him then if he hadn't told me Mona and Toby would see that he got custody of both kids. I had every reason to believe him. And I'd have walked over hot coals to keep that from happening."

Camp stopped dancing. He cradled Emily's face between his hands, and without breaking eye contact, he bent slowly and kissed her softly. At least, it started out soft. As her warmth seeped into his pores, his hands slid down her neck, over her shoulders and fanned across her back, which deepened the kiss. He held her so tightly he felt her lashes brush his cheek as her eyes drifted shut. Spinning out of control, Camp knew he wanted more than simple kisses from Emily Benton. He wasn't sure what made him finally lift his mouth from hers to take in air. It might have been a change in the beat of the music, or a subtle shift in the dancers. But when Camp looked up, he and Emily were standing alone under a blue spotlight. As he peered dazedly through a break in the crowd, his eyes connected with those of a shocked Megan Benton. Her lips were pressed so tight a white ring bled into a face red with anger. Near her stood a stunned Brittany.

His hands grew sticky with sweat where they'd slid to Emily's narrow waist. The instant he cleared his throat, her eyes popped open and she blinked several times, out of touch with her surroundings.

"What's the matter? Are you embarrassed?" she asked quickly.

"Not me. The girls."

She leaned out, still in the curve of his arms. One look at the unforgiving faces, and Emily groaned.

Camp's hold on her rib cage tightened. "We did nothing to be ashamed of, Emily. We're both single and certainly past the age of consent."

"You're right," she said firmly.

However, Camp noticed she wasted no time disengaging their limbs before she selfconsciously straightened her blouse. Her cheeks were crimson.

"Their cowboys must have called it a night," he said crisply. "I don't feel we have to explain ourselves, do you, Emily?"

"No."

As it turned out, that was the last word any of them spoke on the long walk back to the wagons. The girls said nothing. It was a silence brimming with accusations and loathing and it spoke for them as they set a punishing pace.

Emily, head held high, marched three steps behind them and two ahead of Camp.

A charley horse in Camp's right calf irritated the he
out of him and kept him from catching up.

Thunder rumbled in the distance. Every now and then
a flash of lightning cut through the black sky. There were
no stars out, and the moon, which had been bright earlier,
had gone into hiding. Camp tasted dampness in the air
with each indrawn breath. Before now he'd given little
thought to the summer storms that frequently rolled across
the plains. In the eerie quiet, broken only by their rapid
footfalls, he recalled an incident from a pioneer journal.
A man's hat had blown off in a high wind. His horses
had spooked, causing the entire wagon train to stampede.
One wagon turned over, leaving a young mother and child
dead.

Camp rubbed at the ache in his hip. It must be the mood
he was in. Thunder didn't mean the storm would pass
through the area.

With effort, Camp managed to close the gap between
himself and Emily. "Robert probably double-checked the
stock, but I think I'll have a look around. Maizie planned
to visit friends in town. She may or may not be back yet."

Emily nodded. "Sherry and Gina are both staying in
town. Mark's in charge of Gina's wagon. Brittany should
take care of Sherry's—if it enters her mind. Since Megan's sleeping there tonight, I'll make sure everything's
tied down."

"You'll be alone in your wagon?"

"I didn't say that to give you ideas," she hissed. "A
kiss is not an invitation to share my bed."

"I never thought it was," he said gruffly. "The prospect of a storm is making everyone edgy. I was merely
going to say that if you're as wide-awake as I am, maybe
we could fix a pot of coffee and sit outside for a while."

"Herb tea would be nice. I need to unwind." She

anced at the sky. "We may get rained out. I wonder if ae wagons leak."

"The original ones were waterproofed. I assume these are. Maizie has run the Oregon Trail with the same wagons. I'm sure it rained on those trips."

"She doesn't strike me as a woman who'd be deterred by little things like flood and famine."

"Flood? Did you have to say that? I figured our biggest worry would be lightning."

They laughed together, and both girls turned around to glare.

"All that over a kiss?" muttered Camp. "I thought kids who had three holes in each ear were unshockable."

"Megan's never seen me kiss any man before. I imagine it did come as a shock."

"Never? Really?" Camp caught her elbow and turned her toward him.

Emily hoped it was dark enough to hide the heat she felt spreading from her neck into her cheeks. "I explained that Dave and I were little more than strangers living under the same roof. Since his death, what with juggling a job, kids and the squabbles with my in-laws, I haven't had the energy to date."

Camp picked up her hand and kissed the palm. "I figured I'd have to fight my way through a crowd of men at your door."

They felt the first splat of rain on their connected hands before Emily broke free. "I know how many miles there are between your house and mine, Camp. Don't tease."

He shook off raindrops that seemed to fall faster, cursing his leg that had cramped up again. "I'm not teasing, Emily," he whispered, huffing to keep in step. "From the first minute I laid eyes on you, I felt...interest. I know you didn't then, but you have to agree it's there between us now. The last thing I want to do is rush you or scare you. So say the word and I'll back off.''

They were nearing the copse of trees where the wagons waited. Emily hunched against the increasingly fierce rain. "Everything would be simpler if you *were* the chauvinist Sherry described," she said with a sigh. "To use kind of a dated term...."

She sounded so earnest Camp hated to laugh. It was just that he'd never thought of himself that way. He gave women colleagues as much credence as the men in his department. It wounded him to think Sherry would say such things to someone she'd only met at the start of this trip. So they didn't see eye to eye on everything. Camp had thought most of their bickering had been in jest. Sherry had to know he'd move heaven and earth to keep her safe—to keep every woman on this trip safe.

"I see I caught you off guard, Camp. I'm sorry. Sherry said something about sibling rivalry. Or maybe it was gender rivalry."

"Listen, Emily. If there's any rivalry, it's all on her part. I'm proud of Sherry's accomplishments. And I thought she was proud of mine. Obviously we're coming at this reenactment from different angles."

"Don't tell her I said anything. I'd hate to be the cause of some new feud."

"There isn't an old feud. Believe it or not, this trek was Sherry's brainstorm. She and I definitely need to talk. Enough said. Do you still feel like sharing a cup of coffee with me? Er...I mean, my coffee, your tea. While I'm checking the horses, you'll have time to change into jeans and grab your slicker."

"All right." Emily saw that Megan and Brittany had already climbed into Sherry's wagon and had lit a lantern. "After I have a word with the girls, I'll build a fire and put on a pot of water. I know Sherry has instant coffee. I'll borrow some while I'm there."

"Emily, I will build the fire and put the water on," he declared. "I don't want you to assume I brought it up so you'd fix my coffee."

"Have it your way. You won't catch me stepping on a man's toes when he's trying to prove a point."

Camp heaved a sigh as she scurried off. Obviously he *hadn't* gotten his point across. She still believed Sherry, or she'd never have made that parting comment. As he followed the gentle sway of her hips, Camp realized he wanted Emily to think well of him. Better than well, he admitted unabashedly.

He wandered among the restless horses, absently checking hobbles. A jagged bolt of lightning forked across the sky, illuminating the grassy slope where the animals grazed. Sweat broke out on Camp's upper lip. Damn, the storm was breaking fast. He wondered if the horses would be all right out here in the open. He stuck around for a few minutes, but when there were no new bursts of lightning he circled the herd one last time before heading back to the wagons. The smell of coffee wafted out on the wind, teasing his nostrils.

Feeling guilty for loitering after making such a big deal of building the fire and fixing the coffee himself, Camp veered off to wash his hands in the stream. It surprised him to see water lapping to the top of the bank. Earlier, when he'd collected water to shave, the current had flowed gently with barely a ripple. Now, unless he was way off base, the creek had risen considerably. In Maizie's absence, he needed to alert Robert.

Emily smiled as Camp charged out of the trees. "I was about to go looking for you. I wondered if a wild animal had carried you off." Fat raindrops hissed and spit as they hit her fire.

"The stream's climbed the bank by about six inches. I'm going to tell Robert."

"I'm surprised you didn't pass him on the trail. He and Maizie went to check. Maizie heard about the storm while she was visiting friends. She said if the rain doesn't let up by morning we'll have to cut short our stay in Council Grove. According to Robert she took plenty of flack about that."

"Tough. I'm sure we know who complained. Philly. Did Maizie say what problems we might face?"

"Not specifically. I gather she was concerned about the lowlands near Diamond Springs. Robert said it's pretty hard crossing the Arkansas River in a storm."

Camp squatted on his heels and accepted the cup Emily handed him. "I thought that's the reason they equipped our wagons with balloon tires instead of the standard wagon wheels. So we wouldn't bog down in wet weather."

"I don't know. They'll be back this way," she said, pouring water over her tea bag. "You can ask them then."

"Um." Camp blew on the liquid to cool it. He hoped they wouldn't come back too soon. If Maizie said to leave, they'd leave. But the rain wasn't too bad yet, and Camp wanted this time alone with Emily.

"You look uncomfortable. Here, I got out four lawn chairs, Camp. I couldn't find Sherry's instant coffee, so I brewed a pot. And I invited Maizie and Robert to stop by for a cup of tea or coffee."

"Um," Camp mumbled again.

He'd no sooner accepted a chair and sat than he saw Brittany jump from Sherry's wagon and head their way. "Our idea seems to be turning into a full-scale party," Camp muttered. "What do you suppose *she* wants?"

Emily crossed her legs. Mild curiosity appeared on her

face as Brittany waltzed up and helped herself to a chair, wedging it between Emily and Camp.

"I smelled coffee over Megan's nail-polish remover. I always have a cup before I go to bed. It seemed stupid to build a fire just for me. I didn't figure you'd mind my horning in." She produced a cup from her jacket pocket and filled it to the brim.

Camp looked irritated, Emily merely amused.

"The rodeo was awesome," Brittany exclaimed, facing Camp. She deliberately presented her back to Emily as she regaled Camp with details of each event, barely pausing to take a breath and an occasional sip of her coffee.

Feeling ignored, Emily got up once and paced to the trail head and back, checking for Robert and Maizie.

Camp leaped up at the same time to stoke the fire. "Can't you send her to bed?" he implored Emily out of one side of his mouth.

"Me?" Emily darted a glance over her shoulder at Brittany's carefully composed face. The girl was the picture of innocence.

"Yes, you. After all, she's here at Megan's request. No doubt to act as chaperone."

"Yeah." Emily looked over at the wagon where Megan was reportedly doing her nails. She saw a dark head jerk out of sight. "I suspect that's exactly what's going on."

"Shall we try and outwait them?" he whispered.

"Hey, you two," Brittany grumbled. "No fair keeping secrets. Here, Camp, I brought you my data sheet." She pulled some crumpled papers out of her pocket. "And Sherry's. Oh, and she said to give you Gina's."

Emily bit her lip. "Darn, I didn't fill mine out. I'll go do that now."

Camp reached for her arm to tug her back, but it was too late. She'd set her cup on a log and sprinted for her wagon dashing between raindrops. Reluctantly, he gave the fire a last jab before returning to sit beside Brittany.

She refilled her cup, casually scooting her chair closer. "What kind of papers will I have to write for your fall class? I figured I'd get a head start. With your help," she added.

Camp choked, spewing his mouthful of coffee all over his jeans. In the classes Brittany had taken from him, she'd never once handed a paper in on time.

"I'm turning over a new leaf," she said sweetly, as if reading his mind.

"That's good." He plastered on his best professor's smile. "We'll be doing a unit on forts. There are several on this trip. I can't give you special tutoring, though, Brittany. It wouldn't be fair to other students in the class. The stuff you just told me about the rodeo might make a good English composition. You should go back to the wagon and jot everything down. Otherwise, you run the risk of forgetting."

"Yeah, right," she drawled. "You want me out of the way so you and Mrs. Benton can make out."

Camp was about to tell her in no uncertain terms that what he did and with whom was *his* business and nobody else's, but he'd no more than opened his mouth when Maizie and Robert clomped into the firelight bringing the smell of wet forest.

"Welcome to Grand Central Station," Camp muttered, his eyes tracing Emily's return from her wagon.

Oblivious, Emily passed him her data sheet. Her attention shifted to the mother and son who scraped layers of mud from the soles of their boots. "I scribbled my first impression of things we saw on the tour," she said absently. "I'll add more tomorrow if you need it."

"We'll be pulling out at first light," Maizie rasped. "The Neosho is rising and spilling into our creek. I'm gonna wake everybody now and give them the news. Robert's riding into town to tell those at the hotel. Take your coffee with you, son.''

"What about Gina?" Emily asked. "Shouldn't she rest another day?"

"I wish she'd stay put, but as Robert said, we still have to drive her wagon to Santa Fe. All eight wagons are booked for the return trip. Mark can pick her up on our way through town in the morning. We won't drag her back here tonight."

"Mark isn't an experienced driver. Do you expect a lot of problems due to the weather?" Emily automatically moved closer to Camp.

He slid an arm around her waist. With his free hand, he filled cups for Maizie and Robert. Robert thanked him, waved backward as he slogged off through the puddles.

Maizie took a bracing sip before answering Emily. "I always expect problems with the weather. Sometimes I'm pleasantly surprised. Sometimes not. We're a whole lot better equipped than the pioneers. If we can't ford the Arkansas, well, at least we won't be fighting cutthroats and thieves. Thanks for the coffee, Campbell. Fill a Thermos or two. It's gonna be a long night."

Camp jerked the pot and slopped the coffee. "What do you mean, long night?"

"Hear that thunder gettin' louder?"

He acknowledged by dipping his chin.

"Well, till Robert makes it back, I'll need your help keeping those horses in line. Can you sing, boy? Cowboys sang ballads to quiet their stock during thunderstorms. I sound like a damn cat that's got his tail caught in a door."

"You're kidding, I hope," Camp flared. But even as the words fell from his lips, he saw that she wasn't.

"Wish I was. We'll be in a helluva fix if those horses stampede. How was I to know Philly wouldn't be worth a tinker's damn or that I'd have our group all split up when it decided to storm?"

Emily hovered on the balls of her feet. "I'll help ride herd, Maizie."

"You will? I appreciate that. With two of us riding in opposite directions around the horses, that'll leave one to keep the coffee hot and the fire stoked. We'll trade off, one every half hour, until Robert returns."

Camp grasped Emily's wrist and swung her around. "You'll do no such thing. The middle of a potential stampede is no place for a woman."

The light of battle sparked in Emily's eyes. "What does that make Maizie?"

He gulped. "I...I'm sorry, Maizie. But you're an old hand at this."

"And you're Clint Eastwood?" Emily smirked, dander clearly rising.

"Emily, be reasonable."

"I am being reasonable. You're the one spewing testosterone. And for your information, I can even sing on key."

Maizie tipped her face to the rain and laughed. "Entertaining as this is, I gotta break it up. That last bolt of lightning hit yonder in those trees. Emily, you and I will take the first shift." Maizie grinned at Camp. "Give you time to cool down, sonny."

Taking Maizie at her word, Emily folded the extra chairs and tipped them up next to the wagon so the seats would stay dry.

Brittany dragged her chair closer to the fire. "Who cares if Emily wants to pretend she's Annie Oakley? I'll keep you company, Camp."

Maizie lifted Brittany out of her chair, one hand tucked firmly in the girl's armpit. "If you're gonna stay up, you can help ride herd. Four makes trading off easier."

At first Brittany acted as if she thought Maizie was joking. As soon as it became clear that she wasn't, Brittany pulled loose and flounced off.

Frustrated by Emily's stubbornness and the sudden crash of thunder that shook the ground, Camp pushed his face into Maizie's. "There's nothing I can do to stop Emily. I won't, however, sit by the fire while you ladies risk your necks."

A gleam flashed in the older woman's eyes. "Then quit flappin' your gums and saddle up. The closer the riders, the less chance those big brutes'll bolt."

By morning, Camp was so cold, weary and saddle-sore that he hardly knew which end was up. It didn't help that the park floated in three inches of water where the stream had overflowed its banks.

Sometime during the long night, the heavy rain had put out Emily's fire. Between the thunder and the lightning, they'd had their hands too full keeping the teams clustered to even worry about the absence of coffee.

Emily tried to assist Harv, who was attempting to start a fire.

"Forget it," snapped Maizie. "We'll grab coffee in town."

Mark and Jared complained about having to forgo the catfish breakfast. By the time they hitched the horses, drove to town and picked up Gina, not even their slickers warded off the rain that washed down in torrents.

At noon the wagons were mired up to their hubcaps, and there wasn't a tree in sight to give travelers or horses any relief from the steady downpour. For lunch, Camp ate a cold hot dog, plain. He figured the bun would be soggy before it hit his mouth.

Tempers were so short that Maizie called a halt to the day's travel before they reached the Arkansas River. "We won't be able to cross anyway," she said in explanation.

"How do you expect us to start a campfire in this crap?" shouted Philly.

"I'll show you," Emily told him. "We all have tarps. Let's string a couple of them between two wagons."

Camp stood in awe of her spunk. Despite his tiredness, he did as she asked.

Everyone admired Emily's resourcefulness in using dry wood from her wagon to build a fire in the largest of her cast-iron pots. She soon had coffee perked and passed around. Then she proceeded to mix a huge batch of scrapple, which she cooked and served to everyone.

"I'm impressed, gal," Maizie said between bites of the leftover cornmeal mush seasoned with ham and onions. "I told Robert to hand out beef jerky. But it's nicer having something hot to warm the innards."

Others heaped praise on the cook. Yet no one except Camp offered to help her wash up after they'd cleaned their plates.

"Don't you have sense enough to go in out of the rain?" Emily yanked the stack of plates out of his hand and dumped them into a pan of hot water.

He smoothed a hand down her rain-wet cheek. "Not if it's the only opportunity I have to spend time alone with you."

Emily's stomach did a jig. A pocket of heat warmed her from the inside out as he bent down to join their cool lips. She didn't even notice that water dripped down their noses from the bills of their caps.

Neither was aware that the dishpan began to fill with rainwater. They strove to bond tighter as the kiss wore on. Megan's petulant voice finally drove them apart.

"Mother," she whined from the wagon, "Are you planning to stay out in the rain all night?"

Breathing hard, Emily clutched her slicker with one hand. She didn't know how or when it'd fallen open. Her

yes searched Camp's and found them dark and dangerous.

"It's pouring," she whispered. "What are we doing?"

"All that steam isn't coming from the dishpan, Emily.
I'm not ready to go inside and leave you. Tell Megan to
buzz off."

"I would, but if we stay out in this we'll catch pneu-
monia."

He could see that she felt as reluctant as he did to call
a halt. It was enough for Camp. At least, for now. "Your
mother'll be in once we finish the dishes," he called to
Megan. "Unless you're volunteering to come out here and
take my place."

As Camp expected, his challenge was met with silence.
He managed to steal several more kisses from Emily before an awful deluge forced them to say good-night.

For the second night in a row, he didn't sleep. But this
time the taste and scent of Emily Benton filled his head.
He was getting in deep. Maybe too deep for someone
who'd landed on the bad side of Emily's firstborn pride
and joy.

"It's been said that women had little to do at river crossings except knit. The men did all the dirty work."
                    —*Something Sherry read in a* non-fiction
                                book she bought in town.

CHAPTER NINE

FOR FIVE DAYS the column wound slowly through water-logged farmlands. Wagons got mired up to their hubcaps in muddy sinkholes. Regardless of age or gender, everyone scrambled through the muck to help unstick wagons. The single most important goal was to keep moving.

Brittany and Megan moaned, groaned and griped so vocally, they alienated people who might have been inclined to agree that the trip was no longer fun.

Camp, especially, felt like throttling the less-than-dynamic duo. It was as if in addition to complaining from dawn to dark, the two had appointed themselves watchdogs over him and Emily. The girls found ways to foil his carefully engineered plans to spend time alone with Emily, sabotaging his schemes almost before he set them in motion.

Emily merely chuckled. "I'm enjoying this immensely, Camp. Normally Megan does her best to ignore the fact that I exist."

Camp rolled an empty water barrel to the lip of Gina's wagon. "I'm glad you find their Hardy Boys surveillance techniques amusing."

Nancy Drew," she said, breaching his wrath to help the barrel down.

"What?"

"A girl sleuth—not boys."

"Before this trip, I never realized it was so easy to step on toes in the battle of the sexes. Let go of that barrel. Even one end is too heavy for you." He bent and rolled it toward Terrill Boone's water wagon. Maizie's middle son hadn't had an easy time delivering fresh water to their stopover on the outskirts of Fort Larned. He'd also brought a vet this visit. Bad weather had taken its toll on the horses. The vet retired several of the big animals due to strained ligaments. Camp figured if he hauled many more of these oak barrels full of water, he'd have to be retired, too.

"Who keeps the battle of the sexes alive?" Emily asked. "Not women."

"An interesting observation. One I'd gladly explore more fully if we ever managed any time alone. We need to talk, Emily."

"About what? The fact that you're going to kill yourself with these barrels? Why don't you fix some sort of skid?" she suggested matter-of-factly. "I saw an old snow sled at an antique store in town this morning when some of us went to do laundry. Wouldn't its runners slip through the mud as well?"

"Might." Camp turned the idea over in his head. What he found even more appealing was the fact that he'd require Emily's help locating the store. "After I fill this barrel, maybe you could show me where you saw the sled."

"Sure." Her smile broke slowly. "I swear I can hear the wheels turn in your head, Campbell."

"Shh. Not so loud. The wind around here has ears."

"Ah...you plan to ditch our spies?"

"You've got it," he said. "Let's meet at the bri[d]
that crosses the Pawnee fork."

She squinted at the sky, face hopeful. "The rain ha[s]
finally let up. I wish we could visit the wagon ruts tha[t]
are supposed to be near here."

"Your wish is my command. Sherry rented a car to
take Gina, Doris and Vi to the fort. No reason we can't
rent one, too. Terrill's laying over tonight. I'll fill barrels
later. Let me wash off some of this sludge in case we
want to eat in town."

"I look so scroungy no self-respecting café would let
me in the door."

"No, you don't." He eased the barrel onto the filling
rack, his gaze cruising slowly over her face and down her
body. "You look grr...eat."

"Stop, you're making me self-conscious."

Smiling, he placed gloved hands on her shoulders. In-
tent on kissing her, he jumped a foot when Megan Benton
leaped out from behind the truck.

"Mom," Megan cried, virtually yanking Emily right
out from under Camp's nose. "I changed my mind about
seeing the fort. Can we go now?"

Emily swept the hair from her eyes—while her feet
remained firmly rooted. "This morning you stomped
around and refused to talk about visiting the fort with
Sherry. Now I have other plans, Megan."

"What plans?" The girl threw a mean look at Camp,
who tried valiantly, behind Emily's back, to signal her
silence. Without success, apparently.

"This morning," Emily said, "I discovered a sled in
an antique store that I think will allow the men to haul
water more easily. I was just about to show it to Camp."

"Well, no problemo, then." Megan snapped her fingers. "Brittany and I will go with you. We'll leave him
at the store and go on to the fort. All right, Brit?"

At the sound of her name, the second girl appeared m behind the truck.

Camp busily filled the barrel. He felt Emily's beseech-ng eyes on his back, but he wasn't up to dealing with another of Megan's manipulative displays. "You ladies go on. Take in the sights. Robert and I can manhandle the rest of these."

Sorrow washed over Emily. Spending the afternoon with Camp had sounded exciting. Megan's sudden interest in the fort didn't fool Emily. Although—she sighed—the sole reason for making this trip had been to build a better rapport with her kids. "I'll go run a comb through my hair and grab my billfold," she said resignedly. "If you change your mind about the sled..." She turned to Camp. "The store is on Eighth."

He nodded, not trusting himself to speak. A longing glance in her direction revealed her looking back wist-fully. Their eyes clung for several seconds. Breaking the contact, he encountered the smug coconspirators. It was all Camp could do not to vent his anger on them. Except that fighting with Megan wasn't the way to win Emily over. Camp forced himself to say generously, "Have a good time, kids."

"Absolutely!" Megan's tone hadn't dipped so much as an octave.

THEIR SECOND MORNING at Fort Larned brought clear blue skies and the return of a bloodred sun, giving the weary travelers a new lease on life. Dodge City was their next stop. Maizie promised a break that would extend over the Fourth of July week-end.

All day they trudged through fog curling damply off the saturated ground. Camp spent his time plotting to fi-nagle time alone with Emily in Dodge. The very name, Dodge City, carried a certain romantic mystique for Old

West aficionados. Camp thought surely Dodge—the ¦
called Cowboy Capital—would offer enough diversio⌐
to capture the interest of two impressionable girls. To sa⌐
nothing of a huge fireworks display attached to the Fourth
of July celebration.

If all of that failed, he could spirit Emily off to the old
fort. The girls had complained at length about their boring
visit to Fort Larned. Megan announced that if you'd seen
one fort, you'd seen them all.

Camp was beginning to feel desperate.

The column of wagons was met on the outskirts of town
by the mayor and hordes of curiosity seekers. For the first
time Maizie did circle the wagons. She passed the word
to unhitch and hobble the horses in the center, saying the
mayor planned to present her with the key to Dodge City.

"This is perfect," Camp whispered to Emily. "After
the hoopla, we'll slip away. No one will notice we're
missing." *Please,* his eyes begged.

"You're sure?" Emily didn't sound convinced.

Camp didn't dream his own sister would scuttle his
plans.

"Ladies," Sherry called, sidestepping city dignitaries
as she rounded up Emily, Gina and the elementary-school
teachers. "What do you say to renting a car again?
There's a metal sculpture at the local college campus—
The Plainswoman. From there we can visit the Kansas
Teachers' Hall of Fame and then go on to the old fort."

Emily's despairing eyes sought Camp.

With a sinking feeling, he realized it'd be impossible
to object to Sherry's agenda. Pioneer women *were* the
focus of his study, after all. But he proved to be quick-
witted. "Hey, sis, do you mind if I tag along?" He hoped
he sounded casual.

Brittany barged in and jerked a thumb toward Sherry.

e invited Megan and me to go first. Unless you sit on
neone's lap there won't be room."

Sherry Campbell stuck a finger in her ear and shook it
s if something was wrong with her hearing. "Excuse me,
Brittany. Five minutes ago you said in no uncertain terms
that you and Megan wouldn't be caught dead traipsing
around with a group of 'brainbuckets.'"

"We, uh, we talked about it, and agreed it'd be good
research for school." She kept her eyes on Sherry, refusing to meet Camp's hard stare.

"I have an idea," he said, crossing his arms. "I'll rent
a van. That way we can accommodate everyone. We'll
get one with a lift for Gina's wheelchair."

Gina beamed. "Great idea. We had problems at Fort
Larned. I told the boys I wasn't going today, and they've
been moping around ever since."

Camp was careful to cover his glee at outsmarting girls
who thought they couldn't be outsmarted. "Then it's settled. I'll meet you in front of the Santa Fe Railroad depot
in half an hour." Whistling, he strode off before Brittany
and Megan found a way to scuttle his plans to spend the
day with Emily.

They all fitted nicely in the twelve-passenger minibus.
Camp knew the girls were bent out of shape about the
fact that he'd maneuvered things so Emily sat up front
beside him. The others were so busy loading Gina's cam-
eras that no one noticed Megan's and Brittany's pouts.
Camp did, but he was through playing into their hands.

"Hey, ru...le," Mark bellowed as later Camp drove
into the parking lot at the Teachers' Hall of Fame.
"There's a gunfighters' wax museum next door. Can me
and Jared go there while you visit the college and the fort?
Look, we're right across from Boot Hill Museum. Okay
if we bum around town and meet you for the fireworks?"

Since his plea was directed at Emily, Camp continued

to search for a parking place. When he'd found a
Emily still hadn't answered her son. Both boys sat o.
edge of their seats, waiting. Camp suspected she was v
ried about allowing kids that young to run loose in
crowded streets.

"Maybe Brittany and Megan would prefer to check ou
the gunfighters, too, and maybe poke around those old
board-front stores at the museum village," Camp said
lightly. "The mayor said there'll be gunfight reenactments
and other entertainment all day." He worked to keep from
sounding as if he had an ulterior motive.

Unwittingly Sherry aided his cause this time.

"You want them to ogle Miss Kitty and her cancan
dancers? How educational can that be? Honestly, Nolan,
it's just another amusement park."

Camp spread his hands. "You're right. They'll get
more out of a visit to the fort than watching actors sen-
sationalize legends that may or may not be true."

"To say nothing of missing a trip to the old wagon
swales," Doris added.

"So what?" Mark whined. "Do me and Jared have to
traipse out to dumb old ruts 'cause Brittany and Megan
hafta act grown up?"

"If only this wasn't a holiday weekend," muttered Emily. "There're so many people in town...."

"If I didn't have this bum leg," Gina said flatly, "I'd
go with the boys. I'd rather ride in a real stagecoach and
learn to do the cancan," she said, surprising everyone.
"The mayor's wife told me Miss Kitty's girls give free
dance lessons."

Megan and Brittany exchanged pensive looks. "Free
lessons?" Brittany ventured weakly. "What do you think,
Megan?"

Camp sensed the girls wavering. Acting deliberately
uninterested, he thrust open the driver's door. "Stay here

rgue if you like. I'm going to see what's so great
Kansas teachers."

nothing else, that tipped the scales for the girls. Im-
diately they clamored to go with Jared and Mark.
We're doing this so you won't worry, Mom," Megan
old Emily.

Oh, sure, Camp thought. But he didn't let his reaction
show.

"Yeah, Mrs. B.," Brittany chimed in. "It was a tough
decision. Say, why don't you come with us? Then tomorrow we'll all go to the fort—like we did at Fort
Larned."

"Brittany!" Megan shook her head.

Camp held his breath as he helped Vi climb down. He
willed Emily to refuse the girls' suggestion.

"Uh, thanks for asking, Brittany. But you two hated
Fort Larned. And there are other forts along the trail. Go
on, have a good time today. But I want everyone to meet
inside Boot Hill Village at five. Do...do any of you need
money?"

Camp knew better than to offer any this time. Heart
soaring, he happily kept a low profile.

With the youngsters gone, the adults paired up to wander through the teaching museum. Sherry pushed Gina's
wheelchair. Vi and Doris fell into step. That left Camp
and Emily bringing up the rear. Any guilt he suffered for
wishing the kids out of the way was lost in the joy of
simply being in Emily's company. Even though they
spoke little, they shared an occasional touch or a quick
smile. By the time the group finished the tour, Camp and
Emily had fallen into an easy camaraderie.

"I'm hungry," Gina announced after they'd left the
sculpture and headed for the fort. "Hey, look there! A
salad bar with a wheelchair ramp."

Sherry craned her neck to see. "Sounds good."

Vi clapped her hands. "It's next door to the steak h[ ] a friend suggested."

Emily screwed up her face. "I'm not very hungr[ ] There's a frozen-yogurt place across the street with table[ ] outside. Maybe I'll just enjoy the sun."

"That'd suit me." Camp rubbed his flat stomach. "Someone set a time to meet back here."

Emily jerked her gaze away from Camp's midsection.

Sherry checked her watch. "Steak will take longest to fix and eat. Will an hour and a half give everyone time enough? We passed an interesting clothes store down the block. Gina and I'll check it out after we eat. Do you want to go, too, Emily?"

Camp resigned himself to losing her. He hadn't met a woman yet who'd pass up an opportunity to shop. She surprised him.

"There's nothing I need, and I don't want to be tempted. Maybe I'll talk Camp into visiting the Carnegie Center for the Arts."

"Fine with me," Camp put in. "Although I find it hard to believe Carnegie funded a center for the arts in a lawless cow town."

"The lawless era ended twenty years before Carnegie issued the grant," Doris chided.

Camp grinned. "I stand corrected."

Sherry rolled her eyes. "Some historian. We'll have to preview the paper he's writing. Emily, make sure you set him straight."

Camp dropped an arm around Emily's shoulders. "It's a tough job, but you picked the right lady. This one has a backbone of steel."

Laughing, Emily jabbed him in the ribs. When it failed to dislodge his arm, she gave up. "We'll see you all later. If we don't get moving, our free time will be gone." As

loped across the street, both missed the curious look
rry aimed their way.

Instead of sitting in the sun with cups of yogurt, Camp
nd Emily got waffle cones and wandered the tree-shaded
boulevards, stopping to read historical markers. Down the
street a long drumroll sounded. Very soon a brass section
struck up a patriotic tune. The music faded as they crossed
to look at the Carnegie Center, and grew louder again
once they'd cut across a cobblestone street to peek into
the Ford County Courthouse, where so many outlaws had
met their fate.

"Can't you almost feel the ghosts of all those old gunfighters?" Emily asked in hushed tones.

Camp swallowed the last of his sugar cone and grasped
Emily's hand. "Kind of a shivery feeling? Like a breeze
cooling your body, only there's no wind?"

She nodded, automatically seeking his warmth.

He smoothed a hand up and down her arm. "That's
what I experienced the time my high-school history club
visited Meramec Caverns outside of Sullivan, Missouri.
Our adviser said the caverns had been a hideout for Jesse
James. The first cave I looked at, I saw huddles of frightened slaves. They seemed so...real. It shook me. I didn't
mention it until after the tour. Our guide admitted Union
troops stored powder kilns there during the Civil War, and
that the caves were part of the Underground Railroad.
Jesse James really visited there only once, briefly." He
paused. "Needless to say, for the rest of that trip, everyone avoided me."

"Oh, Camp. It must have frightened you."

"Yes. But my folks had a plausible explanation. Of
course, they come from an intuitive Scots ancestry. Dad
said strong souls from past eras reach out to the future so
we can build on what they learned. It made sense to me."

"Ye...s," she said slowly, thoughtfully.

"You're not put off?"

"No. Should I be? I don't understand, though—with a that Scots blood, why weren't you cursed with red hai and freckles, Nolan Campbell?" Reaching up, she ruffled his dark hair.

He exhaled explosively, all but hearing Greta's snide comments. "Here I thought you were getting ready to say I had a screw loose. What's wrong with freckles, I'd like to know? *Yours* are nice."

"Ha! Kids didn't call you carrot top and measle face."

Camp studied her upturned face so long and hard, and with such hunger, it had Emily sucking in her breath.

The moment was lost as the band they'd heard earlier now rounded the corner. A brace of coronets, trumpets and slide trombones made the sidewalk vibrate. The musicians led a full-fledged parade flanked by a gaggle of followers.

Camp found himself irritated at a clown who darted up and made Emily laugh out loud by finding coins behind her ear. Or maybe it was the garish stalk of fake flowers that the guy pulled from his sleeve to give the "pretty lady."

With a delighted smile, she stood on tiptoe and kissed the clown's cheek, heedless of the white greasepaint. Jealous, he wanted to buy her a million real bouquets; even more than that, he wanted to be clever enough to drive her cares away. She should laugh more often.

Still smiling, Emily tapped her watch and shouted over the din that it was time to meet the others. In fact, they had to run.

Partway down the block, Emily dropped her paper flowers and tripped on them.

Camp caught her before she fell. He scooped up the colorful bouquet and held it away from her, demanding a kiss for its return as he jogged backward.

She danced around him, trying to grab her flowers. Convinced he wouldn't give them back until she complied with his zany request, she threw her arms around his neck and kissed him full on the mouth.

For a minute Camp's hand went limp and he nearly lost the flowers. In the nick of time, he clutched the stalk, awkwardly flattening it against the small of Emily's back as he claimed the kiss he'd craved all day.

Hard to say how long they would have remained locked in their embrace if a passing teen hadn't shrilled a wolf whistle.

Groaning, Camp released her slowly. And happened to glance over her shoulder into the dismayed faces of their companions, who'd gathered at the van.

Sherry appeared the most confused. "What was that about?"

More for Emily's sake than his own, Camp wagged the bouquet under the ladies' noses and explained that the amorous clown had led to his teasing kiss.

Emily snatched the flowers from his hand so quickly, Camp wasn't sure she appreciated his efforts on her behalf. But it was for her sake that he kept quiet about their relationship—if relationship it was. For one thing, he didn't want his sister giving her a hard time. And judging by the speed with which Sherry lay claim to the front seat, Camp knew he'd handled the explanation correctly.

"Where to now?" he asked briskly, as if Emily and Sherry hadn't clammed up.

"To the fort, Romeo," Gina sang out, making matters worse. "From there we'll visit the swales. It'll still be light enough for taking pictures."

The old fort sat between U.S. highway 154 and the Arkansas River. Its buildings, made from limestone, had been quarried north of the city. This time, as they piled out of the bus in the parking lot, Sherry hooked arms with

Emily. "Come across the street with me to the cemete
I heard Bat Masterson is buried there. You can help n
find his headstone. Nolan, I trust you'll stick with Gina
The cemetery ground is too soggy for her wheelchair.
She'd better stay on the walkways inside the fort."

Camp agreed. What else could he do? Still, he deeply
resented the roadblocks his sister placed between him and
Emily. He understood Megan's attitude, and even Brittany's, who had fancied herself in lust with him. But what
was Sherry's problem? Racking his brain, he drew a
blank.

However, once he resigned himself to not making
waves, he got on well with Gina. She knew a lot about
the history of Dodge City. Camp, Gina, Vi and Doris had
nearly completed a circuit of the outbuildings by the time
Emily and Sherry reappeared.

"All that trouble for nothing." Sherry sighed. "The
cashier in the gift shop said it wasn't Bat Masterson buried here, but his brother who was once the marshal in
Dodge."

"Why are you so interested? It's not as if we're related," Camp said jokingly.

"No. But as a kid you got all pumped up over moldy
museums. I found gunslingers intriguing. Be still, my
heart," she said with a laugh.

Camp snorted. "I guarantee if you ever met one of
those tough hombres from the Old West, you'd run so fast
smoke would roll from your boots."

"In your dreams, brother. I held my own in neighborhood brawls. I guess you've forgotten that I smacked Roy
Keller in the teeth my senior year and walked home from
the Sadie Hawkins dance."

"I remember. All because the poor joker ran out of
gas."

"Well, he tried to take some squirrelly way home. His

ry sounded flaky to me. So I took off. It wasn't my
ult he had to push his car for miles.''

The women tittered over Sherry's escapade all the way
to the van. Camp barely managed to herd everyone
aboard. Their jovial mood lasted until they disembarked
at the wheel ruts carved by the wagon trains that had
passed through Fort Dodge.

There were no buildings to block the wind. They
stepped into hip-deep prairie grass that undulated across
the flat land like breakers on an incoming tide. Deep
swales, six abreast, disappeared from the naked eye to a
point where the purple horizon met a floating sea of grass.
In the silence, Camp thought he heard babies crying. Or
was it the tears of pioneer women torn from their families?

The minute his eyes met Emily's and he saw the sheen
of tears, he knew she felt the connection, too. He put out
a hand, and she slid hers into his larger palm. They stood
like that, joined to each other and to the past by a thin
thread of emotional understanding, until Gina cleared her
throat and Sherry coughed, interrupting the moment.
Camp struggled to reconnect with the here and now.

Powerful feelings lingered. No one spoke on the last
leg of their journey. It was as if each person sat wrapped
in his or her own cocoon. Camp dropped the women off
at the entrance to Boot Hill Museum while he turned in
the rental. He was sure Emily would stay in the van. But
no, she let Sherry entice her out.

Dusk fought for possession of an orange sky as Camp
hurried back on foot. He entered the museum village as
electric lights winked in the stores lining the main street.
Camp soon found the others. They'd stopped to listen to
a variety of barkers hawking their wares.

Mark and Jared dashed up, apologizing for being late.

Megan and Brittany arrived just as Emily was ready
send out a search party.

"Sorry," they breathed as one. "We had to see the end
of the gunfight. Those guys die so cool," Megan explained.

"There you go." Camp nudged Sherry. "A chance to
get yourself a gunslinger."

"I've got dibs on the one in the black hat," said Brittany. "In fact, we want his autograph. If you let us go
back, we'll stake out a place to watch the fireworks in
front of the Long Branch Saloon."

Mark tugged Camp's sleeve. "Have you guys seen the
neat old steam engine parked at the north end of Main?"

Camp shook his head.

"It's the train that replaced the Conestogas on the Santa
Fe Trail. Me and Jared climbed all over it. Mom, you
oughta come look, too."

"Gina? Are you interested in seeing the train?" Emily
turned.

"I'd rather the girls parked me outside the saloon. I'm
running out of steam."

"The saloon serves sarsaparilla," Megan announced.
"I'll get you one if you'd like." Everyone gaped at the
girl who never volunteered to help with anything.

Sherry placed her hands on the handles of Gina's chair.
"A drink would hit the spot. You kids take off. Maybe
Gina and I will find out if the Long Branch serves some-
thing stronger than sarsaparilla. How about you, Emily?"

"I'll go with the boys. I'm hungry, and I smell corn
dogs. Save me a place to watch the fireworks, all right?"

"Sure," Sherry agreed. "Are you ready for a cold beer,
Nolan?"

"No," he said without hesitation. "Mark wants to
show me the train." He walked off before Sherry could
come up with another excuse to separate him and Emily.

The train engine truly was an old iron horse. The boys importantly demonstrated all they'd learned for the adults.

Emily and Camp were properly appreciative. They admired everything, then were ready to move on.

"Can we stay awhile?" Mark begged.

More easily convinced this time, Emily nevertheless extracted a promise to meet outside the Long Branch before the fireworks started.

She and Camp picked their way through the crush of people. "There's the vendor with the corn dogs." Camp took Emily's hand and pulled her along. "Or there's hot pocket sandwiches if you want something that'll stick to your ribs."

"Look." She slowed. "A booth selling baked potatoes. If I buy a potato and you get a hot pocket, we can trade bites."

Camp would have bought sushi, which he hated, to please her if she'd asked. He couldn't take his eyes off her as she stood in one line and he in the other. Afterward, totally immersed in each other, they wandered along the board walkway.

Camp stole kisses every chance he got. Or maybe they weren't stolen. After the first one, Emily rose to her toes, clasped his shirtfront and did a little kissing herself. During one such silly exchange they parted to find Sherry, Gina, Brittany and Megan bearing down on them.

"Oh, no," Camp groaned. "Not *again.*"

"Where have you been?" demanded Megan. "Mark and Jared came back ten minutes ago. We lost our good spot for watching the fireworks 'cause we had to hunt for you."

Camp deposited the remains of their meals into the trash. "I can't speak for Emily, but I haven't lost my way since I was a kid."

"How fitting," Sherry murmured. "You're both acti▪ like adolescents."

Gina wheeled to the front. "Love scrambles the sanes▪ brains."

"*Love?*" The word erupted in chorus from three sets of pursed lips.

The only thing Camp noticed, however, was how quickly Emily denied any involvement. Out popped that reserved coolly private second side of her again.

Just then the crackle of rockets overhead kicked off the fireworks display. Funny, he hadn't exactly labeled what he felt for Emily. Camp did know she made him feel young again. And happy. And a little reckless—which made him wonder what, if anything, she felt for him. Suffocating smoke from the Roman candles falling around them—not to mention the presence of their companions—precluded his asking anything so intimate.

On the brisk walk back to the wagons after the finale, he and Emily were kept apart, constantly surrounded by others. He couldn't say with certainty whether this was by action or design.

Determined to have a word with her, he whispered a hurried invitation to meet outside his wagon for tea after everyone had gone to bed.

She nodded, seeming as anxious as he.

Restless, Camp set about brewing her favorite tea. He'd even drunk some of the nasty stuff by the time she showed up.

"Whew!" Short of breath, she accepted the steaming cup he handed her. "I haven't sneaked out of bed to meet a boy since eighth grade."

Camp was taken aback to think she ever had. Realizing he didn't know her at all, he decided it was time to bring whatever it was between them into some kind of perspective. "I'm not a boy, Emily. We're adults, you and I."

Sensing a subtle shift in his tone, she set her cup aside without a word. He did the same in time to catch her as she walked straight into his arms.

"It doesn't sit well with me to sneak around." Camp leaned back and framed her face with both hands.

Heart speeding, Emily murmured agreement as she stretched up to capture his lips.

She sighed when Camp slipped open a button on her blouse and rubbed a knuckle over the aching swell of her breasts.

Needing desperately to feel his flesh, too, Emily tore a button off his shirt, in her haste. She had barely reached her goal of touching his skin when a series of small pops culminating in a loud explosion shattered their treasured interlude.

"What the—" Camp released her abruptly as a horse screamed in fright and lanterns winked on in nearly every wagon.

"Firecrackers," Emily gasped hoarsely as another series of loud pops sent two of the mighty Belgians plunging against their flimsy ropes.

"Damn those boys." Camp fumbled at his shirt. "I'll wring their necks."

"If I don't beat you to it." Emily tidied her blouse as she ran toward the tent Jared and Mark had erected near Gina's wagon. Seconds later she backed from the enclosure shaking her head. "They're both still sleeping like the dead."

"Then who?" Camp frowned.

The who really didn't matter. Robert Boone hollered for Camp to help corral two horses that'd managed to break loose. The chore ended up taking Robert, Terrill, Camp, Emily and Sherry all night.

Near dawn, the crisis was controlled. The gritty-eyed

men and women dragged back into the wagons, onl
have Maizie greet them with a troubling announceme.

"I've called a meeting," she said sternly. "It's tir
we talked straight about responsibility to one another. An
we need to take a hard look at our route."

The wagon master's word was law on the trail. He ruled
with an iron fist. *His* way or they parted ways.
—*From one of Camp's reference books.*
(All his sources assumed that, without
exception, wagon-train bosses were men.)

CHAPTER TEN

MAIZIE SAT ATOP her wagon seat and gathered everyone
around. "Serious mischief afoot last night. We're lucky a
horse didn't break a leg."

"We know who done the deed," shouted Philly.
"Them brats. Make their parents pay. Teach 'em the consequences of having the little buggers."

Camp was supremely glad to hear that Philly and his
wife hadn't spawned any more of their kind.

Mark, his face pale in the cloudy light, stepped closer
to his mother. "Me 'n' Jared didn't set off any firecrackers," he insisted, even though his voice quavered.

Jared concurred in a stronger voice.

Emily brushed at the cowlick that set Mark's hair awry.
"He's telling the truth. Camp and I were up having...tea," she said, stumbling over the partial lie. "The
boys slept through the whole thing."

"Ha!" yelled Philly. "I'll bet they were playing possum."

"My son doesn't lie." Robert Boone loomed over the

other man, his hamlike fists knotted. "It could hav
kids from town."

Maizie stuck a thumb and little finger between
teeth, emitting a deafening whistle. "Those who di
know." Her gaze drifted to where Brittany and Meg
huddled against Sherry's wagon, faces pinched.

Camp saw the girls turn several shades grayer. He wondered why he hadn't thought of them sooner. Setting off
fireworks at that strategic time was obviously another attempt to drive Emily and him apart.

All heads turned to follow Maizie's faintly accusing
stare. It wasn't hard to tell from the girls' guilty expressions who the culprits were.

"In my day girls played piano and crocheted things for
church bazaars. We didn't run the streets causing trouble," lectured Philly's wife. "Those two should be pun-
ished."

"Make them groom the horses for a week, and scrub a
few pots and pans," shouted her husband. "It'd kill 'em
to get their hands dirty."

Camp listened to the undercurrent of remarks, expecting Maizie to call a halt. When she didn't, he did. "Setting firecrackers isn't a capital offense, folks. I'm sure
they're sorry." Although from their mutinous expressions,
Camp wasn't sure at all.

"Nolan's right." Sherry insinuated herself between
Harv Shaw and the girls. "We've risen above making
outcasts wear scarlet letters. It's over. Let's get on with
business. Maizie, you said you wanted to discuss our
route. Is there some problem?"

"Before we do that," Emily said, holding up a hand.
"If my daughter set off those cherry bombs, she *will* suffer the consequences."

Maizie crushed the rumble of voices. "Then that's
that." She jumped down and unfolded a large map, which

...ned to the wagon canvas. "The long-term weather ...ast is for a series of storms rolling up across Texas ...i the gulf. They may peter out. They may not. It's ...ing buckets in the Oklahoma panhandle right now—...ading our way. Rain here means snow over Raton Pass. ...o we take the longer northern route, or the shorter Cimarron cutoff?"

"The Cimarron route has more creek and river crossings," Robert said. "If they're swollen that'll slow us down. We could spend days waiting for the rivers to drop."

Maizie broke off a piece of tobacco and started to put it in her mouth. Then, catching Camp's eye, she tossed it into the fire, unwrapping two sticks of gum, instead. "In bad weather neither route's a clambake. Personally, I'd rather dry a wagon out than lose it over the edge of a thousand-foot precipice because the tires slipped on ice."

"Speaking as someone responsible for women, kids and four wagons," Camp said, his voice quiet but firm, "I vote for the cutoff. We know we can make it through ankle-deep mud."

Sherry strutted into the circle. "You think we women are afraid of a little snow, Nolan? If the pioneers scaled the pass, so will we."

Camp refused to be provoked. "From accounts I've read, both routes were used equally by the pioneers. Wagon trains suffered loss from outlaw and Indian attacks on the cutoff. But more people died in treacherous snowstorms on the mountain trail."

"Will taking the cutoff be cheating?" Emily calmly injected a note of reason. "I'm talking about your article now." She took a deep breath. "What bearing will changing routes have on your work?"

Brittany shoved her way through the huddle. "Don't listen to her. She's looking for more time to make out

with him.'' She jerked a thumb at Camp. ''Ask him
those two were really doing when those firecrackers ʋ
off.''

''Why can't we just go home?'' Megan delivered dir
looks at Camp and Emily.

Mark Benton's eyes popped. ''You mean Mom and
Camp—hey, ru...le.'' The boy gazed adoringly up at
Camp. ''All ri...ght!''

Sherry gaped as if Emily had suddenly turned into a
two-headed snake.

Emily's cheeks reddened. Neither she nor Camp con-
firmed or denied anything.

Maizie snapped her fingers to gain attention. ''Pioneers
faced floods and cyclones along the Cimarron. If you're
dying for adventure, there'll be plenty. Either way, this
train is going on to Santa Fe.''

''And we don't have all day to decide.'' Robert stroked
his unshaven jaw. ''Guess I'll stand with Camp on this
one.''

Doris and Vi quickly sided with the two men.

''We were promised a trip over Raton Pass, and by the
devil, I want what I paid for,'' Philly insisted.

Terrill Boone, who had rounded up the lame horses to
drive home, announced that he was leaving. ''Why not
review the weather at Caches? That's where the trail
splits,'' he said for the benefit of those who didn't know.

''I need a consensus now,'' Maizie said stubbornly. ''I
don't want to wait until we hit bad weather, then have to
make snap decisions. Take a look at the sky off to the
south. We're in for a squall.'' As if to prove her point, a
black cloud obliterated the horizon and began to spit rain.
''Well, what'll it be?'' she pressed.

Gina hobbled forward on her crutches. ''I'd hate for
anyone to have to haul my bag of bones up nearly eight
thousand feet over Raton Pass.''

...lly's wife urged him to reconsider voting for the ...ter route.

"You're all a bunch of wimps," he snarled. "I'm call-...g the Better Business Bureau the minute me and the ...issus get home. None of our friends'll fork out dough for this rip-off trip," he said, climbing into his wagon.

"News to me that he has friends," Emily muttered.

Camp cornered Maizie. "If we decide on the cutoff, will that allow us some extra time here? Some of us need sleep. And I'd planned on hitting the Laundromat this morning. This is my last pair of jeans." He pointed to the mud-caked denims he wore.

"Depends on what the rain does to the river. I'll give you as much time as I can. Long as you agree to take your clothes wet and leave without question if I say so." She let her gaze touch each individual. "That means no aimless wandering around town. I don't want to chase in ten directions if the Arkansas starts to rise."

"I missed doing laundry in Fort Larned," Sherry said. "But I'm beat, too."

"Throw your clothes in with mine. I'll do them," Camp offered.

"Not on your life, big bro. You'd love a tidbit like that for your paper."

"Must every issue be confrontational, Sherilyn? What sense is there in both of us sitting around a Laundromat?" Seconds slipped by and she didn't answer. "In that case—" he grinned "—how much'll you charge to do my washing?"

"You don't have enough money. Not even if you throw in your trust fund from Gramps. I believe in total equality between the sexes. When I get married—I'll do my laun-dry and my husband will do his. Put that in your old report."

"All I can say is get it in writing, Sherry, *before* the ceremony," Gina shouted.

Camp reached into his wagon and hauled out two duffel bags of dirty clothes. "You forget how well I know you, sis. I have never in my life dry-cleaned my jeans, while you—"

"I do that so they'll stay new longer. So there."

"Enough." Maizie held up her hand. "Quit bickering, you two. Time's wasting."

Camp backed off. Later, at the Laundromat, he filled a third of the washing machines and sat by himself, while Sherry and Gina talked quietly in a corner. Between cycles, he daydreamed about Emily. Why were so many people conspiring against them? Megan probably felt threatened. With one in three marriages splitting up, kids discussed the trauma of bad experiences with their peers. And around the college, he'd heard all manner of stories dealing with wicked stepmothers and equally wicked stepfathers.

Sherry's attitude puzzled him. They'd had a stable home, where affection was openly shown. Their parents were still deeply in love. He'd entered graduate school the year Sherry started high school. Camp recalled a flock of boys hanging out at the house on weekends. These days, of course, they moved in different circles at work. To his knowledge there hadn't been anyone serious in Sherry's life during the last few years—although he tried not to listen to scuttlebutt on who dated whom. The rumor mill in that place could be vicious, he'd had a taste of it after Greta threw him over.

"We're leaving," Sherry trilled near his ear, causing Camp's eyelids to fly open. "I fed your dryers with my leftover dimes. It'll cost you a king's ransom to dry eight pairs of jeans. Don't fall asleep and let them lock you in here. On the door it says they close at noon on Sundays."

He stifled a yawn. "If I don't put in an appearance in the next hour—or as long as it takes to use another roll of dimes—will you send the dog with the brandy?"

"I'll send Maizie. Brr," Sherry said as she maneuvered Gina's wheelchair out the door. "That rain's flat-out comin' down."

Forty minutes later, Camp's clothes were dried, folded and stuffed back into the two duffel bags. He was soaked again by the time he'd gone two blocks—as were his canvas bags and most of their contents. Compared with the previous day, the streets of Dodge were near deserted.

Not so the wagon circle. It was a beehive. "What's up?" Camp cornered Jared, who led two of the spirited new Percherons toward the wagons.

"Maizie's got it in her head to ford the river ASAP. Some old geezer she talked to said the level's risen six inches in two hours."

"Well, there goes my nap," Camp grumbled.

"You're right about that. Don't even talk to my dad. Gram woke him up and he's growling like a bear who got rousted out of hibernation." A horse snorted and danced around Jared, tangling the lead line.

"The Perches are going to be hard to control," Camp noted. "Why don't you split them up? Maybe the Clydesdales will calm them down."

Jared untangled the ropes. "I was going to give 'em as they are to ol' Philadelphia." A twinkle shone in the youth's normally placid eyes.

Camp looked away, over Jared's head. "Can't fault your reasoning. But who has to make sure everyone crosses the river safely?"

"Hadn't thought of that. S'pose I'd better give one to you and the other to Dad then."

As he nodded absently, Camp's gaze lit on Emily. Coatless, hatless, she flew across the field toward him. His lungs cinched so tight it hurt to breathe. Darn, he wished Jared would take those horses and go. The kind of welcome he had in mind could use a little privacy.

Emily skidded to a stop in front of him. It wasn't joy Camp saw in her eyes, but dark waves of worry.

"Camp, I'm so glad you're back! Maizie says we have to leave, but I can't find Megan anywhere."

Camp dropped his duffels and swept a glance over the wagons, as if expecting Megan to materialize out of thin air. He took a mental count of the saddle horses and felt better noting they were all there.

"You've checked everywhere?"

"Yes." She clasped her hands nervously. "I thought maybe you saw her walking into town. According to Brittany, Megan said she wasn't going one step farther."

"That's hotheadedness talking. Who does she know in Dodge? Nobody, right?"

Emily shrugged, looking miserable.

"You're soaked to the skin," Camp said softly. "Find a jacket. I'll toss my bags in the wagon and meet you back at Maizie's. We'll have her call a meeting. People may know more than they've let on."

"You mean Brittany?"

"Or someone who might not have realized that she was doing anything out of the ordinary."

"Oh, Lord, I hope so. It's such a helpless, awful feeling."

Minutes later, a sour-faced Maizie clanged the bell, calling everyone together.

"That river's rising higher by the second. If anyone's seen that girl today, spit out when and where. If we don't cross the Arkansas within the hour, we don't cross. So if you're covering for her out of loyalty—don't." The wagon mistress pinned Brittany, then Mark and Jared, with a steely look.

"I told you what I know," exclaimed Brittany. "She said she wasn't pushing wagons through the mud ever again."

Mark, eyes big in his face, simply shook his head.

Philly hitched his belt over a protruding belly. "The brat probably stowed away on Terrill's wagon. Everybody knew he was heading home."

Emily ran up just then. "Megan didn't take any clothes that I could tell. But she rooted through my purse and has my phone card. And she has Mona's credit card number."

"Credit card info, but no clothes. Hmm. Maybe she figures on taking a bus or train," Camp said, sliding a thumb over the itchy stubble on his jaw. "Maizie, you and Robert start the wagons rolling. Emily and I'll swing by the depots. If we don't turn something up, I'll let Jared handle my wagon and I'll ride after Terrill."

"Camp, you're dead on your feet," Emily protested. "She's my daughter. If anyone rides after her it should be me."

Camp shook his head. "We'll talk about that if the need arises."

Maizie added more gum to the wad already in her mouth. "I don't like splitting a tour group. 'Specially not with a flooding river between. I hope you find the sassy little miss. And when you do, I'm gonna give her what for."

Emily's sigh could be heard over the clattering rain. She and Camp gratefully donned slickers that Sherry produced.

"Don't be too hard on her when you find her," Sherry murmured. "According to Brittany, Megan was smarting from Philly's drubbing. I gather the firecracker incident scared the girls as much as it did the horses."

"Pray we find her, Sherry. I know Megan talks big and

she tries to act tough. But she's lived in a small town her whole life." Emily's voice cracked.

Camp touched Emily's arm, indicating they needed to go. He heard the splash of the lead team being forced into the swollen stream as they set off down the trail.

Outside the bus depot, near a bank of phones, the two of them sighted their quarry at the same time. Megan's auburn hair clung wetly to her neck. She was hunched under a dripping overhang, looking cold and slightly dazed.

Camp couldn't be sure from this distance if that was rain or tears tracking down her cheeks and dripping off her chin. In case it was tears, he put out a hand to caution Emily. "Let's hear her side of this before we pounce."

Emily indicated that she understood, but her steps quickened. "Megan, honey..."

The girl covered her face with her hands and began to sob—sad, gulping sobs. She didn't, however, object when her mother gathered her close.

Camp, never comfortable with women's tears, stood back feeling powerless. He didn't know how much time had elapsed before he made sense of Megan's words through her hiccups.

"I—I thought Mona would c-come for me," she cried into Emily's shoulder. "But she has an appointment in St. Louis tomorrow at the spa. She...she sa...id I should find my own way home. Toby's busy, too. Tomorrow's his poker night. He said he'd wire me money. That's their answer to everything."

Emily could have told Megan that—had tried to in a hundred ways or more. Maybe she'd been wrong not to strip the kids' blinders off after Dave's crash. She hated hearing her daughter's heartbreak.

Camp didn't want to interrupt, but the rain was falling harder. "Emily, I know you two have a lot to discuss.

Can it wait? If we don't leave now, I'm afraid the river'll be too high to ford.''

Megan scrubbed at her eyes. "What's he doing here? Mark thinks he's so great, but I want him to leave us...leave...*you* alone." She wailed the last.

A couple walking down the street turned to look, and hesitated as if considering whether or not to intervene.

Camp broke from his frown to give them what he hoped was a reassuring smile. As they seemed inclined to linger, he whipped off his yellow raincoat, threw it over Megan's shoulders and hustled both women back to the park.

Maizie alone paced the clearing. One wagon remained on this side of the Arkansas. It was Camp's.

"You three are a sight for sore eyes," Maizie rasped. "We got no time for palavering. The river's running fast and she's running high. Robert had his hands full crossing Emily's wagon. River carried him downstream to where the bank was almost too slick for the horses to climb out."

"Well, what are we waiting for?" asked Camp. He boosted Emily and Megan into the back of his wagon and motioned for Maizie to join him on the seat.

Camp fought to keep the horses lined up with the tire tracks emerging on the far side. His jaw and his muscles ached by the time he pulled to a stop next to his sister.

Sherry let out a whoop on seeing Megan huddled between them.

If Camp thought Maizie would let them rest once they cleared the difficult crossing, he'd called it wrong.

"Snap to it," she said, gritting her teeth as she jumped down into the mud. "I want to see everybody driving his or her own wagon. This ain't the only river that'll be over its banks today. I know some of you haven't slept in twenty-four hours. I can't promise it won't be twenty-four more. I never claimed to be able to control the weather. What you see is what you get. Let's roll 'em."

Camp wanted a word with Emily. But that wasn't to be. She handed his slicker back with the barest whisper of thanks and climbed aboard her own wagon. He noticed Megan slunk into her mom's wagon bed, looking neither right or left.

Next thing Camp knew, Emily had pulled in front of Sherry.

As if the day hadn't started out rotten enough, the clouds sat down even lower and rain lashed them with all the fury of hell. Midafternoon, instead of allowing a break, Maizie handed out small bags of dried fruit. There'd be no hot meal, not today.

Rain poured without letup. If they made two miles today, it'd surprise Camp. The flat prairie offered no shelter, and the day turned into one round after another of stuck wagons. He'd never dreamed that a reenactment could be this realistic.

When Maizie finally consented to calling a halt that evening, not even Emily could coax a fire to start. Everyone fell into bed, too tired to even gnaw at the beef jerky Robert Boone said they needed to eat for energy.

Camp slept like the dead.

Morning produced a break in the rain, but no slack in the schedule. Maizie whipped them in gear after insisting they eat bread and jam for breakfast.

Noonish, a pale sun came out. Hordes of mosquitoes descended on the spot Maizie referred to as Middle Crossings. There, drivers toiled to ford an engorged Cimarron River.

Under the wet cottonwoods on the opposite bank, the humidity rose even higher. And tempers rose right along with it—as the first wagons to cross had to wait for the others.

Megan Benton, who'd spent the morning riding with Sherry and Brittany, cried over ugly red lumps that itched and marred her pretty face. Camp and Robert took the brunt of the girl's griping as they strained to dislodge Sherry's wagon from a sinkhole in the center of a swift-running river. "I want to go home," she cried.

Brittany and Megan clung to each other. "I hate you, Nolan Campbell," Brittany sniffled. "If the pioneers did this voluntarily, they were nuts."

Camp and Robert ignored her comments and put shoulders to the wheels. The minute they got the wagon ashore, Megan ran to Emily. Camp suspected it was because the girl didn't want anyone to see how the bites had left her face splotched and swollen. At the moment, he had more to worry about than mosquitoes. Several wagons had shipped water during the crossing. Maizie consented to an early stop in order to dry things out. It wasn't just clothing that'd gotten wet. Doris and Vi lost all their oatmeal. Sherry's flour was ruined, as was Gina's sugar.

Philly had insisted on fording the swollen river without help. He nearly capsized his wagon and wasn't half so belligerent when he caught up to the others.

The heat remained unbearable. Steam rose from everything.

Maizie gathered the disgruntled group for a pep talk, pointing ahead to a desolate, barren plateau. "It's gonna be hotter than a pig fry tonight. I recommend tearin' off some cottonwood branches here. They'll dry fast. You can throw your sleeping bags on top of 'em and sleep under your wagons tonight. Wet canvas blocks the wind—not that there'll be any. Inside, the wagons'll be virtual bake ovens."

"What about critters and creepy crawlies?" Brittany inquired in a small voice. "Jared said he saw coyote tracks along the river."

Emily put a hand on Brittany's shoulder. "Animals like

coyotes, badgers and racoons are more afraid of humans than we are of them."

"A lot you know," sulked Megan.

Camp smiled at Emily to bolster her spirits. She'd come through this rough stage of the trip without one complaint. "Listen to Emily," Camp urged the girls. "And while you're at it, take some lessons. She has her fire started and black-bean soup cooking. Smoke drives off mosquitoes, too." He glanced pointedly at Megan.

"Yippy skippy." She twirled a finger in the air, stuck out her tongue at Camp, then ran off toward a steamy field of flowering weeds.

Emily exchanged a worried glance with Camp. It was the first time she'd looked directly at him in two days. He took advantage of the crack in her resistance. "Give her time, Em. When she starts to sweat, she'll see the wisdom of bedding down under the wagon. Mmm. That bean soup smells tasty. I swear I don't know how mountain men survived on beef jerky."

"Are you angling for dinner?" she asked, tilting her head like the Emily of old.

"I sure wouldn't turn it down," he drawled.

"Stop by with your bowl in about an hour. I'm offering to feed everyone tonight."

His smile froze. Well, if that didn't put him in his place, Camp didn't know what did. Maybe she'd be more amenable if he won Megan over first. He angled toward the field, hoping for a chance to discuss how he felt about Emily.

A few yards into the meadow, Megan ran screaming toward him. Swooping behind her was a black swarm of bees.

Camp grabbed her, zigzagging past the swarm and going in the opposite direction. He set her on her feet a safe distance away. She didn't even thank him.

"Megan, I wish..." He grappled for words to alleviate the strain between them. But she sailed off, refusing to listen.

At wit's end, during dinner Camp asked Emily to collect the data sheets. He figured she'd bring them by his wagon and he could convince her to stay for tea or something. No such luck. Emily collected the sheets and sent Mark to deliver them.

"You and my mom have a fight?" Mark asked Camp bluntly.

"No. Mark, I like your mother a lot. A whole lot, for that matter. And you kids, too. When this is over, I'd like for us all to get together more."

"Ru...le." Mark's teeth glistened white in the firelight.

"Tell me, Mark. Is Megan afraid I'm trying to take your dad's place?"

Mark's freckles stood out in stark relief. "Mona and Toby have her brainwashed. My dad..."

"Yes?" Camp prompted after a moment of silence.

"He...he was my dad and all—but he wasn't very nice to Mom."

Camp put out a hand, then pulled it back and rubbed his forehead. "Son, it's okay to love someone and not like the way he acts or some of the things he does. I know it sounds weird, but give it time. You'll understand."

"O...kay," Mark said shakily. His head came up as his name was called. "Gina," he said. "I promised to fix her bed under the wagon. Say, Camp, I heard what Brittany said. Are there varmints around?"

"Would Maizie suggest sleeping out if she thought there were?"

"No. Hey, thanks, Camp. You never treat me like a kid. I hope you and Mom...well, you know." Blushing, he left.

It was some time before Camp managed to wipe the

smile off his face and settle down to read the papers Mark
had dropped off. He finished adding his observations, then
crawled under his wagon. Only when he lay back on a
crackling bed of branches to stare at the black underbelly
of the wagon did he try to analyze his feelings for Emily
and her kids. Megan as well as Mark. If anything, Megan
needed unconditional love more than her brother. She
needed someone to care, yet be firm in guiding her. As
sleep stole over him, Camp vowed to set things right with
Emily before many more days had passed.

Except that bad weather continued to dog them. At
Lower Springs they almost didn't get across Sand Creek.
Ugly yellow mud sucked at their boots and stuck to their
tires like glue. Maizie ordered teams rotated twice. Camp
understood why they'd rented so many extra horses.

Four days later, they faced the swiftest section of the
Cimarron, and Maizie expected them to be ecstatic over
two giant boulders barely visible to the naked eye. They
poked out from the waterlogged grassland still ahead.

"Point of Rocks," she said proudly. "Pioneers cried
over those boulders. Meant they were looking at Colorado
and within spitting distance of Oklahoma. Also means
we're still on the Santa Fe Trail." She chuckled.

"Was there any doubt?" Camp asked, almost too tired
to appreciate a joke.

"Navigating by the sun and the stars is tricky, boy. By
tomorrow afternoon we'll cross the Cimarron one final
time. This rain doesn't slack, she's gonna be boiling. The
ground twixt here and there is like a sponge. I want y'all
looking out for one another."

Camp took her at her word. And the person he planned
to look out for was Emily. So instead of bringing up the
rear as he'd been doing, he forced his team past Sherry's
wagon. Pulling even with Emily, Camp smiled across the
space between them, which dragged a reluctant smile

from her. He regaled her with funny stories and soon had her in stitches. For over an hour they were so engrossed in conversation, neither noticed that Sherry's wagon had fallen behind.

In fact, Camp didn't discover it until they stopped for the night. "Where're Sherry and Brittany?" he asked Emily, peering behind them down a stubbornly empty trail.

"I don't know. Oh, Camp, wouldn't we have noticed if Sherry'd had trouble?"

"Maybe she's admiring the sunset. If she doesn't show by the time we finish unhitching, I'll saddle Mincemeat and ride back."

"I'll go, too. Now, don't say no," she admonished, well aware before he said anything that he was going to object. "Four hands are better than two if Sherry needs help. I'm going with you, and that's final."

His shoulders fell as if in resignation. "Yes, ma'am," he grinned. He'd take time alone with Emily any way he could get it.

"By 1867 women traveled across the plains in comfort. It was so safe they could serve their men off china plates."
—*Sherry cut this out of a book, taped it to her data sheet, noting that it was a big, fat lie.*

CHAPTER ELEVEN

SHERRY'S TEAM, a mix of Percherons and Belgians today, was much harder to handle than her teddy-bear Clydesdales. After the trial at the river, her arms felt like lead weights, and she knew she and Brittany were falling behind.

"Brittany, I can't see the main body of the train anymore. Won't you please drive for a while? These brutes are yanking my arms from their sockets."

"I told you I don't feel good."

"Well, I'm not surprised. You haven't eaten anything to speak of in three days."

"I hate fruit. And that awful jerky about pulls the caps off my teeth. My folks put a lot of money into them. A fortune, according to my dad."

"If they put that much into them, the caps should hold if you ate shoe leather. You're not anorexic, are you?" Sherry asked all of a sudden.

"No! Who can eat food covered in flies and mosquitoes as big as a barn? Who *wants* to eat? Everything smells like horse shi—"

"I get the picture, Brittany. Oh...damn!"

"What's the matter?" Brittany peered through the opening with frightened eyes.

"Conquistador is limping. I think he picked up a stone." Sherry yanked the animals to a stop. "Will you find me that thingamajig Maizie gave us to dig them out?"

"I don't know where it is. Have you done this before?"

"No. But I've watched Robert. How hard can it be? If you can't find the pick, give me your nail file."

"It's diamond and it's new!"

"It can be platinum-covered gold for all I care. We aren't going another step until that stone comes out."

Brittany threw the file onto the seat. "You owe me a new one."

Sherry soon discovered the task was nowhere near as simple as it had appeared. The horse wouldn't stand still, and the rock was embedded in gunk. Every time she cleared the area around the stone, Conquistador jerked loose or set his foot down. Patience thinning, Sherry hiked the foot onto her knee and started over.

A ghostly fog had moved in by the time she finally removed the rock. Sherry's jeans were caked with mud, her fingers scraped and frozen.

Throughout the entire ordeal, Brittany griped incessantly.

"If you're not going to help, be quiet," Sherry finally snapped.

"It's eerie here," Brittany whined. "How soon before we catch up to the others?"

"Do I look like a psychic? Frankly, I thought Nolan would have come by now."

"Ha! He can't see beyond Emily."

Sherry tossed the file on the seat and unwound the

reins. "You keep saying that. Em's had one bad marriag
She's not about to get tangled up with another man."

"Are you blind? The only reason they're not sleeping
together is that Megan pitched a royal fit. But kids only
count for so long."

"Enough. I know Emily. Wow, it's turning to pea soup
out there. We must be closer to the river than I thought.
What time is it? I took my watch off to work on that stone
and now my hands are too icky to dig it out of my
pocket."

"Six o'clock."

"It can't be! We were supposed to cross the Cimarron
by four!"

Brittany shoved her watch under Sherry's nose. "Six,
see! And in case you haven't noticed, it's getting dark."

"You're right. Hear that?" Sherry led the team a few
wagon lengths and cocked an ear. "I can't see it, but I
think the river's just ahead."

"All I hear are dogs. Or coyotes! Do you hear that
yipping?"

Sherry did, and tried to forget accounts she'd read in
that book she'd bought. "We have wood in the wagon.
Let's build a fire. I know someone'll be back for us
soon."

"They won't. We're lost for...ever. We're going to
die—I know it."

Gritting her teeth, Sherry looped the reins over a cottonwood branch, electing to keep the team hitched. Brittany's theatrics grated on her nerves. Sherry grew even
more agitated when the wood she'd dumped in her big
metal pot refused to catch fire because the heavy mist that
blew around had drenched it.

Suddenly, a figure parted the fog. Sherry glanced up
eagerly, expecting to see Nolan. A gasp tore from her
lungs as she scrambled away from a tall stranger. A giant

a man, bearded and dark. Unkempt, dishwater-blond hair straggled over the collar of a scruffy jacket. His ripped pants were dirtier than his rundown cowboy boots. In the swirling mist, he looked positively frightening.

The stranger ripped off a muddy glove and reached for something in his belt.

Oh, God—a gun. Sherry fought the fear welling in her throat as Brittany screamed bloody murder, leaped from the wagon seat and slumped against Sherry in a dead faint. "Oh, good grief." Sherry staggered under Brittany's full weight.

"I'll be doggoned. A couple of women out here alone on a night not fit for man or beast." He stopped, discovering the Conestoga. "Is one of us caught in a time warp?"

He had a deep, slow drawl and teeth that flashed wickedly white from the depths of the beard.

Shaking in her boots, Sherry shoved a piece of kindling she still clutched into her jacket pocket. "Don't come any closer," she warned. "I swear I'll shoot."

"Now, hold on." He backed into the thick fog until all that showed were laser-blue eyes and the ragged outline of his bearded jaw.

Brittany roused enough to stand on her own. Babbling hysterically, she threw up her hands and ran behind the wagon.

"Come back here, you coward," Sherry muttered out of the side of her mouth, afraid to take her eyes off the man, who'd begun to speak in that lazy voice again.

"You ladies are a long way from civilization. Suppose you tell me what y'all are doing out here alone in that confounded contraption."

In a flash of genius, Sherry made up a lie. "We're part of a huge wagon train. The others crossed the river. Our husbands will be back for us any second.'' She waved her free hand to indicate herself and the now-absent Brittany.

"A wagon train, you say?" He crouched next to the black pot in which Sherry had sheltered a pile of twigs. Snapping open a cigarette lighter, he started the fire that'd only sizzled damply for Sherry. "I'll just keep you company until your menfolk show up." He rose, cool gaze affixed to Sherry's ringless left hand.

Behind the wagon, Brittany began to wail and carry on. "We'll all be killed—I told you so. He'll leave our bodies out here to be picked clean by buzzards. I'm too young to di…e!"

Edging carefully backward, Sherry reached out and yanked Brittany up on the balls of her feet. "Hush," she hissed. "Don't give him any ideas."

Brittany only blubbered harder.

Sherry wrapped a hand in the front of the girl's jacket and shook her hard. "Listen. I told him the men have already crossed the river and they'll be right back for us. Quit bawling and act like it's true."

The stranger poked his head around the wagon, straight brows pulled together in a fierce frown. Both women screamed and clung together.

"Whoa." He held up grimy hands. "I'm just an ordinary guy from down in Huntsville, Texas. Been up river-panning for gold."

His lopsided grin was far from reassuring to Sherry. The one and only thing she knew about Huntsville, Texas, was that it housed the state's maximum security prison. What if this man was an escapee? He wouldn't let people who could identify him just wander off! In a blind panic, she snatched a bigger chunk of wood from her supply and whacked him upside the head. He toppled like a rock. She heard a splash and knew how close they were to the Cimarron.

"Hurry, Brittany. Climb aboard! Let's make tracks. Duck if you hear shots." Boosting the younger woman into the seat, Sherry felt her legs almost give out. Nevertheless, she untied the reins, scrambled up herself and forced the horses into the murky water. She wasn't sure, but she thought the man had begun to move. Whipping the team into a frenzy, she never looked back, only hunched against expected gunfire.

As they bounced and jolted through the river, spraying water every which way, Sherry gasped out her fears to Brittany.

"You mean he's an outlaw?" shivered Brittany.

"Or a low-down murderer." Sherry gripped the leather straps more tightly and shuddered. "Let's hope he's on foot and doesn't have a horse to follow us."

As if on cue, above the thud of the team's big hooves, they heard a sharper, lighter clippity-clop through the fog. Sherry urged the already blowing horses faster. Brittany mewled louder.

The dark shape of a saddle horse appeared so quickly in front of them that it took all of Sherry's limited power to swing the team to the right and avoid a disaster.

"Oh, God, it's him," Brittany shrieked as the phantom horse swerved and gave chase. When the darkly silhouetted rider leaned out of his saddle, grabbed the harness of the lead horse and fought to bring the team to a halt, Brittany's wild screech drowned out their captor's voice. "We're dead meat! De...ad!"

"Whoa. Sherry, pull up. Dammit, stop! Are you two hurt?" Camp threw his weight against the bit. "What in thunderation is wrong with her?" He squinted at the cowering Brittany.

Sherry couldn't say how or when she recognized her brother's voice. By then she was shaking so hard she had almost no muscle left to do as he asked. But in that last mad race, they'd driven out of the mist. The moon and stars winked in an inky sky as finally Camp and Sherry brought the huge beasts to a standstill.

Emily cantered up on the opposite side of the wagon. "Runaway team?" she asked Sherry.

Camp vaulted from the saddle, uncaring that he landed in a mud hole as he swung up to see why Sherry wasn't talking. He barely caught her when, with a strangled cry, she launched herself at him from the high seat.

"It's okay," he breathed, hugging her and patting her awkwardly. "You're safe. What in blazes happened? I didn't realize you'd fallen so far behind until Maizie signaled to stop for the night."

"We met an escaped convict with a gun," Brittany cried. "A murderer."

Camp pried Sherry away from his chest. "Murder..." Seeing his sister's white face, he stared at the mist boiling behind them. "Escaped convict? How do you know? You wouldn't be putting me on?" Camp frowned, meeting Emily's eyes over Sherry's head.

Sherry pressed a hand to her throat. "He didn't have on black and white stripes, or the orange coveralls you see on TV. But he said he was from Huntsville—and he had the...the *look* of an escapee. Oh, Nolan, let's leave, please."

"Sherry smacked the guy with a piece of firewood. He fell in the river. I hope he drowned," Brittany announced without a shred of compassion.

"You what?" Camp again glanced at Emily as if for verification.

"He...he looked disreputable. All right?" Sherry tossed an uneasy gaze over one shoulder. "In the fog, everything was creepy. I...he said he was panning for gold. I mean...really, in this weather? Can we just go?"

Camp returned Sherry to the seat. "Emily, lead them

to Cold Springs. I'll take Mincemeat and have a look around.''

"No," all three women exclaimed at once.

"Camp..." Emily rode around and blocked his leaving. "Why would anyone be in this desolate area all alone?"

He caught her restraining hand and kissed her fingers. "Probably some innocent old prospector. If Sherry injured him or worse," he said, "somebody'll have to ride into Ulysses and report it to the police."

Sherry blanched. "God, I never thought. Nolan, I didn't mean to hit him so hard. And he wasn't, you know, old, the way I picture a prospector. That was p-part of the problem. I'm sure he was armed. Oh, I wish you wouldn't go."

"Careful, sis, or I'll get the idea you care." Turning to Emily one last time, Camp murmured, "I'll be fine. You take it easy, too."

"I will, Camp. You can count on me."

He waited long enough to see them move out, before breaching the wall of fog. The idea of an armed prospector sounded ludicrous. But again, they were forty miles from civilization. Something *had* happened. He'd never seen Sherry so rattled. *She hit him,* he mused. Exactly how a pioneer woman would have handled things. That was certainly going into his paper. Too bad he wasn't writing a book.

Grinning, he flipped on the powerful construction flashlight he'd borrowed from Robert before he and Emily left. Sherry's wagon tracks stood out clearly on the muddy ground. The river tumbled and eddied in front of him, shrouded in fog.

He found where the wagon had left the water, but the beam refused to penetrate the cottony mist. Step by wary step his horse moved into the river. Camp thought about what awaited him on the other side. A dead man, or a furious one.

Camp touched his heels to Mincemeat's sides to speed their progress. On the far bank he discovered Sherry's large cast-iron pot lying on its side. He smelled recent smoke, but saw no fire. Another whorl of mist obliterated the scene. Dismounting, he combed the river's edge on foot. Thank goodness he didn't stumble across any dead body. To the right of Sherry's tire tracks he saw signs that something heavy had crawled a short distance through the mud. A tracker he wasn't, but Camp bent and followed the snaky trail.

Finally, footprints.

The ice melted from the solid wad in Camp's chest, and he stopped expecting to find a dead man slumped behind every pile of rocks.

Pushed on by the horse's hot breath on his neck, Camp literally tripped over a heap of wet clothing that in all probability belonged to the person he sought. His light beam swept up and over a shivering naked man. A guy about his own age who hopped on one foot, trying to stuff his wet legs into a dry pair of jeans. Beads of water caught in the man's too-long blond hair. Blue eyes blinked rapidly in the bright light a moment before the figure lunged for an army knife Camp saw lying open on the hood of a bright-red Jeep.

"Hold on there, buddy," Camp growled. "You've got no call to fear me."

Relaxing, the man dropped the blade, leaned against the vehicle and finished pulling up his trousers. "For a minute I was afraid you were that crazy lady who tried to brain me." The man's last words were muffled as he shrugged into an out-of-shape sweatshirt with a college logo on the front. "If you're her man," he muttered, yanking on socks and a battered pair of sneakers, "you have my condolences. Last I saw of those two wild women, they were driving a team across the river like two bats out of hell. I would have followed to see they didn't break their fool necks, but the dark-haired one decked me." He touched a spot above his left ear and grimaced.

"Uh-huh." Camp found himself uttering Maizie's stock reply. Whatever the blond stranger was, Camp judged, he wasn't an escaped convict.

"Don't blame you for not being in a hurry to catch her," the man said with a smile. "If you give me a minute to stoke the fire, I can offer you coffee. Or there's beer if you'd rather. The name is Lock. Dr. Garrett Lock." He leaned forward and extended a broad hand, which Camp accepted.

"Doctor? Medical, dental or academic?" Camp released the cold, damp fingers, looped his reins over the Jeep's bumper and began to loosen the saddle girth.

Hunkering down to fan a low, smoldering flame, the man in the sweatshirt pointed to the logo on his shirt. "Assistant dean of collaborative programs in Huntsville, Texas. At the college," he added in afterthought.

"Really?" Camp glanced at the overlong, dirt-caked hair, the Jeep and the worn tent. "Quite a ways from home, aren't you, Lock?"

"Yeah. My son and I pan for gold every summer. He's eight. This year, my ex-wife decided to get married. Carla—that's her—hasn't seen Keith since she walked out. Because she's marrying again, she's exerting her rights under our shared custody agreement. Insisted I send Keith to Saint Louis for the summer, so he could meet the jerk she's marrying. I should have canceled this trip, but after two weeks of rattling around the house alone... You have any kids?" He looked at Camp. "Sorry, here I am rambling, and I didn't even catch your name."

"Nolan Campbell. And no, I don't have children. I'm

also a Ph.D. History." Leaning on the Jeep's fender, he crossed his ankles and supplied the name of his college in Columbia.

"No kidding?" Lock peppered him with questions as he tossed out old grounds and deftly assembled a new pot of coffee.

Camp answered the rapid-fire queries about his campus, a slight frown creasing his brow, furrowing deeper with each successive question.

"It really is a small world, Campbell. The night before I left Huntsville, I sent in my application for the dean of human services vacancy at your college." He sighed. "Don't get me wrong—I like what I'm doing. But with Carla making noises about seeing more of Keith, it'd behoove me to move closer to her. Not that I'd want to be in the same town. Columbia's a good compromise. So I called the college job line and learned the dean's position had just been posted."

"Um." Camp stared at his boots. "I didn't realize our dean was leaving." The position Lock had mentioned was the one currently held by Sherry's boss. Camp wondered if she knew. Wouldn't that be something, if her so-called outlaw ended up her boss? A bizarre coincidence, to say the least.

Lordy, Camp could visualize how the fur would fly. But he was jumping ahead of himself. A dean's opening meant hundreds of applicants. Maybe Lock was qualified, but it was a long shot to assume he'd get the job. "Maybe I will have that beer," Camp decided aloud.

"Sure." Lock's teeth gleamed evenly white as his lips parted in an apologetic smile. "Hope you don't mind drinking alone. After that dunking, I need something hot."

"I understand. I've frozen my buns more than once on this trek." Briefly Camp outlined the paper he was writing

and how he'd come to be out here in the wilds himself.
In the interest of self-preservation he refrained from mentioning that one of his subjects—the wild woman with the
dark hair—was his sister.

Garrett Lock disappeared into his battered tent. He
came out with a beer and two folding stools. He also
handed Camp a business card. "Whether or not I'm cho-
sen for the position, I'd like to read your published piece.
I'm kicking around doing one on displaced homemak-
ers—women reentering the workforce after years spent at
home. We're quick to hand them grants to continue their
education, but we ignore their low self-esteem and in
some cases, their lack of assertiveness. Obviously not a
problem in your group." He ruefully touched his head
again.

Camp waited while Garrett poured a mug of steaming
coffee, then he lifted his can in a toast. "To the women
of the Santa Fe Trail—then and now. You know, Lock,
my colleagues expect the women on my expedition to fail.
I admit I had my doubts at first, too. I've since changed
my opinion."

Lock didn't smile. "As a sociologist, I try to keep an
open mind. Although in my own situation, I'm afraid I'm
only human. To tell you the truth, I'm furious with my
ex. Carla's been so wrapped up in becoming a big-shot
bank officer, she neglected our son. Till now."

Camp took a swig from his beer and thought about
Emily's bad experience with her husband, and now with
her in-laws. "Speaking as someone who has feelings for
a lady with two kids—one of whom would rather her
mom got involved with a space alien than me—I'd guess
your ex is going through some rocky times, too."

"Maybe. Hey, how did we hit on this depressing subject? Tell me more about your college and Columbia."

Camp did just that. Then they touched a bit on academic philosophy. Camp enjoyed their conversation immensely. He almost hated to leave. But his beer was finished and he knew the others would worry if he didn't get back soon.

Standing, he tightened Mincemeat's cinch. "I don't have one of my cards with me, Lock. If you decide to take an unofficial look at the campus, I'm in the phone book."

"It helps just knowing there's a friendly face among the faculty if I reach the interview stage. Y'all take care on your trip. I have a shortwave radio, a ham operator out of Houston passed along information of hurricane activity. I was debating whether to head home about the time I met your...friends."

Camp's ears perked. "Hurricane? We still have to cross the North Canadian River twice and the Carizozo."

Lock whistled softly. "'Course, that doesn't mean the rains will blow inland."

"No, but thanks for the warning. We're trying to simulate what the pioneers would have gone through as closely as possible, but that doesn't mean we want to risk anyone's life." Reaching out, he clasped Lock's hand. "Good luck on the job hunt."

"Tell the wildcat she may get another crack at me." As Camp swung into the saddle, Garrett added, "I never asked if she lived in Columbia. Am I liable to run into her in a dark alley?" His face split in a purely male grin.

Camp thought briefly about his direct omission—in not mentioning Sherry's position at the college or her relationship to him. But chances were slight that a man who looked like Grizzly Adams would be offered a job by the staid board of directors at his institution. Smiling, Camp shook his head.

"That's good," Lock said, lifting two fingers in salute.

"If she crossed gloves with Evander Holyfield, my money would be on the brunette's knockout punch."

As Camp kneed his mount into the dark river, Garrett Lock faded into an opaque haze. Looking back, he thought it was as if the scene had never happened. Maybe it hadn't. Maybe he'd dreamed the entire thing. Sherry certainly wouldn't believe him if he told her the man she thought was an escaped convict actually had visions of replacing her boss—a guy who wore Italian silk ties and custom-made suits.

Once Camp left the river, the stars popped out overhead and the moon sent silvery shafts of light dancing in and out of the rain-drenched prairie grasses. Gazing at the panorama of stars, he found it difficult to imagine a storm headed this way.

At the outskirts of the row of wagons, Sherry ran to meet him. Her face was pale in the moonlight and dark circles ringed her eyes. "Where have you been? I imagined you lying out there somewhere, shot dead."

Camp climbed off the pinto. "Then you ought to be ecstatic when I tell you I saw nary a dead body nor a man with a gun."

Her hands fluttered to his sleeve. "Thank God. So I didn't kill him. Oh, Nolan, I've been so worried."

"About me or him?" he teased.

"You first...and him. Both." She swallowed several times before throwing her arms around him and planting a kiss on his cheek. "I'm sick from worry. I'm going to bed. Everyone else has. Oh, Emily saved you some hash and asked if you'd please bank her fire."

His eyes automatically swerved to the one remaining campfire. His heart had kicked over like a newly wound watch when he'd thought of Emily waiting up. Now his pulse dropped back to normal. He looped an arm around Sherry's neck and aimed a kiss at her forehead. "I have to see to my horse. Then I'll tend Emily's fire. Honestly, I'm too bushed to eat.''

"I'm sorry to have sent you on a wild-goose chase, Nolan. You can bet I'll keep up from now on.''

"Good. And I'll keep better watch. Sherry...''

"Yes?'' She turned at his serious tone.

"I know we have a tendency to argue. In case I haven't said it in a while...I do love you.''

"Are...you...all right, Nolan?''

He caught up, snagged her neck with one hand and pretended to shake her. "I'm fine. Can't a guy tell his sister he loves her once in a blue moon?''

She fidgeted. "Yeah. And same to you, Campbell. Don't let it get out, but I like knowing you'll always be there for me.'' She gave him a crooked grin. "Enough of this sentimentality. I gotta run.''

Camp's bemused expression gave way to one of exasperation as she dashed away. She'd been a difficult baby, too. And an independent teen.

"That was sweet of you,'' said a soft voice from the shadows of his wagon.

"Emily?'' His tone showed his delight at having her appear after all.

"Sherry likes everyone to see her as strong and tough. Underneath she's a marshmallow. A lot lonelier than she lets on.''

His head came up as he lifted the saddle from the gelding. "Pretty deep assessment of somebody you've known less than six weeks.''

"Camp...I...'' Emily almost told him she'd known Sherry a lot longer. That they were friends and had served on intercollegiate committees together. But Sherry didn't want him to know.

"Hey, I didn't mean to take your head off. I forgot you psychologists love to probe a man's soul.'' Grabbing a brush, he groomed the horse before leading him to a deep patch of grass and affixing his hobble.

Emily remained where he'd left her, hands linked loosely in front of her, a faint crease between her brows. "We were talking about women. I'd never presume to second-guess men. God knows I made a royal mess of that once."

"Don't be so hard on yourself. I really didn't mean to snap. I'm tired. It's been a long day."

"I know." She sighed. "When we got back home, Brittany carried on for an hour. I'm glad you didn't find anything."

"Nothing of consequence." He suppressed a shiver of guilt at the lie, but decided he really couldn't tell her about Garrett Lock—and risk Sherry finding out. He glanced up at the sky. "Did Maizie mention the possibility of another storm?"

Emily followed his gaze. She grabbed the lapels of her jacket and pulled it a little tighter. "The wind's picked up, and it's gotten colder. But no, she didn't say anything. At least not to me. Come sit by the fire. You must be hungry as well as tired. I saved a plate of hash."

He stopped her with a hand at her elbow. When she turned, he curved a palm around her cheek. "Thanks for looking out for me, Emily. I've wanted a chance to talk. About us."

Her lips turned down and sadness darkened her eyes. "There can't be any us, Camp. Megan may seem all mouth and bluster to you, but this thing with Mona and Toby really shook her. I can't do anything that'll threaten the little security she has."

"You're entitled to a life, Emily."

"I have a life. I have my home, my children, my work."

He felt her tremble at his touch. "Is that enough, Em?

What about five years down the road when your nest is empty and your job becomes routine?''

"In five years Mark will still be in high school. I'll grow with my job," she said desperately.

"I'm sure you will. I won't argue with you, Emily. It's not my aim to make your life more difficult. Say, where's that food you promised a starving man?"

She took a deep breath and let it struggle out in a thin laugh. "Don't be so damned accommodating, Campbell. A woman likes to have the illusion that she's worth fighting for. And you know perfectly well where I cook the food."

She would have whirled and marched off toward the flickering fire, but he snatched her hand. "Who do you want me to fight? Megan? Your in-laws? I intend to talk with Megan. And I won't say it hasn't entered my mind to steal you away. All of you."

Another sigh trickled through her lips. "I said it before and I'll say it again—you're a dear, sweet man, Nolan Campbell. But talking to Meggie is like batting your head against a stone wall. Stealing me away is a nice fantasy, but I learned a long time ago that you can't run from your obligations. You're good for my ego, though. I was feeling quite sorry for myself."

"That's the last thing you should do, Emily. Will you stay while I eat? I hate to ask—I'm sure you're beat, too. You did more than your share today, helping dig Gina's wagon out of the mud, and then, riding out with me to find Sherry and Brittany."

"I'm a night owl. It doesn't seem to matter how early I get up, sleep doesn't come easily."

"Something else we have in common, insomnia. Except, when I do drop off, I could sleep till noon. You're up with the roosters. Before the roosters," he corrected.

"Holdover from growing up on a farm. We had to *feed* the roosters."

"And milk the cows and walk nine miles to school in the snow." Mouth quirked in a teasing smile, Camp leaned close to the pot, sniffing the hash as he dished it up. He was grateful that because of Terrill's strategic visits they had more plentiful and more varied meals than had been available to the pioneers. "This smells great. I didn't realize I was so hungry." Taking the fork Emily handed him, he sat back and dug in.

"You know, Camp, I didn't mind life on the farm, although we worked constantly. Oh, I grumbled at the time, I'm sure. All kids faced with chores do. But this trip reinforces the basic values I learned."

Fork halfway to his mouth, Camp stopped to stare at the woman curled comfortably in the lawn chair. Her eyes sparkled like the stars; her cheeks glowed with good health. Suddenly he imagined her puttering around his big old country kitchen. Imagined her capable hands planting flowers, and maybe a garden. He saw Mark chasing down to the stream, fishing pole in hand, followed by Pilgrim, his golden lab. Megan...didn't quite fit. Her image was fuzzy, not clear like the others. He shook his head and quickly took another bite.

"Is something wrong?" Emily shifted in her chair and placed a hand on his arm. "Did the hash dry out? I can scramble some eggs."

"It's not the food. Would you like to live in the country again, Emily?"

She stiffened, then lifted one shoulder slightly. "I haven't thought about it. I've thought of running away to a desert island, or to a remote cabin in the mountains. But I learned from my dad, who farmed and dealt with the fickleness of the elements all his life, that you have to face trouble head-on. He always said you could leave your problems behind but not your conscience. In my case, they amount to the same thing."

"I assume you mean you've dreamed of escaping, of leaving behind your husband's debts—and your in-laws."

"That's all it is—a dream. In today's world it's impossible for an honest person to simply disappear."

"But what if someone paid your in-laws every last cent you owe?"

Face wreathed in smiles, eyes dancing, she said, "That mythical white knight on a fire-breathing steed? I know he doesn't exist."

Camp brooded a moment, trying to fit himself into that armor she teased about. He hadn't tapped the trust fund his grandparents had set up. His folks and Sherry thought he should use some of it to hire a construction crew to finish his house. He'd much preferred doing the work himself. Now...

Emily rose, stretched like a contented cat and took the empty plate from Camp's nerveless hands. "Talk about a tough day. You look positively catatonic. Nice as it is to sit and solve the problems of the world, I suggest we call it a night."

Studying her bright hair and slender back as she efficiently set the pots and bowls to soak, Camp realized she didn't have a clue as to the thoughts running through his head. And because she didn't, he decided to bide his time. No sense jumping the gun, scaring her off. He had several weeks left on this trip. Time to talk Megan around. Time to let all the pieces click in his own mind. Although his arms ached to hold Emily close through the chilly night, he settled for an unsatisfying hug and a friendly good-night kiss.

Emily watched him put out the fire, wondering how even the simplest kiss from him ignited such a blaze inside her. She wrapped those feelings close as he escorted her to the back of her wagon. And thanked him politely when he offered her a hand up. But she sat in the darkness for a long while, listening to her daughter's even breathing, fancying she'd just left that knight on the fire-breathing steed.

Ah, but she was a fool. If Nolan Campbell hadn't found a damsel in distress to rescue in his thirty-eight years, he wasn't likely to start with a widow who had two kids and more than her share of troubles.

"Not even the toughest men who sought to tame the West messed with Mother Nature."
— *Awakened by a storm, Camp recalled this relevant tidbit from one of his lectures.*

CHAPTER TWELVE

WIND, blowing things around outside, jolted Camp into wakefulness. He'd sat up long after parting from Emily, integrating Sherry's account of her meeting with Professor Lock into his notes. Sherry skirted certain facts on her data sheet. Brittany's diatribe would make a movie. And then there was his own encounter with the man....

Yawning, he climbed from his sleeping bag, immediately registering a severe drop in temperature. Now he knew why Maizie had insisted they stock up on long underwear. His were still in plastic bags. "Brr!" He rubbed his pebbled flesh. Once he had the long johns out and on his body, he applauded Maizie's foresight.

Outside in the biting wind, Camp grabbed for things such as coffeepots and aluminum lawn chairs that whizzed along the ground. When the wake-up call sounded, he'd collected quite a few, including two webbed chairs belonging to Maizie, whose wagon sat the length of a football field away.

"Thanks, sonny," she panted, running up. "Glad you're up and around early. Don't know if we're in for a major blow, or if this is a lagging tail from yesterday's storm."

"I heard rumors of a gulf hurricane," he said.

"Don't like the sounds of that. Nosirree!"

"Should we batten down the hatches and stay put?"

Maizie's faded eyes probed the blustery sky that had begun to lighten. "We're sittin' geese here. If we leave soon, with any luck we can make Round Mound or Rabbit Ears before she really cuts loose."

No sooner had she spoken than Robert hurried toward them, resembling a bear in his leather hat with ear flaps and his heavy, plaid mackinaw. "Putrid-looking clouds to the southeast. What's your take on them? Are we headed into trouble?"

Maizie unwrapped a square of bubble gum. "Campbell heard there's a hurricane in the Texas gulf. I figure we got seven, eight hours of drivin' before we know whether she dies on the vine or not. You two tell everybody we're rollin'."

Roll out they did after sorting through the tangle of property. They made short work of necessary chores, and no one mentioned breakfast. Even the horses sniffed the wind and laid back their ears. As usual, the Clydesdales took things in stride. The Belgians and Percherons frisked around, edgy as spring colts.

Camp stopped Mark before he pulled out. "Seems we'll be bucking a stiff head wind, son. Fall in behind Robert. Let his wagon block the wind."

"What about Sherry and the teachers? And Mom's driving four Belgians."

"I know." Camp rested a hand on Mark's arm. "They're all good drivers. Jared's a backup if anyone needs a break. Our first scheduled stop is McNees Crossing. We'll touch base then."

"Okay. And Camp, thanks for not making me turn this

wagon over to Jared now. I know he's older and has more experience.''

"You're doing fine, Mark. Just remember, a real man recognizes his limitations. He's not afraid to ask for help.''

The boy bobbed his head. "I understand. You never preach like Toby. When you say stuff, I understand what you mean. I wish you were my dad, Camp.''

Hunched inside his jacket, Camp massaged the back of his neck. "I'll keep that in mind.'' As he stood dumbly watching Mark guide his team into line, Gina Ames poked her head through the back canvas.

"If it matters, Campbell, you get my vote, too. The way Sherry talked before the trip, I figured you for a real chauvinist. Always nice to be pleasantly surprised.'' Disappearing again, she tied the canvas closed.

Stunned, Camp moved toward his wagon. What did Gina mean? It sounded as if she and Sherry had been in contact prior to the trip.

"Camp? Is something wrong?'' Emily slowed her wagon.

"Nothing.'' He strode to her side and covered one of her gloved hands with his own. "Are you wearing long underwear?'' All the trekkers but Emily looked as if they'd gained five pounds overnight. Camp didn't want her suffering if she'd forgotten.

"What a thing to ask.'' Her husky laugh volleyed on the wind. "Mine are silk,'' she said, smoothing a hand along her thigh. "Not as bulky as cotton, and warmer.''

"Pu...leeze, Mother!'' Megan stuck a tousled head out into the blustery wind. Just as fast, she withdrew it. "If I told a guy what underwear I had on, you'd have a cow.''

Emily blushed furiously and slipped a neck scarf she had hidden beneath her jacket up over her ears. She slapped her reins repeatedly and the wagon lumbered off.

Several heartbeats skittered by before Camp blocked out the vision of *his* hand sliding over Emily's slender thigh. Giving himself a firm shake, he followed her lead. As if his team sensed something in the air, they lunged against their traces.

Mile after brutal mile, the wind clawed at the drivers' clothing. Less than two hours on the road, the canvas ripped loose from one side of the teachers' wagon. Sacks, papers and clothing blew out and fell with a thud or danced across the prairie. The entire train stopped. Mark and Jared ran to corral the flapping, ghostly apparitions before they spooked more horses. The heavy canvas bucked and leaped constantly as Camp and Robert fought to tie it down.

Emily and Sherry parked, joining the chase for free-floating debris. They returned with the booty, breathless, faces red and chapped.

"Whew!" Emily rewrapped her neck scarf. "Now I know why pioneer women looked old before their time. This wind is murder!"

Sherry pulled out a tube of lip balm. "I'm sure this is cheating," she said, aiming a grimace at her brother. "But I never agreed to end this trip looking like a crocodile."

He turned up his sheepskin-lined collar. "I don't recall asking you to."

"You said women couldn't give up creature comforts for the time it'd take to go from Missouri to Santa Fe."

"Lyle said that." Camp stripped off one glove. "If you share that stuff, I promise this weak moment will never find its way into my sordid tale."

"Go ahead, tell the world I'm a wuss." Sherry slugged him on the arm before she handed over the tube.

"Ouch." He rubbed the spot. "Hit some poor devil in the head with a slab of cordwood, and now you beat up

on me. Maybe I should warn the world about this strea
of violence in Sherilyn Campbell.''

She two-stepped around him, thumbing her nose as if
ready to box. ''Yesterday was self-defense.'' Pausing, she
eyed Camp and Emily, who laughed openly at her antics.
''You two look so...so outdoorsy. Like you enjoy this
misery.''

Camp rested his forehead against Emily's. They both
grinned foolishly.

''See what I mean?'' Sherry groaned. ''There you go
again. What's with you two? Anybody would think
you're...involved or something.''

Camp hurriedly smeared balm on his lips.

Emily hunched against the wind. 'I don't like storms.
But...I feel alive out here. Free. You know how tense
I've been, Sherry.''

Capping the balm, Camp flicked a puzzled glance between the women. ''That gives the impression that you
two go back a ways.''

''Oh.'' Emily covered her lips. Why had she promised
Sherry that she'd hide their friendship from her brother?

''Didn't you think Emily seemed tense the first time
you met her?'' Sherry asked breezily.

Her reply was too cavalier to suit Camp. He'd wondered before if Sherry and Emily had met through work.
Perhaps they thought it'd skew his results. Or his percep-
tions. He'd have to consider whether it would.

Camp was glad that Maizie cupped her hands and gave
her famous ''Roll 'em'' yell just then. He wanted some
time to mull over how Emily's comment fitted with
Gina's earlier statement. Or even *if* it did. It stood to reason that Sherry and Emily might have met at a conference,
but how would either of them have known Gina?

What bothered him most was the fact that they'd—
probably—lied. In some sort of conspiracy, yet, orches-

ated—probably—by his loving sister. However, he
didn't have time to worry about any of this now.

"See you at McNees Crossing," he said, giving each
woman a brisk nod. "Can't say I like the color of that
sky."

"Maybe it's the sun trying to break through the
clouds," Emily murmured.

"Maybe." Camp didn't tell her that the only other time
he'd seen a sky like that, a twister had demolished his
uncle's new brick house while the entire family huddled
next door in the garage. Camp had been twelve, Sherry
just a child. They'd gathered for a Campbell reunion and
had steaks barbecuing on the outdoor grill, he recalled,
when his mother noticed the muddy yellow sky. The
group barely had time to seek refuge before a funnel cloud
appeared out of nowhere. He'd never forget the wreckage.

Camp wished he'd made time for a word with Maizie
about that sky. But he didn't want to pull out of line and
leave Emily unprotected.

Everyone was jittery, miserable and starved by the time
Maizie called a short break at McNees Crossing. They sat
on a wind-buffeted promontory looking down on the
North Canadian River, now a mass of boiling whitecaps
and deep whirlpools.

"Get these wagons across to the other side and keep
moving," their leader ordered. "If you've got something
to nibble on, do. We're not stopping."

"It's inhumane to drive us like donkeys," Philly
shouted. "We need rest and food. We ought to rebel."

Maizie blew a giant pink bubble. The wind popped it.
"Fine. Go ahead and stay. Prove you're a jackass. If
you'd ever had the pleasure of butting heads with a
twister, Philadelphia, you'd be shakin' your bootie. I sure
don't fancy being caught on this plateau."

"Twister?" Harv spit. "Those clouds are miles away.

You're bluffing. Running us to death because we lost time on account of those brats.''

"Uh-huh! It's your pee...rogative to believe what you will. Ford this river one wagon at a time. Robert, you first. Stay east of that scrawny patch of rabbitbrush, and try not to drift downstream. Mark, can you make it on your own?''

Mark huddled in his fleecy jacket. His freckles stood out rust-colored against a pasty face. "I'm pretty tired. If Jared doesn't need to help my mom or Sherry, I'll ask him to drive a stretch for me.''

In her aviator's cap that buckled firmly under the chin and a down coat pulled on over her fringed leather jacket, Maizie looked like an unhappy troll. "Emily and Sherry, listen up. I want one person per set of reins. Emily, you're the experienced driver so you take the downriver side, giving Megan the up. Sherry and Brit, do the same. Doris, you and Vi decide which of you has the most power. Jared, give Mark a hand.''

Camp looked at the grim faces of the people Maizie had singled out. Megan seemed close to hyperventilating. Brittany's face was a frozen mask.

Robert drove in close to his mother. "What if Camp and I tie the saddle horses to our wagons, cross, then swim them back to drive the women's wagons over?''

Her eyes turned flinty. "Extra time we don't have, Robby.''

"You're the boss,'' Camp grunted, still disturbed by the bruised-looking sky.

"Glad somebody recognizes that fact.'' Maizie glowered at Harv Shaw. "Here's the plan. Robert leads, followed by Emily and Megan. Then you, Camp. Sherry and Brittany next. Jared and Mark. Doris and Vi, then Harv. I'll ford last, pushing spare stock ahead of me. Hop to it,'' she yelled.

Robert made it across without incident. Emily's lead horse stumbled and went to his knees.

Behind and upstream too far, Camp felt powerless to render aid. He continued on, teeth clenched, feeling Emily's struggle to help her horse. Camp's facial muscles didn't relax until the front wheels of Em's wagon found purchase in the shallows. He ran to her, shouting, "Good job!" Megan literally fell into his arms. Surprised, Camp offered comfort. The minute she realized what she'd done, she shoved him aside.

Midpoint in the raging river, Sherry battled her own demons. Brittany stared at the water as if entranced. The lead horse on her side reared, ripping the reins from her limp grasp. Snaking leather confused the team. They panicked, then stopped. No amount of coaxing on Sherry's part could set the animals in motion.

Robert grabbed a rope and ran along the crumbling bank. Slick as any cowboy, he twirled a noose and dropped it neatly over the balky Percheron's head. Between Robert and Camp, who threw his weight into the rope, they forced the team ashore.

Sherry wanted to throttle Brittany. But then the younger woman fell apart, and Sherry felt bad. "It's all right, Brit. We made it okay. Don't cry."

Though shaken by Sherry's experience, the others crossed safely.

"I know you're all right proud of yourselves," shouted Maizie, her words torn from her by the wind. "That storm is moving faster than we are. Save your attaboys and girls till we're in the cradle of Rabbit Ears. Twixt here and there is open prairie. Line up four abreast. I'll bring up the rear again. Anyone spots a funnel, yell like crazy. Everybody up on the seats, ready to jump and roll under the wagons if need be."

"What about me?" Gina tapped her splint and her cast.

"I'll help you," Mark said staunchly. "I won't leav
you. That's part of what you're paying me for."

Emily's pride in Mark's mature response was replaced
by distress as Megan began to weep. She dragged her
daughter closer, taking her own comfort from the warm
hand Camp pressed to her shoulder.

Harv Shaw hitched his pseudo-western belt buckle
higher on his paunch and swaggered over to Maizie.
"Your brochure didn't mention tornadoes."

"Sorry, they're hard to order for every trip," she
drawled sarcastically.

His bulbous nose flared. "This isn't funny."

"Damn tootin' it's not. My neck's on the line, too. So
quit palavering and hit the road. The sooner we find cover,
the better."

"Why did you let all these women and kids come?
They'll slow us down."

"Shut up." Camp stalked around Emily and grabbed
Harv by his jacket front. "These women aren't pitching
half the fit you are. They're doing their jobs! And to top
it off, they aren't your concern."

Emily applauded, slow and loud. Sherry and Gina
joined in.

Philly brushed Camp's hands aside. He stomped off,
muttering darkly. "Far as I'm concerned, it's every man
for himself. Don't expect me to baby any damn-fool
women. Me and the missus are taking off. Catch us if you
can."

"Hold on a dang minute." Maizie chased him. He
scrambled onto the high seat, cracked his reins and
bounced his wagon off across the open plains.

Maizie spit her wad of gum in his wake. For once Camp
wished it'd been a stream of tobacco.

"Want me to catch the jerk and shake some manners
into him?" Camp asked.

"Nah. Let him go. There's one on every trip. He's been obnoxious a heap o' years. We aren't likely to change him."

Camp noticed how the women, including Brittany and Megan, suddenly sobered, their fear replaced by grit and determination. He was both humbled and proud, and wished Lyle Roberts could see this display of courage. Modern women might enjoy modern comforts, but these ladies had guts with a capital G. As they moved forward, Camp raised a closed fist to the advancing storm and issued a rebel yell.

With Philly far out in front, the others filtered into two lines. All twenty-eight horses strained against their harnesses. Yet they were driving into such heavy, gusty winds, there were times it felt as if they were standing still.

Except for wild cotton and an occasional tuft of primrose, the grasses had been beaten down by the rain. Before the travelers often saw silos or farms in the distance; now they might have been the only humans on the planet. They had all bent to shield their faces from the harsh wind, so no one realized the Shaws' wagon had hit a scrub manzanita and blown a rear balloon tire. Not until the first row of wagons practically ran the Shaws down.

"The rest of you keep truckin'," Maizie yelled over the wind's howl. "Robert and I will change that tire. I've got a couple spares in my wagon."

"I'll help, too," Camp shouted.

Maizie waved him on. "You stay with the women. I've seen at least two funnel clouds pass behind us. See? Directly south is Rabbit Ears."

Peering through red-rimmed eyes, Camp saw the protruding rocks still some distance away. Nodding, he motioned for the others to keep moving. He didn't like the thought of leaving anyone behind.

Emily's Belgians arched their thick necks and heav
forward. Sherry's team fought their bits, circled an.
nearly ripped the traces out of her hands.

Camp pulled alongside. "Let's trade wagons, sis. We
can't risk getting stuck out here."

"No. I'll show them who's boss." Muscles bunched,
Sherry forced the cantankerous animals into line.

"Maizie said there's a cut between that rounded rock
and the flat-topped hill that forms the ears. Head there.
Unhitch the teams," he bellowed. "The horses will do
better unencumbered. We'll take shelter in the rocks."

Each driver flashed him the thumbs-up sign.

The closer they got to the rock formation, the more
wicked the lightning. Hail rained down in large white pel-
lets. Thunder hammered. Peal after peal blended with the
pounding gallop of the horses' hooves.

Off to his left, Camp saw a twister unfold. It hovered
five or so feet above the ground. For a minute it seemed
to chase Mark's wagon. Just as quickly, it veered off and
whistled across the open prairie. Camp swallowed a lump
lodged in his throat. Sweat popped out on his forehead
despite a sharp drop in temperature. Still he urged his
team faster. His shoulders ached from the pull of the lath-
ered horses. He honestly didn't know how the women
managed with their lesser strength. But they did.

At last Mark's lead wagon entered the dark crevasse
snaking into the only shelter for miles around. Camp
breathed a little easier after Emily reached it, too. Doris's
team disappeared next. Sherry's wagon made the turn seconds before Camp's own. There was no time for congratulations. No sooner had they all freed their teams than
there arose a fiendish howl accompanied by thick, churning black clouds.

Stunned, the bedraggled group watched small trees being sucked into a gyrating funnel tearing along the pass.

d dirt swirled as angry black clouds swallowed light-
ng bolts and put on a laser show. Rumbling, tumbling
oward them, it ate the earth like some greedy late-show
monster.

Camp screamed for everyone to take cover. No one
moved. Instead, they all seemed paralyzed, staring in horror. Except for Emily. She shoved those closest to her flat
to the ground. Once she'd helped Sherry and Brittany,
Emily ran to assist Gina down from the wagon.

Adrenaline pumping, Camp tore up the rocky trail. He
flung Doris, then Vi, into a rocky hollow. With seconds
to spare, he used his own body to shield Mark, Jared and
Megan. Over the noise, he heard a horse scream in fright,
but dared not raise his head as thick, humid air whistled
above him like a banshee.

A saddle horse, tied to the back of Camp's wagon,
broke his rope and bolted. At least two of the freed teams
galloped wildly back the way they'd come. The most
Camp could do was pray he hadn't led his party into a
death trap. And what about Emily? Had she reached
cover? Last he saw, she was attempting to help Gina.

It seemed that he clung to the sharp rocks forever, listening as the cries of his fellow travelers competed with
the ear-splitting shriek of the funnel. In reality, the hide-
ous experience lasted less than twenty seconds. Even after
silence descended, it took time for them to untangle their
limbs and stop shaking enough to assess the damage.

"It tore the water barrel off the side of my wagon,"
Gina reported, hobbling along the rutted, cratered ground
the microburst had left in its wake.

"We lost the front third of our canvas," Vi relayed
anxiously. "Our team looks dazed, but intact," Doris
added.

Drained of energy and color, Emily clamped a shaky
arm around each of her children. "What's important is

that we all came through unscathed. Has the da
passed enough for one of us to ride out and see
Robert and Maizie are doing?" she asked Camp.

"I'll go see in a minute," he said, giving in to a de
perate need to touch her hair. "We need to round up a
the horses before they break a leg in potholes left by the
twister."

"I'll help." Mark pulled from Emily's grasp.

Seeing the concern cross her already pinched features,
Camp turned the boy down. "You and Jared start a fire
so we can dry things out. Seems the sky is clearing to the
south, but we're not necessarily out of danger. I'm assuming, after all that's happened, Maizie'll decide to dig in
here for the night."

"You can't handle bringing in all the runaways by
yourself, Camp," Emily said quietly. "Once the boys get
a fire started, Doris and Vi can break out packets of soup.
I'll go with you after the horses if you like."

He did like. The thought of the two of them sharing
the one remaining saddle horse—no matter how
briefly—appealed immensely to Camp. It took only moments to capture the surefooted gelding he'd snubbed to
Mark's wagon earlier. He boosted Emily onto the broad,
bare back, then swung up behind her, asking Sherry to
hobble and feed the horses that had begun to mill about.

"Do you suppose everyone who got caught out in the
open is all right?" Emily asked worriedly the minute they
cleared the outcrop of rocks.

"Yes. See?" Camp directed her gaze. "They're driving
in now. Looks like all are accounted for." He felt a sigh
of relief whisper through Emily's frame.

"Thank goodness. I had visions of us having to try to
bury someone on the trail the way the early pioneers did.
We may be more technically advanced, but when it comes
to the elements we're still at their mercy."

Ve certainly are." He laced both arms around her
der waist. "I'm ready for this trip to end, Em. What
omething bad had happened to you or the kids? Or to
.yone I talked into coming?"

"You didn't talk us into anything. We volunteered."

"Why did you? You'd have made a lot more money
teaching summer school."

"The truth, Camp," Emily blurted out, "is that Sherry
twisted my arm and Gina's. I'd told Sherry I wanted to
spirit the kids away from my in-laws. And Sherry met
Gina when Gina attended her program after a rough divorce. It was your sister who convinced her to backpack
in the Sierras. Sherry's counting on us to prove that
women are tough. The joke's on us. Stacked up against
Mother Nature, we aren't tough at all."

"I'll be damned. So Sherry did load the scales. I never
would've believed she'd be that devious. Or that you'd
all go along with a lie."

"I wouldn't call it devious...exactly. And we didn't lie
on our applications. You weren't exactly playing fair, either, Camp. To be totally unbiased you should have
booked an equal number of men. Randomly selected, of
course."

"Of course," he said, sounding irked. "There's one of
our runaway teams. Do you want to walk them back to
the cut, or should I?"

Emily started to slide off the gelding. Pausing, she
turned and gazed into Camp's eyes. "Sherry did me a
favor. I'd never have met you otherwise."

Camp felt the tension leave his body. Swinging down,
he took Emily in his arms and kissed her tenderly. "I
have a distinct feeling Sherry isn't nearly as pleased about
that as we are. If you want the whole truth, I can't be too
mad at her, either."

Emily leaned an ear against his chest and listened to

his reassuring heartbeat. "She probably considers ⸱ traitor. Then there's Megan. If looks could kill we'd ⸱ be dead. What are we going to do, Camp?"

He rubbed his hands over Emily's back. "I'll talk Megan, Em. She's part grown-up, part child. I'll find time when she's not hanging out with Brittany. Maybe tonight."

Emily gazed at him somberly. "My kids have been through so much turmoil. How can I put them through more?"

He drew her up on her toes and covered her mouth fiercely. He would find time to talk with Megan, he vowed, releasing Emily's limp form to stride away.

BUT THE TIME didn't present itself. There was too much work to be done to repair the damage. Relations within the group as a whole were strained, even though preparations for a celebratory dinner were under way by the time Camp brought in the last strayed horse. Dinner for all but the couple from Philadelphia, Camp noticed.

Emily baked the last of her cake mixes. Vi contributed the honey-almond topping. Gina broke out a special blend of coffee she'd been hoarding.

Philly and his wife were very pointedly excluded from the festivities.

"Let's not be petty," Camp said, wanting to ease the rift. "We should all be thankful to be alive." When it became clear that his efforts at mediation had failed, he excused himself to go work on his report. But the words he needed to describe the day wouldn't come. He fell asleep staring moodily into his flickering lantern.

Emily stayed up after the others had said good-night. Memory of the twister remained too real for her to sleep.

Camp's light still glowed. She wondered if he, too, worried about another storm. Tiptoeing to the back of his

n, she parted the wet canvas. "Camp?" she whis-
d. He didn't stir. Emily realized he'd fallen asleep
n his lantern burning. Afraid that might be dangerous,
e climbed over the feed trough and crept toward the
ght.

She'd lowered the flame when Camp suddenly bolted
upright, tumbling her headfirst into his supplies. A small
scuffle ended as he emerged from his stupor and felt her
curves crushed beneath him.

"Emily?" He blinked sleepy eyes, carefully scanning
her damp hair and pale face. With a shaking hand, he
smoothed his fingers down her cheek. "It's really you.
You were just in my dream."

"A nightmare, you mean?" Her eyes crinkled at the
corners. "I missed your help with the dishes. Everyone
else always disappears after eating."

He kissed her softly. "Why didn't you wake me
sooner?" he murmured, nibbling at her neck.

"Camp, it's late. I should go back to my wagon."

"Why?" He nuzzled her ear, drawing in the scent of
her perfume. "You smell like raindrops and jasmine.
Mmm, my favorite scents."

"What I smell like is horse," she murmured.

Kissing her arched brow, he eased her out of her jacket,
tossed it aside and covered her with a portion of his down
sleeping bag. He pulled her against his chest. "You scared
me today. What if I'd lost you?" He rubbed his chin over
her bright hair.

Sighing, she stretched like a cat. "Don't make me too
comfortable. I can't stay."

"Really?" He divested her of her plaid shirt, hesitating
when he ran into the silk of her long johns.
"Darn...getting you out of these is going to take some
fancy contortions." While she pulled the top over her

head, Camp let his lips skim the flesh she uncovered, bit by bit.

As the offending article dropped away, Emily brushed her fingers through a lock of his dark hair that had fallen rakishly over his forehead. Suddenly she was struck by a blinding need to feel the naked chest that rose and fell beneath his waffled underwear. Hands unsteady, she worked the hem of his shirt out of his jeans and smoothed her palms over the rough thatch of hair beneath. Heat built within her. Places that obviously still had life. Her urgent reasons for leaving his wagon dimmed as her limbs grew both liquid and weighted. She hadn't felt like this in so long. Too long, she thought, moaning with pleasure.

Camp wasn't a man to make love lightly. By the time their combined breathing had grown ragged and begun to steam the lantern's glass, the thundering of their hearts told him exactly where such explorations would end.

Emily's appearance in his wagon was a gift. A gift he wanted to unwrap slowly and savor to the fullest. "Are you sure?" he breathed against her ear as her questing fingers succeeded in opening the top button of his jeans. "Because if you're not, you have two seconds to say no."

Nothing had ever felt more right to Emily. But they hadn't discussed the important things lovers were supposed to discuss in this day and age. The evidence of his arousal, pressed close to where she was wet and ready to receive him, threatened to make Emily ignore all the facts she preached to her students.

In the nick of time, his question stirred her guilt. "I'm...not...on anything, Camp. I'm sorry." She started to roll away, her body shaking with need and regret.

He tugged her back. "Don't apologize," he murmured, his kisses greedy and desperate. "I should be the one. I wanted this...hoped for it. I...I bought something that day in Dodge." Behind her, he fumbled for a sack. He ripped open the box inside and scattered half the packets, and then, in a fever, they managed to shed jeans, as well as the remaining long underwear, and tear apart one slick packet to sheathe him.

They made slow, delicious love. Giving, taking. Murmuring words of love.

Afterward, Emily lay curled contentedly in Camp's sheltering arms. They talked in fits and spurts and made elaborate plans for their future well into the rainy night.

Twice Emily said she needed to dress and go back to her wagon. Both times Camp wrapped her tighter and kissed her until she snuggled against him and agreed to stay a little longer. Together they laughed over how the wind rocked the wagon like a cradle, never guessing it would lull them to sleep.

"MO...TH...ER!"

Emily woke abruptly to a drizzly gray dawn and Megan's frantic shout. In a panic, Emily frantically collected the clothes that lay strewn around Camp's wagon bed. Her cold silk underwear refused to slide onto chilled flesh.

Not sharing her sense of urgency, Camp leaned over and kissed the creamy base of her spine. "Come back to bed," he mumbled.

She shook him off. "Are you crazy?" she hissed, yanking on panties and jeans. "What will Megan think? I've never spent the night with a man."

Camp's lips curved as he sat up and filtered his fingers through her sleep-tangled hair. "Kids are probably more accepting of sex than we are, Em."

Because he'd begun to hunt for his own clothes, he didn't realize that she stiffened when he used the word *sex* to describe what they'd shared last night.

Camp dressed hurriedly and vaulted out of the wagon first. He raised both arms to help her down just as Megan, accompanied by Brittany and Sherry, slopped through the puddles between the two wagons. Megan skidded to a stop. The others piled into her.

Color drained from the girl's face. "I didn't know where you were!" Disgust replaced the fear in her eyes. "You slept with him. How could you?" Covering her face, she ran blindly through the rain.

Camp shielded Emily as best he could. He expected Sherry's support and was disturbed to hear her side with Megan.

Clutching Brittany's arm, Sherry stared at her brother and her friend in confusion. "Find Megan," she urged Brittany. "Tell her she can bunk with us for the time being."

"Yeah," Brittany said stoutly. "This is totally gross. And I'm never going to take another of Nolan's stupid classes."

"That's a relief," Camp murmured to Emily. "I guess that means she's over her crush." When Emily didn't respond, he bent for a closer look at her face.

She tried to wrap her jacket tighter and wad up her wrinkled long johns. Her eyes looked dead. "Oh, see the mess I've made of things!" she cried. "I've played right into Mona's and Toby's hands."

Camp attempted to enfold her again. To his surprise, she shook him off. "I'm not blaming you, Camp. Last night was as much my fault as yours. But I have to consider what to do now. Please, just leave me alone."

Numbed, he watched her splash through muddy bogs to her own wagon.

Last night, they'd talked about seeing each other after the trip. They'd made firm promises, or so he'd thought. Now, in just a few words, Emily had reduced the special experience they'd shared to a one-night stand, and Camp didn't like it. He didn't like it at all.

"Women would have been quicker to go West if it wasn't for the rat-finky men who led the expeditions."
—*Brittany wrote this in block letters across her data sheet, leaving the rest blank.*

CHAPTER THIRTEEN

AS THE MORNING SKY lightened, a brisk southerly wind blew the rain clouds away. A beautiful double rainbow arched high over Rabbit Ears, promising hope for a better day. Few noticed. They were too busy choosing sides in the latest skirmish.

Camp wallowed in a black mood, but at least he'd built a fire and fixed coffee. Emily didn't even do that. She was hiding, as if they'd done something wrong. That was ridiculous, he fumed. They were adults. Unattached, responsible adults.

In the course of sipping coffee and grumping, Camp noticed a lone rider canter in. Not Sherry's gold-panning professor. A stranger. Maizie's problem, not his. Rising, Camp tossed the last dregs from his cup and hauled out his shaving gear.

Emily crawled from her wagon just as he propped his mirror on his feed trough. She immediately ducked back out of sight.

"Wait!" Camp slung the towel over his shoulder and lunged for her. He grasped her wrist. "Emily, this is crazy. I love you! But it's as if you're willing to throw away everything that's happened between us.''

Her throat worked convulsively for several seconds before any words came. "Love? You can't. I...can't. Oh, Camp.'' Tears glistened in her blue eyes.

His fingers tightened. "*We* can. Together. You're not fighting alone anymore.'' Releasing her, he cupped her chin.

Her lower lip trembled. "Don't do this, Camp. Don't make me choose between you and Megan. I stayed in a bad marriage for years because I couldn't...wouldn't forsake my kids. I won't do it n—''

"Hush.'' He brushed his fingers over her lips to silence what he didn't want to hear. "How could you even think I'd ask you to? You and the kids are a package, Emily. We'll work things out. Have faith.''

Sherry and Megan rounded the wagon. Megan's mutinous expression forced Camp to drop his hands. The two skirted Emily as if she had some communicable disease. Their actions made Camp furious.

"Megan's gathering some of her things,'' Sherry said stiffly.

Emily hopped down and walked away.

Camp stood his ground, facing his sister once Megan had climbed into the wagon. "I'm serious about Emily. I want to marry her, Sherry.''

"Marry...?'' He watched the reactions flitting across Sherry's face. Shock and bewilderment. Camp waited, expecting congratulations to follow. He waited to no avail. Megan handed an overflowing duffel and a cosmetic case out to Sherry. Then, as if he hadn't spoken, the two brushed past him and disappeared.

So...he and Harv Shaw were to be tarred with the same brush. Social outcasts. Camp steamed all the while he shaved. But...hadn't he read in pioneer journals that women united behind one of their own whom they felt was being mistreated? And men were blackballed for being too familiar. But that was then, not now, dammit! He hadn't mistreated Emily, and his intentions were honorable. In fact, if they'd had more time to talk, he'd planned to discuss paying her debts to free her from Toby and Mona.

"You're sure looking sour today, boy. What's got your tail in a crack?" Maizie sauntered up behind him.

Startled, Camp felt his hand slip. The razor nicked his chin. "Ouch!" He dabbed at the blood. "Do you mind honking or something? Scare a guy out of ten years' growth, why don't you?"

"Sorry. You look full-growed to me." She slapped him hard enough on the shoulder to splatter shaving cream down the front of his clean shirt.

He scowled harder. "You're in fine mettle. Is that why we're dinking around here giving the flies and mosquitoes a field day? Shouldn't we hit the road?"

"I figured after the day we put in yesterday, we all deserved to sleep late. I can see an extra hour's shut-eye didn't improve *your* disposition. I thought you'd be walkin' on air after the helluva job you did herdin' people to safety. I hope you gave yourself credit for heroism in that essay you were workin' on last night. Burned the midnight oil, didn't you?"

Memory of how he'd spent the long night slammed through Camp. "Uh, thanks for the praise, but the piece I'm writing isn't about me. It's about the women. And they deserve most of the credit for the way they handled themselves."

"Yeah. Share the glory—that's fine. Hey, I really came for a different reason. From here to Ute Creek we're on private farmland. The owner sent a rider with an invitation to join 'em this afternoon for a barbecue. Palmer declared a holiday in our honor."

"How'd he know we were here?"

"He had a plane up at first light checking crop dama. The pilot relayed how close we'd come to the path of t. tornado. I know Palmer. He's probably majorly gratefu that he didn't have to deal with our dead bodies strewn over his new-plowed ground." She guffawed heartily.

Camp couldn't resist a grin. "He's not alone in that."

"You got that right, sonny. With Philadelphia ready to call his lawyer as it is, I shudder to think what would've happened if you hadn't gotten the others into the rocks as fast as you did."

"Isn't there some way to muzzle that nincompoop?"

"Last time I checked we still had freedom of speech in this country."

"Too bad." Camp dabbed at the dot of blood again. "Won't attending this barbecue put us farther behind and give Harv more to bellyache about?"

"The ground's a hog-wallow anyway. What's eatin' you, boy? I thought you'd be happy as a possum in a strawberry patch. The farmers on the trail always threw a wingding for passing wagons. Can't get more authentic than Palmer's hospitality."

"Sorry. Guess I'm not in a party mood. I'd be more inclined if my sister and her pals quit acting as if Emily and I had smallpox."

"Don't they appreciate that you saved their sorry hides?"

Camp's hungry eyes devoured Emily as she sat beside Mark's fire, brushing curls into her gleaming, just-washed hair. "The two are unrelated, Maizie."

"Uh-huh," she grunted. "That ol' green-eyed monster, then?"

He eased out a breath. "Are they right to object? Lord

there's reason enough on both sides to avoid en-
ement, I guess.''

Well, if it means anything...when you turn your back
t lady looks at you with her heart in her eyes. Now, it
n't my business, mind you, but seems to me two college
rofessors oughta be able to figure a way around most
any problem.''

Camp's gaze remained locked on Emily as Maizie
walked away. Obviously she didn't understand the extent
of Megan's dislike for him. It presented a critical hurdle.
However...there'd been a time he was a pretty fair hur-
dler.

He repacked his razor while Maizie spread the word
about the barbecue. Plainly, her message perked up everyone else's spirits. Only, his mood remained pensive. Already he missed Emily's quick wit and her bubbling
laughter. To say nothing of the sense of well-being that
came over him when they were together. But he'd worked
with enough teens to know that it'd take more than a smile
or a teddy bear to win Megan's favor. He just wished he
knew what it *would* take.

Out of habit, he kept tabs on Emily in the line of wagons. Long after he ceased to see her profile, he imagined
how her lips had felt last night on his bare skin. His mind
relived every moment in her company as the train wound
through miles of fields laid waste by the storm.

The smell of barbecue smoke reached the column before anyone could see the Jones farm—which turned out
to be a huge, multipillared estate with wide verandas rem-
iniscent of Southern plantations.

Palmer and Evelyn Jones were nowhere near as osten-
tatious as their home. ''Welcome, welcome,'' he boomed
in a jocular voice. ''Climb down and sit a spell. We'll
have that side of beef cooked faster'n you can say bar-

bee-cue!'' Jones sported a snowy beard that contr
with leathery skin toasted to the color of teak.

"According to my pilot, you're all luckier than a sn
in the Garden of Eden. Storm reminded me of the t
twister we had in '52.''

"Palmer, dear, don't get started. At least let them ea
before you bore them.''

He turned to his wife, a plump woman with warm
brown eyes. "All right, Evie. Bring on those horse-
durveys you and Cora've been fussin' with all morning.''

At that signal, a row of duded-up farmhands lounging
against the fence doffed summer straw hats and rushed to
help the women from their wagons.

Camp watched three cowboy-types stumble over their
polished boots trying to be the first to reach Emily and
Sherry. He wasn't at all pleased with the gallant giant—
a younger version of Clint Eastwood—who won the stampede to Emily.

The saving grace was that Megan Benton looked as
miffed as Camp felt. Although that was probably because
the cowboys had unmistakably relegated her to the status
of kid.

Oblivious to any undercurrents, the locals boisterously
led the way to a side yard set with long picnic tables,
leaving Camp and Robert to unhitch the wagons. Even
Mark and Jared went after the tempting canapés Mrs.
Jones and Cora had begun to pass on trays. But when
Mark chanced to glance back, he returned to the wagons
to pitch in.

They released the horses into a field of deep grass
where Jones had told Maizie to let them graze. Several
such fenced fields circled the house, making a lush oasis
on the endless brown prairie.

Moments after the last horse was turned out, Mark and
Robert joined the revelers. Camp, slower to seek the

...ter that rang out from the side yard, plucked a piece ...veet grass to nibble. That was when he noticed Megan ...mped against Sherry's wagon, tears streaking her ...eeks.

In view of her continuing hostility, he could have left ...he girl to her own devices. But it went against Camp's nature.

"Megan..." He tossed the stalk of grass before he sauntered toward her. "Sometimes it helps to get frustrations off your chest. As a teacher, I've developed an impartial ear. So if you feel like talking...."

"Butt out," she sniffed, gouging a knuckle into very red eyes.

"If I had a dime for every time a student started out saying that, I'd be a millionaire. Come on, Megan, you don't have to like me to talk to me."

"Why are you so cheery? Mom took up with that other dude fast enough. She doesn't know *you're* alive, either."

Camp heard the bitterness in the girl's hoarse voice. "'Took up with' is a strong term for someone she's just met. I imagine the young man was just flirting with her because Mr. Jones asked his staff to make us feel welcome—that's all." He tried not to grit his teeth. "Anyway, Emily called for you. I heard her."

"She didn't mean it. Because...because she hates that I look like my dad. Mona said. She didn't even cry when they told her Daddy died."

Mona again. "I'm afraid I can't comment on that, Megan. I do know that sometimes people are too shocked to cry at first. I'm reasonably sure you were aware that your parents were having a tough time before the accident. Your grandmother can only guess what your mom felt inside."

"But it's true she hated my dad. They didn't even sleep together," Megan cried.

"When a marriage breaks up, it's never one-" Camp weighed his next words carefully, eventua~ ciding to lay his cards on the table. "There's no que that your mother loves you, Megan. This morning she that if she had to choose between you and me, I co take a hike."

The tears dried on Megan's cheeks. "Is that why yo~ let the dude horn in?"

Over the top of Megan's flyaway mahogany curls, Camp had been following the outline of a man jogging through the field next to the one with the horses. He'd burst from a small stand of cottonwoods. Camp found it curious that the rail fence surrounding that parcel of land was interspersed with barbed wire.

His gaze left the man momentarily to snap down and clash with Megan's accusing eyes. "That's not it at all. Emily is worth fighting for—even if that means fighting with *you*—until the cows come home. I just can't conceive of doing anything to hurt her." *There, let her chew on that!*

A shout for help interrupted Megan's reply. It came from the puffing man Camp now identified as their obnoxious wagon mate from Philly. Charging fifteen feet behind him, with massive horns lowered, was the biggest, ugliest bull Camp had ever seen.

"Quick, call Mr. Jones or one of his men," Camp ordered Megan over the enraged bellow of the bull. Expecting her to obey, he took off at a run.

"Why would you help that jerk?" Megan yelled.

Believing the panic on Harv's face spoke for itself, Camp scrambled over the fence and dropped inside. Shaw, who carried fifty pounds of extra weight, had begun to flag. "Hurry, man, " Camp shouted. "Don't stop now. Here…I'll give you a boost."

Face as red as the shirt he was wearing, Harv had his

...ll trying to keep a grip on his unzipped pants. He ...s grip and they floated down around his knees. It ...e take Einstein to figure out why the man had made ...p into the trees.

...Damn, Camp didn't see how he could distract the bull ...d heave himself, plus someone who outweighed him, ...ver a six-foot fence topped with barbed wire. Rivulets of sweat ran into his eyes as he ducked behind Harv and tried to heave him over the fence.

Harv grunted. "I'm caught on the wire."

Out of the corner of his eye, Camp saw the bull change directions. And he saw two other things. First, the seat of Harv's pants was firmly caught in the top strand of barbed wire. Second, Megan still stood outside the fence, doubled over laughing.

Worse—much worse—the snorting, drooling, plunging bull pawed menacingly a few yards away. Camp shoved frantically at Harv again. His flabby butt bounced immediately back. Camp decided this whole thing must resemble The Three Stooges.

Harv's shouts finally penetrated the party noise. Harv's wife, Sherry and Emily dashed pell-mell toward them.

Just as the bull lowered his head to charge, Camp saw Emily vault the fence.

"Don't just stand there, Campbell," she shouted. "Haul ass."

"No way! Get out of here." He made a move toward her.

"My dad raised Charolais," she said. "I used to run circles around guys like that." She inclined her head toward the bull, which had stopped to paw again.

"Yeah. Well, in another life I medaled in the hundred-yard dash. So you help Harv. I'll distract the bull and hightail it over the gate."

"Too far," she muttered. "Uh-oh. Time's run out trying to act macho. Harv's too heavy for me to buc

Before Camp had time to think, she darted at the mal, flailing her arms. Left little choice, he climbed two rungs so he could better reach the impaled ma. Above the sound of blood rushing in his ears, Camp hear people shout. He wanted to check on Emily, but he almost had Harv free. Besides, having seen Emily in action during the tornado, he had to believe she could do what she said.

And she would have if the bull hadn't swerved around her and charged the men.

"Ah!" Camp felt Philly disconnect from the barbs and fall into his wife's waiting arms. Camp should have followed. Instead, he glanced over his shoulder to check on Emily—and smelled the hot, putrid breath of the bull. Next, he heard denim rip, and a searing pain tore up his calf. If not for the hands dragging him over the fence, he'd have lost purchase and become a rag doll for three thousand pounds of royally ticked Santa Gertrudis.

Camp clutched a torn, bloody pant leg, noting with relief that Jones and some of his men had arrived and gotten Emily out, too.

It was Megan's white face that Camp noticed, even more than the sticky blood seeping through his jeans. She was literally shaking. Then Emily appeared, blocking his view. She brushed his hands away and began to mop at blood with a handkerchief that smelled of jasmine. Camp gave himself over to her ministrations.

"The brat just stood there and laughed." Harv's eyes bulged. He'd zipped his pants, but still had a large L-shaped flap in the seat, exposing his underwear.

"I'm awful sorry." Her guilty eyes flew to Camp. "I—I didn't think anything bad would hap-happen," Megan stammered.

...mp felt sorry for her. Anyway, why hadn't Harv ...d to use the bathroom in the house? At the very least ...hould've realized the barbed wire wasn't for looks. ...mp thought maybe he was more willing to be magnanious toward Megan because he felt protective of her. Or ...ecause Harv Shaw had been a horse's patoot from the get-go. "Come on, Harv. Where's your sense of humor? We must have looked pretty funny. And you can't blame the bull when they're probably barbecuing his brother. I don't know about you, but I've worked up an appetite. What say we put this aside and go eat?"

Had Camp imagined it or was there a modicum of respect along with the regret in Megan's eyes? Before he managed to ferret it out, Mark ran up, asking if he could bring Camp a soda or anything.

"No, but thanks, sport. I'll be fine once I get this leg taped together. Please, everyone—go back to the party."

Surprisingly, Megan came forward. "Mom, I'll go get the first-aid kit."

"Uh, thanks, honey. We'll meet you at the wagon." Emily helped Camp to his feet. She shook off the hand of the cowboy who tried to take Camp's weight—the young Eastwood who'd been following her around. "Go back to the barbecue, Dylan. My kids and I can manage."

The man's gaze bounced from Emily to Mark to the retreating Megan. "They're yours? But they're...you don't look old enough," he burst out.

"Megan is fourteen, and Mark is twelve. Believe me, I've earned my parenting badge for every one of those years, and then some." She would have slipped her shoulder under Camp's arm again, but Sherry nudged her aside this time.

"You go with Dylan, Em. I know how fussy Nolan is about his clothes. I'll see him back to the wagon, tend his leg and find him a clean pair of jeans."

Some of Emily's joy folded in on itself. But to make a scene. And if Camp wanted her h Sherry's, he didn't say so. She pasted a smile on h "Let me stop and tell Megan not to bother wi first-aid kit, Dylan."

"Sure. Sure. You go on. Uh, do the other ladies have kids, too?"

"Not Sherry or Brittany. Sherry just took off with h brother, and it appears you'll have to pick a number to wait for Brittany." Doing her best to keep a straight face, Emily pointed out the young woman already ringed by admirers.

Leaving Dylan to his fate, Emily hurried to where Megan waited. "Sherry's taking care of Camp's injury. Why don't we go eat?"

"I'm not hungry. Mom...could we maybe grab some time later to talk? I mean, just the two of us?"

Emily sucked in a sharp breath at Megan's earnest tone. "Why, ye-yes. Any time. I'm always available for you and Mark. You know that, don't you? Your welfare comes first with me."

"Really? Then do you mind if we talk now? Otherwise, I—I might lose my nerve."

"This sounds important. Shall we walk?" Emily linked her arm with Megan's and they strolled back the way they'd come. "Avoiding the bull, of course." She smiled.

Megan looked troubled. "Camp asked me to go for help. I didn't."

"Oh." Emily's loose hold on Megan's arm tightened. "I wondered what Harv was yammering about. This time, your decision had serious consequences. You need to realize that, Megan. Is this what's bothering you?"

"Yes and no. Tell me why you and Daddy lived like strangers in the same house," she blurted.

"Sweetheart..." Emily's voice was strangled. "I, ah, I

...have a right to know.'' Little by little, as they ... she unveiled the truth about Dave's decline and ... money his parents had handed him only made ... de into booze easier and faster.

...es huge and weepy, Megan asked in a shaky voice, ... ny didn't you just take Mark and me and leave?''

...Emily attempted to explain the far-reaching influence ... Megan's grandfather in terms she hoped made sense to ... fourteen-year-old.

"Toby and Mona are awful," Megan burst out angrily. "How could you let me believe them all this time?"

"How could I not? Don't you understand, Megan? They had...still have the power to take you and Mark away from me."

The girl threw herself into Emily's arms. "Mama, I'm sorry. I'm so sorry that I help...helped them."

"There, there, hon." Emily hugged her tightly. She, too, cried. "That's why I chose this trip. I'd hoped—but what on earth happened today to bring this about? Not that I'm complaining." She sniffled, wiping first Megan's eyes, then her own.

"Camp's the reason."

"Camp?" Emily drew back. Her heart began to hammer. Did that mean he had talked with Megan? That they'd buried the hatchet? She was almost afraid to hope.

Megan wriggled out of her mother's arms. "He, uh, caught me feeling sorry for myself. I don't 'xactly remember what all he said—except that you loved me enough to tell him to flake off. Gosh, Mom, I figure you *must* love me bushels to dump him like that."

Emily's heart wrenched. She felt it tear in two. She had to force her arms around Megan this time. But she should have known better than to wish for too much good luck. Why wasn't it enough to be mending bridges with Meggie?

It was, and yet...

The piece of Emily's heart that Camp had beg
thaw didn't want to go back into cold storage. Unfo
nately, Megan hadn't minced words over the reason
her abrupt turnaround. Emily dared not even contempla
risking the loss of her daughter's tenuous trust. She simpl
had to avoid Camp at any and all cost.

The remainder of the day posed no problem. Megan
never left Emily's side, and Camp spent the bulk of his
time in the company of their host.

Prodded by the hot, drying winds that blew in, Maizie
announced they'd leave at dawn. At first there were grum-
bles, but after cleaning up and delivering a profusion of
thanks to Mr. and Mrs. Jones, everyone seemed ready to
turn in.

Morning brought harsher winds. No one complained.
They were just glad the monsoons had passed. Maizie said
there'd be three days of hard driving to reach Wagon
Mound, at which point, weather permitting, they'd take a
side trip to Fort Union.

Camp half expected Emily to fuss over his injury—
would have welcomed it. But she seemed preoccupied. So
he left Sherry's original bandage in place.

At their few brief breaks and throughout lunch, Camp
observed that Emily and Megan appeared to be tighter
than ticks on a hound. That was good. He assumed he'd
played a small part in bringing about their reunion, so
Camp was at a loss to understand why Emily now went
out of her way to avoid him.

Dammit, he'd ask her outright at supper. That plan got
sidetracked by a sandstorm that drove them all inside their
wagons for the next two days.

Early the third morning, Maizie clanged them awake
before dawn. "Rise and shine," she roared in a voice loud
enough to wake the dead. "We've gotta make fast tracks

unless we want to bog down in the shallows of the Canadian River. If this sand keeps rolling we'll be up to our armpits.''

"You do have a way with words," Camp grumbled, poking his sleep-rumpled head through the canvas. Sand trapped between two wagon bows dumped on him.

Mark and Jared hooted with laughter at Camp's expense. The others were a little more restrained, except for Sherry.

"At last!" She said, laughing. "God finally agrees that you should bathe. I understand not wanting to wet the cut on your leg, but did you break the arm that holds your razor?''

Camp snorted. "I only let shaving go for two days. Besides, I distinctly remember hearing you say how sexy George Clooney looks with stubble.''

"George has that helpless I-need-a-keeper look," Sherry said. "Sorry, bro. You look more like a gorilla.''

"Well, since we're related..."

Maizie stuck her thumb and finger between her teeth and whistled shrilly. "Save the family squabble till we hit Wagon Mound. Then you two can trade insults all you want. You'll need that excess energy to push these wagons through sand.''

That sobered everyone. Camp withdrew to check the covers on his stores. Emily might act aloof; Sherry, however, seemed more her old teasing self. What was up with Emily? Camp gave up trying to figure her out in the face of hordes of giant blackflies that swarmed around horses already edgy from stinging sand. With each successive break they took, Maizie's temper mushroomed.

"Keep that rear in gear," she yelled at Camp after he slowed his team to a walk in order to check on Emily, who had all but stopped her wagon.

Camp's own composure snapped. He was drenched in

sweat and his leg throbbed like the very devil. "V
got women driving three wagons, Maizie," he said
grily. "Maybe *you* have the strength of two mules,
they don't."

Sherry swung around and attacked Camp. "Pu...leez
Speak for yourself. We didn't come this far to wimp ou
now. Feel free to quote me in your paper."

"Forget my paper, Sherry. Can't you see that Emily's
played out? Last time we switched her teams, she got
stuck with four ornery Belgians. They'd pull my arms out
of their sockets, too, for crying out loud. It has nothing
to do with gender."

"Ha! You say that now, but what's to prevent you
changing your tune when you actually write about this
incident?"

Emily glanced at Sherry's red face and the tired lines
fanning from Camp's eyes. "Why would he be dishonest,
Sherry?" Emily asked quietly.

"Yeah, sis. I'm not the one who loaded the dice here.
You'd better ask yourself how many friends you'll have
if you kill off Emily and Gina."

Sherry sucked in a sharp breath, once again feeling be-
trayed by Emily. And by Nolan. "I thought they *were*
friends," she said in a shaky voice. "Apparently I was
wrong." Swiftly, she moved up in the line. She wouldn't
let them see her tears.

All Camp saw was a flicker of pain that sliced through
Emily's blue eyes. As for his sister, he didn't know her
anymore. "Emily...I..." He stretched out a hand. It hung
in the wind as Emily slapped her reins. And as she'd done
on their first day out, she left Camp in a film of red dust.

Who'd have thought that one simple academic paper
had the potential for causing so much trouble? Camp
sighed. He knew he only had until Santa Fe to set things
right with Emily.

on, lethargy crowded everything else from Camp's
as their grimy column limped toward the rock for-
on. Early pioneers had named it Wagon Mound be-
se its outline resembled a Conestoga pulled by a brace
oxen.

Oddly enough, someone driving more modern convey-
ances—off-road vehicles—had beaten them to the long-
awaited shelter. Eight to ten men milled aimlessly beneath
a gaudy blue cabana. It looked surreal and out of place to
Camp. As the wagons lined up and stopped, flashbulbs
suddenly winked in rapid-fire succession.

"What in blazes?" Camp worked to calm his high-
strung team. Had they stumbled into a movie set? When
the spots before his eyes cleared, the first person he saw
was his history colleague Lyle Roberts. And Jeff Scott.
Their clean clothes left the biggest impression on Camp.
He passed a hand over his bloodshot eyes, wondering if
they were a mirage. But no, reporters swarmed the wagons. One particularly aggressive journalist badgered Gina
to tell him about her injured leg. The few men Camp
didn't recognize turned out to represent syndicated news-
papers.

Imprinted on Sherry's grim features, Camp saw a firm
belief that he'd arranged for this welcoming committee.
Groaning, he dropped the reins long enough to massage
his aching leg. Whoever engineered this twist of fate had
ruined everything. After this, it was unlikely Sherry *or*
Emily would ever speak to him again.

Philly was the only one delighted with the invasion. He
swooped down, taking his day in court, so to speak. If
there was any part of the trip the man *didn't* bitch about,
Camp couldn't figure out what it'd be. But for the life of
him, he felt too beat to care.

"Exploring the Santa Fe Trail is still a huge adventure. Not for the fainthearted."
—*Caption beneath a newspaper photograph of Camp.*

CHAPTER FOURTEEN

LYLE ROBERTS STARTED to clap Camp on the shoulder, then encountering his filthy shirtsleeve, drew back and dusted his hands. "Congrats on making national news, buddy. Our boss is rolling in clover. He loved having the department's name splashed all over TV. But why give so much credit to the women? Outrunning a tornado should have scared them into dropping this project faster than last year's wardrobe."

"What the hell are you talking about? We weren't on television."

"Indirectly you were."

Camp wondered why he'd never noticed before that Lyle had an oily smile.

"An Oklahoma news team interviewed a pilot. He and his boss, some farmer, expounded at length about your escapades. They were unduly impressed that women drove some of the wagons. That's why I rounded up this crew—to counter the damage, so to speak. These women won't look quite so impressive when these guys write their articles."

Grabbing Lyle by the front of his spotless jacket, Camp

ɔut yanked the shorter man off his feet. "See here.
paper isn't a hate vehicle against women."

Lyle's Adam's apple bobbed. "No? At least a *them and*
s piece, then. I thought that was the whole idea."

Camp tightened his grip. "Your attitude toward women
stinks. The group did a damn fine job coping in every
instance. Don't you dare knock them until you've trekked
this trail yourself!" Releasing Lyle before he lost it totally, Camp rolled his tired shoulders and limped off to
tend to his horses.

Jeff Scott, who'd witnessed most of the byplay, ap-
proached Camp. "This publicity gig on the heels of your
run-in with a twister was probably bad timing. I'll pass
the word. We'll leave now—save our brouhaha for your
arrival in Santa Fe."

"You do that," Camp snapped.

"Ah, what's your expected ETA?" Jeff jumped back
as Camp detached the forward singletrees, freeing the first
two of the giant, dust-covered Percherons.

"Next Friday, barring any other unforeseen problems."
Camp's irritation cooled. He'd always found Jeff to be
reasonable.

"If by unforeseen you mean stormy weather, relax. The
five-day outlook for this area is much improved. Sun, sun
and more sun."

"It's not just the rain," Camp said wearily. "Wagons
break down. Horses go lame. Sun blisters. This wind
stirred up a dust bowl. Good water is scarce. Along the
Santa Fe Trail, conditions haven't changed much in a hundred years. That's what I'll explain in my paper. And we
had advantages the pioneers lacked. More towns. Better
supplies. And no worries about attacks by renegades."

Jeff's jaw tensed. "But you ran afoul of an outlaw. Or
so Sherry said."

Camp's shoulders stiffened. He'd forgotten Garrett

Lock, Ph.D.—the fellow scholar. Since he couldn'
of a way to set the record straight without embarra
Sherry, Camp let Jeff's remark pass. Still, Camp had
ond thoughts about letting these guys walk away with
story. Who knew what they'd print?

"Say, Jeff, why don't you and Lyle tag along with u
from here to Santa Fe? Tomorrow we're visiting Fort Union. Frankly, I've always thought a discussion of the frontier escort provided early traders would make a publishable paper."

"I don't know..." Jeff raked a dubious eye over
Camp's dirt-encrusted face.

"Come on. Before Lyle spouts off about my group's
performance on the trail, he ought to observe them in
action."

"I suppose. But we didn't bring any camping gear."

"You're welcome to use my wagon. I'll bunk with
Robert Boone."

"Ah, we don't have food, either," Jeff added hastily,
as if searching for an excuse.

Camp grinned. "No problem. Men are born hunters,
right? We're natural providers. Isn't that what you told
Sherry at the college Christmas party?"

Jeff's face turned a sickly green. "Did I say that? I've
never shot a gun."

Emily appeared in Camp's peripheral vision. The red
dust had coated her normally shiny hair. Untidy or not,
she still looked beautiful. When she finally reached him,
Camp reined in the warm greeting that rose to the tip of
his tongue, lest Jeff see the truth of his feelings. No telling
what mischief the men could make of that.

"Emily, you met Jeff Scott in Boonville," Camp said.
"I've taken the liberty of inviting him and Lyle to join
us for the rest of the trip."

ly's eyebrows shot up. "Maizie's not too keen on
blabbing to the press, Camp. Maybe—"

"'ll talk to her," Camp broke in smoothly.

"Okay. So how many are staying for dinner? We're
ing potluck tonight. Something simple. Potato-cheese
up and corn bread."

Jeff patted his stomach. "Gr...eat! All we've eaten today is snacks. Your train showed up three hours later than
we calculated. By the way, it's good to see you again,
Mrs. Benton," he said effusively. "I'm not the best in the
kitchen," he added. "But I can manage a potato peeler."

Emily looked Jeff over thoroughly, her eyes revealing
nothing of her assessment. "Fine. The rule on the trail is,
if you want to eat, you help. Camp, Maizie asked if you,
Mark and Jared would hunt up something to burn. We're
out of firewood."

"Will do. As soon as I picket my team." It was all
Camp could do to hide a grin. He'd bet Jeff had no idea
how many potatoes it took to feed this crowd.

"Say, Jeff. Send Lyle and your newshounds to Maizie
for a list of chores. She assigns nightly duties. Or Lyle
could pull the rocks out of the back of my wagon, build
a fire ring and start coffee. Coffee beans are in the canvas
sack. The pot and grinder should be there someplace. Water's in that barrel." Camp pointed to the dirt-caked oak
container lashed to the right side of his wagon.

Jeff's eyes widened as he darted a quick glance to Lyle
and a photographer, swaggering along the row of wagons.
"I'll tell him, but I wouldn't recommend drinking the
coffee. Lyle can't even boil water." With that, Jeff trotted
off.

Emily's eyes crinkled at the corners as her gaze met
Camp's. She opened her mouth to speak, but closed it
promptly when Sherry stalked up.

"Hobnobbing with the enemy again, Em?" Sherry

whirled on her brother. "Having those macho jerks ▬
us here was a low, sneaky blow even for you," she ▬
cused in a hurt voice.

"But I didn't—"

"Like they just happened to drop out of the sky? Yeah
sure." She turned her back. "Come on, Emily. If we whip
up a meal fit for a king, we'll present Lyle Roberts with
a culinary feat that'll put his great-grandma to shame."
Sherry virtually dragged Emily away.

Camp's weariness struck again with a vengeance. He
fed and hobbled his team, giving a lick and a promise
with a dandy brush to knock the worst of the red dirt off
their once-sleek coats. Tired as he was, maybe he'd skip
supper and go to bed early. He didn't have the stomach
to listen to Sherry and Lyle sniping at each other all evening.

Emily let Sherry pull her back to the fireside because
fixing food for their added guests would take all hands.
But she hadn't liked the pallor of Camp's skin and decided to keep an eye on him. Was he coming down with
something? He and Robert had done the greater share of
the physical labor these last few days. If she'd done any
shirking it was only because she'd been preoccupied with
Megan.

Megan. If only there was a way to make her judge
Camp favorably. Ha! Scant chance of that. She had a better chance of being run over out here by a bus.

While Emily blended ingredients for the soup, Camp
dropped off braids of tallgrass to burn in the absence of
wood. He came by twice; neither time did he linger. Later,
she noticed him carting things from his wagon to Robert's. He'd washed, shaved and put on clean clothes. Was
his leg bothering him? It looked as if he was limping.

Maizie clanged the bell announcing supper. Emily got
busy dishing up soup and corn bread and lost sight of

..p. When all bowls were filled and everyone seated, ...awned on Emily that he hadn't shown up. *Where was* ...? Strangely, it was Megan who threw out the question. "Where's Mr. Campbell?" Her voice carried just enough to interrupt the talk and laughter being exchanged around the campfire.

Vi glanced up in surprise. "He brought us a huge armload of those grass things to burn. I haven't seen him since."

"Nor I," said Gina. "He refilled my feed trough while the boys braided grass."

Robert paused in the act of pouring honey over his corn bread. "Far as I know, he turned in. He's bunking with me tonight. Gave these guys his wagon." A jab of his knife singled out Lyle, Jeff and the young college reporter who'd elected to stay with the train. "Camp told me the others are leaving after they eat."

"Camp's not sick, is he?" Emily broke in, unable to contain her worry.

"Didn't say so if he is." Robert quirked a brow at Mark and Jared. "Did he mention being sick to you guys?"

The boys stopped shoveling soup into their mouths. "Nope," they chorused.

Emily continued to fret. Since Doris and Vi volunteered to do the dishes, Emily went to check on him. Not wanting to call attention to her concern, she skirted the people who sat around the fire talking after the reporters had taken off.

She peeked into Robert's wagon, but it was too dark to see if Camp looked feverish. Was his breathing normal? Emily listened carefully, the way she did if one of her kids was sick. But Camp wasn't a child, nor was he hers to worry about. Wishing wouldn't make it so. Turning to sneak off as quietly as she'd sneaked over, she ran into Sherry Campbell.

"What are you doing?" Sherry whispered.

Unconsciously, Emily raised a protective hand to throat. "I, um, saved your brother some soup."

"Why? Megan said you'd come to your senses. Y have, haven't you, Em?"

Emily's lashes dropped over suddenly wet eyes. "I...I..." Clutching the bowl of soup more tightly, she started past Sherry.

"I don't understand any of this, Em. I'd hate for either you or Nolan to get hurt."

Emily's steps dragged. "Where's the hurt, Sherry? I don't see."

"After all the times you've said you don't think you'll ever recover from a rotten marriage? Well, Nolan's suffering the aftereffects of a broken engagement, too."

"He was engaged?" Emily's chin quivered. "Recently?"

Sherry shrugged. "She married someone else last year. Nolan doesn't talk about it. It's a case of them being mismatched. She expected candlelight and wine from somebody who doesn't have a romantic bone in his body."

Emily recalled the tender way Camp made love. She'd thought him terribly romantic. Although, who was she to judge? Odd that he hadn't mentioned an engagement. But then, men rarely talked about their failures.

"Have you forgotten how upset you were when you thought I asked you on this trip to set you up with Nolan? I'd feel horribly responsible, Em, if either of you got hurt."

Emily felt an old, familiar frustration. The type that occurred whenever she tried to please and appease. "The last thing I want," she mumbled, "is to jeopardize our friendship."

, too." Sherry looped an arm through Emily's and
r away.

ULTRY MORNING added to the edgy tempers. Camp's
leagues and the college reporter did nothing, but ques-
oned everyone. Tired of it, the members of the wagon
rain voted to get under way early.

Maizie was bordering on apoplexy. She was furious
that the reporter took down every word Philly said and
ignored her remarks completely.

The majority blamed Camp for the burgeoning rift, so
he kept to himself.

Try as she might to forget him, Emily's eyes involun-
tarily tracked Camp. The deep lines bracketing his mouth
concerned her. His normally warm eyes were dull. However, he cooked breakfast for his pals and hitched his
team.

If Emily had known how much effort it took Camp to
carry out each of the duties he performed, she'd have been
really worried. This morning he'd finally gotten around to
changing the bandage on his leg. The lower half of the
cut where the bull's horn had gouged deepest looked
swollen and badly infected. Camp cleaned it with alcohol,
and just about flew through the canvas roof. He smeared
the area with antibiotic cream from his kit and covered it.
The rest seemed to be healing.

Lyle's litany of complaints kept Camp's mind off his
throbbing leg as the column lumbered steadily across the
cracked, baked earth.

"My butt's about to break," Lyle groaned. "I wish I'd
hitched a ride back to Santa Fe with the reporters."

"Stuff a sock in it," Jeff warned. "Keep bitching, and
if Camp doesn't plant you in that cemetery, I will." He
pointed off to the right. "See those hand-carved head-

stones? Let's walk a while. Hey, wouldn't it be
we stumbled across some old bones, Lyle?''

"*Our* bones, if this keeps up," Lyle said. "I
Camp puts in his paper that weak pioneers were prob.
shaken to death.''

Camp roused enough to get in a jab. "Women pionee
right, Lyle? You said there were no weak men.''

That shut Lyle up. He clambered out with Jeff, muttering that a walk would do him good. Camp wallowed in
the silence. During the brief respite he discovered Emily
leaning out every so often to look at him. It cheered him
to know that if he fell off his wagon, he wouldn't go
unnoticed.

His two talkative colleagues rejoined him much too
soon to suit Camp. Especially as it ended Emily's checking on him. It was another five miles before he managed
to divert their attention to the vastness of the blue sky.
The men failed to see any beauty in scenery. They did
shut up, though, as the column neared Fort Union.

The lead wagon flushed a herd of antelope that'd been
grazing in an uncut field of grain. All drivers slowed, angling for a better look. But the herd took off.

Whooping, Mark dropped back to keep pace with
Camp. "Gina wants to set up for pictures. Man, this is
neat. Those other forts were kinda swallowed by towns.
This musta been what it was like for the real pioneers.''

Camp smiled. What a change from the sullen kid who'd
fractured everyone's ears with his boom box at the start
of the trip. "Once we pass by, Mark, the antelope will
come back. Gina can probably set up a telephoto lens
from the fort.''

"Good plan." Gina poked her head out of the wagon
and waggled an arm. "Hey, Camp, notice anything different? I got rid of the splint last night," she said. "Wish
I could lose this leg cast, too. I'm tempted to cut it off

, but the doctor said not until we reach Santa Fe.
.re a drag.''

.mp's leg wasn't in a cast, but he could understand
feelings. He had zero tolerance for infirmities himself.
turned to a sneering Lyle and said, ''She's one tough
dy. If you believe women today have gone soft, let me
ell you about Gina Ames.'' He described her injuries and
her determination to stay with the train. He broke off as
two members of the Park Service popped out of the visitor
center to greet them.

If Camp's bad leg was a little shaky when he climbed
down, he blamed it on the washboard clay they'd crossed.

''Take the tour,'' Camp told Lyle and Jeff. ''Rusty
picked up a stone.'' He patted the huge horse. Really,
though, Camp wanted to shake them and follow Emily at
his leisure. Boy, he had it bad. In effect, she'd told him
to buzz off, yet he couldn't bring himself to stay away.
He loved how her eyes lit with an inner fire each time
she experienced something new. He'd never met a woman
who derived so much pleasure from simple things. A sun-
rise. A sunset. Wildflowers.

Perhaps some of her ebullience had even begun to rub
off on Megan and Brittany. Megan's face was wreathed
in smiles as she skipped along the cobblestone path past
the crumbling officers' quarters. And Brittany seemed to
be listening intently to what the ranger had to say rather
than flirting outrageously with the young man.

The adobe fort was mostly in ruins. The sun beat down
mercilessly. Camp found his leg buckling far too often.
By the time the rest of the group turned the corner near
the military guardhouse, they were far enough ahead that
he decided no one would miss him if he returned to the
visitors' center. According to the guide, the center boasted
a bookstore and a gift shop.

Inside, his eyes adjusted slowly to the artificial light.

He sat on the floor and leafed through several books. [choosing] two, he hobbled into the gift shop, whe[re] bought small magnets of local stone painted with Co[n]togas for all the women—including Philly's wife. She [de]served a solid-gold Cadillac for putting up with Ha[rry.] Anyway, he'd planned to give some commemorative trin[-]ket to everyone before they parted. Too bad there weren'[t] many items available for men. As he debated between pencils stamped with the Santa Fe Trail Association logo and fake leather coin purses, the clerk called him aside.

"We just got these in, sir."

Camp studied the key chain she held out for his inspection. Around a Conestoga wagon bow were the words *I followed the Santa Fe Trail*. "These are perfect." He told her how many he needed. "And could I ask a big favor? Would you hide the remaining magnets and wait until we're gone to shelve these key chains?"

"No problem." She bagged his purchases and accepted his credit card. They chatted about the secret gifts even as the first wave of the tour group walked in. Emily and Sherry, followed by Megan and Brittany.

Camp and the clerk stopped in midsentence. He realized how guilty they must look. And for such a benign reason, too.

Sherry waltzed up. "Don't be fooled by his pretty face," she told the clerk. "My brother will twist your words to suit his purpose." Winking at Emily, Sherry explained the mission they were on to the startled clerk.

Camp wagged the two history books he'd bought. "With subjects like you, sis, why stop at a paper when I can fill a book? Wait till you see your role."

"You're kidding?" She pulled back. "You're not. Nolan, history texts flat-out lied about women's roles. I'm calling Yvette to have her meet us in Santa Fe with a reporter from the Women's Hub so we'll get some posi-

...ress of our own. Do you have a pay phone?" she
...nded of the clerk.

...et Sherry think the worst of him, Camp mused. Sud-
...ly, though, it seemed important that Emily know his
...ork would be an honest account of the trip. But appar-
...ntly Emily and Megan had also skipped out. He did no-
...ice Lyle standing at the end of the counter. Camp swore
to himself.

"You'd better muzzle these women, Camp. By the time
we roll into Santa Fe, that Yvette will have undermined
you so much, you'll probably even be blamed for the tornado."

"Lyle—" Camp grabbed for the corner of a card rack
to keep from falling as an unexpected pain knifed down
his leg. "Can't you get it through your head that I'm
writing a true comparison-and-contrast, not an exposé? I'll
admit that at the time I got roped into this deal I had some
reservations about the women holding up. Now, the main
thing I've learned is that when the going gets tough, so
do the women."

Lyle snorted.

"Don't take my word," said Camp. "See for yourself
on the long haul over Glorieta Pass. I'd advise you to
sleep well tonight if you don't want the ladies showing
you up." Sweeping Lyle aside, Camp limped out the front
door.

Concealed behind a row of books, Emily heard everything that was said. Her heart tripped and stumbled in her
chest. Oh, why was Sherry never around when Camp dis-
played the fine traits Emily had come to respect? Well,
Sherry might not have been, but Megan and Brittany had
returned in time to hear the men's exchange. Emily
thought they'd been suitably impressed. She wouldn't
pressure Megan just now to revise her opinion of
Camp—but soon. Before they parted in Santa Fe. Emily

intended to tell Camp that she would see him after they returned home.

Camp begged off joining the others for supper. Once again he missed how closely Emily monitored his every move. In Robert's wagon, Camp rebandaged his leg. It annoyed him that there was no noticeable improvement.

"Maizie, how did Camp seem tonight?" Emily asked out of earshot of the others.

"Fine, I guess." She unwrapped a new pack of gum. "Quiet, maybe. We didn't talk. But then, I'm torqued at him for givin' that jackass from Philadelphia an outlet for his complaints. Why do you ask? Is something wrong with the boy?"

Emily shoved leftover biscuits into a plastic bag. "I'm probably making a mountain out of an anthill. We had words a few days ago. He may be avoiding me."

"More'n likely he ate something that didn't agree. A steady diet of camp cookin'll do that. Or maybe he's plain tuckered. Heat'll do *that*."

"Um. Probably that's it." Emily struggled to contain a yawn. "Mercy. Hiking around the fort today wore me out. Believe I'll turn in, too."

"Do that. Next couple days are gonna be monotonous as hell. You'll see why some folks went crazy trekking this trail. No hills, no trees, no water until we make the bend and start the climb over the pass at San Miguel."

Emily wrinkled her nose. "That ought to test our grit."

"Test more'n that. It'll be a miracle if I don't strangle Philly."

"Or if Sherry doesn't throttle Lyle Roberts. I thought she was going to dump bean soup over his pointed head tonight."

"Yeah," Maizie chuckled. "And every woman here'd be cheering her on. Good night, girl. Can't wait to see what develops tomorrow."

NOTHING DEVELOPED. Except the day was long and monotonous. First, Sherry's wagon broke an axle. It took Maizie, Sherry and Emily three hours to fix it; Sherry had refused help from the men. Then Philly's lead horse stepped in a gopher hole and pulled a tendon. Maizie raked him over the coals for his carelessness. He cried foul, claiming she'd led him across that particular piece of ground on purpose.

Camp was awfully glad when Robert insinuated himself between those two. Today, Camp's head felt the size of a barn door, and he was sweating like a bay steer. Not surprising. The sun hung in the sky—a red ball of fire. Emily slathered sunscreen on herself and the kids so many times, they all resembled greased pigs. Watching her fingers slide over her skin alternated joy with pure torture.

Few words passed between the travelers after Maizie stopped for the night. Not even mosquito netting deterred the bugs that descended on them. The flies were horrible. Camp burned his dirty bandage to keep the flies off it. It was such a disgusting process that he decided to leave his wound unbound.

ABOMINABLE WAS A TERM Camp jotted in his journal numerous times over the next two days. No one in the group escaped visible scars—welts dealt them by repeated strafing missions of flying insects. The only good that resulted was that everyone expended so much energy outwitting the bugs, they had no stamina for backbiting. For once Philly's lip was zipped, as was Lyle's.

On the third day out, the ragtag party reached San Miguel. There, at least, was something of interest to break the tedium of the prairie.

"Whoee! Is that a mirage?" shouted Gina, pointing to the silhouette of an old adobe church that broke the flat, continuous skyline.

"I'll give you half an hour to take pictures," Maizie shouted. "By two o'clock I plan to be well into Glorieta Pass."

The women tumbled out of their wagons, laughing and cavorting like kids who'd escaped a school bus after riding three hours to a field trip.

The men, normally more reticent, climbed down and ran through the old plaza and down a slope to where the Pecos River was little more than a muddy ribbon. All except Camp. His leg still oozed in spite of the antibiotic cream. Thank goodness there were no red streaks that would indicate blood poisoning, but neither was it healing.

On her way back from the river, Emily realized he still sat on his wagon seat in the shade of a gutted adobe house. Screening her eyes with a sunburned arm, she assessed his condition. "Camp, are you sick? Have Jared spell you."

Camp blinked at the soft outline of the face he loved. Heat devils glistened and quivered around Emily's slender body, splintering his concentration. "I'm fine."

She put her hands on her hips. "If this show of machismo is for the sake of your book, it's plain asinine. I'm calling Jared now. So you climb into the back of that wagon. Go on." She gave a nervous laugh. "I must sound like your mother."

He didn't laugh with her. Instead, he tossed her the reins with a sigh and climbed into the wagon box.

Sherry ran up, dashing water from her dripping wet hair. "I never thought I'd soak my head in filthy water. Frankly, it felt better than sex." Not receiving the expected response from her friend, Sherry sobered. "What's wrong? Why are you holding Nolan's team?"

"He's not feeling well. Will you go ask Jared if he'll drive?"

Sherry frowned. "I don't remember Nolan ever being

sick a day in his life. But...he spent hours in those last two rivers, ferrying everyone safely across. Who knows what awful germs lurked there. Look at me. I'll probably die of some amoebic invasion." She spiked her muddy hair. "Okay, I'll hunt up Jared before I wash. Nolan will be all right?" It came out in the form of a question.

"Yes. And hurry with Jared. I hear Maizie giving her rebel yell to move out." Emily worried her bottom lip. Camp had caved in too easily. Surely he'd say if something serious was wrong, wouldn't he?

Maizie chafed as the drivers dawdled. But at last the column stretched out for miles across a fallow, arid field. She'd instructed them to leave plenty of room between wagons for the tough pull up Glorieta Pass—where, because of drop-offs on both sides, they had to parallel the highway. In many places on the long upgrade, the drivers found it difficult to stay on the extrawide shoulder. Passing cars honked, making the big horses jittery and hard to handle.

At three o'clock, when they were midway up the steepest slope, automobile traffic going both ways ceased to exist. The drivers began to relax.

All at once a boom shook the ground. Even those lucky enough to be driving teddy-bear Clydesdales fought to keep them from bolting. The earsplitting rumble had barely died away when two bigger booms thundered in succession. The last explosion catapulted a bleary-eyed Camp from his bed.

"What in blazes happened?" he bellowed, scrambling to sit beside Jared.

"Dunno." Jared set the wagon brake and took a firmer grip on the reins. "Yonder comes a couple dudes in hard hats. Looks like they're talkin' to Maizie."

Word eventually filtered down to the end of the line. The pass was supposed to be closed for the next twenty-four hours so that workers could blast a train tunnel through one of the canyons. The signal crew wasn't happy that members of the wagon train had somehow missed posted signs. "Absolutely no one's allowed beyond this point," one disagreeable hulk of a man yelled, waving his hairy arms at Maizie.

She promptly went from wagon to wagon with the news. To Camp, she said, "I'm madder'n a mama wasp, but my sting won't do a lick of good. This is a heckuva place to try to stake our horses. Just do the best you can. The hulk promised to check with his crew chief to see if they'll grant us time at daybreak to cross the pass."

Gina climbed down from her wagon, using crutches to traverse the rough incline. "If we're going to stop for any length of time, I'd like Mark to set up my tripod. The least grouchy of those workmen pointed out that the last of the old wagon swales are visible in the valley off to our left. I figure with my strongest telephoto lens and a four-to-one converter, I can manage a fair picture."

"Fine by me," Maizie said gruffly. "Might as well get something out of this damned inconvenience."

Camp leaned against his wagon, silently cursing further delay. In the last ten minutes he'd begun having chills. He realized his body needed more help fighting off the infection in his leg than the antibiotic cream provided. He let Lyle's bellyaching go in one ear and out the other.

Unexpectedly, the entire hillside shook with the loudest blast yet. Horses whinnied and reared. The report that followed rattled Camp's teeth.

Mark Benton's team bolted. Thrown off stride, the boy wasn't able to stop the runaways headed on a collision course with his mother's wagon.

In a frantic effort to remove her wagon from Mark's path, Emily snapped her team of four bullheaded horses into gear. She didn't realize that Megan had stood to see what was happening, until the right wheel of her wagon struck a granite boulder. "Me...gan, sit," she hissed.

Then Emily felt the balloon tire rupture; she felt the metal rim grate on the rock outlining the precipice. In spite of the fact that she grappled with all her strength to turn the team, Megan bounced up and out of the wagon. She hung in the air a moment, then flew over the embankment.

The girl's high cry of terror mingled with the sounds of panicked horses and Emily's bloodcurdling scream.

Charged with a burst of adrenaline, Camp arrived at the ledge while several others, stunned by the accident, huddled, looking horrified. He threw himself flat to the ground. "Be careful. Stay back," he warned Emily, who had somehow landed beside him.

"I'll take care of Emily's horses and wagon," shouted Robert.

Inching forward so he could look down into the canyon, Camp gave thanks that his hastily muttered prayers were answered. Megan's fall had been broken by a scrubby bush that grew on a narrow lip some fifty yards below. While Camp assessed the situation, she moved and tried to rub her elbow.

Camp cupped his hands around his mouth. "Lie still. Don't move a muscle. Please, sweetheart. We'll come after you real quick, I promise."

Emily, flanked closely by Sherry and now Mark, let her shaking hands drop from her mouth. "She's alive," Emily gasped. "Oh, how will we get her? From here to there is a sheer drop!"

Camp scooted back. Cold fear licked at his veins. Another shot of dynamite would shake Megan off her precarious perch. Aware that time was the enemy, he scrambled to his feet. The first jolt of adrenaline had faded, leaving him hot and icy at the same time. All that prevented him from vomiting was the more immediate fear for Megan's life. Even as he pulled Emily into a comforting embrace, he began to dispense orders like a drill sergeant. "Em, you and Sherry go tell those signalmen to radio ahead and stop blasting. Robert, bring the longest, sturdiest rope we've got. Jared, find a sound tree or a solid rock to lash it to."

White-faced, Emily reached out and clutched Sherry's hand. The two seemed in shock. Camp dredged up an encouraging smile.

"I'm going down," he muttered out of Emily's earshot. "Megan's stuck on a narrow ledge that could give way at any time."

"All's well that ends... Happy trails to you... Women can do anything!"

> —*Possible endings for Nolan Campbell's paper, uh...book???*

CHAPTER FIFTEEN

CAMP WAITED to talk rescue strategy with Robert Boone until Emily and Sherry had left on their mission. Thankfully, the schoolteachers diverted Brittany's and Mark's attention as Maizie ran up carrying three ropes. Camp, who'd never been in the Boy Scouts or the navy, tied them solidly into one. He wouldn't let anyone else touch them.

"You ever done any rappelling, boy?" Maizie asked.

Camp shook his head. "Have you?"

"Nope. Why don't we wait to see if that blasting crew can helicopter in a team of paramedics? We don't need two casualties."

Camp's gaze never wavered. "You know how wiggly kids are. All that's holding her is one unhealthy-looking creosote bush. If I didn't try and Megan fell, how could I ever face Emily?"

"If you two don't beat all. Maybe after this you'll quit square dancing and admit you're crazy about each other."

He'd already done that. The problem was Emily's. And everything hinged on the girl stuck on a ledge. The feisty, pretty, scared kid who needed his help. In the silence that followed, Camp knotted the rope around his waist. He

concentrated on the task ahead, oblivious to the ring o
pasty faces watching his every move.

Jeff, Lyle, the college reporter and the pair from Philadelphia, stood apart from those involved in the rescue
attempt.

Robert twisted the rope securely around a sturdy boulder. Slipping on a pair of leather gloves, he braced his
feet, looped the sisal around his shoulders and prepared
to play it out a little at a time for Camp's descent.

Just before Camp stepped over the side into midair, he
saw Jeff Scott align himself with Robert. Oddly enough,
the big man from Philadelphia did the same. *Well, would
wonders never cease?*

As Camp dangled in space, grabbing at a bush here and
there to keep from bouncing off the granite wall, his mind
raced on fast-forward. What if Megan had broken bones?
Or internal injuries? Camp worried that maybe he
shouldn't have been so quick to play hero. Moving her
might do permanent harm. He wasn't a paramedic. He
couldn't even heal a damned cut on his leg!

On the other hand, he'd already heard her happy cry,
probably at the sight of any warm body coming to her
rescue. Besides, it didn't make sense to let her wait alone
until help from another avenue could arrive.

Camp was close enough for Megan to guide his landing. "Swing left. Can you grab that skinny bush?"

"Thanks. Will I have a ledge to stand on?"

"Some. Boy, am I glad to see you! Standing up in the
wagon was pretty dumb, huh?"

"You're outta rope, Campbell," Robert yelled from
above. His voice echoed back to Camp three times from
a yawning cavern below.

Camp settled his feet securely on the thin shelf before
answering. "It's okay, Robert. I'm down. Just give me
time to catch my breath and check Megan over."

"You got it."

Again the muffled echo seemed to leapfrog spookily in space. Something in the way the outcrop on which he stood sheared off sharply, and the way blue sky and jagged rock formations tilted crazily every time he looked down, shifted Camp's pulse into high gear. He hung on to the rope, worried that he'd pass out.

"Can I sit up now?" Megan begged. "Oh..." the young voice quavered. "You only got one rope. How're we both gonna get to the top?"

Trying to get over feeling as if he was Spider Man stuck on a vertical wall, Camp could manage only a lame chuckle. "Good question, Megan." He couldn't believe that with so many creative minds topside, no one had thought of that very important detail. "We were all too shaken by your nosedive to think clearly. Anyway, don't sit until I decide if it's safe to move you. Is there space for me to kneel?"

"I can't see too good. But if you turn a little toward me, maybe there is. Just be careful. The rocks are sharp."

They were more than sharp; they were knife-edged. And slippery. As Camp turned slowly, his boot slid on loose shale. One rock shot over the lip. They heard it ping off the cliff wall—followed by one distant thump, then another. After that, no noise at all but the sigh of the wind. Sweat popped out on Camp's forehead.

"Wow. Must be a long ways down." Megan's shaky voice barely rose above a whisper.

"Don't think of that," Camp ordered. "Your mom'll kill me if I don't get you back in one piece."

"I guess she probably went ballistic, huh?"

Camp read guilt in the girl's tone, but at least her volume was stronger. His own heart had almost stopped the minute she'd flown over that embankment. He'd come within seconds of hurling himself over the precipice, filled

with visions of snatching Emily's daughter back with h
bare hands. If that was the description of ballistic, then i
wasn't just a mom thing. "Your mom, Mark, me, everyone was scared to death. So let's give you a look-see,
then figure out how to lift you out."

Camp did a check of Megan's extremities. She had a
scrape on her cheek that was already beginning to bruise.
Her left arm and hand were scratched. Not deep, and the
blood had already dried. There was a ragged tear in her
shirt and another in her jeans. But as Camp gently tested
each joint, Megan didn't yelp with pain. "Do you hurt
inside? Stomach? Chest?"

She shook her head.

"Your back? Your neck? I need the truth, Megan."

"I hurt, but I can wiggle my toes...and my ears." Red-
tinted lips curved in a cheeky grin.

Tipping his face toward the row of faces peering over
the rim, he shouted, "No serious injuries. When I give
three pulls on the rope, it means I'll be sending her up."

"Yo!" was the single word that drifted down.

Megan dragged a grimy wrist across her nose and
sniffed loudly. "You mean I've gotta go up alone?"

Camp, who suddenly felt a stab of vertigo, said curtly,
"You didn't have company on the trip down, did you?"

"N-n-no." Huge tears spilled from eyes very like Emily's. "But then I didn't have time to think about falling.
I just did."

"I'm sorry, sweetheart. I didn't mean to bite your head
off. You've been very brave. Hang tough a little longer."

"O...ka...y."

His fingers were so slippery with sweat that Camp had
a hard time untying the knots he had so carefully fashioned. The minute he freed the rope from around his
waist, he underwent an odd sense of impotence. Standing
there defenseless, Camp had a flash of insight. He knew

...actly what he'd write. It would have nothing to do with who was stronger, man or woman. But rather how it took everyone working together for people to build on what they'd learned, to survive. That was what the pioneers' quest had been about.

"It's time," Camp muttered. "Let's hoist you back to your mom so she'll breathe easy." Using the utmost care, he twined the crudely fashioned harness around Megan's narrow chest. Repeatedly, he checked the strength of the knots he'd tied.

"I know you didn't have to come after me," she said, clutching his hand.

He gave the second of the two sharp tugs on the rope. "Of course I did. I love your mother, Megan. Everything about her. And that includes you kids." He felt compelled to hug the girl awkwardly and to say, "Tell her for me again, will you?"

"I'm sc...ared. Please, come with me and we'll both tell her."

"Too much weight for those guys to handle." Camp gave the last yank. "Once you're up, they'll toss the rope back down for me." He tried to straighten from his crouched position—to help guide her away from the first outcrop of rocks as the rope tightened and slowly began to lift her from the ledge. A sharp pain knifed through his calf. It hurt so badly it threw off balance. He let go of Megan and grabbed at his leg. Releasing her allowed the rope to arc. Her feet struck his shoulder, interfering with his already weak hold on the bush. A brittle twig broke off in his hand. Camp felt both his boots slipping.

"Oof." He flailed for a handhold but grasped only air. Megan's scream floated above and below him. His death knell, he thought as wind rushed past his ears. But, dammit, he wasn't ready to go until he heard Emily admit that she loved him. His feet connected with rock. Then his knees did. Then his head. Sky, sun and visions of Emily smile converged in darkness.

"MAMA, MAMA," Megan shrieked as several sets of hands hauled her out of thin air onto solid ground. "Oh, Mama," she sobbed as Emily's strong arms enveloped her, "He...Camp fell off the ledge. We've got to help him. We've just got to."

The group that pressed in on the rescued girl splintered. Robert, Sherry and Maizie ran to the precipice, flopped prone and draped their heads over the edge.

"Nolan," Sherry called frantically. They heard nothing but the squawk of a bird and the rattle of wind rustling through scrub cedar dotting the hillside. Sherry's voice, uneven with panic, wafted right and left as her brother's name danced around the canyon.

Then...nothing.

Robert cupped his mouth with his hands and yodeled Camp's name three times. The results were the same. Mocking echoes.

Tears coursed down Megan's cheeks. "Mama, he said he loved you. And Mark and me...hateful as I've been. It's my fault. He didn't have to help me—but he did."

Mark clung to his sister's arm and to his mother's hand. Emily noticed that he stoically refused to cry, while she had no defense against the tears that filled her heart and clouded her vision.

"Well," she said, forcing her focus on the next logical step. "Hunt up more rope and a first-aid kit. Camp needs us. I'm going down."

Maizie placed a gnarled hand on Emily's arm. "We'll tell those men to order up a medivac chopper out of Santa Fe pronto. It oughta reach us before dark."

Emily retreated behind a determined smile. "We're wasting time."

"Em, for crying out loud." Sherry waded through the thicket of people clustered around her friend. "He's my brother, but I agree with Maizie. We already know a chopper is on its way. They ordered it for Megan. Oh, sure, I talked big, bragging that modern women are as capable as the pioneers—but what you're proposing...Em, listen to me. This is a job for professionals."

"Save your breath, Sherry," Lyle Roberts snorted. "Look at her eyes. The woman is crazy."

"Crazy in love with Camp," Robert said. "C'mon, Jared...Mark. Let's scout out extra rope."

The three left at once.

Sherry stared at Emily, and feelings of desolation stirred alarmingly in her breast. Her brother and her best friend. Suddenly she felt like an outsider. As if she'd stumbled into emotions she knew nothing about. Perhaps there was time. Most of the women she met through her job suffered from the negative fallout of having loved unwisely. Emily had been one of those women—and she was a counselor, too.

The thought of Nolan with Emily meant she'd have to reexamine all her ideas and beliefs. But that shouldn't matter, she told herself. Not as long as her brother survived this.

Racked with uncertainty, bereft, sick with worry, Sherry crept off to wait alone.

Robert and the boys returned with seven sturdy lengths of rope. Maizie's son knotted them, testing each one. After he'd finished and the rope lay coiled neatly at the foot of a strong cedar, Emily stepped into the harness that'd served both Camp and Megan. Donning gloves, she shrugged off the anxiety she felt emanating from the silent watchers.

Maizie draped a small pair of binoculars around Emily's neck. "Time to call a spade a spade, girl. We don't

have any idea how far he fell. If you haven't found
by the time the rope's played out, use the glasses to
to get a fix on him. Memorize landmarks. Maybe save t.
rescue team shootin' in the dark.''

A chill swept over Emily. The combined weight of the
binoculars and the first-aid kit clipped to her belt seemed
to press in on her, causing panic. Then her two children
stepped up and hugged her.

''It's kinda scary swinging out there. But these guys
won't let you fall.'' Megan gazed with trust at the men
handling the rope. ''I know Camp will feel lots better
having you there. He can't have fallen far, Mom. We
heard a rock tumble and bump forever. But there weren't
any echoes when Camp fell. Only one bump.''

Emily stored that information. ''Just promise me you
kids will stay back from the edge.'' She trailed a loving
hand down their earnest faces. After they nodded, Brittany
Powers, of all people, stepped forward, saying the three
of them would go recheck the whereabouts of that medivac helicopter. And Emily knew it was time to go.

She'd watched rappelling on TV. That was how she
went over the edge. Feet flat against the granite wall, facing those she left behind.

''Good luck,'' called Gina. ''Tell that lunkhead to hurry
back here and collect the best darned data sheets yet. Tell
him I won't even charge him for the pictures if he decides
to write a book.''

A smile found its way to Emily's lips. Bless Gina. Emily no longer suffered the niggle of fear that had been
eating at her insides. She would find Camp alive. He had
an unfinished mission—to write this story. To tell the truth
about men and women—modern and pioneer.

Foot by foot she sank into the canyon. She breathed
easier after passing the ledge that'd broken Megan's fall.
Below that, a grassy slope about four feet wide curved

a bulwark of rocks. Emily saw now that it was a ꞁacomb of caves. Unexpectedly her rear, descending ꞁead of her legs, struck bedrock. The blow was sharp ꞁough to bring tears to her eyes. As the rope coiled over ꞁer knees, Emily glanced around and saw Camp's crumpled form about three feet below her and off to the right. He lay facedown, half in, half out of a granite cave. He lay as still as death. Except for a splash of red that ran from his forehead to his chin, his face was devoid of color.

Emily's heart banged in her chest. Her pulse sounded like a thundering waterfall in her ears. The red was blood. Some dried. Some fresh. She barely had the wherewithal enough to lift her hands to her mouth and yell in a shaky voice, "Stop the rope. I've found him." She recognized her own fright in the echoing words, the reverberations circling like vultures. By the time Robert's question concerning Camp's condition floated down to her, Emily had steeled herself for the worst and scrambled on her hands and knees to press three bare fingers against Camp's jugular. She paid scant attention to the sharp rocks that ripped through her jeans and her gloves. The joy she experienced on feeling a thready pulse overrode all discomfort.

"He's unconscious," she shouted, ignoring the salty tears wetting her cheeks and lips. "But *he's alive*." Those two precious words exploded on a heartfelt sob of relief. "I'm going to try to determine how badly he's hurt."

The roar of approval raining down from above spurred her onward.

Working swiftly, Emily covered him with the light Mylar blanket from her first-aid kit. It would help retain his body heat and ward off shock. Even now, the sun was sliding out of sight over the ridge, and a cool breeze had risen up. She checked his arms and legs, not feeling any obvious breaks. The knees of his jeans were ripped, but so were hers. These rocks were jagged.

Carefully, Emily tore open medicated pads to wipe the blood from his face. As she touched the large goose egg on his temple that still oozed blood, Camp mumbled and stirred. He flopped from his stomach to his side.

She dabbed at the spot again with the cool sponge. He moaned, blinked twice, then stared at her with huge dark pupils that all but erased the liquid brown of his irises. "Go away, angel," he ordered in a gravelly voice.

"Camp, it's Emily. You lost your footing after you saved Megan. You have a huge knot on your head. Do you hurt anywhere else?"

He closed his eyes, and for a moment Emily thought he'd slipped into unconsciousness again. Her heart pounded as she stripped away the blanket and began a thorough inspection of his torso and stomach for internal injuries.

"Emily?" Her name sounded thick on his tongue. "For an angel you're stomping all over my pride."

"Oh, Camp." She leaned forward, trailing her fingers across his lips. "You frightened us. Me!"

They both gave a start as a helicopter dipped into the canyon, and the loud whump-whump of its rotors stirred up dust. Like a giant, noisy bird, it hovered at eye level for several jolting heartbeats. Then, as swiftly as it'd swooped in, it rose and disappeared over the ridge.

Before they had time to comment to each other, Maizie's voice warbled. "The rescue team has a fix on your position, Emily. Can you help Camp into a basket if they drop one? The spur you're on isn't wide enough for them to set down another man."

Emily telegraphed Camp a questioning glance.

He said nothing. As she continued to study him, brows furrowed, he sighed and nodded. "I hate going out of here trussed up like a damned Thanksgiving turkey. But I suppose there's no other way."

She shook her head.

"I'm awake," he hollered. "If they toss out a double harness, they can pluck us both out."

"Oh, Camp. Are you sure?" Emily demanded. "That's a nasty head wound."

"Not nearly as bad as the wound to my dignity. I intended to save Megan, and in so doing earn your undying love—and hers." He grimaced in disgust.

"You did."

"Did what?" Camp's eyes rose to meet her steady gaze.

"Earned Megan's and my undying love."

The sound of the helicopter starting up drowned out his rebel yell. He squeezed her arm and shouted, determined to settle this before the chopper whisked them away. "Are you saying Megan no longer objects? Emily, will you marry me?"

For some reason, the helicopter shut down its engine just then, and the rotors quieted enough that Camp's plea bounced off the cliff walls.

Emily's face flamed red in the last vestiges of sun, and so did his.

"What did she say?" demanded a chorus from above.

"Mom," came the thin voices of Megan and Mark. "It's okay with us."

"I...well, marriage is a big step," Emily whispered. "There're the problems with Mona and Toby. To say nothing of the huge debt I owe them."

The helicopter roared to life again. This time it lifted off and moved out over the canyon.

Camp feared that if he didn't demand a commitment *now*, while she was weakening, it'd be too easy to lose everything they'd gained once life got back to normal. He drew her lips to his and put all his dreams and promises into a single kiss.

They disregarded the downdraft from the rotors that whipped Emily's curls from his hands. Yet he didn't release her until the first cable and harness plopped into her lap. "Say yes," he shouted in her ear. "After all of this, do you believe there's any problem we can't overcome?"

Hands shaking, Emily buckled his safety harness and reached for the second one tumbling from the copter's belly. All through the process of shedding the original rope and connecting the cable straps to her harness, she made him wait. Then, as they wrapped each other in an embrace, ready for the scary upward jerk, she said, "I will marry you, Camp—as long as you publicly admit there's not one darned thing wrong with modern women. I owe your sister that."

He endeavored to land a happy kiss on her mouth, but they were spinning too fast and her eyes were closed tight. Giving up, he growled, "Tell me you know I would have done that anyway."

He felt the rumbling of her laughter. *She did know.* For the first time in longer than Camp cared to remember, in spite of his injuries, all felt right with his world.

On their landing, the chaos he'd predicted set in. Hands of family, friends and strangers wrenched them apart the instant their feet touched the ground. The paramedics who'd flown in examined Camp in one wagon and Megan and Emily in another.

Emily protested, insisting she was fine. And she was. Megan's minor cuts and bruises were treated, and they were both allowed to go.

In the other wagon, Camp didn't fare as well. The blow he'd taken to the head continued to leak blood. But the paramedics were more concerned with the infected cut on his leg.

"We should transport him to Santa Fe," the medics' leader told Maizie. "The blasted man says he won't desert

...he wagon train. He needs vigorous antibiotic therapy or ...hat wound on his head may end up infected, too.''

Maizie unwrapped a stick of gum and folded it into her mouth. "I can hear what he thinks of your idea." She grinned. "The whole world can hear." She winced, listening as Camp's vocal objections burst through the wagon canvas.

"I understand what you're saying, sonny," she commiserated with the medic. "But I got a policy in this outfit. The customer is always right. Now, we have clearance to scale the pass at daylight, lookin' at maybe an eight-hour trek into Santa Fe. We started this trip together and we'd sure like to finish the same way. Any chance you can give him a shot to tide him over till we reach a doctor? We've got another casualty who'll be goin' to have a cast removed." For Maizie, that was a long-winded speech. She stuffed two more sticks of gum in her mouth, waiting for the medic's reply.

The others crowded close. First the teachers put in a good word for Camp, then Robert.

"Campbell did me a good turn," Philly added gruffly. "It's beyond me why he'd insist on sticking this out. It's the most uncomfortable vacation I've ever taken. However, he wants to stay, so he ought to be allowed."

Emily almost didn't believe her ears. "We'll take care of him," she vowed. "Isn't that right, Sherry? That's what our pioneer sisters would have done."

Lyle Roberts threw up his hands. "You'd let the man die to prove a point. I give up. You win. You're all as tough as shoe leather. And you're also nuts. I intend to tell our department chairman that you all belong in the loony bin."

Almost before the words left his lips, Lyle struggled against an angry press of bodies. "Who knows this pip-squeak is here?" muttered Gina.

"Yeah. We could sort of nudge him over the ledge,"
Brittany proposed gleefully. "Students would cheer. From
what I hear, his classes are totally boring."

Lyle shrank back. "Jeff. Do something."

"Um." Jeff pretended to ponder. "What if Lyle promises to keep his trap shut?"

"He'd better." Mark puffed up like a rooster. "Camp's
gonna be me and Megan's new dad." As if that in itself
said everything.

"Then the poor sap's getting what he deserves," Lyle
said. "Let him write his paper. Nobody who's studied
history will believe him." He shoved past Robert and
Jared Boone.

The paramedic shut his case and checked around for
his co-workers.

Emily pulled him aside. "Don't listen to Lyle. First of
all, he's wrong—women's history is a huge new field.
And this trip is a history study. Camp's study. He's gone
to considerable trouble and expense. How would it look
if he didn't finish?"

"Sure you're not in sales?" The medic laughed. "All
right. Fine. I'll give Campbell a whopping-big shot."

"Thanks. I'll watch him tonight, and re-dress both
wounds if they need it." Emily sought out Sherry with
her eyes, daring her to object.

Sherry nodded. It looked as if, no matter what, she was
gaining a sister. So why did it feel more like she'd lost a
best friend and a brother?

Maizie whistled between her teeth. "We haven't
reached Santa Fe yet, folks. Don't think because of all
this excitement you can slough off chores."

While the medic dispensed Camp's shot, the others
picketed horses and readied a makeshift resting place for
the night. After the strain of the day, people mostly kept
to their own wagons.

Emily cooked for herself, Megan and Camp. She didn't know who fed Lyle, Jeff and the reporter. Maybe Sherry had. Emily noticed the young college reporter had been following Brittany with his tongue hanging out.

Camp drifted off to sleep before he finished eating. Emily quietly removed his plate and cup. She blew out the lantern. "I'm going to throw my sleeping bag under his wagon, in case he needs me during the night," she told Megan.

"Me, too. In case *you* need me," Megan said. "I apologized to him for everything, Mom."

Emily hugged her child and kissed her on the forehead. It was the first time in over a year that Megan didn't pull away. Emily stayed awake long after Megan's breathing evened out in sleep. So much had happened in such a short time. But she felt good about it. Better than she'd felt about anything in years. Her first marriage had begun with an elopement to Atlantic City. After a quickie wedding, Dave spent what should have been their honeymoon meeting with casino developers.

Yawning, Emily wondered if Camp would mind having a church wedding with all the trappings. A winter wedding. Sherry'd look wonderful in dark-red velvet—provided she'd be maid of honor. Megan and Mark could give her away. Emily fell asleep dreaming of red roses and white carnations.

IN THE MORNING, Camp claimed he felt as good as new. Well enough to drive his own wagon.

"I thought you'd ride with me," Emily said. "I told Jared he could drive yours. There's some young lady he met in Santa Fe on his last trip. Imagine what it'll do for his image to drive a wagon in." Nervous today, she talked in spurts. "Besides, we only have these last few hours to be together. We have a lot to discuss."

Camp threaded his hands through her spiky curls. "We have the rest of our lives, Emily."

"Yes, I know. Oh, Camp. Do what you want, of course. We can talk about a date for our wedding later."

"You're ready to set a date? In that case, Jared, my man—you're welcome to my wagon."

Emily gave a self-conscious laugh. Nevertheless, they whiled away the remaining miles in chatter. In the end they chose Thanksgiving break for the wedding. Both agreed, along with Megan, that it was important to spend Christmas as a family.

"I want you to move to Columbia right away, Emily. I'll take a room with my folks and let you and the kids have the house. After we furnish it fully, that is."

"Kick you out of your house?" Emily shook her head vigorously. "Why can't we all live there?"

"We're doing everything by the book, Em. So your in-laws haven't a prayer of charging you with misconduct. And the first thing we're going to do is pay them off."

She gasped. "But how?"

"My grandfather left me money in trust. His only stipulation was to use it for something that would make me happy. That's you and the kids, Emily."

Her eyes filled with tears. He was offering her love and freedom. No one had ever given her so much. For the remainder of the drive, they hammered out the intricate details. Emily didn't want to go back to the town where her in-laws wielded so much power. Camp agreed. If an opening came up at his college, she could apply or not. As far as he was concerned, it was Emily's choice.

They were surprised to top a rise and see the first of the wagons pull into the outskirts of Santa Fe. A crowd had gathered to greet them. Bands played. Dogs barked, and children stared at the dusty wagons in awe.

Camp spotted the reporters who'd talked to them after

ne tornado; they were converging on the front wagons with cameramen in tow. "Come on, Em. Let Megan watch the team for a minute. We need to be sure those fools get things straight. It took all of us working as a team to reach Santa Fe. Even Philly came around. That's the story I want told."

"Good luck. You'll have to muzzle Lyle. And isn't that Sherry's friend Yvette? Sherry asked her to bring a staff reporter from the Women's Hub."

They watched Yvette greet Sherry. Camp and Emily were still too far away to hear what the two friends said.

"You actually completed this whole smelly trip," Yvette exclaimed. "You've never looked better, Sherry—outside of those abominably dirty jeans. You've lost weight."

"Maybe five pounds." Sherry wrinkled her nose. "I *feel* good, but you won't *believe* everything that's happened."

Yvette grasped her arm. "Neither will you. Your boss announced his retirement, just as you suspected. I'm glad you filled out that application and left it for me to drop off. You'd have missed the filing deadline by hours."

Sherry clapped her hands. She'd thought her dean might retire. Now that he had and her hat was in the ring, it changed things. Her heart skittered. So Nolan wasn't the only one with good news. Only...what if she didn't reach the interview stage? Guys like Lyle would rub it in forever.

"Yvette, you haven't told anyone I'm applying for the dean's slot, have you?"

"No. But why wouldn't you broadcast such great news?"

"Because." She half turned and saw her brother and Emily coming toward them. "I can't explain now. Please,

Yvette, don't spill the beans. Listen to what Nolan has to
say. Then you'll understand.''

"Married?" Yvette gaped from Camp to the woman
who stood at his side. She clucked sympathetically. "Another good woman bites the dust. Well, congratulations...I guess.'' She slid a glance at Sherry, who'd turned
back to her wagon. Camp and Emily left to talk with the
reporters.

For the next hour, everyone jabbered at once. Until the
outfitter collecting the wagons to make the return trip to
Missouri arrived, and the pain of parting struck them all.

"I won't really turn you into the Better Business Bureau,'' a very subdued Philly promised Maizie. "This trip
proved what a man's made of. Uh, and a woman,'' he
added, gazing sheepishly at Sherry. "If any of you are
ever in Philadelphia, look me up.'' He passed everyone a
business card.

Camp stuffed the card in his pocket. "I hate goodbyes.
Anyway, you're all invited to Emily's and my wedding.''
He named the date in November. "It'll be a great reunion.
I'll send everyone a copy of my paper, too. Is that fair?''

"Suits me,'' said Maizie. "I want you to know that this
trip is one for the books. I owe you my thanks, Campbell.
The last few days I haven't even missed my tobacco. Robert's gonna buy me a year's supply of gum before we
head home.''

"Hip hip hurray!'' Vi and Doris led a cheer.

Brittany and Megan squeezed into the circle. "We want
to confess to the firecracker caper. We're sorry.'' They
grinned at each other. "Even with all the stuff that happened, we agree this summer's been boss. Rule! The
best,'' Megan interpreted.

Gina limped forward, aided by a cane. "Camp and I,
we have a date with the doctor. Oh, and my gift to each
of you is going to be a framed picture. I'll mail them.''

"Gifts. That reminds me." Camp snapped his fingers. "Hey, Mark. Toss me that blue duffel, will you?"

Gazing adoringly at the man he'd soon call "Dad," Mark brought the bag.

Camp found the sack with the gifts he'd bought at Fort Union. He even gave key chains to the three men who'd joined the excursion late. The reporter, Jeff Scott and Lyle Roberts didn't know what to say. Each looked floored by Camp's generosity as they pumped his hand.

To break the silence, Emily rose on her tiptoes and kissed Camp. Out of breath as she pulled away, she whispered, "That's thanks from everyone for sponsoring the trip. I'll save mine for later. In private." Blushing, she added more loudly, "*After* I edit his academic paper, of course. While he's with the doctor, I'll collect the last data sheets. So make them count, ladies. Make them count. We don't want history repeating itself."

Camp kissed her then. The kiss went on for so long the others drifted away. The couple surfaced and found themselves alone. Laughing, they linked arms and strolled toward the doctor's office.

"The past defines the present, Emily. And the present determines how we look at the past. Lyle is dead wrong about people not paying attention. Our paper will shake a few trees."

"*Our* paper?" Emily's steps faltered. "You actually will let me edit it?"

Camp flattened his hand comfortably at the small of her back. "Oh, did I forget to mention that you and I are going to coauthor this piece? Plus, I really do have an idea for a book that I'll need your help with."

Grinning, she leaned into the hollow of his shoulder. "That book will dislodge a few opinions and revise a few so-called facts. And when the dust settles, Camp, maybe we'll influence the future."

"I think we influenced some people on this trip. gardless, we'll influence the future of our kids."

"Mark and Megan, you mean?"

"Um...and others." This kiss made him late to see the doctor. Very late, but he didn't care. Professor Campbell felt he had the world by the tail.

* * * * *

Watch for Sherry Campbell's story, coming from Superromance in August, 1998.

HARLEQUIN SUPERROMANCE®

Hope Springs

Hope Springs Eternal...

Faith O'Dare loves living in the tiny town of Hope Springs, where all good things happen. But now things are happening just a little too fast. It seems as if half the women in town are pregnant—and only one of them is married.

Faith believes her out-of-town boyfriend will *want* to marry her, though—until she finds out he's already found wedded bliss with someone else. His law partner, Sean, wants to make amends for his wayward friend, but what can he do...apart from help decorate her nursery, raise her child and marry her himself?

March 1998—**BABY BOOM** (#780)
by Peg Sutherland

Look for further tales from Hope Springs
in the coming year.

Look for these titles—
available at your favorite retail outlet!

January 1998
Renegade Son by Lisa Jackson
Danielle Summers had problems: a rebellious child
and unscrupulous enemies. In addition, her Montana
ranch was slowly being sabotaged. And then there was
Chase McEnroe—who admired her land and desired her
body. But Danielle feared he would invade more than just
her property—he'd trespass on her heart.

February 1998
The Heart's Yearning by Ginna Gray
Fourteen years ago Laura gave her baby up for adoption,
and not one day had passed that she didn't think about
him and agonize over her choice—so she finally followed
her heart to Texas to see her child. But the plan to watch
her son from afar doesn't quite happen that way, once the
boy's sexy—*single*—father takes a decided interest in *her*.

March 1998
First Things Last by Dixie Browning
One look into Chandler Harrington's dark eyes and
Belinda Massey could refuse the Virginia millionaire nothing.
So how could the no-nonsense nanny believe the rumors that
he had kidnapped his nephew—an adorable, healthy little boy
who crawled as easily into her heart as he did into her lap?

BORN IN THE USA: Love, marriage—
and the pursuit of family!

DEBBIE MACOMBER

invites you to the

HEART OF TEXAS

Join Debbie Macomber as she brings you the lives and loves of the folks in the ranching community of Promise, Texas.

If you loved Midnight Sons—don't miss Heart of Texas! A brand-new six-book series from Debbie Macomber.

Available in February 1998 at your favorite retail store.

Heart of Texas by Debbie Macomber

Lonesome Cowboy	February '98
Texas Two-Step	March '98
Caroline's Child	April '98
Dr. Texas	May '98
Nell's Cowboy	June '98
Lone Star Baby	July '98

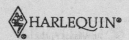

HARLEQUIN®

HPHRT1

KEY TO MY HEART

Unlock the secrets of romance just in time for the most romantic day of the year—Valentine's Day!

Key to My Heart
features three of your favorite authors,

**Kasey Michaels,
Rebecca York
and Muriel Jensen,**

to bring you wonderful tales of romance and Valentine's Day dreams come true.

As an added bonus you can receive Harlequin's special Valentine's Day necklace. FREE with the purchase of every *Key to My Heart* collection.

Available in January,
wherever Harlequin books are sold.

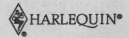

WELCOME TO *Love Inspired* ™

A brand-new series of contemporary inspirational love stories.

Join men and women as they learn valuable lessons about facing the challenges of today's world and about life, love and faith.

Look for the following February 1998 Love Inspired™ titles:

A Groom of Her Own
by Irene Hannon

The Marriage Wish
by Dee Henderson

The Reluctant Bride
by Kathryn Alexander

Available in retail outlets
in January 1998.

LIFT YOUR SPIRITS AND GLADDEN YOUR HEART with *Love Inspired* ™!

Steeple
Hill™

LI298